THE
REDEMPTION
GAME

A FLINT K-9 MYSTERY

THE
REDEMPTION
GAME

A FLINT K-9 MYSTERY

JEN BLOOD

Adian Press
Maine

For my friends and family
in Midcoast Maine.

1

IT WAS THE KIND of summer day that makes a body glad to be alive, and even more so to be alive in coastal Maine. Sun shining. Birds singing. All right with the world.

Except for, of course, the chorus of fifty or more dogs barking nearby and a stench to rival what you might find at a full-fledged, badly funded zoo. Which was, more or less, where we were headed.

I walked beside Jack Juarez, FBI Special Agent recently turned private investigator, along a deeply rutted dirt road off another deeply rutted dirt road off an infrequently traveled secondary road in Cushing. It was June, the sun reflecting off the deep blue of Muscongus Bay just across the way. On the other side, the barking of the aforementioned fifty or more dogs got impossibly louder the closer we got to our goal.

Bear, my eighteen-year-old son, walked on my other side, though he'd been quiet since we'd gotten out of the van. My own tension ratcheted higher as we approached our destination: a once-grand Victorian home that had long since gone to seed, set on ten acres of prime coastal real estate and flanked by two equally rundown old barns.

A surge of mangy-looking dogs of all shape and size

rushed a rickety gate that barely looked sturdy enough to hold them back. I registered Jack's flinch beside me, though to his credit he didn't turn around and run.

"I'm going to check around out back," Bear said to me. "I want to get a look at the farm animals before Nancy comes out and runs us off the property."

"Be careful," I warned him. Nancy Davis was the owner of this ruin of a place, and was definitely not known around town for her hospitality. "If she comes out, tell her you're with us and don't engage. Just come find me."

He nodded without actually agreeing, but I had to hope he was smart enough by now to know when it was worth arguing with me and when it was better to just do as he was told.

Bear managed to skirt around the side of the building just as Nancy stepped out her front door and stood on the sagging stoop glaring at us. The dogs' snarls and yowls got worse as soon as Nancy set foot outside, as though they were drawing on their owner's ill will.

"Why are we here, exactly?" Jack asked me under his breath, his tone wary as he eyed the old woman now striding toward us.

"To evaluate the dogs. See if there are any we can take on at the island and rehabilitate there."

"My dogs don't need rehabilitating," Nancy shouted at us, still ten yards away. She had to be nearly seventy-five, but clearly her hearing wasn't suffering for it. Apart from that, though, Nancy wasn't wearing her years well. She wore a tattered house dress with a bathrobe over it, her white hair stringy and thinning across her scalp. Her right arm was in a cast, and she walked with a limp. The dogs in the yard—I counted twenty of them at first glance—vied for her attention, occasionally snapping at each other in the chaos.

"You know what's happening, Nancy," I said, my own tone softer than hers. There are times when I'm grateful for my Georgian accent, though I haven't lived in that part of the country for going on twenty years now. My drawl is gentler than the Maine accent, making me seem more compassionate than I necessarily am. This morning, I used that to full effect.

"You've got a choice," I continued. "Either find a place for the animals or the State will intervene and take them. Wouldn't you rather know where they're going?"

A dog who looked like a mix between a Sheltie and a rat came up to her and took a corner of her robe between his teeth, pulling at it with menacing little yips and growls.

"Knock it off, Oswald," she said, though there was tenderness underlying the words. "You wanna play, go find Albie. I ain't got the time."

Albie was Nancy's youngest son, a quiet, tense man with a number of cognitive challenges that had kept him reliant on his mother into his adult years. Discouraged, Oswald shifted his focus to us, still outside the fence. He nosed through the chicken wire, his attention fixed on Jack. The ex-agent took a step back. Jack Juarez had seen plenty in his day, I knew, but Oswald still seemed a little beyond him. I heard him curse under his breath, and he glanced at me as he bent to clean dog crap from his leather shoes.

"Have you thought about what we talked about the other day?" I pressed Nancy, ignoring Jack and Oswald for the moment. "If you can find a place for, say, three quarters of the dogs—"

"They're special needs," she said immediately, cutting me off.

Regardless of her animosity, she opened the gate and ushered us in, hollering and kicking at any dogs who dared try and escape. I glanced at Jack to see if he was still on board, but there was no time for a discussion. Game as always, he followed me through the gate and into territory I was sure was completely foreign to anything he'd ever seen before.

Two stunted pug mixes had taken up the charge with Oswald, successfully herding Jack back toward the gate before he'd managed more than a couple of steps into the yard.

"Nobody's gonna take them dogs," Nancy continued. "Half the ones in the house have health problems. And nobody's house trained in the lot. You tell me, who'll take that on but me? Besides, they've only ever known me."

Jack managed to extricate himself from the dogs, albeit momentarily, and stepped forward with the beguiling smile that was precisely the reason I'd asked him along in the first place.

"This is quite a setup you have here. If you don't mind me asking, how many dogs do you have, exactly?"

Nancy stared at him with dark, withering eyes for a full two seconds before she turned to me. "Who in hell is this?" So much for Jack Juarez's irresistible charm.

"Jack Juarez," I said. "He's helping me out today."

"Well, he doesn't need to be here." She stopped speaking altogether, arms folded over her bony chest while she waited.

"Why don't you go check in with Bear?" I said to Jack, nodding toward the back of the property. "I'll let you know when I need you two."

"You're not going to need them at all," Nancy said. Jack started to protest, but thought better of it when Oswald and his pack approached again.

"You know where to find me," he said. I waited until he was out of hearing range before I shifted my focus back to the old woman.

"What in Hades are you doing here, Nancy?" I said. I tried to infuse some compassion into the question, though that wasn't easy. "You need help here—you must see that. You've got dogs literally busting out the seams of that house, not to mention the state of the farm animals out in the field. Have you looked at those cows? I can count their ribs from here. The llamas' teeth need filing. The sheep need shearing..."

The more I went on, the tighter Nancy held herself. I watched the dogs circling around her, their attention shifting to me: the interloper. Someone their person clearly wasn't happy to see. A Newfoundland the size of a small pony, his coat patchy with mange, worked his way from behind a piece of cardboard and duct tape that patched a broken window in the house. At sight of Nancy, he loped our way with tail waving.

"Get back in there, Cody," she told the dog. "Go on, now."

The Newfie ignored her and headed for me. He would be magnificent if not for his circumstances, and a fresh surge of rage ran through me as he bumped his massive head into my stomach, nearly taking me down. "Do you know how many people are in line for rescued Newfoundlands?" I demanded. "Someone would take him in a heartbeat."

"I don't need anybody to take him. To hell with all of you," Nancy said. "You damned bureaucrats forget we're talking about living creatures here."

"Since when have I been a bureaucrat?" I returned. "And I think you're the one who's forgotten they're living creatures. You've saved their lives, and I thank you for that, I really do. But what kind of quality of life do they have now, if half of them are sick and all of them are starving?"

I stroked Cody's head, noting the ribs clearly defined through his ruin of a coat. A dog like this should be at least a hundred pounds, but I doubted Cody was more than sixty.

Nancy's lips tightened. She raised her good arm and pointed toward the gate. "Get out. You're no better than my son, trying to steal my animals and move me out of here just so he can have my land. He doesn't give a rat's ass what happens to these animals. None of them do."

"None of whom, Nancy?" I asked wearily. I'd known Nancy for a couple of years now, in some capacity or other. I was well acquainted with her conspiracy theories.

"Developers," she said. "Barbara and her fancy-fairy husband've got them sniffing at my land. She's been on me for months now to sell her this plot so she can expand her place. And it's not for my own good, I'll tell you that much."

I didn't know Nancy's neighbors—Barbara and her "fancy-fairy" husband—beyond maybe being able to recognize them in a police line-up, but I was sure this wasn't the whole story.

"So, don't sell," I said regardless, seizing the moment. "But don't try to do this alone. I thought Fred was helping you. Didn't he come back to try and sort this out?"

Fred was Nancy's oldest son, a strange, precise little man in his forties.

"He left," she said, with a trace of scorn. "Couldn't take it. Didn't even say goodbye. Just packed his things and left one night, just like his daddy did years before. Sent me a note from Cleveland, wishing me luck. Then next thing I know, I hear from his lawyer saying he wants to evict me and Albie. From my own damned house!"

"I'm sorry," I said, and meant it. Cody lay down in front of me, directly on my feet. "But maybe this is the only way he knows to help you. If not, there are plenty of other people around here more than willing to lend a hand. I've got space on the island to take some of your animals and work on training, and there's a whole network of others who'll pitch in. We'll clean this place up, set you up with a number you can actually handle."

She stepped forward silently and grabbed Cody by the collar, jerking the dog to his feet. Cody followed her willingly, then sat beside her and leaned against her hip. Nancy didn't say anything for a minute or more, still tense, before I noticed the sheen in her tired eyes.

"Please, Nancy."

She shook her head, more against the tears than my words. "If I weren't so damned old," she said. "I used to be able to handle it, you know. Could've run this place in my sleep."

This was actually true, I knew. Nancy had been doing animal rescue in the area for over twenty years, long before I came on the scene. She traveled around the country helping with cruelty cases; up until a couple of years ago, she'd run this place as smoothly as the proverbial Swiss watch. Her stellar track record was the major reason no one had shut her down sooner after it all got away from her.

"Does that mean you'll let me help?" I asked.

She took a deep breath, and looked around. Oswald and his buddies had returned, which made me wonder where Jack and Bear might be. They paced around us with a dozen other barking dogs, watching my every move. Cody ignored them completely.

"Is your friend gonna help?" Nancy asked.

"Jack?" I said. "I don't know. Maybe."

"Looks like he's being tracked by a grizzly bear every time Oswald looks at him sideways, you know."

I squelched a smile. "He does a little bit, yes."

"Nice to look at, though," she noted.

"Don't start."

She looked at me innocently, a trace of mischief in her eyes. "What? You don't think I notice something like that? I'm old and maybe half nuts, but I'm not dead. I can still appreciate a good-looking man when one comes around."

"You know I haven't forgotten the question," I said, getting us back on track. "Will you let us help?"

A few seconds of hesitation followed before she finally nodded. "Come back tomorrow—"

"We're here now. You know the police are set to come in tomorrow."

"Come back tomorrow," she repeated firmly. "Give me a few hours to pull myself together, talk this through with Albie and my other babies here."

Despite my reservations, I nodded. "We'll be back first thing," I said. "And we'll get this sorted out, all right? This can be a good thing."

"Sure it can," she said grimly.

Moments later, Nancy and Cody retreated back into her ruined house. I picked my way through rotting dog food, animal crap, and the carcasses of multiple rats—at least I hoped they were rats—toward the back of the property in search of Bear and Jack. I found them in a soggy pasture out behind the house, where Bear was giving an overgrown sheep a once-over while Albie—Nancy's younger son—

looked on, arms crossed over his chest, face dark with anger. He wore a green sweatshirt with a pirate on the front, BUC PRIDE in large white letters across the bottom. It looked as old as the hills, and just as dirty.

Jack, meanwhile, crouched beside a grizzled black and white tomcat with one missing ear. The dogs that had been pursuing him, I noted, were now keeping a safe distance.

"I see you met Cash," I said.

"Is that his name?" Jack asked. The cat butted his over-large head against the palm of Jack's hand. "I'm not positive, but I think he saved my life."

"Cash keeps everyone in line here. They didn't mean you any harm, though," I said, nodding toward the pack of little dogs watching us from the fence line. "But you do give off a vibe. They can sense your fear."

"I'm not afraid of them," he said, a trifle indignant.

"Of course not."

"Now you're just patronizing me." He shifted his focus back to the cat. "What's his story?"

"Long-time neighborhood stray," I said. "He got into it with a coyote, though. You should have seen the coyote." Jack smiled faintly, focus still on Cash. "Nancy raised the money to cover the vet bills, and added him to the menagerie."

Jack nodded with apparent approval.

"So, what are we doing?" Bear interrupted us, returning from the field with one massive black and white sheep tottering along beside him. "Some of these guys are in bad shape. We need to get them out of here, but Albie's giving me a hard time about it."

Albie had followed Bear back toward us, his entire body coiled as tight as a rattlesnake about to strike.

"We're coming back tomorrow morning," I said. Bear started to protest, but I held up my hand. "Nancy needs a few hours to pull herself together. That's all she's asking. One more day won't kill these guys."

Bear looked at the ram beside him doubtfully. The wool was so thick I couldn't imagine what we would find underneath. Unlike wild sheep, which shed their wool naturally the same way a dog sheds its coat, domesticated sheep have been bred so that the wool will continue to grow until someone intercedes. If no one shears them, the coat can become so overgrown that flies lay eggs in the moist folds of their skin. Maggots hatch, and literally eat the animal from the outside in. Based on the smell coming from the poor thing, I was guessing we could well face a situation like that here.

"Do you think there's any way we could take him now?" Bear asked, nodding toward the sheep. "Therese should take a look at him. I don't think he should go another day."

Therese was the vet out on Windfall Island, our base of operations for Flint K-9 Search and Rescue and a growing animal rescue Bear had started. She was on standby today, with full knowledge of what we could be up against with Nancy's animals.

"I might be able to arrange something," I said. I surveyed the rest of the pasture, taking stock of the donkeys, llamas, cows, sheep, and goats in turn. "What about the rest of the place? Is there anyone else you think needs to come now?"

"There's a dog," he said. "They keep him chained out back. We should get him out of here as soon as we can."

"I'll check with Nancy. Anyone else?"

Bear took the place in critically, his gaze intent. "There

are a couple of llamas that really need to get out of here sooner than later. Those, and that miniature donkey farther out." He nodded toward a thin, shaggy donkey at the back of the field. "You think you can talk her into letting them go now?"

"Mom says everybody stays," Albie ventured, joining in the conversation for the first time. He avoided my eye when he spoke, his gaze locked on the ground, arms still wrapped around his chest. "Nobody goes. This is the best place for everybody. Anybody who leaves here, they get killed."

"That's what we're trying to keep from happening," Bear said, with surprising gentleness. "You're a smart guy—you know some of these animals aren't doing too well right now. And your mom's having a hard time, too. We're just trying to help."

Albie took this in, glancing up to look at Bear for a split second before he looked back at the ground. "It's not safe," he said, half to himself. "Out there isn't safe. In here is the only safe place for us."

My heart clenched at the dangerous message Nancy had taught him over the years, and I struggled to find some way to reach the man. "I like your shirt," I finally said lamely, gesturing to his chest. "The pirate there…"

His face transformed in an instant. "Buccaneer," he said. There was reverence in the word. "It's a buccaneer, not a pirate. People always get that wrong. Coach gave it to me." He turned around, pointing awkwardly at the back. MVP was written at the top, with A. DAVIS and the number 7 beneath it. "You know what that means?" he asked.

"Most Valuable Player," a girl's voice said, behind us. I turned in surprise. A pretty blond girl likely a little younger than Bear strode toward us, taking Albie in with a casual nod. "Albie got MVP when he was in high school."

"Georges Valley," Albie added. "I went to Georges Valley High School. Class of 1990. Coach Pendleton. I played outfield on the baseball team."

"Hey, Bear," the girl said to my son, who nodded in her direction but otherwise remained mute. She cast a long look in Jack's direction, then shifted her attention to me. "I'm Julie Monroe," she said. "We live next door. My mom wanted me to come over and see if I could help."

"You're not supposed to be here," Albie said, in a whisper directed at Julie. "You know you're not—"

"I know, I know," Julie said, waving the comment away carelessly. "I'll go. I just figured if you need any help..." She let the statement trail off.

I watched with interest as she worked her way a little closer to Bear, who looked decidedly uncomfortable at her approach. Bear is a good-looking kid who hasn't quite figured that out yet, but it's bound to sink in eventually. Especially with the attention of girls like Julie Monroe.

I thought longingly of Ren Mensah—another member of the Flint K-9 team, and to date the only girl to steal Bear's heart. She'd left Windfall Island just over a month ago for California, where her father had just relocated. Ren was hard working and thoughtful and bright, and the least manipulative person I'd ever met. I could handle Ren dating my son.

I didn't have a clue what to do with girls like Julie Monroe.

Thankfully, based on the somewhat wild look in his eyes, Bear was even more clueless than me.

"I'll talk to Nancy about the llamas and the donkey," I said to Bear. "Go on over and check on this dog you want us to take, and I'll meet you there."

Bear nodded. Albie's momentary transformation at the memory of his glory days in high school was forgotten quickly at my words. He fixed me with a long, hard stare. "Nobody goes," the man said quietly. "Everybody has to stay."

"Everything will be okay, Albie," I said. "We'll take good care of anyone who leaves here. You don't have to worry about that."

He turned his back on me, visibly seething. A crawl of uneasiness ran through me, but I pushed it aside. Bear went to track down whatever dog he meant to save, while Julie tagged along beside him. I couldn't shake my anxiety when I saw Albie take off after them.

"You want me to go, too?" Jack asked. He stood with Cash still threading between his long legs, a throaty purr audible from a few feet away.

I nodded, relieved. "If you wouldn't mind, that would be great."

"No problem." He paused. I thought he was concerned about the dogs again, but when he shifted his gaze back to me it was clear that wasn't what was on his mind. "Be careful, all right? I don't have a good feeling about this."

"Yeah," I agreed with a sigh. "Same here. Watch your back."

We parted ways, and I headed back to the house in search of Nancy. A sheep, two llamas, a donkey, a dog... Would she actually agree to let any of them go now? Or at all, without a fight? It was distinctly possible that she was just telling me what I wanted to hear so we would leave her alone. Once we were gone, who knew what lengths she'd go to to keep us from coming back again.

I was just a few feet from the shaky-looking front stoop, trying to decide whether I should brave the steps or simply call to Nancy from outside, when I heard shouting somewhere in the distance.

"We're taking him! Now," Bear said, loudly enough to be heard across the yard.

Wonderful.

"You're not taking anybody!" Albie's voice countered, louder even than my son.

I winced at the look on Nancy's face as she came flying out of the house, a lot faster than I would have thought she was capable given her condition. Well, hell. Nothing could ever be easy, could it?

"Albie?" Nancy called, forehead furrowed and lips set in a thin line. Mama was mad.

"He's trying to take Reaver," Albie shouted in reply.

Uninvited and largely unnoticed, I followed Nancy around the corner. Instantly, my own rational thoughts left me. I'd been here before, damn it, and I hadn't liked it any better the first time.

Albie stood with a gun pointed at Bear, who stood in the way of a big, block-headed dog. The last time Bear did this was just under a year ago, and it had gotten him shot and taken hostage. The boy never does seem to learn.

"What's going on, Bear?" I asked. It was a struggle to keep my voice steady.

Bear stood with his hands up in front of a snarling, snapping pit bull staked in the middle of a circle of mud and feces. A mountain of a dog, with gleaming teeth and the kind of muscle that would make anyone think twice before approaching. That impression was only intensified by a mangy coat and ribs standing out clearly in the once-powerful frame. Presumably, this was the dog Bear was so committed to saving. Jack, meanwhile, stood close by with his own hands raised, though to his credit he appeared a lot calmer than anybody else in our little tableau. I waited for Nancy to intervene; to tell her boy to put the gun down and be reasonable.

She stood beside me, breathing hard from her dash to reach Albie. Not a word passed her lips.

"He wants to take our animals," Albie said to his mother. The gun wavered. It was a shotgun, double-barreled and, I had no doubt, fully loaded. He hefted it back up, pointed in Bear's direction once more.

"This dog is starving," Bear said. Despite the gun pointed at him, his voice betrayed his anger. "Just look at him. He's dying right in front of your eyes."

"He'll die anyplace else," Albie said, his own voice rising. "They'll kill him. They'll kill anybody who leaves here. Right, Mom? That's what they do. They kill all God's creatures."

He was talking too fast, hands shaking. Any glimmer of rational thought I might have glimpsed before was gone now. I glanced at Nancy, and my stomach tightened. She was smiling. Pride shone in her eyes.

"That's right, baby," she agreed. She shook her head sadly—purely for effect, it seemed to me. "They kill all God's creatures out in that cruel world."

"That's not what we intend to do," Jack intervened. His

voice was even. Quiet. The kind of voice you can get lost in. Or maybe that's just me. "Why don't you put the gun down, and we can talk about this."

"He's just waiting for me to do that so he can take Reaver," Albie insisted.

I assumed Reaver was the dog, who frankly looked like he had no intention of going anywhere. I shoved my own anger down at sight of a prong collar biting into the dog's neck, his body lousy with sores and mange. He couldn't be more than four or five—a dog in the prime of his life. At the sight, I understood all too well my son's rage.

"Look at him!" Bear said, directing the words to me. "They've half killed him. They tortured him, for God's sake."

"We saved him!" Albie said. "We got him down South. That man was killing him, and we got him away and we saved him. We brought him home and took care of him. And now you want to take him away from us."

"Saved" was a relative term. Surely the hell they had created for Reaver and the other animals here couldn't ever be viewed as anyone's salvation.

"Nobody's taking anyone right now," Jack said. "Bear is just worried about you and your mother, because it seems like you've gotten in over your heads here. Like maybe there are more animals than you can handle."

"We were handling everything just fine until the State started sending people out here to drive us nuts," Nancy said. "If you just leave us alone—"

"People would leave you alone if you'd stop taking in animals you can't take care of, and do something about the ones you already have," Bear said. His voice was still tight, his body just as rigid. Albie kept the gun on him, unmoved by our arguments.

The other dogs on the grounds, meanwhile, had caught wind of what was happening. Oswald and his gang of rat dogs barked ferociously at Jack, Bear, and me, though they thankfully had the good sense to keep out of reach of Reaver. The dog looked like he was prepared to rip to shreds the first thing that came within striking distance.

"Bear, keep still," I said, infusing the words with my best no-nonsense, I'm-your-mother-and-you'll-do-as-I-say tone. "Albie, what are you going to do after you shoot Bear? Because if you do that, the police will definitely come, and they'll take you away from here. You don't want that, right?"

Amazingly, logic actually seemed to have an effect. The man looked at me, working through the question before he shifted his gaze to his mother. The question was clear in his eyes. *What do I do?*

I wanted to throttle the woman when her mouth remained shut, lips pinched tight. One word from her, I knew, and the standoff would be over.

The seed of doubt had been planted, though. Jack stayed with it.

"Jamie's right, Albie," he said. "We don't want to see you and your mom separated. You obviously take good care of her."

Jack stepped in front of the man, effectively blocking Albie's shot of Bear. The former FBI man reached his hand out, his dark eyes as compassionate as I'd ever seen them.

"Please, Albie. Put down the gun. Then we can go home, and you and your mom can get back to your lives."

Another tense second, possibly two, passed. I hoped to God Bear didn't take it upon himself to argue Reaver's plight again. Thankfully, he did not.

Slowly, Albie lowered the gun. He looked exhausted.

"We're trying to take care of them," he said quietly, to no one in particular before his gaze locked on Reaver. "We saved Reaver, but he won't let us near. We're trying to help him."

Jack took a step toward Albie, and very calmly took hold of the gun now pointed at the ground. "I know you are," he said. "Now, I'm just going to take this before somebody gets hurt, and I'll put it back in the house for you. Okay?"

Albie nodded numbly, releasing the gun.

"You're not setting foot in my home," Nancy said. "Put the gun over by the barn, and get the hell off my land. We don't want and we don't need help—not from you, and not from anyone."

Jack did as he was told, showing only a hint of uncertainty at the tide of small dogs that surged forward when he stepped away.

Bear, meanwhile, almost immediately turned his attention back to Reaver. The dog had barked himself hoarse, the prong collar pressing deeper into his larynx the more he strained. To my astonishment, however, he fell silent the moment Bear turned to him.

"It's okay," Bear said quietly to the dog. "We're getting you out of here. You'll be all right."

Bear took a step toward the dog. Reaver didn't bark. Didn't bare his teeth, or back away. He didn't cower. Instead, I watched as the dog's head came up. His tail waved hesitantly.

"Do you know this dog?" I asked Bear.

"Ren and I came to help out here a few times this winter," he said. He took another step, until he was inside Reaver's circle. My son crouched, turned sideways with eyes lowered and hand extended.

Reaver went to him without a second of hesitation.

"He's been trying to get that dog from me for months," Nancy said. There was a trace of spite in the words. "I told him before, and I'll say it again. He'll get that dog over my dead body."

Bear looked her in the eye, his voice even. Reaver remained close by his side. "Fine with me."

My son, the diplomat. Before things could escalate again, I interceded.

"Nancy, you know what happened here today is only going to be worse tomorrow. But if you refuse to be reasonable about this, you're bringing it on yourself."

"I'm not leaving my home or my animals without a fight. If you learned nothing else today, it should be that. Now, get out of here or I'll get the shotgun myself. And I won't take the coward's way out like Albie here. Once I pick up that gun, I'm not putting it down again."

"Come on, Jamie," Jack said. "There's nothing more that can be done today."

I considered Nancy's words, and the reality of what would happen tomorrow. Animal welfare and the local sheriff's office were set to come in. Nancy knew this. I couldn't imagine her letting that happen without an outright war.

I nodded, with no idea what else to do. "Come on, Bear," I said.

He looked at me, torn, with Reaver still beside him. "But—"

"Now, Bear. He'll be all right."

An empty promise if ever I'd heard one.

Bear leaned in and whispered something in Reaver's ear, while the dog rested against him. He stroked the pit bull's head, took a deep breath, and stood.

We left the grounds, the three of us, without a single soul saved of the hundred-plus animals that Nancy held captive.

2

JACK, BEAR, AND I WALKED the mile trek back to the main road in silence. The sun was still shining, the birds still singing, but the day seemed darker than it had when we'd first set out.

When we got to my truck, I wasn't surprised to see others alongside it, including a sheriff's car and a pickup bearing the local Humane Society's logo. A cluster of people had gathered beside the vehicles, the sheriff and the director of the Humane Society among them. In addition, a blond woman in her forties stood alongside Julie Monroe, the local femme fatale we'd met earlier. Based on the resemblance to the older woman, I assumed this was Julie's mother. Beside them, a clean-cut man with his hair tinged with silver watched the proceedings with clear interest.

"Any luck?" Sheriff Chris Finnegan asked. There was no mistaking the unhappiness in his eyes. He didn't look hopeful.

"She wouldn't budge," I said.

The sheriff grimaced.

"Told you," Julie said, somewhat defiantly. Her eyes drifted to Bear, who didn't look like he'd even noticed she was there. Still brooding over Reaver, I wasn't sure he realized any of us were.

"Where does that leave us?" the unknown man asked.

Tracy Rodriguez, director of the Humane Society, glanced at Sheriff Finnegan before she spoke. "We have fosters standing by, but we don't have a head count. Did you get any idea while you were there?" She directed the question to me, but I shook my head.

"Nancy wouldn't say, and I couldn't get a look inside the barns. By the sound and smell of things, I'd say they're full up, though."

"They've got twenty-eight dogs in the big barn," Julie volunteered. "Albie doesn't know how many cats are in the other barn, but he thinks maybe sixty. Twelve dogs in the house, and a bunch of rabbits in one of the rooms there. Plus three cows, five llamas, a donkey, and a bunch of goats—nine, maybe?—in the field. And a sheep."

All eyes turned to the girl, who flushed slightly.

"Albie likes to talk if I'm around," she explained.

"I thought I told you not to go over there," the woman said. The sound of her voice confirmed my original theory: definitely the mother. I'd know that tone anywhere.

"I didn't go over there," Julie lied. "I was just hanging out by the fence, and Albie came to me. It's not my fault if he wants to talk. I never left our property."

"Sorry," Sheriff Finnegan interrupted, looking at me. "I should introduce you. This is Barbara Monroe, and her daughter Julie. And Hank—Nancy's neighbor on the south side."

Hank and Barbara both nodded a greeting. I recalled Nancy's mention of Barbara and her husband trying to get her to sell her place. Thinking of the kind of nightmare scene we'd just left, I couldn't blame them for wanting to be rid of her.

"I hate that it's come to this," Barbara said.

She was a striking woman, with a slender build and thick, carefully coiffed hair that fell to her shoulders. I was surprised to find that I believed her.

"She brought it on herself, Babs," Hank said to her. "How many times did we tell the damn fool woman she needed to get rid of some of those animals? Or, at a minimum, stop taking any new ones in?"

"God knows you've done everything you could," Tracy said to Hank sympathetically. "Short of going to work for free over there twenty-four/seven, you couldn't help those animals any more. The whole thing just got away from her. You have no idea how fast that can happen in this business. It doesn't mean she's completely right in the head, but there's more to the story than just that. She started out with good intentions."

"Sorry I got out of there when Albie went nuts," Julie said, her voice lowered, directing the words to Bear. I listened in unabashedly. "He can be scary if he gets mad enough. Especially if his mom is around."

"It's all right," Bear said, his own voice just as quiet. "I was glad—it was the right move. I wouldn't have wanted you to get hurt."

At which point, Julie Monroe turned into a puddle of goo—something Bear was doubtless oblivious to.

"So, what's the plan here?" Hank asked, pressing Sheriff Finnegan. I forced myself to focus on the conversation, shifting away from the teens.

"I'm going to take some time to talk things out with Jamie and Tracy before we make that call," the sheriff said. Hank nodded, but I noticed that Barbara didn't look too pleased at the idea of being cut from the conversation.

"I'm happy to lend a kitchen if you need a place to stretch out or whatever," she said. "Tim's out of town, so it's no trouble. There's plenty of room."

To my relief, Finnegan shook his head. "Thanks, but no. I'll give you a call if I need anything. Otherwise, just sit tight. We have things under control."

As they were leaving, Julie asked Bear to come over to check out something in her barn—which, frankly, is just the kind of request that makes mothers the world over cringe. I expected Bear to make some excuse and stick with us, since Julie didn't seem like the kind of girl whose barn he'd normally be interested in. I was mistaken. He mumbled something to me, eyes downcast, and followed Julie and her mother into the horizon.

Once they were out of earshot, Jack and I broke the news to the others:

Despite Sheriff Finnegan's earlier assurances, we very much did not have things under control.

"You really think they're a danger?" Finnegan asked, after Jack and I had given him the unsavory details on everything that had happened at the Davis house.

"Albie had a gun on us," Jack said. "And he might have been hesitant about what to do, but I've been in the situation enough to know that Nancy, at least, was serious. If we had pushed hard enough, she would have snapped."

Tracy frowned. Finnegan looked at her searchingly.

"I thought you said they were stable."

"I never said any such thing," Tracy said. She looked peeved at the mere suggestion. "I said I didn't know what she was physically capable of, since her health is so compromised. But that doesn't matter, as far as I'm concerned. We've done these animals a disservice too long. We have to get to them."

"I thought I was getting through to her at one point," I said. "Before we heard Bear and Albie fighting, it seemed like she might be open to accepting help."

"Right," Tracy said, with an implicit eye roll. "Let me guess. 'I used to be able to handle this all on my own. Nobody cares but me. It just got away from me. If I could get somebody to come in a couple of times a week...'"

"You've heard that song before," I guessed.

"More times than I can count," she agreed. "It always ends the same way. We get a crew in there to clean up. Take some of the animals off her hands. Somebody from the community volunteers for a week or two, maybe a month, before Nancy runs them off.

"Next thing we know, we get word that she's taking in animals again. We start the whole dance all over again. And in the meantime, it costs animals pain and suffering, the state in police enforcement, and my shelter is stuck with the bill to clean up the mess—again. I'm done. She needs to get out of there, and every one of those animals needs whatever shot they can get at a healthy, loving forever home."

I'd been thinking much the same thing myself, so I was grateful to have someone on the team with that level of clarity. It wouldn't make tomorrow any easier, though.

"Okay, okay," I said. I held up my hands in surrender. "You've convinced me—though it wouldn't have taken much, after seeing the condition of those animals. But at the very least, it seems like a mental health professional should be on hand tomorrow when all this goes down."

"We've got a woman we work with," Finnegan said with a nod. "She's familiar with Nancy's case. They've even talked a couple of times without Nancy getting the rifle out and threatening to blow her head off. I'm hoping that will count for something."

I hoped so, too.

"What about the animals?" I asked, directing the question to Tracy.

"I've got vans, volunteers, and livestock trailers ready to roll first thing tomorrow morning. If Julie's numbers are on target, I think we have enough foster homes to deal with everyone, though it's hard to know for sure. We're just going to have to let things play out. I've contacted a couple of outside organizations that have said they can come in and help out if needed."

"That's the best we can do, then," the sheriff said. He looked back down the road, in the direction of the Davis home. In his mid-forties, he was a big, burly man with a young face that looked inordinately weary today. He sighed. "Damn, but I'll be glad when this is over."

I nodded in silent agreement. Looking around, it was clear that everyone shared that sentiment.

●

After the others had gone, I paused outside our truck to say goodbye to Jack, who'd met us here in his own car. The truck was idling with Bear at the wheel, and I was painfully aware that my son was watching my every move.

"Thanks for helping out today," I said. "I appreciate you coming along."

"It was interesting. And I told you: even though I'm doing the P.I. thing now, you should call me if you need me. I like working with you."

For a brief time, Jack had considered working for me

with Flint K-9. Ultimately, it became clear that search and rescue wasn't really his forte and he made the decision to establish himself as a private investigator in the Rockland area instead—probably a good choice given his reaction to Nancy's pint-sized crew. He'd been here for nearly three months, though I wasn't sure how many cases he'd actually worked in that time. Selfishly, I couldn't deny that I was glad to have him close by. And not just for the helping hand he provided in a pinch.

"So, I guess I'll see you around, then," I said.

"I was planning on coming out tomorrow, actually," he said. "In case you need any help."

"That's all right," I assured him, thinking once more of the look on his face at Oswald's advances. "There's a good local team of volunteers and workers that will come out with the Humane Society. Plus Sheriff Finnegan and his team. I'll let you know if we need you."

He frowned. "Okay." His hands were deep in the pockets of his jeans, a pensive expression on his face. I got the sense there was something more he wanted to say, but Bear honked the horn impatiently and broke the spell.

"Thanks again, Jack," I said. I leaned up on impulse and kissed his cheek. "Call me soon, okay? Maybe we could get coffee…"

"That would be good," he said. And then, also seemingly on impulse, he added, "Or dinner? I'd like to take you out. For dinner, I mean. Not coffee."

"That sounds good," I agreed. Despite the horror show we'd just left, I felt a flutter in my stomach at the thought. "Call me. We'll set it up."

"I will." He grinned. I grinned back, feeling giddy and more than a little bit foolish.

"Mom!" Bear called from behind the wheel. "Therese is

waiting for us back at the island. I've got a million things to do to get ready for tomorrow."

I rolled my eyes at Jack. "Duty calls. I'll talk to you soon."

"Soon."

I climbed back into the truck, neatly avoiding Bear's eye, and resisted the urge to look back to see whether Jack was still there, watching us go.

Twenty minutes later, we were headed across Muscongus Bay to Windfall Island.

Therese, our on-site veterinarian, was waiting at the wharf when we docked the boat that afternoon. She was a short, round French-Canadian woman with little to no people skills and gray hair that she wore in a buzz cut. She was amazing with the animals, though. Since that was my priority in this business, I'd hired her the moment I knew I had the funds to staff the vet position full-time. Now, she took one look at Bear and frowned.

"Where are the animals? I thought the plan was to bring at least a few back here today."

"Nancy wouldn't let them go," Bear said shortly. "They'll be here tomorrow, though. I'll make sure of it."

"What shape are they in?" the veterinarian pressed. "And what kind of numbers are we talking about?"

"They're bad," Bear said. "I'm going to go up to the kennels and see how much space we have." He'd gotten progressively quieter on the journey back to the island, his tension worrying me. Now, he brushed past both Therese and me and strode up the steep hill back to our newly built headquarters.

Therese looked at me questioningly. "I see he hasn't gotten any sunnier."

"Sorry," I apologized. "I know he's not a treat right now.

I don't know that anything short of Ren coming home will change that." She nodded, but made no comment. I shifted gears once more, returning to the animals that would soon be under our care.

"I'm not sure how many we'll need to take," I told Therese. "Tracy already has fosters lined up from the Humane Society network, but I know she's counting on us, too."

"Sure," Therese said. "I've been out to Nancy's before. I know what kind of operation she's running—and the kind she used to run. It's a damn shame it got away from her the way it did. She used to do good work."

"So I've heard. The rescue business isn't for the faint of heart, that's for sure." I thought once more of the animals suffering under Nancy's care now. "Do me a favor, Therese?"

She looked at me expectantly, waiting for me to continue. "If it ever looks like we're taking on more than we can chew or I'm neglecting any of these guys, give me a swift kick in the butt, would you? You're right, rescue is tough. But there's no excuse for what Nancy is putting her animals through now, no matter how much good she might have done in the past."

"Oh, trust me, you'd hear from me," Therese assured me. "Don't worry. You and Nancy were always cut from different cloth—that woman's got something dark going on in her head. Always has."

We returned to the business of figuring out where we would put all the new charges we'd soon be taking on, though Therese's words stayed with me while we worked.

At the moment, our numbers out on Windfall Island were already impressive. Bear and Ren had set up both a wildlife rehabilitation center and a farm animal sanctuary, which meant that on any given day we had everything from injured peregrine falcons to abandoned pygmy goats under our care.

The island had been donated to the organization by a friend, and a couple of grants along with private donations and my own funds all helped to make the place what it was today. Volunteers and staff worked together on an extensive garden to keep the humans on the island well fed, and we had just put in the last solar cells needed to ensure we could fuel the entire place on renewable energy. Windmills installed off the coast helped considerably with that, something Bear had been instrumental in getting under way. It was the culmination of years of hard work for me, but it was unquestionably worth it.

That night, it was after midnight by the time we finished feeding and exercising everyone on the island and then prepped for new arrivals. With Phantom—my stalwart K-9 partner, a German shepherd I'd saved from euthanasia seven years before—by my side, I limped wearily back to the dormitory-style barracks recently completed for Flint K-9 staff who lived out on the island.

The dorms are more monastic than many would like, I'm sure, but personally there are times when I find the simple twin bed, bedside table and lamp, and my little salvaged dresser a welcome relief from the overstocked world on the mainland. Tonight was one of those times.

I changed into T-shirt and yoga pants while Phantom took her rightful place at the foot of my bed, and I got under the covers. Phantom inched her way up to a spot by my side, and sighed heavily as she lay her head on my pillow.

During our search in Bethel over the winter, Phantom

had had a scuffle with a coyote. She'd recovered nicely from that by now, but there was no question that time was catching up to my nearly ten-year-old K-9 partner.

"Night, sweet girl," I said to the dog.

I felt her tail thump against my leg as her eyes sank shut. Phantom was asleep long before I was that night. The last thing I remember thinking before I finally sank into dreamland was, *I wonder how in Hades we're gonna get those animals away from Nancy tomorrow. And whether she'll survive losing them.*

I didn't have to wait long for my answer.

3

IT WAS THREE-THIRTY the next morning when my cell phone rang, the bedroom pitch black. Phantom woke at the sound and was immediately on her feet, breathing down my neck as I answered. She knew what a middle-of-the-night phone call usually meant:

Work.

"Flint K-9," I answered, my voice clear despite my grogginess. In this business, you learn to wake up fast.

"Jamie?" It was Tracy, from the Humane Society. I recognized the voice immediately. My head cleared, dread dawning.

"What's wrong?" I asked. Somehow, I was afraid I already knew.

"Something happened over at Nancy's," she said. "The animals got out—or someone let them out, looks like. They could be all over the county by now."

"Where are Nancy and Albie?" I asked.

A full three endless seconds ticked by before she answered. "Albie's missing. And Nancy... I'm not getting a lot of details so far. Maybe a heart attack. The coroner's not talking."

"You're saying she's dead?"

"I don't know anything more than that," Tracy said. "Everything's kind of crazy right now, and they're not releasing any official information."

She sounded exhausted. "The problem now is that all of those animals of hers are scattered to every corner of the county. You think you can come out and lend a hand rounding them up?"

"Of course," I agreed. "But you said Albie's missing? Do they need dogs looking for him?"

"The sheriff didn't say, but you may be getting a call. You know Albie: I don't think he would have gone far. My priority right now is the animals."

I was already thinking ahead, caught up in what we would need; what we would face. How many of Nancy's dogs might be reactive to other dogs? Or aggressive toward people? And now they were running loose, Nancy no longer there to be their buffer from the outside world.

"You want dogs or just extra hands?" I asked.

"I'd leave the dogs behind unless you want one of Nancy's wolverines to shred them to pieces. Just bring anyone on your team you think can handle themselves. I've already got someone alerting the area, so locals will hopefully get their pets inside and keep the doors locked until we can do something."

Good luck with that, I thought grimly.

"Okay," I said. "I'll get there as fast as I can. Are you telling people to keep their guns locked up and their knickers on straight? I'd like to take as many of these animals alive as possible."

"It's Maine. There are a lot of people out there who

won't think twice before pulling the trigger on an animal if they think they're trouble. You know that."

I did know that. People in this area loved their animals, but Nancy's mangy, snarling renegades were hardly the kind of fluffy puppies that would tug most people's heart strings.

"I'll get there as fast as I can," I repeated, even more determined now.

I went to Bear's door, just across the hall from mine, as soon as I was off the phone and had pulled on proper clothes. To my surprise, I got no response when I knocked. I tried again. Bear has always been a light sleeper; it used to drive me nuts trying to keep him down when he was little, back when we shared a studio apartment in Washington State. Knocking more than once to rouse him for a call was almost unheard of.

Regardless, I got no response the second time around, either.

Uneasy now, I pushed the door open.

His bed was unmade, but that was hardly unusual—left to his own devices, my son isn't exactly a neatnik. He and his dog Casper were nowhere to be found, and there was something eerily uninhabited about the room.

You'd do well to keep an eye on my son, Brock Campbell said in my head. I tensed, a wave of nausea accompanying the sound of the familiar voice.

I'd first heard Brock's voice during a search in Bethel over the winter, when a group of battered women on a dogsledding expedition had gone missing. Since that search ended, I hadn't heard Brock often—but I had heard him. I knew he wasn't gone; knew that, when the circumstances were right, he would be back.

Knowing that didn't stop my churning stomach or the pounding in my head that inevitably accompanied every visit.

Ignoring the voice, I pulled my phone from my pocket and selected Bear's name on my contact list.

To my relief, he picked up on the second ring, sounding distant and nonplussed.

"What's up?" he asked, nothing light or welcoming in the tone. I frowned.

"Where are you? We got a call to head over to the mainland."

"Couldn't sleep. I was over at the galley, talking to Ren."

"At three in the morning?"

"It's three hours earlier in California," he reminded me.

"Okay. So, at midnight? Doesn't she have work?"

"She was up, okay? Geez. You said we got a call?"

"Yeah. Put Casper in and meet me at the pier. Something happened at Nancy's."

I expected a barrage of questions, Bear's usual response to a call. Instead, he said only, "I'll be right there."

He disconnected without another word. I put my phone away, unable to shake the feeling of dread that lingered in the silence that followed. I waited for Brock to return, every muscle knotted.

This time, he didn't come.

By four a.m., the island had mobilized and my crew was headed for the mainland to help with the search for Albie and the escaped animals. Unfortunately, right now that crew was seriously shorthanded. Ren and her dog Minion were both gone, though I hoped they would return eventually. We still weren't sure what she would be doing in the fall, and I knew the uncertainty was taking a toll on Bear. Her father, Carl, had also been an important part of our team. With the two of them gone and no new hires brought on board yet, every call was a challenge in logistics.

Regardless, we made do.

Our ragged team piled into the Flint K-9 cargo van while it was still dark outside. Monty Caldwell, an ex-con who was now my second in command at Flint K-9, was behind the wheel with me beside him in the passenger seat, Bear and another of my most reliable hires— Sarah Prescott— beside him. Sarah was short and slender, with innumerable piercings, tattoos, and—today, at least—pink hair shaved almost to her scalp. The shade changed regularly, though this had been her preferred style for some time now. Therese climbed into the back with her cell phone glued to her ear.

I'd gotten my phone out twice with the intention of calling Jack before ultimately returning it to my pocket. Maybe I would call him once I had a better idea of what we were facing. For now, it seemed silly to get him out of bed just because I felt better having him around.

I'd been getting periodic updates via text about the status of the search since first hearing from Tracy. So far, all of the farm animals had been located, along with twenty-two dogs and a dozen cats. I thought of the two immense barns with animals coming out the seams, and shook my head. It still boggled my mind that someone would have seen fit to set every one of them loose.

"What's the count on the animals again?" Monty asked me as he pulled out of the Littlehope town landing parking lot.

Bear recited the numbers Julie had given us the day before, then added, "The numbers are always changing, since a lot of animals die on Nancy's watch. It's all just best guess, basically."

I thought of Bear's apparent familiarity with Nancy's place the day before. "You said you and Ren went there before? Without me, I mean?"

There was a pause, and I realized he was trying to decide how much to tell me. I missed Ren immediately. Where Bear can be secretive, forever trying to solve his problems on his own, I could always count on Ren to come to me when it mattered most.

"We thought we could convince her to give some of the animals up," he finally confessed. "Or at least, maybe we could help her with them. We went there a few times this winter."

"When was the last time the two of you went?" I asked.

He thought for a second. "End of April, maybe?"

"Why did you stop going?"

He didn't say anything. I thought back to that time frame, and recalled one Saturday afternoon in particular. Bear had come home with bruises, and a dog bite on his ankle that he'd been far too vague about explaining.

"The bite you had to get stitches for?" I asked. "Did that happen at Nancy's place? You told me it was a dog training client."

"If I told you it was one of Nancy's dogs, you would have freaked out. Reaver didn't mean anything by it, just got nervous because I made a sudden move. It was my own fault."

"That was a deep wound," I said. "You needed half a

dozen stitches. Did you even find out if he'd had his shots? What the hell were you thinking?"

"Ren followed up with Nancy," Bear said, his voice tight in defense. "And she was obsessed with making sure it didn't get infected—you know how Ren is. I watched the bite, was up to date on my tetanus… Ren would have made me say something if anything went wrong."

"That wasn't her call, though," I said. The rest of the van was quiet, and I knew this wasn't the time or the place to be having this discussion. Regardless, I wanted to make sure Bear had some idea of how serious the consequences could have been for this kind of omission. "I know you two are used to dealing with a lot of responsibility—a hell of a lot more than most kids your age. That doesn't mean you can just go around me when the truth is inconvenient. It's still up to me to keep you safe."

"I'm eighteen now," Bear reminded me unnecessarily. Like I wasn't there eighteen years ago, when he was tearing up my insides on his way out. "It's not up to you to do anything at all for me. It hardly matters anymore, though, does it? Ren's gone. You don't have to worry about us going around you anymore."

His tone was sullen, like he was just spoiling for a fight. He'd been going back and forth between two moods ever since Ren left, like he couldn't decide whether he wanted to beat the crap out of somebody or just curl up and cry. Personally, I wasn't crazy about either choice.

"I miss her too, you know," I said. Though it was dark in the van, I could see Bear shift in his seat. "But you don't see me being a jerk to everybody around me because of it. And as for your being eighteen meaning I'm not responsible for you anymore, that's a load of horse crap and you know it. Just because legally I may not have to put a roof over your head now doesn't mean I'm not going to worry about every move you make. I don't get to retire just because you had a birthday."

"Mm hmm."

So much for that conversation. I chose not to push anything further in the presence of the others, but I really wasn't loving this brooding, humorless new side to my son. He'd always been serious, but this was ridiculous.

"Well, however many animals she had out here," Monty interrupted, steering us along an almost-empty stretch of Route 97 as the sun came up on the horizon, "it hardly matters. Chances are, she didn't even know how many there were. I still don't understand what she could have been thinking, letting things get this bad."

Monty had been working with me for seven years now, and there was no mistaking the disapproval in his voice. I'd hired him the day he was released from the Maine State Prison, on a recommendation from a friend who ran a canine training program with the inmates there. He could be irreverent and outspoken, but so far I hadn't had a single moment's regret since bringing him on board.

"She was crazy," Bear said. "Trust me, there was no reasoning with her. We should have taken them all yesterday."

"We weren't getting them out of there without a fight yesterday," I said. "This was the only way."

"Yeah, this is so much better than getting a few cops involved and just getting it over with when we were already there," Bear said dryly.

"Hindsight's twenty-twenty. If I'd known something

like this would happen, I would've pushed her harder. We couldn't have known."

"I still don't get how anybody could do this," Bear said. "She claimed she loved them, but you saw them yesterday. Animals half dead, starving, mangy, with who knows what kinds of diseases. Killing each other, biting anything that moved... If she loved them, she had a funny way of showing it." The anger hummed from his body.

"It's not up to us to figure out what she was thinking," I said. "We leave that up to the investigators."

"Right," Bear muttered. "We just go in afterward and clean up the mess."

We rode the rest of the way in silence, though Bear's words lingered in my head for the remainder of the drive.

4

NANCY'S HOUSE WAS OVERRUN with police cars, ambulance, and fire trucks when we arrived shortly before six that morning. There were plenty of civilian cars as well, most of them equipped with at least one dog crate or a stack of cat carriers, while volunteers stalked the premises in search of one more rogue dog, cat, cow, or rabbit to save.

"Where are the animals you've already gotten?" I asked Tracy when I reached her, standing beside the Pope Humane Society van. Her dark hair was pulled back, and she wore jeans and a man's flannel shirt—both of them filthy. The day hadn't even started yet, and it had already been a long one.

"We're triaging out back," she said. "Thank God, the animals in the barns and the farm yard were right where Nancy left them—looks like it was just the guys in the house who got out."

"There's a fence, though," I pointed out. "Wouldn't they have just been confined to the yard?"

"Front gate was open, too," she said, grimacing. "Whoever did this, I don't know what in hell they were thinking. But then, I almost never do where people are concerned. Animals are so much easier to figure." She took a second to get herself back on track, then added, "I have three stock trailers people have donated. The problem is, a couple of fosters backed out at the last minute, and we found a bunch of animals at the back of the big barn nobody seemed to know about. Which means I have a few more placements to deal with."

I glanced at Therese, standing beside me with arms crossed over her ample bosom and a knowing expression on her face.

"How many can we take?"

"Realistically?" She weighed the question. "Bear already committed to a donkey and ram he checked out yesterday, I guess. We have room for a couple more of the farm animals. Maybe the rest of the sheep. We need to redo the fencing out on that northern pasture on the island. Our pygmies have trashed it."

I grimaced. We'd been having fencing wars with Randy, Rowdy, and Piper, three rescued pygmy goats, since Bear got them from a hoarding situation in New Hampshire last fall.

"We're in good enough shape to take the whole sheep herd here and not be stretched too thin, though," Therese continued. "I know there are a couple of cows—"

"Already got placements for the cows, the chickens, and the rabbits," Tracy said. The beauty of living in a rescue-friendly rural community. "We need a place for the dogs—at least the ones the police say aren't a danger."

"We've got an entire building with empty kennels," Bear said immediately, leaping into the conversation head first. "We can take whoever you need."

"Not so fast," I stopped him. "We have a new shipment of trainees coming next month. We tell the shelters we're not taking them, and those dogs die."

"That gives us a month to work with these guys. We can figure it out."

At Flint K-9, we work with high-kill shelters around the country to find dogs with the right energy, build, and temperament for search and rescue, police work, or to serve as therapy or assistance dogs. We pull those dogs off the euthanasia list, bring them to our facility out on Windfall Island, and then work with the dogs on the basics—housetraining, basic commands, and socialization—before either training them ourselves for search and rescue or sending them to affiliate groups who will train them in another specialty. It's a constant juggling act to ensure we have the space to take in new dogs when necessary while still making sure we're turning out top-notch working dogs who will go on to live out happy, healthy lives in forever homes once they make the transition from Flint K-9.

Therese raised her eyebrows at me, but said nothing. I did the calculations. It was true: right now we had twenty empty kennels, and were in a rare position to be able to work twenty-four-seven on rehabbing and re-homing these dogs. Dogs who had, up until last night, known only one kind soul in their lifetimes—and that kind soul had nearly killed them.

"We need to approach this with as much organization as possible," I said, my focus on Bear. "That means you're in charge—completely—of house training, nutrition, socialization, and everything else that goes along with this. You don't have Ren to help you, but you have access to our staff and resources to make things happen. All that said… This means you're responsible for coordinating this whole thing. It's a big job."

"I can handle it," he said, without a second's thought.

I have faith in my kid, but I definitely had some

reservations this time around. Regardless, I nodded. "Okay, then. We can take up to twenty dogs that you think we can either re-home given the right training, or send to long-term foster placements if that's the better solution. I leave it up to you to decide how to run things from there."

He grinned at me, dark eyes alight. After the way he'd been acting for the past month, that light was a relief. Bear has always loved a challenge.

"You got it," he said. And then, almost as an afterthought, he added, "Thanks, Mom."

I nodded. Most parents dread the question, "Mom, can I keep him?" I have no sympathy until their kid starts asking, "Mom, can I keep the whole kennel?"

Monty had been back in triage checking out the other animals, but now he returned to me at a light jog, phone in hand. "They just got a call about a rabid dog over on River Road, about a mile from here. Said it's a giant tan and white pit bull, frothing at the mouth."

"The dog that was chained out back—Reaver," I said to Tracy. "Is he still here?"

Tracy shook her head. "No. We've gotten complaints about him before, so that was one of the first things I checked. Somebody must have let him loose."

"You think that could be him over on River Road?" Monty asked, then reconsidered. "Giant pit bull frothing at the mouth sounds about right, I guess."

Tracy frowned. "There's some cowboy who's afraid of dogs who lives not far from here. He's got guns, and he's certainly not shy about using them. Hank, Nancy's neighbor, is already over that way trying to catch another couple of dogs spotted over there. I'm sure he could use some help. I was just about to head over myself."

"I'll go," Bear said.

"You stay here," I said quickly. After the bullet Bear had taken when another cowboy with a gun took a shot at his dog, there was no way I was letting him go that route again. "Take care of the dogs we've already got here, and start working up assessments. Tracy and I will handle Reaver."

To my surprise, he didn't argue. In fact, he looked a little relieved. Maybe Bear didn't come through everything in Vermont last year quite so painlessly after all.

"Let's go, then," Tracy said to me. "I don't know how much time we've got before somebody decides to take matters into their own hands."

●

The sun was just coming up over the ridge on River Road when we got there, a ball of pink and gold that hovered above the tree line. Cushing is a fishing village—and not the kind tourists flock to. It's a rough town that keeps to itself, somehow managing to maintain an air of unapproachability when neighboring villages very much like it have been overrun by wealthy out-of-staters. Land is cheap and life is tough, but the area is beautiful.

Hank was waiting for us when we got there, smoking a cigarette as he leaned against a red pickup parked on the side of the road. He tossed the butt on the ground and stubbed it out with the toe of his Bean boot, then glanced at me when I glared at him. After a second-long standoff, he bent with some effort and picked it up.

"Thanks," I said.

"You'd think littering was a federal offense, the way some people carry on," he said.

"It's a hard world when a man can't even dump his toxic crap on the ground without being called on it," I said.

He grunted.

"No in-fighting now, you two," Tracy said. "It's bad enough I've got to deal with it with the animals. My people better pull themselves together and get along. You two met, right? Jamie Flint, Hank Williams. Hank, meet Jamie."

"We met," I confirmed. I raised an eyebrow at Hank. "Hank Williams?"

"No relation to the singers. My mom was just a fan. It's good to meet you, officially. I've certainly heard enough about you and your crew out on the island."

I wasn't sure whether what he'd heard was good or bad, and he didn't elaborate. Instead, to my relief, he got down to business.

"We already caught three of the dogs out here—I just sent Mandy back with those. The pit bull seems to be the last of 'em. He was out that way last I saw him." He nodded toward the west. "Running deer, so you know nobody'll stand for that too long."

"No," I agreed, grim. "What did he look like?"

"Big brown and white pit bull, mangy and half-starved. It's Reaver all right."

"I take it you heard about Nancy," Tracy said.

Hank grunted again. He patted the front pocket of his flannel shirt, pulled out a pack of Marlboros, and lit up. "They know who did it yet?"

"They haven't given us any details yet," Tracy said. "I heard rumblings that it was a heart attack. You heard different?"

"Just rumors down to Bob's Market. Nobody knows anything for sure. I heard tell from one of the deputies though, off the record, that there was some cleanup that needed to be done. Blood. Used the words 'brain matter.' That doesn't sound much like a heart attack to me."

My stomach turned. It was just rumor, I reminded myself, and rumors run rampant in small towns like this. Still… They usually have some basis in truth.

Up on the ridge, I saw a flash of movement along the tree line. On the move in an instant, all thought of gossip forgotten, I touched Tracy's arm as I passed. "I think he's still up there."

"You want me to bring my gun?" Hank asked. To his credit, he didn't look happy at the idea. I shook my head.

"We've got tranquilizer darts. No need for anything stronger. We want to take him alive."

"And you don't think I do?" he asked, grim.

Together, the three of us trudged up the ridge toward the forest. We'd barely cleared the tree line before I saw him: as skinny and mangy as Hank had said, but twice as big as I remembered him in Nancy's yard.

"Shit," Hank said, under his breath.

"Just give him a minute," I said. "Nancy couldn't handle him, but Bear was able to establish a bond." I didn't mention the scar on his ankle, courtesy of this dog.

"Bear's not here, though, so that doesn't do us much good," Hank pointed out.

"She means if Bear bonded with him, he's capable of establishing that bond with others and he clearly has some attachment to humans," Tracy said. "So, what's our plan here?" she asked me. "I have the tranq. Do you want me to try and lure him into the open?"

"I don't have any other ideas," I said. I looked at Hank pointedly. "Are you sure you want to be here? It could be dangerous."

"You want me to sign a waiver?" he asked. "If we don't get him, some asshole will shoot him for sure. I don't much care to see things end that way."

Neither did I.

Sobered, slow, and steadfast, we moved forward.

We followed a trail through the brush as the sun rose higher on the horizon, warmth coming up from the forest floor. I heard rustling in the distance, and looked at Tracy. She froze at the same time I did, and Hank bumped into my back. He started to grumble, but I held up my hand. He fell silent. Not far from us, I heard a low whine in the brush. Tracy looked at me quizzically. I shook my head, equally uncertain. I motioned the others to stay back, and moved forward on my own.

"Reaver," I said quietly. The whining stopped. Everything went still. I tensed, unsure what I would come up against if I took another step. Tracy hung back, her tranq gun down. If Reaver was in there and he wasn't in the mood for visitors, it would take him no time to do serious damage to me if he had the mind for it. I might be able to squeeze off a shot, but whether that stopped him in time was anybody's guess.

I remained still, holding my breath. Waiting.

There was more rustling in the bushes, accompanied by that same whine. And more movement.

And then, a grizzled head appeared. Reaver stared at me warily. Rather than look at him head-on, a threat among canids, I looked away. Shifted where I stood, so my body wasn't square with his. He whined again, and took a hesitant step forward. Once he'd cleared the brush, I got a good look at him and felt my eyes well.

There was a fringe of crimson on his chest, dried now. His coat was patchy, raw pink skin showing through on most of his body. I knelt slowly and lowered my head, still not looking at him. Hank started to say something, but Tracy shushed him.

Reaver took another step toward me.

I watched him out of the corner of my eye, noting the way he sniffed the air before moving closer. He looked toward Hank and Tracy, and froze.

No one moved.

Another second passed. Reaver stood, uncertain, his head down and a profound fatigue about him. His ears moved forward, then back. There was a rustle of branches in the distance and he started, his attention riveted in that direction. I thought of his fate if we didn't catch him now, and had no doubt that he would be dead within the day.

"Come on, buddy. Just come with us. We'll get you fixed up—you'll be okay."

He remained focused on me, struggling with his choices. I was amazed he was still here. Either he was worse off physically than I'd thought, or his bond with humans was stronger. I inched my hand toward the treat bag at my waist, while Reaver watched me with naked suspicion.

"You hungry, Reav?" I asked, voice still quiet. "I bet you are. That's why you're out here, huh? You think maybe you can find something…" I got my hand into the bag and slowly withdrew a handful of the bits of jerky I invariably have on hand.

Reaver never took his eyes from me, his nose up and quivering as he sniffed the air.

"I bet Bear's given you these before, huh? Remember them? What do you say, buddy?" I asked. Moving as carefully as I could, I tossed a couple of pieces low in his general direction, then held my breath.

His entire body seemed to tremble as he wrestled with the choice. Finally, after an interminable pause, he stalked toward the food. He gulped down everything I'd put out and then, to my surprise, he raised his head expectantly rather than running away.

"More, huh? All right. I guess I can do that."

I tossed another few pieces, this time closer. Reaver hesitated only a moment before he limped forward and gulped the food.

This was promising, but I knew our time was running out. The longer we were out here, the better the chance that something could spook the dog, and we would never see him again.

Reluctantly, I looked toward Tracy and Hank. Reaver stood there—just stood, immovable. I crouched down and held out my hand, my eyes still averted, my body turned away.

Nothing happened for as much as thirty seconds. Then, still looking away, I felt a warm, wet nose against my palm. The swipe of a soft tongue.

Reaver took the food I gave him, then waited patiently, watching my every move, as I pulled the last of it from my pouch. "You ready to go home, boy?" I asked.

He whined, then lay down.

It looked like I had my answer.

5

JACK JUAREZ LOOKED OUT over Rockland Harbor, where the summer sun shone bright on the water. He was three flights up, with a bird's eye view of the tourists walking the boardwalk below. It looked beautiful out, too.

He could take a walk, he mused.

Rock City Coffee was just down the street. They made great scones, and even better coffee. That would pass a few minutes, anyway.

It was ten past nine in the morning, according to the clock on the opposite wall. He'd rented this apartment with the intention of having it double as office space for his new business as a private investigator, but he was beginning to second guess that decision. Maybe he should have chosen a place more visible to passersby.

Of course, not all that many people hired a P.I. on impulse.

Based on his experiences of the past three months since establishing this business, however, not many people hired a P.I., period. At least, not in Midcoast Maine.

Maybe he should get more plants. Or hire a receptionist. Though he had no idea how he could afford one. Right now, he was eating through his savings at a dizzying rate.

Maybe this whole thing had been a colossal mistake.

A knock at the door interrupted his thoughts, thankfully, before he went spiraling down the rabbit hole of self-doubt completely.

"Just a second," he called. Who would come without calling first?

He thought immediately of Jamie. Whatever his intentions may have been when first making the move to this area—and even he was unclear on what those were, exactly—he had seen very little of the dog handler since moving to Rockland. Despite the filth and the oppressive chaos at Nancy Davis's place yesterday, he'd been grateful for an excuse to be part of Jamie's world once more. He'd told her when he first moved that he was happy to stay on until she hired and trained a replacement who, without question, would be better at K-9 search and rescue than Jack had ever been.

Jack didn't even really like dogs that much.

Jamie, however, seemed to consider their working relationship finished as soon as they left Bethel after a search in February. They'd had time for an awkward cup of coffee here and there since then, but nothing more. Until she'd called him the day before to come lend a hand at Nancy's place, he'd honestly wondered if he would ever hear from her again.

Wrapped up in his tumultuous thoughts, Jack checked the peephole in his door, registered a moment of genuine surprise, and opened up.

Bear Flint, Jamie's son, stood in the hallway looking unmistakably awkward.

"Is your mom okay?" was the first question Jack could think of.

"Yeah, she's fine. She's busy over at Nancy's right now."

Intrigued, Jack stepped aside and motioned Bear in. The young man looked around briefly, but seemed to find nothing worth commenting on as Jack ushered him in and over to a chair.

After an awkward moment trying to decide where to situate himself, Jack settled for the plush leather chair behind his desk. Bear and Jamie were vegetarians. Bear's girlfriend was vegan. Not for the first time, Jack reconsidered his choice in office furniture.

"Is everything all right on the island?" he prompted, when Bear offered no information. He was a good-looking kid, tall and muscular, but right now his eyes were shadowed as though he hadn't slept, and he looked singularly ill at ease inside the office.

"I can't stay long," Bear said, as though Jack had summoned him instead of him simply showing up unannounced on Jack's doorstep. "I need to get back to Nancy's." He sat poised at the edge of his seat before looking at Jack abruptly.

"Did you hear what happened over at Nancy's place overnight? See it on the news?"

Jack shook his head. "No. I usually read the paper, but I haven't gotten to it yet today."

"I'm not sure it's in there," Bear said. "It happened pretty late. But..." He paused, looking around uncomfortably once more. "Well, Nancy's dead. Died in the night. And her kid is missing—I mean, her son. Her grown son. Albie."

Jack felt his eyebrows climb his forehead, honestly shocked. "What happened?"

Bear shook his head. "I'm not sure." He stood, paced briefly, and then plunked himself down into the chair again.

Fidgeted. Wiped his hands on the legs of his jeans, as though his palms were sweating. He looked like he was about to climb out of his own skin.

"Why don't we go outside and take a walk on the Promenade," Jack said. "We can talk while we move."

"That would be good," Bear said. He was back on his feet before Jack had completed the sentence. "No offense. I just… I get a little freaked out inside."

"I hadn't noticed."

•

A few minutes later, Jack walked alongside Bear while the sun shone down, a cooling salt breeze coming off the water. Bear walked with his hands deep in his pockets and his head down, forehead furrowed, utterly oblivious to the world around him. Jack's concern for the boy grew as the seconds wore on.

"So…" Jack prompted, when they'd walked for a few minutes in silence, Bear's focus seemingly directed inward.

"I want to hire you," the teenager said abruptly.

Jack looked at him, surprised. "Hire me?"

"Because of the whole thing with Nancy," he clarified. "I told you: something happened to her, and now Albie's missing. I don't have a good feeling about it."

"How did she die, exactly?"

"I'm not sure," Bear said. "I think she got hit. Her head was bleeding, her skull kind of crushed in." He shifted his gaze from Jack's for a moment, catching himself. "One of the deputies told me that, anyway. We need to find Albie."

"That seems more in line with what you do than what I do," Jack said. "He can't have gone far."

"I don't want you to help us find him," Bear said, somewhat impatiently. "I want you to figure out who killed his mother."

"Bear—" Jack began.

"I can pay," Bear said, cutting him off. "If that's what you're worried about. I've got a shit load of money. I can pay whatever you want."

"Tht's not the issue. I'm just not sure this is worth you spending that money. It sounds like the police are on it."

"They won't do a good job," Bear insisted. "They'll go after Albie or somebody else who didn't do this, I know it. You have to figure out who really did it." He had a stubborn streak like his mother, Jack noted. And a similar sense of justice, it seemed.

"Let's go somewhere a little more private," Jack said, noting the tourists around them. "You can explain your case there."

"I don't really want to go back inside."

"Don't worry about it," Jack assured him. "I know just the place."

The sun was warm but hardly blazing, the sea breeze cooling the air to manageable. Bear wore jeans and a Flint K-9 polo shirt, an ever-present dog training belt with treats and clicker at his waist. They walked in silence past Time Out Pub—where ladies night had a stripper's pole, or so Jack had been told. From there they crossed Main Street, cut through the Rite Aid parking lot, and crossed the street once more at Dairy Queen.

Bear kept up a good pace as the foot traffic thinned along Union Street, apart from a cluster of older women in linen suits and sun hats outside the Farnsworth Museum.

Eventually, they hit Limerock Street. Jack was

momentarily distracted by a crowd of kids at the playground, but quickly refocused on his ultimate destination:

The library.

This time of day, Jack wasn't surprised to find the bench out front empty. Bear looked at him doubtfully.

"No one will bother us," Jack assured him. "Just tell me what you want me to do."

Bear did, with the shadow of the old brick library behind them, patrons coming in and out, strolling by, occasionally casting a sideways glance their way. But, just as Jack had promised, no one disturbed them for the next hour, as Bear continued his story.

According to Bear, Albie Davis was not a violent man. At least, not toward his mother. And certainly not toward the animals in their care.

"But he's been violent toward others," Jack inferred from the phrasing.

"A couple of times," Bear said. He dismissed the incidents with a wave of his hand. "But he's crazy about his mom. He would have been put away years ago if it weren't for her. Why would he kill her?"

"They were going to have to move," Jack pointed out. "Tensions were running incredibly high when I saw them yesterday. Maybe it all just got to him, and he snapped."

"He wouldn't have done that," Bear insisted. "Not to Nancy. No matter how stressed out he was."

"You can't know that," Jack said, as gently as he could.

Bear's jaw tensed, a stubborn cast to his eyes that Jack recognized. Jamie got the same look when she dug her heels in about something.

"Does your mother know you're here?" he asked, rather than waiting for Bear to continue arguing.

"No. This kind of thing is confidential though, right? You can't tell her anything if I hire you."

"That's right," he agreed. "I guarantee confidentiality for any client I take on. But why wouldn't you want your mom to know?"

"I just don't, all right? This doesn't have anything to do with her—just leave her out of it."

The words came out too quickly, and something nudged at the back of Jack's brain. Bear was lying. Or, at the very least, not telling him the whole story. Jack regarded the boy for a moment in silence, considering.

Both Bear and Jamie were "sensitive"—meaning that they had abilities that Jack, to date, still didn't quite understand. One of those sensitivities for Bear was the ability to see, even communicate with, the dead.

"Did Nancy..." Jack began, then fell off, uncertain how to continue.

Bear understood what he meant immediately. He looked down, and Jack saw a flicker of embarrassment cross his face before it vanished. "I saw her, but not the usual way. Like, I couldn't talk to her. She wasn't actually there."

"What did you see? And when?"

"When we were there yesterday, just before we left," he said. "It was just this...flash, kind of. It's never happened to me like that before, so I wasn't sure what to make of it. Usually if somebody appears to me, they stay and we kind of...like, talk. Nancy didn't say anything, though."

"But you did see her, dead."

"Yeah. Her skull was crushed, brains everywhere." He rolled his eyes. "Nice, right? What a great party trick."

"I guess it depends on the party," Jack said. That got just the hint of a smile from Bear. The older man took a breath, considering things before he spoke again. "I won't lie to your mother," he finally said.

Bear perked up, though he remained guarded. "Does that mean you're taking the case?"

Jack thought for a few seconds. It wasn't like his phone was ringing off the hook. If he had to spend one more day staring out the window at the tourists strolling by, he wasn't sure what he would do.

Bear stood and got his wallet from his back pocket. It looked like it was made out of duct tape. The stack of bills Bear took from the billfold was definitely not play money, though.

"I told you," he said at the look on Jack's face. "I have money. What's your retainer?"

Jack frowned. He needed the money, no question, but did he really need it this bad?

"I'm not here looking for charity," Bear persisted. "Brock left me a ton of money when he died. I get all of it when I turn twenty-one, but I've been getting a good allowance every week since Mom moved us back to Maine to stay with him."

Brock had been Bear's father—an abusive brute who had only shown kindness to Bear, as his only heir. The man had been dead almost ten years now. Killed, Jack suspected, by Jamie herself.

"I only spend his money if I can help people with it," Bear said, as though reading his mind. "Anything I need, I earn the money myself or I do without."

"That's admirable."

"The guy was a monster," Bear said with a shrug. "Even if he was my father. I don't need that kind of karma on top of everything else."

He pushed a fistful of cash toward Jack. Though they were reasonably insulated from others, people were definitely beginning to take note.

"Sit back down," Jack said. "My retainer is $1,000, then it's $200 plus expenses per hour. We can draw up a contract with a cap on those expenses when we get back to the office."

"Whatever," Bear said, waving off the details. "I just want you to get started. It's totally nuts at Nancy's place. Who knows what you've missed already."

Bear handed off the retainer, waving off Jack's offer of a receipt, and agreed to meet him at the Davis home in an hour.

By this time, the sun was high in the sky. Jack had already removed his sports jacket, and now rolled up his shirt sleeves. He'd grown up in Miami—at least, he had for the portion of his childhood he remembered, beginning at thirteen years old. Warmth here was a whole different animal, but one he welcomed regardless. He wasn't sure he would ever get used to Maine winters. He wasn't sure he even wanted to.

"I'll need to be out with the dogs looking for Albie for most of the day and night, if nobody's found him yet," Bear said as they parted. "I'm also coordinating with our vet on the island to make sure we're taking as many animals as we can out there, at least until we can find them permanent placements. But you have my cell number. Just call if you have questions. If I'm not in range, I'll check back as soon as I can."

"I'll reach you if I need to," Jack said, unable to hide how impressed he was at the young man's comport. "You're doing good work. I'm happy to help any way I can."

They shook hands and Jack stood by for a moment

watching Bear walk away. He strode forward without looking around him, seemingly oblivious to everything but whatever was waiting dead ahead. Jack took a breath, trying to shake the feeling he'd had earlier that something here wasn't right. Bear was keeping something from him, he was sure of it. What it was and how it related to the job Jack had been hired to do, only time would tell.

6

"SO, WHO ELSE ARE WE MISSING?" I asked Bear wearily. It was nearly three in the afternoon. Bear was covered in grass stains and what looked like a smear of blood on his left cheek, but he looked a lot more energized than I felt at the moment.

"I haven't been able to find Cash yet," he said. "You know, that old one-eared tomcat? Haven't seen him anywhere."

"He probably headed for the hills," I said. "We'll have the volunteers keep an eye out for him, and spread the word that he's missing."

"I've been looking for the Newfoundland," Hank Williams said. He'd remained on scene helping with the animals for the duration of this operation. So far, his knowledge of the place and the animals on it had been invaluable. "Cody."

"Monty caught him about an hour ago," I said. "We sent him out to the island with the last group."

"And he's okay?" Hank asked.

"Scared, mangy, and on the thin side. But in better shape than a lot of them," Bear said.

Hank nodded. "Sure, sure. Yeah, nobody here had it easy." He hesitated. "You know what you're going to do with all those dogs? I mean, once they're cleaned up and whatever? You'll probably want to find homes for them…"

"Are you interested in adopting the Newfie?"

He smiled, and I was surprised at the emotion in his eyes. Not completely, of course—dogs can make the most stalwart among us go a little misty.

"I could fill out an application or whatever. I haven't had a dog in a few years, but I used to have one that'd go on the boat with me when I was out fishing. I think Cody might like that kind of thing."

"I'll talk to Tracy," I said. "She'll get you an application, and we'll need to run some tests on the dog to make sure he's healthy. As long as he is and there are no hitches with your application, I'm sure we can work something out."

"Good," he said, with an abrupt nod. "I feel terrible about what happened here—both with Nancy dying and everything that came before. I know she loved the animals in her way, just didn't have the money to take care of 'em, or sense enough to turn them away. I know she'd be happy knowing they're being taken care of now."

I looked around the dilapidated old house and the muddied front yard. We'd been working hard all day long, and I'd had little time to talk to Bear about any of this. I wondered if he had seen Nancy's spirit anywhere here over the course of the day. I'd have to carve out a little down time later to ask him.

"That's it, then," I said. "We'll come back in the—"

"Jamie!" a voice called. A voice that sounded a lot like Jack's. Which was confusing, since I hadn't even realized he was here. Not only that, but it sounded like he was calling from somewhere beneath my feet.

"Jack? Where are you?" I called back, walking toward the sound of his voice.

"Down here," he called back. "The basement."

Honestly baffled, I walked to the edge of the house and lay down on my stomach in the muck, then peered beneath a sizable gap under the back porch. The smell was rancid, a combination of rotting garbage and dog crap, disease and waste. It was too dark to see a thing, so I shone my flashlight below. Jack blinked in the glare and looked away, while a pair of yellow eyes glowed from his arms.

"What's going on?" I asked.

"He came and got me," he said, nodding toward the yellow eyes. I adjusted the light, and found Cash settled in Jack's arms.

"What do you mean, he came and got you?" I asked. "In Rockland?" It had been a long day; at this point there wasn't much that would have surprised me.

"I heard that something happened and you could maybe use a hand," he said briefly. "Once I got here, the cat found me and led me here when I tried to catch him. You talk to dead people. Don't make fun of me because a cat came to me for help."

As he was speaking, a tiny, plaintive *mew* floated up to me, followed by a chorus of more of the same. Cash answered with a trilling *Prrrt* before he looked back at Jack and me.

"There's a litter of kittens down here," Jack explained. "Five of them. They're skinny, and I don't see any sign of the mom."

Bear had said some cats had been killed here recently;

these babies could well have been orphaned victims of that violence. Cash stood and butted his big head against Jack while the kittens continued their plaintive mewing.

"Bring them out," I said, after only a moment's thought. "We'll send them to the shelter with Cash, and see what we can do from there."

Jack didn't move, though I could make out just enough now to see the horror on his face at the suggestion. "Hang on," he said. "First… There's another problem down here."

Of course there was. I couldn't even imagine what that problem might be, but the number of them stacking up around us was starting to get overwhelming.

"What problem?" I asked.

He hesitated. "There are bones down here."

"There are bones everywhere," I said. "The place is like a pet cemetery—they just forgot to bury most of the bodies."

"This isn't a pet."

"What do you mean, it isn't a pet?"

"They're human, Jamie," he said. A touch of impatience touched his voice. Like I should just assume Nancy Davis had people rotting in her basement. "There are human remains down here. At least a couple of them, possibly more."

I was stunned into silence.

"Hey," I heard Bear say behind me. "What's going on? Monty and I have the trailer loaded up again, but I couldn't find you. Can we go or what?"

I raised a hand, index finger up to indicate I needed a minute. Bear crouched down and peered into the opening below the house with me.

"Hey, Jack," he said. If he was surprised, I heard no

trace of it in his voice. "Is that Cash you've got there?"

"Yeah," Jack said. The kittens started up again, jolting me out of my brief inaction. If we were going to save them, we needed to move now.

"Hand the kittens up here," I said to Jack. "And Cash, if you can get him. Bear, let Tracy know we have another tom and five sick kittens. And then go get Sheriff Finnegan."

"What do we need Sheriff Finnegan for, for five sick kittens and a barn cat?" Bear asked.

"Never mind," I said wearily.

"So they'll take Cash to the shelter, then?" Jack asked. So far, he hadn't moved.

"That's the plan. They'll test him for distemper and FIV, and then maybe someone will take him for the barn cat program."

"He doesn't like being a barn cat, though," Jack said.

"Did he tell you that?"

"Very funny. I can just tell. He likes people too much— if he could be inside, he would." He paused. "What about the kittens?"

Saving orphaned kittens is notoriously difficult in animal rescue. Upper respiratory infections sweep through cat colonies like this, with the most vulnerable members of the colony succumbing within a matter of days.

"Jack—"

"I was thinking maybe we could get Cash tested, and he could come home with me," he said, cutting me off. "Cats are allowed in my building," he added hastily.

"We'll talk to Tracy," I said. "For now, though, you need to get those kittens out of there."

This time, Jack complied. He handed up the first kitten:

a little orange thing that, despite Jack's description, actually seemed to be in good health. He was a little on the thin side, but his blue eyes were wide and clear, the coat surprisingly clean. Based on the weight, I was guessing Mom hadn't been around for feeding for only a couple of days, and Cash had taken good care of the grooming side of things.

Another orange kitten followed, this one purring loudly as I pulled it into the daylight. Cash hopped out of the hole and wound his way around me anxiously, watching my every move.

"It's okay, buddy," I reassured him, as Jack handed off two tabby-colored fluff balls. "We'll take good care of them."

The last kitten was all black, and came up hissing and spitting like a little wild thing as I took him from Jack's hands. With this one, Cash came over just as I was wrangling the little monster into the cat carrier. He bumped against me, purring loudly, and then butted his head gently against the kitten. Instantly, the little guy settled. Cash licked his head, still purring. As if by magic, the kitten stilled.

"Good boy, Cash," I said. "Thanks for the help."

I stood, brushing myself off, and then reached down to offer Jack a hand.

"I'll go back around," he said. "The squeeze is a little too tight for me. I'll meet you out front."

•

"What do you mean, there are more bodies?" Sheriff Finnegan asked a few minutes later, scratching his head. He looked beat, and not at all happy at this latest news.

"Jack said one or two—"

"Three, actually," Jack corrected me, inserting himself into the conversation. He was covered in dirt and cobwebs from head to foot, and he smelled like he'd been nesting in a garbage dump. "That I could see. Where's Cash? And the kittens?"

"With Tracy. She's trying to find a foster placement for the kittens. The fact that they're as healthy as they are actually makes it harder. We need to find a place where they won't be exposed to any illness."

"I was thinking maybe I—"

"I'm sorry to interrupt," Sheriff Finnegan said, "but can we get back to the three bodies in the cellar?"

"At least," Jack said. "Some could be buried, I suppose. These looked like..." He hesitated, unmistakably uncomfortable. "It looks like they died down there."

The sheriff swore under his breath, shaking his head. "The Staties will love that. How much more do you need to do to clear the animals out?"

I surveyed the landscape. The house was now clear— at least as far as we could tell—and so was the dog barn. The barn that held the remaining cats had been emptied as much as anyone could manage, but I was sure we would keep finding cats here for the next month. Maybe longer. The farmyard, likewise, had been emptied. It had taken ten hours to get everyone, but it would take years to address the scars some of these animals carried from the situation Nancy had put them in.

"We're just about done," I said. "No more dogs that we've found. The police can safely start going through everything."

"Safe is a relative term," Sheriff Finnegan replied gravely. "Maybe we don't have to worry about being attacked, but we'll need Hazmat suits to wade through this mess."

I looked around again, at the sea of filth and waste and decay around us. "You're not wrong."

As the sheriff walked away to address the bodies in the basement, I noticed a small, timid-looking man who stood on the sidelines with his hands clasped in front of him. He was speaking to Barbara Monroe, who stood beside him in a crisp summer dress. Her blond hair was pulled back in a chignon as sleek as silk.

When he caught my eye, the man raised his hand hesitantly and stepped toward me. "Excuse me."

When he turned to face me fully, I did a double take. Albie. Or an older, cleaner version of him, anyway.

"Yes?" I said.

He excused himself from Barbara, somewhat reluctantly I thought, and crossed the police line to reach me.

"You're Jamie Flint?" he asked.

"I am. You must be Fred—Nancy's oldest son?"

He nodded. He looked exhausted, and thoroughly beaten. "Yes. I came as soon as I heard. You're working on the search for my brother?"

"No," I said, with a shake of my head. "Right now I'm working with the Humane Society. We're rounding up the animals. A lot of them escaped in the night."

Anger flickered in his eyes for just a moment, then vanished. "Right. God forbid we forget about the animals."

"I can understand your frustration, but most of the animals who were living here are in critical condition thanks to your mother's neglect. This isn't a problem we created."

"I know that," he said, his voice softer. "Trust me, I do. I'd been pushing for months to figure something out with them."

"Yeah. I guess evicting her was one way to do it," I said. Lack of sleep and a day of rounding up animals who may well not survive this had made me testy; I couldn't keep the disapproval from my words. "I know all about it. Maybe if you had—"

"If I had what, Ms. Flint?" he cut me off. "I'd love to hear your ideas. God knows I tried everything I could think of. My pleas fell on deaf ears. I tried bribery; tried threats; tried getting professionals involved. All those professionals did was step in and make this place exactly habitable enough to be deemed safe—barely—for my brother and the animals who lived here. Do you have any idea what it's like, living in a place where the best you can say about it is, 'Well, at least it hasn't been condemned yet'?"

For the first time that day, I thought of things from this man's perspective. What would Bear do, if God forbid I put him in a situation like this? What would anyone?

"I'm sorry," I said, as earnestly as I could manage. "I can't imagine what you're going through right now. It's easy for me to sit in judgment, but I know how difficult your mother could be."

"Thank you. I appreciate that. I just..." He shook his head wearily. "I was at my wit's end. Our father left us rather than stay in this place. My fiancée took off without so much as a note, while we were here trying to get things back on track. God knows what's happened to my brother."

I thought of the remains in the basement. If Fred Davis thought things were bad now...

"Have you had a chance to talk to the police yet?" I asked.

"No. Ms. Monroe caught me as soon as I drove in, and then I spotted you."

He surveyed the scene, taking in the police cars and crime scene van beside the house. With the animals gone, there was a haunted air about the place.

"It seems like a lot of fuss for something that..." He hesitated, realization dawning on his face. "I assumed my mother had a heart attack—she's been on medication for years. Am I wrong about that? How did she die, exactly?"

"You should probably go find the sheriff," I said, as gently as I could.

He looked at me sharply, recognizing something in my tone. A fresh wave of alarm registered in his eyes. "Of course," he said numbly. "Excuse me."

I watched him go, surprised at just how much my heart went out to the man. Then, I looked around and forced another deep breath. Rats scuttled from garbage heap to garbage heap in plain sight, taking their chances now that there were no predators to keep them away. A stench that felt like it had soaked into the very ground itself rose up around me, and I wondered if it would ever truly go away.

I shook my head, squared my shoulders, and got back to work. I'd made little progress before Jack materialized beside me, in a way that had begun to feel almost natural.

"Was that the other son you were talking to?" he asked.

"It is. I'd turned him into a devil based on Nancy's stories and her situation, but I can't imagine what he's going through right now."

"No," Jack agreed. "It seems pretty devastating. And I think it's about to get worse."

I glanced at him. "What—the bodies in the basement?"

"Yeah… That too," he said briefly, averting his gaze.

"Meaning?" He didn't say anything for a second. I raised an eyebrow and ushered him well out of hearing range of anyone else.

"What aren't you telling me?"

"Nancy's apparent heart attack?" Jack said, his voice low. "Yes?"

"They've officially released a statement—it was an attack, but it didn't have anything to do with her heart."

"Someone killed her?" Against my will, Albie's face flashed in my mind.

"Yes. Any thoughts on who it might have been?" he asked.

"It could have been anyone. Hell, it could have been me. No doubt I've wanted to throttle her before, and I know anybody who loves animals has felt the same. Most wouldn't act on that, though."

"Most?" Jack echoed.

I shrugged. "It's hard to know what a body might do in the heat of the moment." The face of Brock Campbell, Bear's abusive father, flashed through my mind, in those final seconds before he closed his eyes for the last time. I pushed the image away.

"They're looking for Albie now," Jack said, oblivious to my own dark thoughts. "The police have some questions."

"I bet." I tried to imagine what the scene possibly could have been before Albie fled. He must have been terrified. "Wait," I said, understanding dawning. "They can't think he had anything to do with this."

Jack shrugged. "You saw how upset he was when we left yesterday."

"Yes, but—" I stopped. The truth was, I had no idea what had happened. And definitely no clue what Albie had been going through in the months and years that led up to this tragic ending.

"I should get back to the island," I said. "Thanks for coming here today. You didn't have to, you know."

"I know," he said. He studied me a moment, and I got the uneasy sense there was something he wanted to tell me. A flicker of guilt crossed his face before it vanished. "I heard about everything that happened, and came out to see for myself. To be honest, I was surprised to hear about it secondhand rather than getting a call from you. I would have come out to help sooner."

"Thank you. But I know you're trying to run a business now. You can't just come traipsing out whenever I get a notion it might be nice to have you on board."

"I'll let you know if I don't have the time," he said. "Let me make that call, okay?"

"Okay," I agreed. "Talk to you later?"

"Count on it. I'm sure I'll need some pointers once I get Cash home."

I smiled, watching him walk away. Try as I might, I still couldn't shake the feeling that I was missing something significant about his presence here today.

7

FOR MOST OF THE AFTERNOON, Jack stayed at the Davis home helping round up animals, clear debris, and whatever else anyone might ask of him. While it was true that he liked being seen as useful, particularly where Jamie was concerned, he didn't fool himself thinking this was altruism on his part. He was here for Bear and the case as much as anything.

He watched Fred Davis, Nancy's older son, observing the man's interaction with Jamie from a distance. He seemed genuinely distraught, as much by his brother's disappearance as the fact that his mother was dead.

After he'd reconnected briefly with Jamie and they had parted ways, Jack made his way over to the spot where Fred Davis and Sheriff Finnegan were still speaking. He lurked discreetly in the background, straining to hear their conversation.

"Will you give us a hand?" Tracy asked him as he lingered by the house, trying mightily to look like he wasn't eavesdropping.

He glanced at Tracy, who nodded toward several pallets of rotting pet food stacked beside the house.

"Of course. What did you want to do with them?"

"There's some food that's still good here—I hate to see it go to waste. A couple of local shelters and pet food pantries got it together for Nancy in the hopes that maybe she'd be able to make it through the winter. I just want to go through and pull the bags out that we can use. The others will be hauled away by the garbage collector in the next few days, if the rats don't eat their way through them before that."

Jack suppressed a shudder, but nodded. He didn't care for rats. Or rot, for that matter. Regardless, he stepped in beside Tracy and set to work, conveniently within hearing range of Fred Davis and the sheriff.

"What happened to her?" Fred asked, his voice more curious than despairing. Which struck Jack as interesting, if not overtly suspicious. People reacted in all manner of ways to grief, in his experience. No one way was really any better than any others.

"I told you, Fred, I'm not going to know anything until the M.E. has a chance to look at her."

"You have to know something, though," Fred insisted. "Somebody said something about a heart attack. You think that's what happened?"

Jack perked up, relieved that Tracy seemed too intent on the job at hand to bother with chitchat.

"Honestly?" Sheriff Finnegan began. "I'm sorry, Fred, but no. It wasn't a heart attack. Can you tell me where you were last night, between the hours of midnight and three a.m.?"

There was a pause. "Me? You can't think I had anything to do with…" Fred paused. "Right," he said, voice resigned.

"Of course you would think that. I'm probably the number one suspect."

"I wouldn't say that," the sheriff said, not without kindness. "But in these sorts of crimes, the family is often involved. I just need to rule you out so I can focus on catching whoever did do this."

The sheriff handled the man well, with just the right balance between compassion and strength. Jack had seen Finnegan in action before, but it had been some time. He was pleased to see that the sheriff hadn't lost his edge.

"Of course," Fred said dully. "I was in Portland last night, and planned to head this way today. I'd just flown in from Philadelphia, where I'm living now."

"Where did you stay?"

"The Hampton Inn by the airport. It was stupid—I knew that. Way too expensive, especially this time of year. I just wanted one more night with sanity and clean sheets before I came back here."

"And you have someone who'll confirm you were there?"

Jack glanced up as he handed off another undamaged bag of dog chow to Tracy. Fred stood facing the sheriff, his shoulders hunched and head down. The body language of a defeated man. So much so that Jack wondered if he might be overselling it.

"Just hotel staff," Fred said. "I got there at a little past ten. Checked out as soon as I got the call this morning, at seven o'clock."

So whoever gave him the news about his mother this morning had decided not to wake him, Jack noted. They had known Nancy was dead and Albie missing by four a.m., according to Jamie. The choice not to call sooner struck Jack as off, though Sheriff Finnegan said nothing.

"Did anyone see you while you were in the room?" the sheriff pressed. "Maybe you ordered room service? Talked to someone at the front desk?"

Fred shook his head. "I just went straight to my room, took a shower, and went to bed. I don't think anyone saw me."

Jack knew that it took just under two hours to get to Cushing from Portland. If Fred had wanted to, he could have checked into the hotel, then gotten in his car and driven straight through to his mother's house. Killed her, done...something, with his brother, and then driven back to Portland. It would have been a long night, but Jack had known plenty of killers who had gone to more trouble to cover their tracks.

He was certain based on the sheriff's lack of response that he was thinking the same thing.

"There's something else I needed to talk to you about, Fred, and I'm sorry about this."

The sheriff glanced in Jack's direction, and Jack quickly returned his attention to the pallets of food before him. Unfortunately, he'd reacted too late.

"Here," the sheriff said, more quietly now. "Why don't you come with me, and we'll find somewhere out of the way to talk about this."

Fred nodded, clearly concerned, and Jack cursed his position. He was used to having a front-row seat to briefings and interrogations, even if local law enforcement hadn't always been crazy about the presence of the FBI. This would take some getting used to.

"Can I give you a hand?" a woman's voice said, just behind him.

"I think we're all right here," Tracy said, before Jack could respond. He turned to find an attractive woman in her mid-thirties, petite and blond, focused on them both. Barbara Monroe, Jack remembered, recalling meeting the woman yesterday.

She smiled when Jack met her eye, and extended her hand. "We weren't really properly introduced yesterday— things were a little bit crazy. I'm Barb. Barbara Monroe. That's our house over there."

She nodded toward an attractive old New England farmhouse on the hill, the yard immaculate and the house clearly well cared for.

Jack shook her hand. It was delicate, the grip firm but distinctly feminine. "Jack Juarez," he said. She smiled but said nothing, waiting for more information. Jack offered none.

"Jack's new in town," Tracy said. "He's lending a hand."

"You're the private investigator, aren't you?" Barb asked, gazing up at him with striking green eyes. "I heard you've been helping Jamie, and then Julie—my daughter—said Bear was talking about your work."

"That's right," Jack agreed, inexplicably self-conscious. It also occurred to him that he couldn't imagine Bear saying anything about him to anyone, much less Julie Monroe. "I just moved to Rockland a few months ago."

She shifted where she stood, her gaze wavering. She had a question; Jack could read her face well enough to see that clearly. Before she could ask it, however, Jack's attention was drawn to a station wagon that had just pulled into the drive.

A small, silver-haired woman got out of the driver's side.

Jack squelched a grin.

He might have been locked out of the investigation before, but his luck had just taken a turn.

"I actually need to speak with someone," he said, addressing Tracy more than Barb. "I'm sorry. I can come back afterward if you still need me."

Tracy waved him off. "The rest of this stuff is no good. I'll have Ronny haul it off when he comes for the rest of the trash."

"Let me know if there's anything else I can do," Jack said.

"Does the offer still stand for you taking Cash and the kittens?"

He hesitated a second before nodding. Tracy grinned outright. "That's good news. I'll let you know as soon as the lab tests come back, probably within the hour. If you could take them as soon as tonight, that would be a lifesaver. We'll send you with food, blankets, cat carrier, and litter pans."

He had a brief moment of panic before he nodded. "Of course. Whatever you need."

Barb had been silent throughout this exchange, but Jack got the sense she hadn't let go of her question, whatever it might be. He gave her another moment, but when she made no move, he left the women and walked as casually as he could toward the house. At the back, not far from where he'd made his exit an hour before, the woman he'd spotted at the station wagon was slipping into a white Hazmat suit that looked two sizes too big.

She was assisted by one of Sheriff Finnegan's deputies and another medical assistant—a young man who was suiting up at the same time. At sight of Jack, however, the woman stopped. Her eyebrows raised, disbelief plain in dark brown eyes.

"Jack Juarez? But it can't be! What are you doing here?" She spoke in rapid-fire French, her eyes alight.

"It's a long story," Jack replied, also in French. "The FBI and I parted ways. I'm working as a private investigator not far from here. It's good to see you, Sophie."

"And you," she assured him with a slip of a smile. "Despite the circumstances. I was vacationing nearby when I got this call—Maine already has a top-notch forensic anthropologist, but she's on leave for the summer. It sounded interesting, and…well, I'm not that good at vacations anyway."

"Shocking," Jack said dryly. "I never would have guessed."

He leaned in and kissed her cheeks, warmed at the enthusiasm of the woman's greeting. Dr. Sophie Laurent was a forensic anthropologist who worked out of Quebec. Jack had worked with her on multiple cases over the years, most recently when he was tracking a serial killer in Northern Maine whose victims had extended beyond the Maine/Canada border.

"So you're here to look at the bodies in the basement, then?" Jack asked. At the look of surprise on her face, he added, "I was the one who found them."

"Of course you were," she said with a smile.

"I don't suppose you need any—"

"I would love some assistance," she said, before he could get the question out. She glanced dismissively at the young man now suited up beside her. "They've loaned me an intern from the medical examiner's office, but I have no idea how that is going to work. I don't know him."

All of this in French, with the unfortunate intern looking on in baffled silence.

"Is there another suit?" she asked the young man, switching seamlessly to English. He looked at her blankly. "A suit," she repeated, gesturing to the one she wore. "I would like my friend to accompany me."

The man looked far from thrilled at this, but Sophie wasn't the kind of woman who ever seemed open to negotiations. Within five minutes, Jack was in a snug-fitting Hazmat suit of his own, following Sophie as she picked her way through trash and ruin back toward the basement. He glanced up in time to see Sheriff Finnegan just coming around the corner, looking none too pleased at Jack's presence. When the sheriff called after him, however, Jack chose to pretend he hadn't heard.

•

Nancy's basement hadn't gotten any more pleasant in the hour since Jack had been in there last. The fact that he now wore a Hazmat suit made him feel slightly more protected, but was about thirty degrees warmer than the fetid air. He struggled for a full breath, and focused on the chaos around him.

"You came down here earlier without gear?" Sophie asked, her voice surreal and distant through her apparatus. Jack merely nodded. She shook her head.

"There was a cat," he said lamely. She stared at him a moment, clearly not sure she'd heard right.

"A cat?"

"And kittens. They needed help."

He thought he saw a faint contraction of facial muscles, though her mouth was obscured. Her eyes sparkled.

"Oh. Well, then…"

She moved on, taking her place ahead of him as they continued deeper in.

Jack waited as Sophie paused at the bottom basement step, taking in the scene. It was jarring, to put it mildly: layers of feces and trash, old mattresses and garbage bags of God-knew-what, soiled clothes and rusted and broken cages.

"Sacré bleu," he heard Sophie say. She looked back over her shoulder at him inquiringly. "Where…?"

He tipped his head forward, indicating they needed to go further in. Sophie stepped from the stairs to the floor with great care and waded into the fray, her feet vanishing ankle-deep into the filth. Despite the warmth, Jack was grateful for the Hazmat suit.

The basement was unfinished. There was a dirt floor somewhere beneath the mess, Jack expected, and rough-hewn rock walls around them. Cobwebs draped the place, murky light just barely making it through the small, single window at the far wall.

Sophie stepped carefully over a rusty bike frame, bracing herself on a broken kitchen chair in order to follow the only navigable path in the place. "How much farther?" she asked, again glancing back over her shoulder. Her breathing was even, her focus absolute. If she was bothered by any of this, she gave no indication.

"There's a room to your right, just up ahead," Jack instructed. Her flashlight beam played along the wall until she found the opening he'd indicated. It was a narrow door, partially blocked off by more detritus. If Jack hadn't heard the kittens mewing so pitifully before, he was sure he would have turned around at this point.

The next room was significantly smaller, no more than ten by ten, with another window at the far wall. This one provided more light, since Jack had removed the pane in order to get Cash and the kittens to safety.

With the sun shining in, it was clear why Sophie had been called: a fully articulated skeleton sat up against one wall, clothing long since disintegrated. Close by, a second set of bones lay among the debris, barely identifiable as human thanks to the degree of decay and the fact that the bones had been scattered far and wide.

"Did you touch anything while you were down here?" Sophie asked.

"Just the cats," he said. Sweat dripped down Jack's forehead behind his mask, the hair clinging to the back of his neck. His back was slick, his skin itching now. He shoved the discomfort aside as Sophie made her way to the skeleton against the wall.

She cast the light along the bones. The head was turned toward the window, the mouth open as though the victim had died mid-wail, eyes cast to the light rather than the nightmare around them. Sophie knelt, all but disappearing in the wreckage, focused on the skeletal mid-section.

"Female," she announced. "Twenties to thirties." She refocused her light on the head, peering into the mouth without touching the skull.

"Teeth are in good shape, but it looks like there was some work done. In conditions like this, it's hard to tell how long she might have been down here. I'll need to get her to the lab to learn more."

"Any idea of cause of death?" Jack asked.

She straightened and took a step back, studying the victim with keen eyes. "Looks like her head took a thrashing—could have been that," she said, indicating a clearly delineated depression at the woman's left temple, where the skull showed signs of spider webbing with the blow. Sophie cast her flashlight beam on the floor. "Looks like there's a bit of blood here, too. She could have bled out."

Her face tightened as she continued studying the woman. "Whoever it was, they didn't go fast. Hard to say just how long, could have been hours or could have been days, but this woman suffered before death took her."

Jack nodded wordlessly. He had come to much the same conclusion.

"And the other?" he asked.

Sophie shifted her flashlight beam to the bones on the floor. "Any sign of a skull?" she asked Jack.

"None that I could find."

She looked around with a grimace. "Well, I suppose we'll find it here somewhere." She knelt beside the bones, without disturbing any of the debris around them.

"Do you know if anyone's been in to document the scene?" she asked.

"No. They haven't known long, and I doubt there's a CSU local to the area. They'll probably be coming in from Augusta."

"That's what I thought." She turned to the intern who, to this point, had gone unnoticed trailing behind them. He hung at the edge of the room looking green, and completely out of his depth.

"We'll need photos of everything as it is right now," she informed the young man. A large camera hung around his neck, sleek and professional looking. He gripped the long lens convulsively at the order and nodded.

"Of course, Doctor."

"And tell them I want everything in the lab—"

His eyes widened. "Everything, as in…"

"Just everything in this room," she said, as though giving him some gift. "I want the rest of the basement documented and the contents catalogued, but I don't need it in the lab just yet."

"Yes, ma'am," he agreed, after a moment. "I'll let them know."

She looked around one more time, then returned her attention to Jack. "I thought you said there were three bodies?"

He nodded reluctantly, his own stomach doing a somersault at the thought. He trudged through the trash to a small alcove at the far end of the room, no bigger than a small closet.

"In there," he said.

She raised her eyebrows at him, and he shrugged. "I wanted to make sure no other animals had gotten trapped down here. God knows what will happen to this place after today."

Jack braced himself as she opened yet another door, this one made of a thin sheet of plywood on rusted hinges. Sophie didn't recoil, but it looked like the intern wouldn't make it out of here with his stomach contents still intact.

"Go get some fresh air," she ordered the man the second she caught a glimpse of what was inside the closet. "Take deep breaths. Throw up if you have to. Just don't do it in my crime scene."

The intern nodded swiftly, ashamed, and headed for the stairs. Jack remained where he was, staring at the body in the closet.

"Male," Sophie said, moving forward with her tape recorder in hand once they were alone. "Hard to say how long he's been dead. With the level of predation and the temperature lately, it could have been less than a week."

She whistled, long and low between her teeth. "They really feasted on you, didn't they?" she asked the body. "I hope to God he was dead before he got down here. It wouldn't have been a good way to go."

"The woman wasn't," Jack pointed out.

"No," Sophie agreed. "But hopefully, the beasts had the good grace to wait until she'd passed before they dined."

Jack's stomach turned at the thought. "Do you think that's likely?"

"It's possible," Sophie said. "If there were cats down here at that point, it's unlikely they would have tried anything until after she was dead. And the presence of the cats would likewise have meant any rats or other small rodents would have stayed away."

"Well, that's something, I guess."

Sophie looked around with a frown. "Precious damned little. But, yes... I suppose it's something."

When they had finished among the wreckage and were outside the house once more, Jack stopped Sophie with a light hand on her arm. She was still suited up, though they had both removed their masks as soon as they crossed the front door threshold.

"Yes?" Sophie said, turning to him with a smile.

He hesitated. If he were still in the FBI, this wouldn't even need to be a conversation. Now that he wasn't, however...

"I know I have no right to ask, but I was hoping you might keep me in the loop on this."

"Because of your client?" Sophie asked. "This mysterious case you're working on?" She eyed him speculatively, taking him in so thoroughly that Jack knew it would be pointless to lie. Nothing ever got past Sophie.

"Partly," he said. "I'm not sure yet, to be honest. I don't know what the bodies in the basement have to do with Nancy—the owner of the house."

"The one who died early this morning," Sophie said.

"Right." Jack paused, remembering that he still had unanswered questions there, too. "Have you seen that body?"

"No, they called me in for the bones. I don't typically deal with fresh remains, you know that."

"Right," Jack said, frowning.

"If you would like, though," Sophie offered, after a moment's thought, "I could get you into the lab while I'm looking over the other remains tomorrow. I believe all four bodies—including the woman who died today—will be in the lab in Augusta. I could give you more answers then, I'm sure."

Jack looked at her in surprise. "That would be great, actually. Very helpful."

He stood a moment longer, unwilling to look a gift horse in the mouth. This generosity still begged the question, though.

She laughed outright, seeing the puzzlement on his face. "Do you remember the case in Black Falls three years ago?" she asked.

"The last time we worked together," he said, nodding.

"It was a difficult case."

"Yes," he agreed.

"I don't know that I would have been consulted as much, involved so intimately, if you had not requested me specifically." Jack started to protest, but stopped at the knowing look on her face. Rather than denying the charge, he shrugged.

"We needed the best for that case. You're the best."

"Indeed," she said immodestly. "But I don't know if you've heard: I recently sold a book."

Jack's eyebrows rose. "I didn't, no."

"Three books, actually. A new mystery series. HarperCollins has been very enthusiastic. And, while I already had excellent credentials, I became much more known after the border murders in Northern Maine. That was what got my current agent's attention." She smiled at Jack warmly. "I owe you a great deal for that case. This is a way I can repay you. I know you would never abuse the information, so if I can help…"

"Thank you," Jack said, genuinely touched. "I'll take whatever help I can get."

Sophie looked back toward the house. There was something both sad and undeniably forbidding about the place, especially now that Jack knew what was inside.

"I have a feeling you'll need someone on this," she said. She didn't look at him, her gaze still fixed on the house. "I don't know what you might have stumbled upon here, but I don't believe it's good. And I think at this point, you've only scratched the surface."

Jack followed her gaze, his own tension rising. He was grateful to have a case, and even thankful that it was such an intriguing one. Sophie was right, though:

This house held secrets, and Jack had a feeling they were buried a lot deeper than today's easy finds might have them believe.

8

IT WAS SEVEN O'CLOCK THAT NIGHT before I was able to get away from the animal rescue operation long enough to help with the search for Albie. There had been a reported sighting along a coastal trail in Thomaston that was under the care of the Georges River Land Trust, so that was where much of the search had been focused throughout the day. There was still another two hours of daylight, the air warm and the sky clear. The biggest issues this time of year in Maine were mosquitoes and blackflies, but a stiff breeze coming off the ocean kept them at bay.

"Have there been any new sightings?" I asked Corporal Lee Todd, a local warden who'd been brought in to serve as Incident Commander for the operation.

Lee was in her mid fifties, short and solid and tougher than just about any of the men I'd known who held this job. She'd been career military before joining the warden service after nearly twenty years of active duty in the Army. Today, she wore her usual khaki Maine State Warden Service uniform, her gray hair cropped short and her cell phone in hand.

"Nothing so far," she said brusquely. "And the sighting this morning was vague at best. A ragged-looking guy with a little ratty dog. Could be him, I guess, but it's hardly a guarantee."

A little ratty dog. Oswald, the rat terrier who had plagued Jack at Nancy's the day before, had never been found. I suspected that he might be the "ratty dog" in question, if this was in fact Albie we were talking about. Lee was right, though: this was hardly proof positive that we were looking in the right place.

"I don't understand why they're not keeping some searchers closer to the house in Cushing. This is ten miles from the Davis home. Albie doesn't drive, and he's not exactly a track star. He's probably scared out of his mind, waiting for someone to come find him."

An image flashed in my mind: Albie in his mother's kitchen. The animals gone, his mother dead on the floor. Was that the way it had played out? Or had he been there before? If Nancy was attacked, had Albie seen the killer?

Or, was it possible that he actually *was* the killer?

Phantom shifted restlessly beside me. Monty had gone back out to the island to get her, Casper, and his own dog, Granger. Phantom's plaintive whine reminded me that we had a job to do, and it had nothing to do with solving the mystery of how Nancy had died. Right now, our number-one objective was to find Albie.

"Sorry, girl," I apologized to the dog. "You're right. Back to work." She looked at me with what appeared to me to be clear reproach. Phantom has a work ethic that would make the best Puritan envious.

I gave her a good whiff of the scent article we'd been

working with: a downright disgusting pair of jockey shorts Fred Davis said belonged to his brother. They were filthy, which made me wonder if the odor might be so strong it would just be confusing for the dogs. Regardless, Phantom sniffed deeply and we set out once more.

Others had been out searching this region since noon, and so far the dogs had yet to pick up a trail. Before we even started, I had my own opinion about whether or not it made sense to be out here. Frankly, I thought the sighting earlier had to be bogus. How could Albie Davis and this little dog of his have possibly made it all the way out here?

Regardless, Phantom and I did our job: we searched.

Before long, Phantom took off along a trail off Upper Beechwood Street in Thomaston, her head up. Would Albie have followed a trail? Who knew how his mind worked on a good day, much less when he was most likely scared just about out of his head. How logically could he possibly be thinking right now?

None of those doubts or second guesses made any difference to the dogs, of course. But it was up to me as handler to take it all into consideration, to make sure I was setting my team up for the best chance of success out here.

We traveled the path for two hours with no luck, as day gradually turned to night. Phantom didn't go far off the path, and it was easy to keep up with her. I took in the smell of sun-soaked leaves and dodged low-hanging branches, thick brambles cutting deep whenever I took a misstep. It had been a long winter, and a hard one out on the island. Now, despite the reasons for why I was out here, I was grateful for the warmth.

This time of year in Maine, Lyme disease is one of

the biggest threats for both dogs and their handlers on a wilderness search. Most of my colleagues wore a kind of permethrin-soaked armor up to their knees—a mesh material sprayed with a Pyrethroid touted by many as safe for people and dogs. Less-well-publicized side effects have been recorded, but chemical companies spend enough money in ad dollars and lobbying in D.C. that those side effects don't seem to get a lot of attention. Regardless, studies linking them to a higher incidence of thyroid cancer, shortness of breath, nausea, and a whole host of problems they create when they come in contact with plants and wildlife alike had convinced me: I would just keep myself covered from head to toe, do regular tick checks, and hope for the best.

Of course, that meant wearing more clothes on a hot summer day than I usually wore mid-winter, but at least they were lightweight. Mostly.

Two hours later, the sun had set, and we had long passed the Thomaston sewage treatment plant that the trail bypassed. We were moving through the woods out behind the Thomaston High School when I heard yapping nearby.

It wasn't the sounding bark of a fellow search dog, surely. There was a tribe of Pomeranians who lived with an elderly couple near here, but this had a deeper edge to it.

Phantom heard it, too. Her head came up, ears working like directional signals, taking in more information than I could have with all five senses working overtime.

"Wait, Phan," I said. She looked behind her, eyes glowing in the glare of my flashlight.

I knew Phantom wouldn't start something with another dog if we ran into one out here, but neither would she back away from an instigator. I thought of Albie's little terrier, Oswald. I definitely wouldn't put it past that dog to look for a fight, especially after a day as hard as he'd no doubt had.

"Heel, Phantom."

The German shepherd hesitated only a moment, clearly reluctant, before she came to a heel at my left side.

"Albie," I called. "Oswald? We're here to help you. Are you there?"

The yapping shifted a tone higher, this time more frantic. It was muffled, though, and I wondered whether I might actually be hearing a dog inside a local house. We weren't far from the neighborhood boundary by this time, so it wasn't out of the question.

Phantom suddenly whirled beside me, head up. She had the scent—I could tell by the way her head moved, nostrils flared. I hesitated only a moment before I let her go. I had to trust that she would follow her training, and come to me if there was trouble.

"Find him, Phantom," I called to the dog.

It was as though a spring had burst inside her. Instantly, she was on the move. I followed as close as I could behind, ignoring the branches slapping at my face or the brambles that snagged my clothing. We were in the thick of the woods, or so it seemed. And then, suddenly, we weren't.

Instead, an open field lay before me, goal posts and a dirt running track at the center.

The high school.

I thought of the conversation we'd had with Albie the day before. The faded pirate sweatshirt he wore.

Buc pride, he had said.

Buccaneers—the mascot of the local high school, or at

least it had been when Albie attended, over twenty-five years ago.

Coach Pendleton gave it to me.

The only place Albie had ever belonged, aside from his mother's menagerie:

Georges Valley High School.

"Albie?" I called. The barking was more frantic now, still muffled but getting clearer. I watched as Phantom made her way toward the equipment shed. She sat, looked at me, and barked twice.

Inside the structure, the barking escalated.

"Good find, Phantom!" I said. At this point, there was no doubt in my mind that she had done the job and found what we were looking for.

I played the obligatory game of tug with the dog, my voice high-pitched and enthusiastic as I forced my aching body to move. Meanwhile, I called Sheriff Finnegan to let him know what I had found, and waited for word back. Going in blind to a situation like this—an unstable suspect and a dog with an unknown history—was hardly ideal.

"You really think you've got him?" Finnegan asked me over the line. Phantom lay a few feet from me now, mouthing at the tug toy with the enthusiasm of a much younger dog.

"Phantom led me to an equipment shed at the high school," I said. "There's barking inside. You knew Albie, right? Is it possible he would have come here?"

"Of course he would," Finnegan said immediately. "I'm an idiot for not thinking of it sooner. Coach Pendleton was better to him than just about anyone in his life. It makes sense he'd go to the field named for the man at a time like this. Hold tight. I can be there with a team in ten minutes."

I told him I would wait, and hung up. Ten minutes is a lifetime when you don't know what's on the other side of a door, though, and tonight was no exception. I took Phantom over to the water fountain for a drink, and studied the broken-down track overlooking a brick homage to 1950s architecture: Oceanside High School, formerly known as Georges Valley. The Thomaston and Rockland school systems had merged in 2011, after a fierce battle by residents of both towns to remain independent.

If Ren and Bear hadn't decided to do home school once we moved to this area just over two years ago, this is the school they would have gone to.

I ordered Phantom to stay by the fountain, and made my way back to the shed five minutes later. I glanced back over to see my dog lying peacefully in the grass, content that her part of the job was over.

Then, I returned to the shed.

I stood outside second guessing myself, talking to Albie and the dog for an endless seven more minutes before flashing lights lit the darkness, sirens sounding through the quiet neighborhood.

"Sheriff Finnegan is here now, Albie," I said through the door. "You guys are friends, right? You don't have to be afraid."

The sheriff strode toward me, flanked by three deputies.

"Has he said anything?" Finnegan asked.

"Nothing," I said. "The only thing I've heard so far is the dog."

"Hang on, Oswald," Sheriff Finnegan called. At his voice, the dog's yapping became a shrill whine. He recognized Finnegan, then—liked him, even.

"Albie," the sheriff continued, "It's Chris Finnegan. You remember that game we won, back in '89? Went into a tenth inning… You were in the outfield. You remember that, Albie? You catching the ball—getting the out that ended the game? Quite a night, wasn't it?"

There was still no response. Frowning, lips pinched, the sheriff glanced at the other deputies and silently motioned them back.

"I'm going to come in now, buddy. I know you've had a rough day. Let's see if we can get you fed, find you a warm place to spend the night. Okay?"

Hesitantly, with one hand on his sidearm, Finnegan moved forward. He said Albie's name again while his hand was on the door handle. "I'm coming in now," he added.

He opened the door.

Instantly, Oswald launched himself at the sheriff, whining desperately. The sheriff motioned to me and I took charge of the dog, who was only too happy to be petted and loved and held by a friendly pair of arms while the sheriff did his job.

There was a stone in my gut as I imagined the worst, while Sheriff Finnegan shone his flashlight past soccer balls and goal posts, field hockey sticks and track hurdles. What if Albie had come here terrified and distraught, and done something desperate? The police had found guns at Nancy's place. What if he had gotten hold of one, and then run to the safest place he could think of?

"It's empty," Finnegan called back to us, just before my thoughts spiraled completely out of control. "There's no sign of him in here."

"He must have put Oswald here to keep him safe, and then kept running," I said.

Finnegan frowned, nodding. "Yeah. But where the hell would he have gone from here?"

I honestly had no idea. Oswald whimpered in my arms as Phantom rose to join the action. I cuddled the little dog closer, murmuring reassurances. We would find Albie; everything would be all right.

I just wished I had some confidence that I was telling the truth.

•

It was nearly midnight by the time I returned to the island that night, after having been up since three a.m. that morning. Monty met me at the waterfront and hopped aboard while I was still trying to lasso the cleat on the dock to secure the boat.

"Thanks," I said, frankly surprised. Monty is great to work with, but he's never once met me at the boat before.

"What's up?" I asked.

He took the rope from me and got it 'round the cleat on the first try, the movement smooth and natural. It had gotten cooler as the night wore on, but he wore a fitted Flint K-9 T-shirt and shorts regardless. Monty is an inch or two shorter than my five-foot-ten, but his body is corded with muscle. His dark skin shone in the moonlight, a tension about him that was unusual for the typically laidback Southerner.

"You work a twenty-hour shift, you rate a welcoming committee," he said. I turned the boat off once we were snug against the bumpers, and eyed him knowingly.

"I've worked twenty-hour shifts before and made it back to base just fine on my own."

He shrugged. "Maybe. But it's a zoo up there—not a lot of down time for silly things like sleep."

We were at mid-tide, which meant the boat was about five feet lower than the dock. We'd had a ramp put in for just this sort of thing, since most four-leggeds aren't great with ladders. Now, Phantom skirted around us and made for the island without waiting for my signal. It seemed I wasn't the only one eager for bed.

Monty and I followed behind the dog, and I wasn't sure which of us lagged more.

"What about Bear?" I asked. "I don't suppose he's seen fit to take a nap at all."

Monty shook his head, eyeing me sideways. Evergreens loomed around us, rising high and gradually closing in as we left the open ocean behind.

"I've been tempted to tranq the little bastard myself today, if you want the truth."

I arched an eyebrow that I knew he couldn't see in the darkness.

"Sorry," he said gruffly. "But the kid is dead on his feet. What time did he turn in last night?"

"I'm not sure," I said. Not a total lie, but it felt like one. I had the uneasy feeling that Bear hadn't slept for a lot longer than me at this point, but for some reason I was hesitant to confess that.

"Well, he's acting like a man who hasn't slept in a week. I used to see that look in the eyes of guys over in Afghanistan. It never ended well."

"I'll talk to him," I promised.

We walked on in silence for a few minutes more. The Flint K-9 base was just over a mile from the dock—a trek I usually enjoyed after a long day. Tonight, it seemed like a lot more than I was prepared for.

Farther in on the island, I could hear dogs barking and what sounded like a donkey's bray; the crow of a rooster; owls, sounding their call overhead.

Monty was right: it really did sound like a zoo.

"So, what else is on your mind?" I asked, when he didn't volunteer anything more.

"Nothing," he said. "What makes you think there's something on my mind?"

"Because we've worked together for seven years now, and this is the first time you've ever met me at the boat without me asking. What's up?"

He hesitated. Ahead of us, Phantom paused on the path, head up, ears forward. I waited for something to spring out at us, but whatever she thought she sensed passed. She moved on, head down once more.

"Have you been following the weather down South?" he finally asked, when the base was in view and I was well and truly ready to collapse.

"The hurricane?" I asked. "Sure. What about it?"

I stopped moving, as did he. Despite the late hour, the place was buzzing—outside lights on, people's voices clear beneath the clamor of the animals. Monty and I faced off on the path leading up to HQ. I noted how weary he looked—something rare, because Monty prides himself on his level of fitness and energy. Uneasiness niggled at the base of my skull.

"My daughter—Grace..." he began.

"Is she all right?" I asked quickly, surprised. I knew about Monty's daughter because he'd elected to tell me during the interview process, but I wasn't sure that anyone else at Flint K-9 even knew she existed. "Is there something wrong? She's not sick—"

"No, nothing like that," he said quickly. "Thank God. But my ex has been having some problems…"

He looked uncomfortable. I waited, quiet now, ignoring the reproach in Phantom's backward gaze when she realized we'd stopped.

"She's dropped out of sight, actually," he said. He cleared his throat, embarrassed. "They're in New Orleans…" He pronounced it N'Awlins, not an affectation since it was actually his hometown. "The hurricane's set to hit there, and they're saying it could be worse than Katrina."

"And you want to go find Grace," I guessed.

"I know it's a bad time."

"Doesn't matter—your kid comes first," I said without hesitation. "When do you want to go?"

"It's slow moving, so I think we've still got a little bit of a window. It could be downgraded, or head off to sea in a couple of days. I just wanted to let you know. I'll keep trying to figure things out from here as long as I can."

"Do what you have to," I said. "But don't worry about us. Family comes first."

"Thanks," he said. "Really—I appreciate it."

I nodded, but before I could offer a response I was pulled from the conversation by a jolt of light. It came fast, violent, inside my own skull, and blindsided me enough that I stumbled. Monty caught me by the elbow.

"Jamie, are you okay?" he asked. It took me a second to realize he'd asked it more than once.

"I am—just tired," I managed when I found my voice again.

He looked skeptical. "Well, get some rest. We're on deck for the a.m. shift to look for Albie unless they find him overnight."

I nodded. "I'll be there." I waited for him to go before I reached for the nearest tree to steady myself, unwilling to let him see that I was not, in fact, as okay as I'd just insisted. The pain was more knife blade than hammer, piercing the back of my skull. I closed my eyes, and listened.

Abusive in life, it seemed Brock Campbell was intent on continuing that trend now that he had my ear in the afterlife. It was telling to me that, even in death, I associated the man with pain.

Now, I held still. Waiting for Brock's voice.

There was silence.

Phantom returned to my side, and the pain in my head gradually faded. The dog gazed up at me, concern clear in her eyes.

"I'm okay, girl."

Keep telling yourself that, James, a familiar voice said. It came from somewhere behind me, or sounded like it had, though I knew that wasn't true. I resisted the urge to turn around, half expecting to find Brock watching me from the trees.

Instead, I forged ahead toward base and the comfort of my own bed.

I stopped outside Bear's room before going to my own. Light shone from under the door, and my heart sank. Bear has never been a great sleeper, starting from infancy. I knocked lightly. When I got no response, I pushed it open as quietly as I could manage.

Casper's head came up when I made an appearance, and

his tail thumped against the bed. I paused, taking in the sight with a rush of gratitude.

"Ssh," I whispered to Casper.

Bear lay on top of the blankets, still clothed, but thankfully sleeping. Casper lay lengthwise by his side, his head beside Bear's on the pillow. I risked a step inside to turn off the light. The room was as much a mess now as it had been when I'd come in nearly twenty-four hours before. Now, however, I noted a stack of books on the desk in the corner. Bear isn't much of a reader—dyslexia robbed him of that particular joy early on, and apart from the stories I'd read to him when he was little, he's never had much time for books. These didn't exactly look like they were there for pleasure, however.

Buckland's Book of Spirit Communications
When Ghosts Speak
Psychic Shield: Personal Handbook of Psychic Protection
Your Psychic Potential

I paused, strangely stung by the titles. I knew that Bear could communicate with the dead—they've been appearing to him from the time he was a little boy. He likewise knew that I had some psychic talents, if you could call them that, but I'd always been hesitant to talk to him about those kinds of things. As a little girl growing up in a God-fearing home in Georgia, I was taught that whatever I might be able to see or hear, sense or predict, it was no gift. I don't believe the things my family believed, but I'll admit that there's still a level of shame, embarrassment, over the phenomena that have followed me my entire life. I knew, despite my best intentions, that those feelings had colored my interactions with Bear on the subject.

Beside the books on the desk was a note. I knew it was past time for me to get out of the room, Casper still watching my every move from the bed. I paused regardless, hating myself for snooping even as I read the note.

I know you don't want to think about these things. But maybe if you just educate yourself, you don't have to look at this as a curse any longer. Just think about it. Love, R

Ren had sent them.

I finally retreated from the room, turning out the light on the way, and closed the door quietly behind me.

I knew nothing about my own psychic abilities, apart from the fact that they seemed to strike at the least convenient times. From the time I was a little girl, I'd had prophetic dreams: dreams that seemed uncannily real when I was sleeping, and then repeated themselves beat for beat in the light of day, sometimes months or even years later. I had occasionally heard people's thoughts, or thought I had, but it happened so sporadically and with such infrequency that I eventually dismissed that particular "power" as a fluke.

In Glastenbury, I'd seen and heard a girl who had been dead some sixty years or more. In Bethel, Brock's voice echoed in my head, repeating the words of the murderer who was stalking a woman in those very woods.

I knew what I experienced, but I never examined it beyond that. Definitely never studied it. The people I worked with knew that I was 'intuitive.' If they were surprised at just how far that extended sometimes, they never said as much.

But then, I didn't exactly invite discussion on the subject.

I went to my room that night with my head whirling, the ache at the back of my skull still there. The voice still echoing within. I shucked my clothes and didn't bother to dig out pajamas. Instead, I allowed myself to crawl beneath the covers, Phantom beside me, and I closed my eyes.

I slept.

9

BEAR WAS ALREADY UP and at 'em when I rose at six the next morning. The sun was up, the island in full swing. Six o'clock is sleeping in for me, and then some. Bear greeted me on the trail to the kennels, five of Nancy's mutts on leash beside him. At sight of me, they all strained at their leads, jumping and yapping at a pitch almost shrill enough to pierce my eardrums.

"You missed the morning run," he said. Every morning at five a.m., regardless of the weather, our team takes as many dogs as we can handle and sets them loose on the island. Together, we all run a three-mile trek over hill and dale, the ocean at our side. Bear studied me, concern clear in his eyes. "You feeling okay?"

"I am, just tired." I thought of the books I'd found in his room. The note from Ren. I had no idea how to bring up the subject, though. "Did you try Nancy's guys on the trail?" I asked instead. Coward.

"Just a few. I temperament tested last night, but only six passed."

The five he had on leash were all little guys. I recognized the pugs and a little Cairn terrier I was sure we'd be able to place with breed-specific rescue in no time.

"These guys didn't make the cut?"

"All passed the bite test," Bear said. The bite test involves using a fake hand on a long stick and going through a series of exercises to see how the dog responds.

"What about the Newfie—Cody? He's spoken for," I said, recalling Hank Williams' request.

"I remember," Bear said with a nod. "He's doing great, just a little stressed right now. I'll work with him, double check to make sure there are no health issues while Tracy checks the adoption forms, and then Cody can settle with Hank. One owner, warm bed and two square meals a day. That's all he really needs."

The quintet had stopped yapping, so I paid a little more attention now that it wouldn't be perceived as a reward for the incessant barking. I checked with Bear for permission first, then crouched with treats in hand.

The terrier came forward readily, tail wagging, but snapped at the others when they tried to do the same. I straightened, and Bear managed to get a sit out of each of them before I gifted them with the jerky I held.

I raised my eyebrows at him, impressed. He shrugged.

"They're all smart, just need some structure and consistency. House training and food aggression will be the biggest challenges. They always are in hoarding cases."

The terrier remained sitting in front of me, runny brown eyes on mine. The pugs were already up again, circling at my feet, whining in the hope of more treats.

"She's smart," I said, indicating the terrier.

"Yeah," Bear agreed. "She's definitely a star in the group. Somebody will be getting a good dog." He hesitated, and I knew there was something more he wanted to ask. Once again, the titles of those damn books flashed through my mind.

He didn't mention them. Neither did I. Instead, he shifted uncomfortably and looked back toward the kennels.

"I was wondering if you could check in on Reaver," he said. "He was sick in the night. Therese has him on IV fluids, but I'm worried." He paused, eyes suddenly old. "Maybe he's just been through too much."

"I'll take a look at him," I promised, rather than offering any false message of hope. Bear was raised in this business; he's seen every aspect of animal rescue imaginable. We both know too well that, just like he'd said, sometimes the animal has simply been through too much.

"I'm scheduled for an eight a.m. shift on the mainland for the search," I said. "I'm assuming you haven't heard anything about Albie being found overnight?"

"No. There was a sighting at Camden Hills, though. That's where the search is focused today, I guess."

"How do they think he got there?" Camden Hills was at least fifteen miles from the Thomaston trails we'd been searching yesterday.

"A couple said they picked up a guy matching his description out hitchhiking on Route 90."

Albie was pretty distinctive. I couldn't imagine many like him were out looking for rides in the area right now. As leads went, it sounded solid.

"Well, that's something, I guess," I agreed. "You planning to go back to help?"

"Yeah. I'll bring Casper—I'm signed up for the same shift."

"Good. I'll meet you at the boat at 6:30, then."

He agreed, and we parted ways. I watched him go up

the path with the dogs, and took a moment to get a read on my own state of mind. The headache and dizziness from the night before were gone, and a solid six hours of sleep had done me good. I felt more energized than I had in a while. I waited for the pain to return—for the voice to return—and was relieved when nothing happened.

Up until recently, it had been at least a month since I'd last heard Brock's voice, and the rare incidents when I did had been few and far between before that. I tried to push away any lingering concerns about my health or sanity, and focus instead on the dozens upon dozens of fuzzy little lives reliant on me and Flint K-9 for their well-being. I barely had time for breakfast; I definitely didn't have time for monster headaches or ghostly visits from my ex from hell.

Our brand-new kennels didn't seem nearly so brand new when I got in that morning. They smelled like crap and mange and unwashed dog, and Therese looked like death warmed over.

"When did you sleep last?" I asked as soon as I saw her. She had to think for a minute.

"A couple nights ago, maybe."

"Go to bed," I said shortly, fixing her with narrowed eyes. "Now."

"There's too much to do."

"I don't care. Sarah and Monty and Bear and I can pick up on things while you're out. It does me no good if my veterinarian burns out now, or kills herself. Hit the galley, find some food, and get some sleep."

She frowned. I crossed my arms over my chest and glared at her. "I'm not your kid. Don't try that look on me," she said. After a moment, however, she added grudgingly, "I guess a couple of hours won't hurt anyone."

"Four," I said. She started to argue, but I stopped her with dead eyes. "I'm serious."

"Fine," she grumbled. "Can I wrap up a couple of things, or you gonna run me out of here now?"

I allowed a smile. "I can be reasonable. Do whatever you need to do. Bear actually wanted me to check on one of the dogs in here. Reaver?"

At the name, a shadow darkened her eyes. "You might want to say goodbye, then. He's not looking good."

"Where is he?"

She nodded to the end of the aisle of kennels. I followed the nod, leaving Therese behind. The last kennel in the aisle had been draped with blankets so Reaver wouldn't be disturbed at sight of the other dogs. I took one look through the gated door, and my eyes welled.

Reaver looked up at me, docked ears tipped forward. He lay on a bare concrete floor, his eyes downcast. He couldn't even lift his head. I noted a canvas laundry bag by the door and looked inquiringly at Therese, who had followed me.

"More soiled blankets," she said. "He hasn't been able to keep anything down—he's gone through six bedding changes by my count so far."

Hence the bare floor, I supposed. "Is there anything else clean?"

"Sarah just brought in a fresh load. I can make a bed up for him."

"You're going to sleep, remember?" I said. "I'll take care of it."

She harrumphed, but it was clear that I wasn't giving up

on this one. After she'd gone, I went to the storage closet and picked out fresh bedding, still in canvas bags and straight from the dryer.

Reaver managed to lift his head when I came in, watching me warily.

"It's all right, boy," I said quietly. "Just setting you up with a fresh bed, okay?"

Each individual kennel was equipped with elevated beds made from PVC pipe and canvas—easy to clean by just hosing them down, and virtually indestructible. Reaver's had been pulled out. Looking closer, it was clear why. This one would need more than hosing down to get it clean again.

"How about we just stick with a bed on the bare floor this time," I said.

My chest tightened when his tail thumped against the concrete. He lay his head back down, eyes drifting halfway shut. I situated a thick, plush blanket on the opposite side of the kennel, then sat down beside the dog. Hesitantly, I ran my hand over the big block head. He closed his eyes the rest of the way.

"What do you think, bud?" His ears twitched at my tone. Eyes opened once more, this time fixed on me. I saw no animosity there. No fear. That was something, anyway. "Bear's worried that you've been through too much. Is he right? Are you done?"

He lifted his head again. I ran my hand over his body, anger rising once more at the feel of his ribs through his mangy coat. He whined. And then, summoning the strength from somewhere deep, he edged closer to me. With a sigh, he lay his head in my lap. Tears filled my eyes.

"Okay," I said. I continued petting him, moving carefully

over his scars and scabs, the thinned fur and flaking skin. "Let's give you some time, Reav. You're not done yet."

He was snoring within a few minutes, his head heavy in my lap. I forgot my own problems, and focused instead on the dog now relying on me for his future. A dog who had every right to distrust every person who crossed his path, and yet here he was—drooling on my blue jeans, body twitching from dreams I would never know.

No. Reaver definitely wasn't done yet.

As I was petting him, my hands paused at the feel of raised skin on his belly. I resituated myself to get a closer look, and frowned. There was what appeared to be a number of some kind tattooed on the skin, though it looked like someone had tried to remove it by burning the flesh there. *People are monsters,* I thought, definitely not for the first time in my life.

A tattooed number, for a dog who clearly wasn't as far gone as Nancy had seemed to think. He'd had some training, I was sure of it—possibly quite a bit of it. This would require some investigation.

10

THE FIRST NIGHT WITH CASH and the kittens, not a lot of sleep was had. The vet had estimated the little bundles of fluff were at least five weeks old, which meant there was no need for two a.m. bottle feedings—or any bottle feedings at all, actually. Regardless, the squalling and cheeps and perpetual mewling coming from the next room were jarring enough to keep Jack—by now well-used to sleeping in an apartment alone—up for the better part of the night.

At six a.m., after a couple of hours of fitful dozing, he gave up and got out of bed. With the sun just coming up, it seemed Cash and his brood had retired. The kittens lay curled around the tomcat, who opened one eye at Jack's approach. Otherwise, he didn't move.

"You need to get them on a better schedule," Jack informed the cat wearily. "You may have been nocturnal before, but things have changed."

He heard a low rumbling purr come from the tom, who stretched lazily. The kittens protested—loudly—and Jack took a step back.

"Okay, fine. Do whatever you think is best."

He ran a hand briefly over Cash's ragged head. The purr

got louder. The kittens began to stir in earnest, which Jack felt bad about. If he thought he wasn't getting enough rest, he could only imagine how Cash's routine must have been impacted by the changes of the past twenty-four hours.

Jack got dressed with the news playing in the background. Network news, on an honest-to-God TV set, not a computer. He knew he was a Luddite; that others had news channels streaming on their phones and iPads and even watches (or so he'd heard), but he much preferred this. Later, he would even read the paper.

Now, however, he would run.

He started a Spotify playlist on his phone. He wasn't *that* out of touch. Jack felt his blood start to move as the first strains of Brittany Spears kicked in. He could almost hear Erin Solomon's voice just under the music. *Seriously, Jack? What is it with you and divas?* He smiled faintly at the thought, and made a mental note to check in with his former girlfriend and her partner, Diggs, soon.

Jamie liked country music, and she liked to sing along when she thought no one was listening. She had a pretty alto that made him think of clear days and sunlight. Secretly, at one time Jack had wanted to be a singer himself, but the nuns at the Miami convent where he'd been raised from thirteen to eighteen hadn't approved of such frivolous daydreams.

He stepped outside and stretched his long legs. Main Street Rockland was virtually empty, apart from a couple of people walking their dogs. It was ten past six when he set out, letting the cool morning air wash over him. He had a long list of things he needed to do today. To be honest, that had been the reason for the sleeplessness last night as much as anything. He was…excited. It had been a while since there had been a genuine reason to get out of bed in the morning.

As he ran, he considered the case. Had the police identified the bodies in the basement yet? Found Albie? Determined Nancy's cause of death? At this stage of any case, the questions were broad, and should be reasonably simple to find answers to. He'd made plans to meet Sophie Laurent at the medical examiner's office in Augusta early that afternoon—at which point, he expected he could start digging into this puzzle in earnest.

He ran along Main Street until he hit Front Street, then turned left to run with the ocean at his side. The waterfront was busy, the fishermen there having already been hard at work for hours by now.

Jack ran the backroads along the water until he ran out of backroads to run, then paced himself along Route 1 until he could get back off the beaten path. He had a strong rhythm going by the time he reached the Rockland Breakwater. He felt the familiar pull in his calves, the strength of a body that wasn't quite breaking down yet, despite the fact that forty was closing in fast.

By the time Jack returned to the apartment, it was after seven o'clock. Traffic had picked up on Main Street, though only marginally. He stopped at Main Street Market for the paper and a coffee, then returned to his place eager for a shower and the ability to finally get down to business.

At the entrance to his hallway, however, he paused.

An attractive blond woman sat perfectly upright in a folding chair beside his door. She stood at sight of him, a cup of coffee in each hand; she started to extend one to Jack, but faltered at sight of the steaming cup he already held.

Barbara Monroe—the Davis's inquisitive neighbor from the previous day.

"Ms. Monroe," Jack said, unable to hide his surprise. "Can I help you?"

"I hope so," she said. He realized as he took a step closer that it looked like she had been crying, her pretty eyes swollen and red. She dabbed at them delicately with a cloth handkerchief. "I'd like to hire you."

His surprise grew tenfold. "Hire me for...?"

She took a deep breath, let it out slowly, and looked at Jack with a degree more calm than he would have expected from the woman. "I want you to prove that Nancy Davis killed my husband."

Jack froze. No clients for three months, not a case in sight. And now, suddenly, he had two clients in the space of twenty-four hours intent on solving a mystery revolving around the same woman.

"Hang on," Jack said awkwardly. "Just let me secure my cat, and you can come inside and start from the beginning."

Once he was sure Cash and the kittens wouldn't bolt for daylight at their first opportunity, Jack led Barbara into his office, where she settled in the chair in front of his desk. He took a moment to clean himself up and change his clothes, then returned to the office with his mind already turning over her opening gambit.

Barbara looked more put together when he returned, and slightly embarrassed for her outburst. "You must think I'm crazy for coming here like this. I can hardly blame you. Sometimes I wonder about that myself, but I just haven't been the same since Tim left. Or disappeared. It's been hard, not even knowing how to react, whether to be angry or worried or just distraught. And, of course, it's taken an even worse toll on my daughter."

"I'm sure," Jack said. "But what you said before, about Nancy... What makes you think she had anything to do with your husband's disappearance?"

"She hated Tim," Barbara said. "I always complained about the animals, but Tim was the one she actually fought with. He was the one who called the police. He was the one who got animal welfare involved. She despised him. And I know that isn't really enough to go on, but I heard about what you found in the basement. There were bodies down there, weren't there?"

Barbara wrapped her arms around herself more tightly, shivering despite the warmth in the room. She sighed. "I know how this makes me sound. Pathetic. Like I simply can't accept the fact that my husband walked out on us."

"Is that what the police think?" Jack asked, as gently as he could. "That your husband left you?"

Barbara nodded. "They've been nice to me about the whole thing," she assured him. "I don't feel as though I've been abused by the system or anything. But I know Tim; they don't. We may have had our problems, but he never would have left Julie like this."

"When was the last time you saw your husband?" Jack asked. He took a legal pad from the top drawer of his desk and a freshly sharpened pencil from a cup of them beside his computer, then looked at Barbara expectantly.

"It will be two months on Tuesday," she said. She appeared relieved that they were getting down to business. "He'd been preparing for a business trip, and was supposed to leave the next day."

"I assume his car was gone. It's not possible that he just left early?"

"That's what the police think," Barbara agreed. "And it is technically possible, I suppose. But he would have waited to say goodbye to Julie, at least."

"I'm sorry to ask this, Mrs. Monroe, but were you and your husband having difficulties?"

Barbara appeared uncomfortable. She shifted in her seat, her gaze settling on the wedding band around her finger. When she looked at Jack again, tears shimmered in her eyes. "Tim and I have been married for over twenty years, Mr. Juarez. Of course, we've had our challenges. What marriage hasn't? That doesn't mean he would be unnecessarily cruel— Tim just isn't that kind of man."

Jack nodded. He suppressed a sigh, recognizing exactly where this case would most likely lead. No one wanted to believe their partner would betray them. But in his experience, that was usually exactly what had happened. Husbands cheated. Mothers ran out on their kids. Lovers killed one another in fits of jealousy. How many times had he dealt with exactly those things in the FBI? Of course, it was true that there were remains belonging to an unidentified male in Nancy's basement, and that man had been killed recently. Technically, it was possible.

"Mrs. Monroe—"

"Please, call me Barbara," she insisted.

"Okay," he agreed. "Barbara. I can't imagine what you've been through in the past two months. I'm happy to look into this for you, but I think you need to prepare yourself for the most likely scenario. Based on what you've told me, your husband was a fit, athletic man in his forties. How do you think an elderly woman like Nancy—with a long list of medical issues—could have murdered your husband, disposed of the body, and then had the foresight to get rid of the car? I hate to be cruel, but I just want you to think about these things before you spend the money on a private investigator."

"How did she kill those other people?" Barbara challenged. "The ones in her basement? Trust me, I've thought about this obsessively for the past eight weeks. I watched Nancy. She was hardly a decrepit, doddering old fool. But I never would have thought of this if I hadn't heard about the remains in her basement yesterday." Her eyes filled suddenly, and she dabbed once more at her tears. "Suddenly, all the pieces fell into place."

She sat up, gathering strength. When she spoke again, her voice was resolute once more. "Maybe Nancy didn't work alone. Albie was there. He would do anything his mother told him to do. She may not have the muscle anymore, but she could have directed him."

She met Jack's eye. The tears were gone now, no hesitation in her gaze. "You may believe I'm throwing my money away, and that's fine. But the reality is that I don't have unlimited resources. My husband's been gone for two months. He was the breadwinner in the family. I make a small amount of money from an Etsy shop, but that's not enough to keep Julie and me going for much longer.

"Tim's vacation time at his job has long since run out, and he was officially fired two weeks ago. We don't have a body, so insurance is refusing to pay anything. If I hire you, at the very least you'll be able to find him. If he's still alive, that's fine—at least I'll know. He'll be financially culpable for Julie. And if he's not alive…"

Barbara remained in her seat, head up and back rigid. Her arms were no longer folded across her chest, but now lay on the armrests, fingernails digging into the leather.

"You say you're out of resources," Jack began. "But my services aren't inexpensive. How much are you prepared to pay for something that could ultimately break you and your daughter's hearts?"

"I'll pay what I have to," Barbara said. "I have a little money set aside, and I'm still quite close to Tim's parents. Naturally, they're as concerned as I am. They will be paying most of this bill."

"I'll need to speak with them, if they're the ones paying."

"I assumed so. I told them as much—they're expecting your call. They're traveling right now, but they're as keen as I am to find out what happened to their son. Whatever any of us can do to help you get to the bottom of this…"

With that out of the way, Jack found himself at a loss. "In the interest of full disclosure, you should know that I'm already working for someone on a case related to this."

"Solving Nancy's murder, you mean," Barbara said with a nod. Jack couldn't hide his surprise.

"It's a small town," Barbara said. "I asked around when I saw you there, but no one could tell me for sure. But once I heard what happened to Nancy, it made sense that you might be there for more than just to help out the Humane Society."

"But you don't see that as a problem," Jack clarified.

"Can you work two cases at once?"

"Of course," Jack said. "I usually had at least half a dozen open cases I was working on at the FBI simultaneously. If you're all right with it, so am I. You should know that all of my clients have full confidentiality, which means I won't be discussing your case with anyone else…"

"So, I shouldn't expect you to discuss the other case with me," Barbara finished for him. She waved off the statement. "Honestly, I don't care who killed Nancy Davis. If I could, I'd thank him myself. It has made my life much easier."

"Him?" Jack asked, caught by the pronoun. He ran through the conversation again in his head, replaying Barbara's words. "You said you heard what happened to Nancy. What was the story you got, exactly?" He kept his voice neutral, making it seem as though he already knew.

"Well, I don't know for sure. I mean, I don't have a coroner's report or whatever. But Jimmy—he works with the EMTs—said they got there and Nancy was dead on the floor with her head smashed in. That doesn't sound like much of a heart attack to me."

"Do you think Albie would have been capable of physical violence against his mother?" he asked.

"God, no. That man's as gentle as they come, and he worshipped his mother. No, I can't see him doing something like this."

"If you'll forgive me saying, you seem pretty intent on keeping Julie away from a man you insist is harmless."

"No, that's fair," Barbara said. If she took offense, she showed no sign of it. "It's not that I'm afraid he would do something to her, but I don't want her giving him the wrong idea, either. Julie always gets mad at me because she feels like I'm not being fair to him, but she's young—she might think she's wise to the world, but she can be awfully naïve."

"So, if you don't think Albie did it, who do you think killed Nancy? You said 'him' before. Clearly, you have a theory."

"I've already talked to the police about my suspicions," Barbara said uncomfortably. "I don't know if it's a good idea talking to you about them. It might end up causing some issues for you."

Jack couldn't hide his surprise. "For me? How would it cause issues for me?"

"I know you and Jamie are…close."

"Jamie Flint? Well, yes. We're friends," Jack said carefully. "I don't see how whatever you have to tell me could have any impact on that, though. Unless you're telling me Jamie did this?"

"Not Jamie," she said. She bit her lip, clearly conflicted. Finally, she sighed. "Jamie's son, Bear. He was there two nights ago. Late. Fighting with Nancy."

Jack felt something thick and unsavory drop in his stomach. "Are you sure about that? What time?"

"After midnight," she said. If there was any uncertainty, she was doing a good job hiding it. "I saw him there. They were fighting on the front steps—I went out because her dogs were going crazy, and I was trying to get some sleep."

"Did you see any kind of physical altercation?" he asked. "Something that would make you think Bear could have done something to her?"

"I just saw them screaming at each other," she admitted. "He followed her inside the house and they were still yelling, but I figured they'd work it out one way or another. I never imagined he might actually hurt her. If anything, I was more afraid for him."

Jack nodded, at a total loss as to how to respond to this information. He needed to talk to Jamie. And Bear—who was, after all, his client. What the hell had the kid been thinking, going over there that night? And what was he playing at, hiring Jack to find out what happened? He had to know Jack would find out about his late-night visit.

"Whatever happened to Nancy has nothing to do with the case I want to hire you for," Barbara said, when he'd been silent too long. There was a note of panic in her voice. "I know there might be some challenge with your other case, figuring out who killed Nancy. But this is about my husband." She got herself under control again and drew herself up straighter. "Can you take my case or not?"

Mind whirling, he took another few seconds to consider. She was right: Nancy may have had something to do with Barbara's husband's disappearance, but it was far more likely that there was no link there at all. Finally, he nodded.

"All right," he said. "I'll take the case. If it turns out that a conflict between this and my other client's case arises, we may need to talk again."

"That's fair," Barbara agreed. She stood. "Now, if you don't mind, Julie is waiting for me. Whatever I need to sign or whatever retainer you need, just let me know."

"I'd actually like to start by asking you a few more questions. I'll need to get numbers for the people your husband worked for, and anyone else you think may be helpful."

"Whatever you need," Barbara said readily. "Honestly, I can't tell you how relieved I am. For the first time, I feel like there's some hope."

Jack shifted uncomfortably. "I just don't want you to get your expectations too high. Resolutions to cases like this aren't always what the client is hoping for."

Barbara looked at him steadily, gaze unwavering. "I'm

not a fool, Mr. Juarez. There is no best-case scenario here. I'm well aware of that. My husband is either dead, or he walked out on me and my daughter. Frankly, I'm not sure which would be worse. Either way, it doesn't seem a happy ending is in the cards for us. I just want to know one way or the other."

Jack nodded. He extended his hand, meeting her gaze. "Then it sounds like we have a deal. I'll start this afternoon."

11

ALBIE'S LAST SIGHTING was actually at the entrance to Maiden's Cliff, a hiking trail on the western edge of Camden Hills State Park. The turnoff comes just at the crest of a hill that looks like you've reached the end of the world and are about to drop into the abyss beyond. Monty turned the van onto the steep dirt drive and stopped the engine when a police officer gave us the signal.

In the back of the van, Phantom, Casper, and Monty's dog—Granger—all took up barking at the same time as Monty rolled down his window. I called back for them to hush, and all but Casper fell silent. It took Bear's command before the pit bull managed to settle himself.

"You're here to join the search?" the officer asked. The FLINT K-9 SEARCH AND RESCUE logo emblazoned on the side of our van seemed to me to be more than enough evidence of this, but who was I to judge.

"That's right," Monty agreed. "We got orders to show up at eight o'clock sharp to get some search time in before the day gets too hot for the dogs."

The officer consulted a sheet of paper pinned to a clipboard, then nodded. "Sure, go on ahead. There's still some parking up there. We're just trying to keep hikers out of the way for the search."

"Any luck so far?" Monty asked, echoing the same question I'd been thinking.

"Not that I've heard," the officer said. "Nobody's sweating too much about it right now. A grown man in this kind of weather, tooling around from town to town before he takes to the woods... I guess we'll catch up with him eventually. Seems like kind of a waste to have this much manpower out here, if you want my opinion."

Monty kind of grunted, and I refrained from making any comments myself. It was true that Albie was physically an adult, but his cognitive challenges combined with whatever trauma he'd experienced the night Nancy died hardly made his safety a guarantee.

The officer stepped out of the way, and Monty drove up the steep incline and found a parking space close to the entrance to the hiking trail. A group of searchers was just emerging from the woods when we stopped the van. I recognized Fred Davis, looking more haggard than he had the night before. He was with Sheriff Finnegan, as well as Nancy's neighbor Hank and Barbara Monroe's daughter Julie.

I got out to check in with Sheriff Finnegan, Bear close behind. Meanwhile, Monty remained with the van getting our gear together and prepping the dogs.

It was still cool out, though the sun was fully up and I knew things would heat up fast. I took a breath and soaked in the world around me, reveling in the peace for a few seconds.

"Glad you could make it," Sheriff Finnegan said, coming

around to my side as I faced into the woods. "Maybe you'll have better luck once you get the dogs on the trail."

"No joy for you guys, then?" I asked, turning to face the sheriff. Fred, Hank, and Julie joined us, while Bear hung back by himself.

"He was definitely here," Fred said. He produced a bit of colorful plastic, and I looked closer. A Scooby Doo Pez dispenser. "He collects these damn things. Probably has two hundred in the house there."

I didn't point out that a lot of other people also collect Pez dispensers—it was hardly guaranteed that this belonged to Albie.

"Any idea why he would have chosen to come here?" I asked instead. Julie drifted away from us, motioning to Bear. Despite the chill of the early-morning air, she wore khaki shorts just past her skinny behind and a tank top that left her flat stomach exposed. Her blond hair was in a ponytail, topped by a Red Sox baseball hat. God, I missed Ren.

"We came camping out here a couple times back in high school," the sheriff said, answering my question. "That's the only thing I can think of."

"That would be enough," Hank said. "He still talks about those camping trips. If he's going back to the few good memories he has outside of his mother, that would make sense."

"When was he last seen?" I asked. I was doing my best to ignore the conversation Bear was now having with Julie, which appeared to be getting heated. She faced off against him, jaw set. Bear looked like he was in way over his head.

"The couple who picked him up left him here last night," the sheriff said with a grimace. "They're not from around here, weren't paying attention to the local news. They saw somebody down on his luck and figured they'd do a good deed."

"They must have been nuts to think that was a good idea," Hank said. "Albie's scary as hell on his best day—no offense, Fred," he said apologetically. Fred shrugged, conceding the point. "After what he's been through, I can't imagine what kind of shape he's in."

"The wife wasn't happy about it, apparently," Sheriff Finnegan agreed. "And she was fit to be tied once she realized who they'd had riding with them."

"Why don't you just say what you mean?" Julie said suddenly, loud enough for everyone to hear. I thought for a moment that she was adding to our conversation, but at the look on Bear's face, realized quickly that they were immersed in their own little drama. Bear blushed, saying something to her that was too low to be heard from where I was standing.

Apparently his response made no impression on Julie, however. She made a face, hissed something unflattering to him that I couldn't quite make out, and flounced away to rejoin us.

Sheriff Finnegan raised his eyebrows in my direction, but I was just as clueless as he was. I shrugged.

"Well, anyway," the sheriff said, "we'd best get you out there while things are still cool. It's supposed to top ninety today—no way those dogs should be out there once the sun is full up. You sure they'll be okay now?"

"I'll keep an eye on them," I said. "Don't worry about it. We have plenty of water, and we'll take breaks. By noon, we'll have to pull them out of the field for a few hours, until things cool off again."

"Do what you need to," the sheriff said. "You know this business just as well as I do, if not better. I've got faith."

"We ready or what?" Monty asked, joining us with all three dogs in tow. They were all leashed, though Phantom was taking to that more kindly than Casper or Granger. Granger was a lanky mix of Catahoula leopard dog and hound that Monty had only been working with for the past year or so, but the dog had a heck of a nose on him.

I took Phantom's leash, and Bear got hold of Casper. The pit bull wound himself around Bear's legs, tail whipping wildly, mouth open in a wide, panting grin and his body wound tight. Ready to work, in other words. Phantom took her place by my side silently. A bystander would have no idea she was the least bit worked up, but I could tell by the way she held her head and tail—ears and tail up, the slightest tension in her aging body. She was just as ready to hit the trail as the younger pups were, she just had a little more dignity about it. I got the rush that always comes at the prospect of another search, and felt myself settling into the center once more.

"Where does Lee want us?" I asked Sheriff Finnegan. "Are we sticking with established trails, or thinking he'll head farther out?"

"He's not in great shape," Fred pointed out. "And he's always worried about falling, so I told Sheriff Finnegan I don't think he'd go too far from the trail."

"But you guys just walked the trail, right?" Bear asked. "It's not like there are that many places for him to hide—it's a pretty straight shot up the mountain."

"True," Sheriff Finnegan said. "But there's always the chance he got spooked and headed farther into the woods.

A person who doesn't have Albie's..." he paused "... challenges is hard enough to figure out. Who knows how Albie might react."

"Forget getting off the trail, I still can't believe he would have stayed out here all night," Julie said. I looked at her, surprised.

"Why's that?"

"Albie hates the dark. He always has to sleep with the light on. Nancy was always making fun of him for it. You seriously think he would survive out here all alone without totally freaking out?"

"People have done a lot more out-of-character things than spend a warm summer night on an easy trail in the Maine woods when they're backed into a corner," Hank said. "To be honest, maybe this time's doing him some good. Giving him a little space to get his head together."

Fred frowned. "My brother isn't some college kid who just went through a bad breakup. Emotionally, he's still thirteen years old, and my mother was his entire life."

"Yeah, I know, Freddy," Hank said, suddenly terse. He lingered over the Freddy, and it sounded like a slur in the stillness. "You forget, I was there. I saw the dynamic between the two of them a lot more than you did the last couple of years—"

"And on that note," Sheriff Finnegan interceded, "why don't you and your team head on up, Jamie? I've been going all night, so I'm going to sit this one out—as are Fred and the others here. Give me a shout if there's anything you need."

I assured him we would do that, and was relieved when he herded Hank, Julie, and Fred to their respective cars.

I noted with interest that Julie was riding with Fred, and made a mental note to find out a bit more about the man's relationship with Julie's mother.

"How do you want to run it, boss?" Monty asked, once it was just us and the dogs again.

"Let's split it into quadrants. They might think Albie would stick to the trail, but we have no evidence of that. I don't want to risk it. Bear—"

"Not the trail," he said immediately. "Please?" To his credit, he did manage to keep his tone even—affable, in fact. "I always get the trail. Instead, how about Casper and I do the rockier outcroppings?"

"You okay with that?" I asked Monty.

"Let the kid do the mountain goating. I'm good with the south corner, see what we come up with there."

"Then it's settled. Check-in every hour, and let's say we meet at the top of Maiden's Cliff, at the cross?"

With route and schedule determined, we parted ways at the head of the trail. I took a centering breath as I watched Monty and Bear take off in separate directions, their dogs leading the way.

"Ready, Phan?" I said. Phantom's tail waved slightly in acknowledgment. I got out the scent article Fred had provided—this time, an old bandanna that was considerably less offensive than the jockey shorts we'd had yesterday—and Phantom poked at it. Breathed it in. And then, she whined. For the first time, she pulled at the lead. I made sure my handheld GPS was working and synced the device with her collar, and unsnapped the leash.

"All right, girl. Let's do this. Find him, Phantom!"

In hiking terms, Maiden's Cliff is what's known as a moderate trail, gaining about eight hundred feet in elevation over the course of a single mile. In spring, it runs along a clear stream, the result of runoff from the snow at the mountaintop. This had been a hot, dry summer, however, and now there wasn't a drop to be seen in any direction.

I followed close behind Phantom, the dog content to stick to the trail and in no particular hurry while she waited to pick up the scent. The relatively warm night air meant scent particles would hover above the ground, since scent rises with the temperature. On cold days, molecules accumulate at ground level and stay there—that's the reason trash smells worse in higher temps while it's barely noticeable in the dead of winter.

As though clear on the science, Phantom kept her nose up most of the time, nostrils quivering as she searched for the scent. Every few minutes, she would raise her head, ears pricked, tuned in to a thousand things I was virtually oblivious to. Meanwhile, I followed behind with growing frustration. If he'd been here, someone should have picked up the scent by now.

We came across a fat porcupine who ambled carelessly across the path, seemingly unconcerned about Phantom's presence. I watched as the spiny behind disappeared into the bushes, charmed despite myself. As a dog handler, I'm well acquainted with the torment of a good quilling. Currently, Casper held the record, with three porcupine crossings in a single summer. As an animal lover, however, I've always had a soft spot for the intelligent eyes and almost puckish personality of the young 'pines. We'd rehabilitated more than one orphaned or injured porcupette, and my memories of the prickly little pups were always fond.

We kept on.

An hour and a half in, after taking several side trips when it seemed Phantom had taken an interest, we reached the old steel cross that marked the crest of the Maiden's Cliff trail. More than a hundred and fifty years before, in 1864, a twelve-year-old girl named Elenora fell to her death from that very spot, supposedly trying to retrieve her hat after it blew off in the wind. It was said that the girl haunted the mountain to this day, though Bear had said more than once that he'd seen no sign of the girl.

Now, I stood a couple of feet back from the ledge, looking down over Lake Megunticook far below. Had Albie come out here? Terrified and alone, seeking some connection to the distant past he remembered so fondly, had he stood in this spot?

I looked down, and fought a wave of vertigo.

There was no safety railing, no rope cordoning off the precipice. If he had fallen, would I sense that now?

If he had jumped?

Stillness fell around us. An eagle soared over the lake, looking for a likely meal. My chest had loosened, tension lessened with the hike, but now I sensed a change in the air.

Something waiting for me.

I swallowed past the fear, bracing myself, but when the pain struck this time it was so sharp, so violent, that it felt like I'd been broadsided. I went down to my knees, stomach lurching, while the blue sea miles below seemed to race to meet me.

Jump, James, Brock said to me. *We can meet on the other side.*

Light exploded in my head. I felt, sensed, Phantom in front of me, her body blocking me from the ledge until I could regain my senses.

And then, it all went away.

Well—all but the pain.

But the lights, the voice, the tension... All of that receded on the wind. I was left still on my knees, one hand on the ground to brace myself.

Fear gripped hold and held fast.

Brock was forty-two when he fathered Bear; I was fifteen, away at a dog-training camp in Maine that Brock founded and ran. At the time, I'd been flattered by the attention—me, a skinny little Georgia nobody, attracting the eye of the dynamic, self-made dog trainer who had taken the world by storm. Of course, I knew now that his training theories were a lot of macho bull that had little to do with behavioral science or any kind of compassion for animals. But then...well. Then, I'd been a child.

I knew why Brock was back—he'd as much as told me during the search in Bethel. He was back because he wanted me to pay for what I did. He wanted me to stand up and tell the world what had happened the night he died in his home almost ten years ago; that the image I portrayed to those around me was a lie.

He wanted me to tell the truth: that I had murdered him in cold blood, while my son slept in the next room.

"You're not taking this from me," I said out loud. Phantom looked at me, clearly uneasy. I forced myself back to my feet. Laughter, hard and mocking, surrounded me.

We'll see about that, James, Brock said. *Think about it. Give me a little time knocking around in that pretty little head of yours. Then get back to me.*

I steadied myself with my hand resting on Phantom's head, stomach rolling, and stared into the abyss.

There had been days, weeks...entire months in the past nine years since Brock's death, when I had thought it was done. I'd killed him. I never told a soul what happened that night—not Bear, not Monty. Not even Jack, and I'd told him more about my relationship with Brock than anyone. I could never find the words to tell him about that last night, though.

But somehow, against all odds, I had gotten away with it. Brock was gone, and I was here.

It was clear now just how deluded I had been. I was still here, but Brock had never really been that far away. The ugly truth had always been there, waiting for me to deal with it. I just wished I had the first clue how to do that.

12

IT WAS JUST PAST EIGHT-THIRTY by the time Barbara left Jack's office. Once she'd gone, Jack ran through a long list of things he needed to do for the day, particularly now that he was suddenly in the midst of two apparent murder investigations. His first call as soon as Barbara was safely out the door was to Bear. He fought the urge to call Jamie instead—not when Bear was his client. This was something between the two of them, at least for now.

Unfortunately, Bear didn't answer. Jack left a message instructing the boy to get back to him as soon as he got the message. Then, he hung up. Should he call Jamie next?

Not yet, he decided. First, he needed to do whatever he could to discuss the situation with Bear. At a loss, he paced the apartment twice before he decided he needed to shift gears to the new charges suddenly relying on him.

He knew he could ask Jamie whatever he needed to about the cats, but there was a problem: if he asked her even a fraction of the things that were buzzing around his brain since Cash came to stay, Jamie would realize he was a complete idiot. At least, a complete idiot about this. In his entire life—at least, that he could remember from thirteen years old on—he'd never had a pet before. When he and his wife Lucia were married, they were both too busy. And after she was killed in Nicaragua six years ago, he never even really entertained the thought. Now, though…

Well, now he realized he'd better learn pretty damn fast. These kittens were relying on him, and they wouldn't feed themselves. The bag of Kitten Chow and pan of litter the Humane Society had provided was all well and good, but he'd seen the disdainful look Jamie had cast in his direction at the meager supplies.

He surfed the internet for half an hour looking for tips on nutrition and care, but there was so much conflicting information that he eventually gave up. At 9:55 a.m., he peered out his window at the darkened storefront of the pet boutique across the street—the Loyal Biscuit. Erin Solomon swore by the place; when they'd been dating while she lived in Portland, Jack had known her to drive the eighty miles each way just to get store brands she could have gotten just as easily in Portland for her dog Einstein.

It's better if it's from the Biscuit. Trust me.

Jamie made most of the dog food for the animals on her team, but he'd seen her pick up treats there in a pinch, when they'd run out of homemade deer jerky or duck hearts or whatever it was she fed her crew. If it was good enough for Jamie, it should definitely be good enough for Cash and the kittens.

So, at 9:59 exactly, just as a petite blond woman put a dog bowl of water out on the sidewalk, Jack was at his door. Cash meowed inquisitively after him, the kittens following with plaintiff yowls of their own.

Who knew a cat could be this much pressure?

To his surprise, the store was already in full swing when he walked through the door two minutes later. A pallet of dog food was in the middle of the floor, with a sign beside it.

Donations for the Davis Animals

A story, neatly typed and pasted on pastel construction paper, followed. The blond he'd seen outside looked up from posting more signage when he walked through the door, keen eyes taking him in with a single sweeping glance.

"Jack Juarez!" she said, with a grin that suggested she knew something he didn't. "Jamie said you'd be stopping by. I hear you got some babies you're looking after."

"Who'd he get?" another woman asked—this one with glasses and dark curls, an air of competence about her that Jack found reassuring.

"The one-eared tom and the kittens," the blond replied. "You remember, Tracy was telling us about them."

Jack racked his brain for names to go with faces. Finally, the blond had mercy.

"I'm Melody. Mel. Whatever. Trust me, whatever you call me, I've probably been called worse. And this is April," she said, indicating the woman with glasses.

April nodded to him. She had a clipboard under her arm, pen in hand. "That's great what you're doing with the kittens. God, what a mess it is over there."

"I told everybody how long ago that that old bat needed to be taken out?" Mel said. April rolled her eyes, with a smile at Jack.

"We know."

"Not that I said someone should actually do her in. But the way she treated those animals? I still don't get why the State didn't do something sooner."

"They tried," April pointed out. "Multiple times. She was pretty slippery about the whole thing. You can't just take someone's property from them—"

"Animals—living creatures," Mel interrupted. "Don't give me that property crap."

"I feel the same way," April said. "You know that. The law doesn't, unfortunately."

Sensing that he might get something beyond just cat food, Jack stuck with the turn the conversation had taken.

"So, do you have any idea who did it?"

Before anyone could answer, a lean, good-looking man with a shaved head, dress shirt, and shorts came to the door pulling a wagon filled with pet food, blankets, and cleaning supplies.

"This is just one side of Main Street," he announced. "PJ and Frank got a bunch of blankets and bedding they said they'll donate, plus a night's stay at the inn for the auction."

He stopped short at sight of Jack, making no attempt to hide his curiosity. "Did you donate?" he asked Jack, nodding to the wagon of food behind him. "Two hundred animals, most of them starving."

"One hundred and seven," April corrected him. He waved off the distinction. "Jack, this is my husband, Mike. Mike, Jack Juarez."

Sudden interest lit his eyes. He studied Jack speculatively. "The P.I., right? Moved here from DC?"

"We were just talking about Nancy," April interrupted smoothly. Jack got the feeling he was being saved from something, he just wasn't sure what.

"Ah—right," Mike said. "Is this for a case you're working on, or you just can't shake the old habit?"

Jack smiled. "Maybe a little bit of both."

"Nice," the other man said. He leaned back against the front counter, but other customers were coming in. Mike frowned, as though they were intruding. "What are you doing for lunch today?" he asked.

The question caught Jack off guard. "Me? Oh. I—uh—have some things…"

"Leave him alone, Mike," April said. She called the words over her shoulder as she inventoried the donations he'd just brought in.

"You want to know who killed Nancy, and why? Nobody knows more dirt about this place than I do."

"That's actually true," April conceded. She took a bag of food still in Mike's arms, plucking it from him as she passed by.

"That's crap," Mel said. "I know a helluva lot more dirt than you do."

"It isn't a competition," Mike said.

"The hell it's not," Mel said. She fixed Jack with a calculating gaze, one eyebrow raised. "Go ahead: what do you need to know?"

●

Jack left the store an hour later with a new cat carrier, a kitten condo on order, a case of kitten food more expensive than most human baby formula, and half a dozen leads to follow thanks to Mike and Mel.

Had he known, for example, that Fred Davis and Barbara

Monroe had once been a couple? Jack assured Mike that, no, he hadn't heard anything of the kind. Not to be outdone, Mel told Jack in excruciating detail about every Loyal Biscuit customer who had made an official complaint to the police or—surprisingly common—made bodily threats against Nancy if she didn't start taking better care of her animals.

By the time Jack left, he had so many leads to follow he wasn't sure where to begin. He opted to go back to the apartment, check on the cats, and figure things out from there.

Whatever else he might have learned, Jack found it hard to dismiss the news that Fred Davis and Barbara had been a couple. Why hadn't she mentioned that this morning?

He tossed the revelation around in his mind for a short time before he dismissed it. Far more concerning than anything Mike and Mel had told him about Nancy Davis was the information Barbara had given him about the night Nancy was killed.

Bear had been there.

Barbara saw them fighting.

Bear still hadn't returned Jack's call. Frustrated, he picked up the phone and put another call through. Though between the search for Albie and everything going on on the island, what were the chances Bear would actually answer?

To his surprise, Bear picked up after the second ring.

"Did you find anything?" Bear asked, without even saying 'hello' first.

"No, not yet," Jack said. "I got some interesting information, though. I was hoping you could shed some light on it."

There was a pause on the line. Jack could hear dogs

barking in the background, and occasional shouts. "Hang on a second," Bear said.

"How's the search going?" Jack asked.

"Well, we're still out here, so it can't be going too great. We got a tip that some tourists had picked him up in Rockland, then dropped him off on a trail in Camden. We're up on the mountain now."

"Well, if anyone can find him..." Jack said. He almost rolled his eyes at the cliché. Bear, likewise, seemed unimpressed.

"You said you had a question?" Bear asked.

"Right," Jack said. "I heard from someone who seems to think you were at Nancy's the night she was killed, around midnight. Do you know why they would think that?"

This time, the pause on the line was so long Jack thought they had been disconnected. Finally, Bear responded. The tension in his voice was unmistakable, and Jack felt uneasiness settle in his own stomach.

"I don't know what they were talking about," Bear said. "I was out on the island that night. I knew we'd have a big day dealing with the animals come morning—why would I go back to the mainland?"

"That's what I was wondering," Jack said. "It doesn't make a lot of sense to me, but this person seemed pretty certain of it. You sure you don't know what they're talking about?"

"No," Bear said. "No clue. Listen, I have to get going. They're waiting for me. Just let me know if you hear anything else."

Jack frowned. It wasn't that he was surprised by the boy's answer, but he was definitely disappointed. He had an uneasy suspicion that however easily Bear might dismiss the allegation, the police wouldn't be so cavalier. And there was no question in Jack's mind that at some point in the investigation, probably not that far down the line, detectives would be knocking on Bear's door.

At shortly past noon that day, Cash and the kittens were sleeping, the apartment was clean, the kitty litter boxes were out, and Jack was ready to hit the road. Sophie Laurent had called and asked him to meet her at the lab at one o'clock, which meant Jack needed to get a move on if he didn't want to be late. He was headed for the exit when a knock at the door stopped him. He frowned. He'd had more visitors in the past twenty-four hours than in the three months previous since moving to town.

The frown vanished when he peered through the peephole, however.

Jamie stood on the threshold when he opened the door, wearing dirty khaki pants and an equally dirty, lightweight white shirt. Her hair was pulled back into a ponytail, and a smudge of dirt on her nose made him grin.

"Hi there," he said. "This is a surprise. Is everything all right?"

A hint of pink touched her cheeks, intriguing him. "It is. I just—I was in the neighborhood. Kind of. I thought I'd just stop in and see how you're faring with the cats." She hesitated, taking in his appearance—jacket on, keys in hand. "I'm sorry, I should have called first. I just thought—"

"No, it's fine," he assured her. "Normally I'd invite you in, but I'm just on my way out to talk to the medical examiner. I thought you were out on the search."

"I am—or I was. It gets too hot for the dogs during the day, so we usually break for a few hours once the sun is full up. We'll hit the trail again this evening, once it's cooler. Monty took the dogs back to the island to give them a break."

"But you didn't need a break?"

She shrugged. "I thought I could just do that here. Two birds with one stone and all that. You're talking to the medical examiner?"

"Yeah. I ran into a woman I used to work with—a forensic anthropologist who's consulting on this case. She invited me to the M.E.'s office in Augusta, and said she'd go over some things with me there."

"Wow. That's a lucky break, isn't it? Just happening to find someone you knew well enough that she'd just invite you in on an autopsy. Or whatever they do with bones."

"It is," he agreed. "You're welcome to stay here while I'm gone if you want, though. You can get cleaned up, take a nap…. Whatever. Make yourself at home." She was already edging toward the door—there was no way she would take him up on the offer, and he knew it. He silently cursed his bad timing. How long had he been waiting for her to stop in, and now he had to rush out the door?

"Or, you could come with me," he said impulsively.

She looked at him in surprise. "To the medical examiner's office?"

"I'll only be there for a few minutes. It would give us a chance to visit. I'll take you out to lunch in Augusta." He glanced back toward the window. The sun was shining, the sky clear blue. "It's a beautiful afternoon for a ride."

"I'm not really in the best shape for the outside world,"

she said, gesturing to her clothing and hair with a broad sweep of her hand. "And definitely not for lunch out."

"Let me call Sophie," he said. Now that he'd come up with the idea, Jack found it too good to let go of. "I'll tell her I'm running a little bit late. You can use my shower, get cleaned up. I promise to save any five-star restaurants for the next date."

"So, this is a date?" she asked. There was still color in her cheeks, and a curious light in her eyes.

He risked a smile, holding her eye. "This is whatever you want it to be, *corazón.*"

She raised an eyebrow at that, but Jack refused to be flustered or apologize for the endearment. A brief silence followed, weighty with unspoken tension, before she wet her lips and took a breath. "Can you give me ten minutes?"

Jack's grin widened. "Absolutely."

Fifteen minutes later, they were on the road. Jamie had showered and changed into clean jeans and a white button-up she'd borrowed from Jack—she'd already used her spare shirt earlier in the day, and Monty was supposed to bring her fresh search clothes that evening. Her hair was down, and still damp. Jack resisted the urge to brush it back from her face, but it took genuine effort.

"Music, podcast, or conversation?" he asked as they set out.

"Conversation," she said. "We can always resort to music if we run out of things to say on the way back."

"Fair enough," he agreed.

They didn't run out of things to say, as it turned out. Jack had been uneasy at first that conversation might veer toward the case he was working on for Bear, but there were so many other things to talk about that they never actually got there. Instead, Jack focused the conversation on the many animals now under Jamie's care out on the island, and Jamie seemed more than willing to go along with that.

"It's pretty crazy right now," she summarized, after giving him a few of the highlights of the past twenty-four hours, "but I think most of the animals we've got out there will pull through. There are a couple of sheep who are in hard shape, and the donkey isn't looking too good. She's eating, though, so that's a good sign. Reaver's my biggest worry at this point."

"The giant pit bull," Jack said. She glanced at him with a smile.

"He's not that big."

"He looked pretty big to me."

"Of course, you looked ready to turn tail and run when Oswald looked at you cross-eyed."

Jack smiled back, not bothering to argue the point. "You don't think he's going to make it, then? Reaver," he clarified. "Not Oswald."

"I'm not sure. He hasn't given up yet—that's something. I was able to spend some time with him this morning, and that was good. I get the sense he's actually had some training, it just got lost under all the trauma Nancy's put him through. Plus, God knows what he went through before. I wish Bear would pay a little more attention to him."

"I thought Reaver was his pet project," Jack said, surprised.

"So did I," Jamie agreed. "Any other time, he wouldn't have left that dog's side once we got him over to the island.

Now, though... I don't really know where his head is. I mean, I know he's busy. We're all busy, and it's true he's taken an awful lot on with this. Still, something's off with him."

"He's been distracted?" Jack asked.

Jamie laughed shortly. "You could say that. He hasn't been the same since Ren left, but the last few days..." She hesitated, as though weighing whether to say more. Jack waited in silence.

"The other night, he never went to bed," she said finally. "I got up to wake him when I got the call about Nancy, and he hadn't been in his room."

Jack tensed, his hands tightening on the steering wheel. He glanced at Jamie, whose gaze was locked on the world passing by outside her window.

"Do you have any idea where he was?" he asked after a moment.

"No," she said. "He was on the island when I called him. Said he'd been talking to Ren on the phone. My guess is that he was with the animals."

She was lying—he knew it immediately, though he had little experience with Jamie's lies. She was usually honest to a fault.

"Mm," Jack said noncommittally.

Silence fell between them. A minute passed, then two. When she still didn't speak, he glanced at her again. She was relaxed, her head tipped back slightly against the headrest.

"Jamie?" he said quietly.

No answer, apart from her even breathing. He smiled at the realization: their first date, and she'd fallen asleep after barely half an hour on the road.

They were nearly to Augusta before she stirred, her

voice a low murmur with an unmistakable edge of distress in there.

"Leave him alone," she said—or at least, that's what Jack thought she said. It was hard to tell, exactly. "Get away from him. Please." She whispered a name, and Jack's chest tightened. *No, Brock. Please, no.*

"Jamie," Jack said. He scanned the road ahead for a place to pull over, and did so with barely a warning turn signal. The car behind blared its horn as it roared past, but Jack paid no attention.

With the car in park, he twisted in his seat to look at her. Her forehead was furrowed as though in pain, every muscle tensed. He didn't touch her, afraid that he would frighten her that much more. Instead, he tried to bring her back with his voice alone.

"You're all right," he said, keeping his tone even. He knew the power of nightmares all too well. "You're safe, Jamie. Bear is safe. Everything's all right."

She awoke with a start, her body jerking convulsively. Only then did Jack risk what he'd wanted to do from the start, laying a gentling hand on her arm as she gradually found her way back to the land of the living.

"You were having a dream," he said, his voice still soft. "That's all it was. You're safe."

"I... Brock was..." She bit her lip to keep from saying more, disoriented.

"He's gone, Jamie. It's over."

She surprised him with a harsh laugh, now fully awake. The protective armor once more in place. "Yeah. Sure it is."

He shifted his hand from her arm to her face, pushing the hair back so that he could look at her. He studied her a moment in silence, noting the furrow that still remained in her forehead. The tension in her body, despite the fact that the nightmare was over. But maybe that's where he was wrong.

Maybe for Jamie, the nightmare wasn't over at all.

"Do you want to talk about it?" he asked after a moment, searching her eyes.

She shook her head. Moved away from him. He let his hand drop. "No. I'm fine. You should get back on the road—you'll be late."

"Sophie will wait."

"She doesn't have to." She managed a smile that Jack was sure was meant to be reassuring. It fell well short of that. "Seriously, Jack. I'm okay. It was just a dream."

When it was clear that she wouldn't say anything more, he put the car back in drive and returned to the road.

"Do you still hear his voice? Brock's?" Jack asked, after several minutes of silence. They were just down the road from the crime lab now, traffic picking up now that they were in Augusta.

"Sometimes," she said briefly. He glanced at her. Her eyes were closed, a sheen of sweat on her face. Jack lay a hand on hers and squeezed, and she turned to meet his gaze.

"Do you have a headache? You don't look well."

"It just shook me a little bit," she said dismissively, trying for a smile. "That's all. Bear was gone… Brock was there." She shrugged. "It was just a dream, Jack."

A few minutes later, he turned into the parking lot for the Maine Crime Lab and found a spot easily enough, since it was a sunny Friday afternoon. No doubt, most everyone in the building was taking a long weekend. Jamie started to reach for the door, but he stopped her with a hand on her arm. She turned to face him once more.

"Have you considered talking to someone? About the dreams, or his voice, or…" He trailed off, uncertain where to go from there.

She laughed briefly. "Right. That conversation would go great, I can hear it now. 'Who does this voice you hear belong to, Ms. Flint? How do you know this man?' What do I tell them? I'm hearing the voice of the man who got me pregnant when I was fifteen? My kidnapper, later in life. The man I k—" She stopped. "The man who made me what I am today, for better or worse?"

"You made yourself what you are today," Jack said evenly. "You did it in spite of Brock Campbell. You made something amazing." He studied her face, the contours and the depth. "You are amazing, *corazón.*"

She smiled faintly. "Corazón," she repeated. "That's the second time you've called me that today."

He pushed an errant lock of hair behind the delicate shell of her ear. "Does it bother you? Me calling you that?"

"No," she said. She studied him intently, her head tilted just slightly. He was caught in brilliant blue depths. "I like the way you say it. It sounds…" she searched for the word. "…sexy. And reverent, both at the same time. Like you're talkin' dirty in church."

He actually laughed. "And that's a good thing?"

"It has its place," she confirmed.

Silence fell once more. She made no move to leave the car.

"How's your head?" he asked after a while.

"It's fine." She smiled at his clear skepticism. "Really.

Jack, I swear. I'm okay. I appreciate the concern, I really do. But it was just a dream. You should get in there, Sophie's waiting."

13

SOPHIE AND THE MEDICAL EXAMINER had already been hard at work for a while by the time Jack got there. Jamie begged off actually going into the lab, and instead settled in a cramped office Sophie showed her to, pulling a Kindle from her bag.

"You're sure you're all right here?" Jack asked before leaving her.

"I'm fine, Jack."

"I won't be long."

"Oh my God." She laughed. "Will you go? I'm okay."

He left her, albeit reluctantly.

"Your friend didn't want to come in with you?" Sophie asked when he joined her.

"No. She's not feeling well."

"Just as well," she said with a shrug. "This may not be as bad as the last case we worked on together, but it's still not for the faint-hearted." She eyed him a moment, then handed him scrubs and a mask. "It is strange, this habit you have of bringing beautiful women with you to the bone yard."

The last time he'd seen Sophie on a case, Erin Solomon

had been with him—at Erin's insistence. Ultimately, she hadn't fared well. He was grateful that Jamie had elected to sit this one out.

"What do you have so far?" he asked, in lieu of a reply.

She led him to a vast, stainless steel exam room, where four gurneys had been rolled out, a body on each of them. An autopsy had already been performed on Nancy Davis, her Y-incision now closed and her body draped.

The two skeletal remains were set out on separate gurneys, the bones carefully laid out to make up two nearly whole skeletons.

Another woman, this one considerably taller and broader than Sophie, joined them.

"Jack, this is Dr. Anna Fuller, chief forensic pathologist here. She's in charge when there's more than just bones we're dealing with. Anna, this is Jack Juarez."

"It's good to meet you," Jack said. He moved forward for a handshake, but paused when the doctor held up gloved hands. He stepped back. "Thank you for letting me get a look at this."

"No problem," Dr. Fuller assured him. "We're always fans of inter-agency cooperation here."

Jack shot Sophie a sharp glare. She was standing just behind the pathologist, and subtly raised her finger to her lips, effectively shushing Jack. He grimaced. This was definitely not what he had intended. Still, it had gotten him a lot farther than his P.I. license would have. Rather than setting the doctor straight on his status with the FBI, Jack kept his mouth shut.

"Shall we, Agent Juarez?" Dr. Fuller said, gesturing to the bodies. Jack nodded, and followed her into the room.

"Do you have cause of death on Nancy?" he asked first, as the pathologist led him to that body.

"We're waiting for the tox results—that's a week to ten days, at least. It looks pretty cut and dry, though. Despite the heart attack, it appears she ultimately died of blunt force trauma."

"Heart attack?" Jack asked, surprised.

"Yes. She had a fairly major cardiac event, and likely would have died of that if she hadn't gotten help quickly. Her assailant either was unaware, or was unwilling to wait for nature to take its course."

"So she was attacked," Jack translated.

"Absolutely," Fuller agreed. "It happened fast, if that's any comfort." Dr. Fuller threw the light on a couple of light boxes, illuminating a set of x-rays. "Point of impact was here," she said, indicating the center of a spiderweb of cracks on the film. "He hit hard enough to drive the skull into the brain, causing an acute subdural hematoma. It may have taken her a little bit of time for her body to fail, but brain death was virtually instantaneous."

"And this couldn't have been accidental?" Jack pressed. "Perhaps she fell while she was having the heart attack."

Fuller pursed her lips, eyeing the films. "There's always the odd chance," she admitted. "Unlikely, though. The angle means she would have had to fall on her head, basically. I'm not sure how that could have happened, particularly given the position of the body when she was found. No— it's more likely that an assailant came up behind her, and smashed her in the head with something."

"Any idea of the murder weapon?"

"My bet's on a fireplace poker." She switched on another

light box, this one containing photos. Fuller indicated a close-up of Nancy's head, after the blood had been washed away and the hair shaved off. "See this," she said. She pointed to a jagged impression next to the wound. "I have a poker like this—the end shaped like an arrow. The full impact would have fallen on the barb of the arrow. This impression here would be from the tip."

Jack didn't bother hiding his confusion. He wasn't surprised when Dr. Fuller went to the other side of the room and produced a long, cast-iron rod with an arrow at the end. She held the instrument aloft for Jack to see, running her hand along the jagged barb that tapered up to the glistening tip.

"If I were bringing this down heavily, the first point of impact would be the one with the most force behind it. That would be here, unless someone was to throw this straight on like an arrow. During impact, the second point to hit would also make a mark. In this case, that would be the tip itself."

She took out a clay human skull and, with more glee than Jack had been prepared for, brought the poker down heavily on the unsuspecting victim. Jack moved forward the moment it was safe, studying the subsequent impression in the clay with interest.

Dr. Fuller was right: the poker was a near-perfect match.

"Did the police find anything like this on the scene?" he asked.

"Not yet," Fuller said. "But I understand they've got a lot to sift through."

"That's an understatement," Jack said. "And the other bodies?" he asked, including Sophie in the question. Up to this point, the forensic anthropologist had been on the sidelines, watching Dr. Fuller with clear interest.

"Why don't you take over, Sophie," the pathologist said.

"Thank you," Sophie said, with a smile. "Don't mind if I do." She walked to the first disarticulated skeleton. The bones had visible gnaw marks, the skull still missing. Jack felt his stomach lurch unexpectedly at the sight.

"This one has been dead a long time—very long. Ten, maybe twenty years. Could have been longer. I'm running some tests to get a more precise date."

"Any idea of identity?"

"Nothing specific. I can tell you he's male. Between thirty and forty years old. No skull means no dental records; no tissue means no tox screen, no DNA, no fingerprints."

"So you don't know who he is, or how he died," Jack guessed.

"Sadly, no. He broke his right femur when he was younger, and it never actually healed right. My guess is he probably walked with a limp. Beyond that, though, I can't tell you much."

"That's all right. I'm sure the police will keep looking for that skull. They're bound to find it eventually," Jack said. He didn't sound convinced, most likely because he wasn't. "What about the other one?"

"I can tell you a little more about her," Sophie said immediately. "Female, twenty-two years old. She was in good health, probably raised with some money—there was some fairly expensive orthodonture, nice teeth."

"Any line on ID?"

Sophie frowned. She went to a steel file cabinet in the corner and took a folder that was lying on top. Wordlessly, she opened the folder, removed a photo, and handed it to Jack.

The young woman was pretty, with a wide smile and sparkling green eyes. Freckles. Red hair. Jack turned the photo over, and paused at sight of the name scrawled in blue ink.

Frances, Age 22

He shook his head. "Frances?"

"Frances Craig," Sophie said. "Her parents reported her missing three years ago in Chicago. No leads turned up, and she'd been distant for a while. They figured she just ran off with someone."

"Did she?" Jack asked. He definitely got the sense Sophie knew more; she was just waiting for the big finish.

"According to the police report, her friends said she'd been dating someone quite a bit older than her. Funny looking little guy, an insurance salesman who lived in Philadelphia."

Jack's eyebrows went up in surprise. "You're telling me this was Fred Davis's girlfriend? The one who left a note and left him three years ago?"

"It appears so. Though I'm thinking that bit about the note isn't quite so clear cut now."

"Not so much," Jack agreed. "Cause of death?"

"Looks like she fell—there's a skull fracture, and the radius is broken. That's consistent with someone putting their hand out to catch themselves. I'm thinking she may have fallen down the stairs."

"Or she may have been pushed?" Jack asked.

"Definite possibility," Sophie agreed.

He sighed, and turned his attention to the final body. Dr. Fuller was working on the corpse, scribbling notes in the margin of a typed report. She looked up when Jack approached.

"You ready for this one?" she asked.

"As ready as I'm going to be," he said. "What have you got?"

"White male, twenty-six years old." She handed him a file, her mouth fixed in a frown. "ID was easy on this one—he's got quite the record."

Jack opened the folder. A black and white mugshot was paper clipped to the upper right corner of several sheets of paper, a young white male staring back at him with hard eyes. "Ray Billings," he read aloud, then scanned the charges. Two counts of domestic violence, one of grand theft auto, and several animal cruelty cases related to a dog fighting ring in Mississippi.

"Any idea on the connection?" he asked. The animal abuse was his first guess, though he had no idea how this man might have ended up in Nancy's basement.

"No clue," Fuller said. "He was due for a court date a few weeks ago and never showed up—there's an arrest warrant out for him. Based on insect activity and the degradation of the body, I'd say he had a good excuse for missing that date, seeing as he was dead at the time."

"How long?" Jack asked.

"Not long," Fuller said. "Two months, maybe three."

"And no one reported him missing?"

She shook her head. "You saw the report. I don't think anyone was crying when he didn't show up to dinner. His girlfriend had a restraining order out against him, and it looks like he didn't have any family—was in and out of the foster care system most of his childhood, before he quit that and headed straight for jail."

Jack went silent, considering all of this. Three victims in

the basement. Had Fred's girlfriend threatened to leave him, and he'd snapped and killed her? It was just as likely that Nancy had done it, but Jack found it hard to imagine that Fred wouldn't have suspected something when the woman supposedly left a note and vanished without a trace. And then there was the other body—the man who had been in that basement for decades. Who was that? And where in hell was the man's head?

"Do you mind if I ask you something?" Dr. Fuller asked, pulling Jack from his thoughts.

"Hmm? No, of course not," he assured her. "What is it?"

"What's the Bureau's interest in this case?"

He hesitated. There was a lie at the tip of his tongue when he tossed it aside. "I'm actually not with the Bureau any longer—I apologize, I didn't tell Dr. Laurent. I'm a private investigator now. My client has an interest in this case."

A shadow crossed Dr. Fuller's face. Jack expected anger, but the woman simply cast a disparaging glance at Sophie and shook her head. "You didn't know, huh, Sophie?" she asked.

Sophie shrugged. "I'm getting old. He may have said something—I guess it just slipped my mind."

"Of course it did," Fuller grumbled. She nodded toward the door. "Well, get out of here before I report you. I could get in real trouble for this."

"I really am sorry," Jack said sincerely. She waved him off.

"Oh, I'm sure you are. Just take your girlfriend and go."

Sophie started to go with him, and Fuller laughed out

loud. "Not so fast, Sophie. I meant the girl in my office. You're not getting off so easy."

"Thank you," Jack mouthed to Sophie, then headed out before Dr. Fuller changed her mind. He hurried to the office only to find Jamie asleep on the sofa, curled up on her side with her arm over her eyes.

He knelt beside her. "Hey," he said quietly, trying not to startle her. Sometimes with Jamie, he felt like he was dealing with a wild animal—one wrong move, and he would send her running from him all over again.

This time, however, she didn't start. She moved her arm away from her eyes, and greeted him with a weary smile. "Hey," she echoed, just as quietly. "You all done?"

"I am. You still up for lunch, or did that headache chase away your appetite?"

She laughed, sitting up slowly. "Nothing chases away my appetite, *corazón.*" She emphasized the word, rolling her tongue on the 'r' as he did. He grinned.

"All right, then. Let's go. I want to get out of here before Dr. Fuller calls the police on me." Jamie looked at him inquiringly. "I'll explain in the car," he assured her.

Jamie stood, and he was pleased to note that she didn't pull away when he slipped his hand into hers. A jolt of electricity ran through him at the contact—the kind of reaction that would have made a lot more sense if he were fifteen again, instead of a grown man. He decided he would need to get used to it, though. Jamie had that effect on him.

14

I SLEPT IN THE CAR on the way home from Augusta with Jack. We'd eaten a good lunch and then stopped for dessert after that, talking all the while. My headache eased with aspirin and food, settling to a dull throb that I barely noticed thanks to the distraction Jack provided.

At the end of our journey, Jack dropped me at my car, parked in the back of his building in Rockland.

"You can come up if you like," he said, the two of us standing outside my truck by the light of a slowly sinking sun.

"No, I should go. They'll be waiting for me."

"You seem tired. Are you sure you should—"

"I'm fine, Jack," I interrupted, before he could go any farther down that road. "I've slept more today than I have in weeks, frankly. But even if I hadn't, I wouldn't do anything to endanger my people or the dogs if I wasn't sure I could handle it."

"No, I suppose not," he agreed reluctantly. I wasn't sure he actually believed me, and the thought rankled. I loved Jack's company, but it seemed sometimes that he was too intent on saving me—casting me as damsel in distress when I had worked hard my entire life to be anything but.

"I'll talk to you soon," I said.

A flicker of confusion crossed his face, but he nodded. "Sure," he said, affecting as casual a tone as I had. "Give me a call, we'll do this again. Minus the coroner's office next time."

"Oh, I don't know. That sofa was awfully comfortable," I said. Despite myself, I was stalling. Should I set a time when we would meet again? I fought the urge to go to him; to lift my face to his, look into his eyes... Let myself feel whatever it was I was trying so hard not to.

Jack's gaze lingered on mine. A smile touched his lips, and his confusion melted away in an instant. It was as though he were reading my mind.

"I'll see you soon, *corazón,*" he said. And oh, the way he said that word. I felt my cheeks heat every time he said it, his voice a low murmur that made me feel my heart beating all the way down to my toes.

He was the one who turned and walked away, leaving me rattled as I climbed behind the wheel and set out. It took nearly the entire drive back to the search before I felt like myself again.

The temperature had dropped to a pleasant seventy degrees by the time the K-9 search teams returned to the mountain. Monty was waiting for me, the Flint K-9 team on their feet and eager to get a move on. Phantom greeted me with wagging tail and an uncharacteristic bounce in her step—my girl is usually too reserved for such displays.

Casper, meanwhile, wove his leash in circles around Bear, the pit bull's body vibrating with energy. Monty's

Catahoula, Granger, howled at the lot of us, pacing back and forth while other search teams assembled.

"Where've you been all day?" Monty asked suspiciously. "You ship me off with the dogs and come back looking fed and rested and just a little…"

I raised my eyebrows at him and shot a look toward Bear. Monty grinned. Message received.

"…satisfied," he finished. "It looks good on you, Jamie."

"Well, I'm not *satisfied*," I assured him. "And I won't be, until we find Albie safe and sound. Where are we with that?"

"We've been over every square inch of Maiden's Cliff," Chris Finnegan replied, in a voice loud enough to include all searchers on the scene. "A couple of dogs were on scent this morning, but nobody's had any luck since then. We're now expanding the search to include all of Camden Hills State Park and the associated mountain range."

"We used to camp in the park when we were boys," a man's voice said, though the speaker was lost among the other searchers. He emerged, and I was surprised to see Fred Davis once again. He wore jeans now, and an expensive-looking LL Bean sweater that wasn't at all suited for a search like this. Both were filthy, his face flushed—clearly, he had been at this for most of the day. He couldn't have looked less comfortable if he'd been in hooker heels and a corset.

"He's always had a soft spot for this area," Fred continued. "Our father used to take us camping here. Dad wasn't much for hiking—he had a limp that slowed him down, but he still loved the outdoors. I could see Albie settling in around here."

Julie Monroe was beside him, as she'd been this morning. She looked decidedly less convinced of this theory. I wondered who knew Albie better now—his virtually estranged older brother, or the underage temptress who lived next door. My bet was on Julie.

"Any thoughts on where he might go if he left the mountain?" I asked, directing the question to the girl. "If he got tired of the woods and decided civilization might be safer?"

"He's got some spots around here," she said. "I'd check those before everybody spends all night walking hell and back up there."

"Spots like where?" Bear asked. A flush of pink touched Julie's cheeks at my son's attention.

"Walker Park in Rockport, for one. The Camden Amphitheatre. Children's Chapel—he likes watching the Belted Galloways. The cows," she explained to Fred, who looked clueless.

"How do you know all this?" Fred asked.

The teenager cast a wilting glare at the man. "He talks to me. And I actually listen."

"Has anyone cleared those spots?" I asked Sheriff Finnegan.

"This is the first I'm hearing of any of it," Finnegan said. "But I'll send someone out."

I considered Julie's theory. God knows I'd spent the better part of the evening doubting this whole search, but I wasn't ready to give up just yet. "We'll finish out our search here," I said to the sheriff. "Julie may be right—it seems like if Albie were out here, we would've come across some kind of scent trail by now. But just in case..."

"Just in case," Sheriff Finnegan agreed. "That seems smart to me."

"Suit yourself," Julie said with a shrug. She sidled closer to Bear. "Do you need a partner? For the search, I mean?"

"You've been out here most of the day, and a good part of last night," Sheriff Finnegan said, including both Julie and Fred in the statement. "I know you took a couple of hours off this morning, but that's not enough down time in weather like this. I want you headed home—both of you."

"I'm not tired," Julie said immediately. "I can keep going."

Despite myself, I felt a tug of sympathy for the girl. She might still look good, but there was no mistaking the fatigue in her eyes. Her arms were covered with welts from bug bites, and heat stroke was far too likely in this kind of weather for anyone who didn't know to take the proper precautions.

"He's right," I said. "You need to get some rest tonight. If Albie's still missing in the morning, you can come back out then. But you need to get something on those bites and get some food into you. Have you been staying hydrated?"

She produced a stainless-steel water bottle from her bag and shook it. Water sloshed around inside. "I've had about a dozen refills today—I must have peed on just about every bush in those woods. I told you: I'm okay."

"I'll take you home," Bear said, to my surprise. And Julie's, based on her expression. "We can check out those places in Camden and Rockport first, then get you fed. Okay?"

Her eyes widened when she looked at him, and she nodded with just a hint of a smile. The girl looked like she'd just won the lottery. "Yeah. Okay, sure."

"You don't need to go out of your way," Fred said

to Bear. "I could give her a ride back." Julie wrinkled her nose—not a lot, but enough that I certainly noticed, and I expected Fred probably had as well.

"That's okay," she said quickly. "I'll just go with Bear. We'll be fine."

Without another word, Bear took off back toward the parking lot. Casper tagged along, looking both confused and deflated. Julie, on the other hand, looked over the moon.

Normally, I would call Bear out for this. There were limited search teams, and we were running on borrowed time as it was. I knew him better than to think he was leaving us on a whim, though—Bear had earned the benefit of the doubt on that count. Wherever he was going and whatever was going on with him, I was certain he wouldn't put his own needs above those of Albie's. Besides which, it seemed to me that, however I might feel about Julie, the girl could use some looking after.

Once we'd determined the area each of us would be responsible for, I was grateful to head out with Phantom all on my own. I can fake extroversion if I absolutely have to, but I'll never be mistaken for a people person. I had a bug net to wear if the mosquitoes got too thick, but thankfully tonight there was a good strong breeze coming up on the mountain. I breathed in deep, let my hand brush against Phantom's head, and set our course.

None of the mountains in the range known as the Camden Hills are that high up, the steepest point being Mt. Megunticook at 1,385 feet. The trails this time of year were well maintained and generally well-traveled, particularly on the other side of the range from where we'd begun, at

Camden Hills State Park. As day bled into night, I was happy to be alone alongside my dog, out in the fresh air and away from the rest of the world. Phantom didn't wander too far ahead, and returned to me frequently for check-ins without being prompted.

"You're as bad as Jack," I told the dog at one point. "How many times do I have to tell you people? I'm fine."

I crouched to give her a thorough head scratching, then checked us both for ticks before we moved on. I found two crawling on her ears, and one making its way up my leg. I'm not squeamish about bugs as a general rule, but I've seen the havoc Lyme disease and half a dozen other tick-borne illnesses have caused. I'm not a fan.

"All right, girl," I said to Phantom, as I straightened and looked skyward at the first glimpse of a crescent moon overhead. "Let's get this done. Find him, Phantom."

Once again, my shepherd headed off into the night.

15

JACK SETTLED IN WITH CASH and the kittens for a couple of hours that afternoon after returning from Augusta, then headed back to the Davis place for another look around at shortly past seven o'clock. A cursory glance when he arrived told him the animals—or all he could see of them, anyway—had been cleared out, and the place seemed virtually deserted. The exceptions were a sedan that appeared to have been fastidiously maintained, and Nancy's ancient station wagon, the windshield smashed and one taillight broken out.

As he approached the house, Jack noticed a solitary figure in the pasture, hands on hips, back bowed in weariness or defeat.

Fred Davis.

"Mr. Davis?" Jack called. He prepared himself for the inevitable challenge of questioning a grieving family member. It was hard enough with a badge behind him. Lacking that, he found himself uncertain of how to begin.

Fred Davis turned, pulled from his reverie. He wore jeans and a sweater, both of them filthy, and looked like a man who had spent a full day—possibly more—on his feet.

The grief had settled fully on his shoulders now, his eyes dark with it.

"Yes?" Davis said, suspicion in the word.

"I was here yesterday," Jack said. "I took one of your mother's cats, and a litter of kittens."

Jack had been hoping this information might be enough to establish the beginning of a rapport, but Davis looked unimpressed.

"If you're having a problem with them, you'll have to talk to the Humane Society. It has nothing to do with me."

"No," Jack assured him. "They're fine, actually. The tomcat does a lot to keep the kittens in line, and they're old enough that they don't require much from me. I'm happy to have them."

"Oh. Well, good." Davis looked slightly more at ease, though only momentarily. "If that's not the problem, what do you want? Like I said, anything having to do with the animals goes to the Humane Society to resolve. If you need the number, I'm sure you can find it online."

"That's all right," Jack assured him. The sun was low in the sky now, but it was still warm outside. Jack had worn jeans and a sports jacket, but wished he had gone for a T-shirt instead. Not only would it have been more comfortable, it would have helped him blend more here.

"I work with Jamie Flint, one of the K-9 search and rescue handlers." Technically, it was the truth. "I just wanted to get a little more information about your brother."

"Of course," Davis said quickly. "Why didn't you say so before?" Why indeed, Jack wondered. "What can I tell you?"

"You know the dog was found in the equipment shed by the Thomaston high school, I assume."

"Sure," Davis said. "I think Jamie was the one who took the dog until Albie gets back, wasn't she?"

"That's right," Jack said. "I wondered if you can think of any other places he might have gone? He was obviously pretty bonded to this coach in high school. Are there any other memories involving that man—Coach Pendleton—that you think might have stuck in Albie's mind?"

"No more than the ones I already told the police about," Davis said. His forehead furrowed, lips pinched with suspicion. "Didn't they talk to you guys about that?"

"They did," Jack assured him. "Just thought I would double check, to see if you had remembered anything more." He paused a moment, letting Davis relax.

"I was also wondering about what happened to your mother," he said. "And the remains found in the basement. Do you have any idea who might have been down there? Who the remains belong to?"

"None," Davis said immediately. His eyes slid from Jack's, and he swallowed convulsively. Jack watched as the man ran a hand through his thinning hair, clearly rattled. "The coroner's supposed to have information tomorrow, and I guess they're looking at digging up more of the place." He paused, wetting his lips. "It's a waste of time, if you ask me. Who knows where those bodies came from. Maybe they were already there when we moved in."

Jack thought of Sophie's conclusions at the lab earlier that afternoon. Male, thirty to forty years old. Dead at least ten to twenty years.

"How long had your mother lived here?"

"My father bought the house when we were kids. Summer of 1976."

"So the idea that these bodies were in the basement, unburied, all that time and no one noticed doesn't seem that likely, does it?" Jack said. He tried to keep his voice neutral. The last thing he wanted was for Fred to feel as though he were being backed into a corner.

"I don't know," Fred said wearily. He shrugged. "I don't know what's likely anymore. I sure as hell never thought I'd find something like this when I finally got my mother out of the picture and could start dealing with this hell hole."

Jack raised his eyebrows at the man, but made no comment. Fred grimaced.

"I meant, after my mother moved out—not after I killed her. God." He took a breath, then released it on a sigh. "I'm sorry. I'm not… I'm still not really clear how I should be acting here. What I should be saying."

"Don't worry about 'should' right now," Jack said, his tone gentler now. "Everyone handles grief in their own way. With everything else on your plate, it's no wonder you're feeling a little confused."

Fred nodded. "Thank you. I appreciate that. I'm not sure what this has to do with the search for Albie, though. Shouldn't you be out in the field actually looking for him?"

Jack hesitated, but only for a moment. It was a risky move, but this area was small enough that word was bound to get back to Fred eventually about his true role in all this.

"I'm not actually working with this search—I do work with Flint K-9 sometimes," he added hastily. "Just, not right now. I was hired by someone who's concerned that your brother might be blamed for your mother's death. My name is Jack Juarez. I'm a private investigator."

Instead of the reaction Jack expected—overt distrust

or abject anger—Fred actually softened marginally. "Who hired you?"

"I'm sorry, I'm not at liberty to say."

"But they want to help Albie," Fred clarified.

"That's right," Jack confirmed. "We just want to make sure Albie is treated fairly once he's found. Do you have any idea who might have wanted your mother dead?"

"I told you," a woman's voice said, from just behind them. Jack groaned inwardly. "There was no shortage of people who wanted Nancy gone."

Jack turned to find Barbara Monroe approaching, looking considerably more put together than she had that morning.

"Not me, of course," she assured them, then added gently, "Hello again, Fred. How are you holding up?"

"I'm all right, Barb," Fred said. The protective mask fell from his face for an instant. Jack saw a flicker of vulnerability when he looked at the woman. Interesting.

"She's not wrong," he said to Jack. "My mother hardly would have won a popularity contest around here. She had more enemies than I can count. That's what I was trying to explain to the police: it could have been just about anyone who killed her. Mom had a way of making you want to wring her neck about five minutes into any conversation."

"Fred," Barbara admonished. "Maybe she wasn't to everyone's taste, but she had her good points. She loved you boys, at least."

Fred nodded. His eyes welled, and he looked away from them both. "Yeah," he said, his voice hoarse. "I know she did, Barb."

"What about recent incidents?" Jack pressed, once Fred

got himself back in hand. "Were there any other interactions that might have something to do with her death?"

"Of course," Barbara said promptly, before Fred could answer. "I told you earlier, exactly who my money's on."

"Who?" Fred asked. "Did you see something?"

Jack frowned, but could think of no way to convince Barbara to keep the information she'd shared with him that morning to herself. Sure enough, the woman continued without pause.

"Bear Flint. He was here the other night, after everyone else had gone. He'd been worked up all day over the animals, and then that night he came out and had a screaming match with Nancy. I guess she changed her mind about letting the police take the animals or something. I don't know, I couldn't hear everything they were saying. But Bear said he would take the animals himself, and there was no way she could stop him. I'll be honest, I was a little afraid of him."

Jack grimaced. This was definitely a change in tone from the story Barbara had given him that morning, when she'd said she was more afraid for Bear.

"Did you tell the police this?" Fred demanded.

Barbara nodded. "Of course. They said they would follow up. There's been so much going on, I'm sure it's taking a little longer than it might otherwise to get their ducks in a row."

"You know this boy?" Fred asked Jack. "Jamie's son?"

"I do," Jack confirmed. "And I'm sure we're not getting the whole story here. I know Bear well—the police are more than welcome to question him, but I know they'll rule him out quickly after that." He was pleased at the confidence he managed to infuse into the words, particularly since he wasn't sure even he believed them.

Barbara started to say something but froze suddenly, a flicker of emotion crossing her face. Fear, Jack realized after a moment. Jack turned just as Bear stepped out of his truck and slammed the door behind him. Julie slid from her seat on the other side, and Jack noted Casper's crestfallen expression at being abandoned in the cab.

"What is it?" Fred pressed, eying the boy himself.

"That's him," Barbara said. The expression on her face left no doubt as to her feelings on seeing her daughter with the hoodlum in question.

Bear hesitated at sight of the trio in the shadows, catching Julie's arm before she could join them. He said something low to her, his head bent to hers.

"Why don't you two excuse me," Jack said smoothly to Fred and Barbara. "I'd like to ask Bear a few questions."

"I'd like to ask a few questions myself," Barbara said grimly. "Julie!" she shouted.

The teenager looked up sharply at her mother's tone, and scowled in their direction. "What?"

"I'll see you later," Bear said quickly. He was headed for his truck when Jack went after him.

Behind him, Jack could hear the raised voices of mother and daughter. He didn't bother listening in, however, sure he already knew the gist of the fight. Right now, he had his own teenager to worry about.

●

"Hey!" Jack said, jogging after Bear when the boy didn't slow his pace. "Will you wait a minute, please?" He grabbed hold of Bear's arm, and Bear jerked it away as he whirled to face the older man.

"What do you want?"

"I want to talk to you," he said, lowering his voice. He looked back over his shoulder, to find that Julie and Barbara were headed for their house. Fred had vanished in the meantime, though Jack wasn't sure whether he'd gone back to his mother's house or was leaving for the night.

"So, talk," Bear said impatiently. "What are you even doing here? Are you just slinking around hoping my mom will show up again, or do you actually have a lead?"

"You mean besides the suspicious-looking kid here the other night fighting with Nancy, not long before the animals were set loose and Nancy was killed?"

A touch of panic flickered in Bear's eyes before he tamped it down. "I already told you: I don't know what you're talking about. I wasn't here. I didn't have anything to do with Nancy getting killed. You know I didn't."

"I don't know that, as a matter of fact," Jack said. He looked at Bear seriously, though he found it hard to summon any genuine anger. The kid was terrified—that much was obvious. "I only know what you've told me, and it turns out you left out a pretty significant part of the story. Why did you really hire me?"

Bear bristled. "I told you: I hired you to find out what happened, so Albie doesn't get in trouble."

"Not so *you* don't get in trouble?"

Bear faltered, but only for a moment before he recovered. Anger flashed in his eyes. "Are you saying I don't really care what happened to Albie? You really think I could have set this up so he took the fall? Why would I have hired you if I did that?"

"I don't think that's what happened at all," Jack said, his own tone measured. "But I need you to be straight with me about what's going on. Why were you there the other night? What possible reason could you have had to go back to the Davis house the night Nancy was killed?"

Bear hesitated. Jack could see him weighing the wisdom of lying versus simply telling the truth. He waited patiently, letting the boy come to the decision on his own. Unfortunately, Bear came to the wrong decision.

"You know what? Just forget it, all right?" the boy said, his jaw tight. "This was a stupid idea, me hiring you. I'll figure it out on my own. I'll pay you what I owe you. Just drop the case—I'll do it myself."

"You'll do what yourself?" Jack asked, his own tone still measured despite his growing frustration. "What does that even mean? I'm not dropping this now—"

"Just forget it," Bear repeated, his voice rising. "Forget the whole thing. I was wrong, okay? Maybe Albie actually did it. Then what am I going to do, pay you to prove it and he gets sent to jail? Just drop it. Let the police figure it out."

"And what if the police end up at your front door?" Jack asked. "Because it sounds to me like that's a real possibility. What do you plan on doing then?"

"Let them come," Bear said, feigning indifference. "I can handle it. I've got nothing to hide. I didn't do anything wrong."

"If you've done nothing wrong, why not just talk to me?" Jack persisted. "We'll walk through the night together. Explain to me what you saw when you were here—"

"I wasn't here," Bear said, reverting to his original party line. "I already told you that. Whoever told you I was was lying. I don't know what they were talking about, but they got the wrong guy."

He tipped his chin up, daring Jack to push further. Jack knew beyond a shadow of a doubt who the liar in this particular situation was, though. And it wasn't Barbara.

"Fine," Jack said. The word came out clipped, angrier than he had intended. "If you want to play it that way, go ahead. But if that's the case, I think you're right: it's probably smarter if I don't work for you. I need to believe my clients are telling me everything when we work together."

He looked at Bear pointedly. The kid didn't give an inch, shrugging. "Fine. Doesn't matter to me. Let me know how much I owe you, and I'll get the money to you."

"I'm not worried about that."

Bear frowned, clearly at war with himself over... something. God knew what, but definitely something. Finally, he shrugged. "Whatever." He looked around, then took his phone from his back pocket and checked the time. "I should get going." Instead of leaving, however, he hung back uncertainly. "Listen," he said, looking more vulnerable, suddenly younger than he had. "Could you still keep my mom out of this, please? She doesn't need to know what happened, right?"

Since in all honesty Jack still didn't have a clue *what* had happened, he nodded without a second thought. "Of course. I gave you my word before. I won't go back on that."

"Thanks," Bear said awkwardly. He nodded toward Jack's car, parked beside his own truck. "So...aren't you leaving?"

"I'll be along soon," Jack said. "I just want to take a look around."

More awkwardness ensued before Bear nodded. He looked miserable. "Oh. Okay, then. I guess I'll see you around."

"I'm sure you will," Jack agreed. Bear turned to go. As he was leaving, Jack called after him impulsively. "If you change your mind about anything, you know where to find me."

Bear nodded, but said nothing as he returned to his truck.

Jack waited until he was sure Bear had gone, but just as he started toward the Davis house Fred appeared on the horizon, watching him curiously. It was barely dusk—he felt far too exposed to continue with the plan he'd initially set for himself. Resigned, Jack waved half-heartedly to the elder Davis brother. Breaking and entering would definitely be simpler under the cover of full darkness.

16

AS THE EVENING TURNED TO NIGHT, despite circumstances I found myself increasingly grateful to be outside. A cooling breeze kept the bugs at bay, and I savored the stretch of my legs with each stride, the feel of my muscles working in concert. Phantom felt like an extension of me, or maybe I was an extension of her... Whatever it was, it was nice to have her beside me.

"Did you have a good day, Phan?" I asked.

I've heard dog owners who'll ask a dog a question, then answer in some silly voice that's supposed to belong to the dog. I understand the charm of that, truly—Bear used to make me 'talk the animals' all the time when he was little. It's always struck me as a little presumptuous, though. I ask the questions, because I'm human and we humans love to hear ourselves talk. But Phantom doesn't answer, because she's a dog—they don't do language as we understand it. I love reading her nuanced body language, though. The tilt of her head, the panting canine grin, the dozen different positions of her ears and tail—every one of which conveys a different meaning.

Now, for example, she looked back at me with ears

forward, tail wagging. She heard me, and she knew I was talking to her about something not terribly important. She seemed happy to simply hear my voice; to share this moment with me. We walked on, quieter, and I felt genuine peace settle over me.

After the sun went down that evening, Phantom and I followed a trail from Maiden's Cliff southeast up to the top of Mt. Megunticook, the highest peak in the range. With darkness upon us, the sound of searchers calling Albie's name took on an eeriness that had been lacking in daylight.

I was relieved when Bear returned to the search shortly after nine o'clock that evening, reporting no trace of scent at any of the places Julie Monroe had said Albie might have gone. Fred Davis had long since gone home, as well. Under cover of darkness, most of the searchers out were professionals either with the state warden service, Flint K-9, or Maine Search and Rescue Dogs, a local organization that had participated in some of the toughest searches throughout the U.S. and Canada.

My headache had dissipated, and there was no trace of Brock's voice in my head. I moved with ease, grateful for the fresh air and the time apart with my dog. The call of searchers and the distant bay of hounds has always been the most beautiful song to me, a lullaby that eases me like nothing else. Phantom continued on with me close behind, the night clear and the ground well illuminated by my headlamp and the stars above.

My enthusiasm had begun to flag as we headed back down the other side of the mountain at around ten-thirty, with the tower at Mt Battie the ultimate destination. Just beyond Adam's Lookout, I saw Phantom pause on the trail ahead of me. Her head came up, tail going stiff.

She glanced back at me once, and then was off. The trail up Megunticook and along the stretch we were on is the hardest in the range, so I was surprised to see Phantom on scent up here. Knowing how out of shape Albie was, I had assumed that he would stick to lower altitudes.

He must have heard people calling for him by now, hadn't he? Must have heard the dogs barking, at the very least. Why would he still be running if he truly had no reason to hide?

I considered the question while I followed Phantom, stopping just shy of a run when she picked up her own pace. With some effort, I put myself in Albie's shoes. A man with cognitive challenges, who clearly had some sensory issues. He would be sensitive to noise, wouldn't he? And he would be terrified out here, regardless of what he had or hadn't seen on the night Nancy died.

Would he come out when people called his name? When he heard hounds baying in the darkness for him? Or would he more likely just curl up and hide, praying it would all just go away?

I pulled out my phone, still on the move, and directed the magic cell god inside it to do my bidding. "Call Bear."

The magic cell god did. Bear answered on the second ring. "Yeah?"

"I'm up on the trail from Megunticook to Mount Lookout. Phantom's got a scent. Call the IC and tell him to shut everybody up, okay? And give the message to our handlers, too. Keep the dogs quiet."

"You think you've got him?" Bear asked.

"Phantom sure does."

"I'll be right there," he said, and hung up. Hopefully, his

first move would be to convey my message before he raced up the mountainside to us.

Up ahead, Phantom was moving even faster. She was definitely on scent now, her focus absolute. I watched as she navigated the trail with ease, keeping her within the beam of my flashlight as much as possible.

I lost her about a hundred yards into her run, and had to content myself with the flashing light on my GPS to guide me to her. The night had cooled, the air almost chilly this high up. I focused on Phantom, and let everything else fall away. I could hear her moving up ahead, though she made barely a sound as she ran. I wanted to warn her to go easy—we didn't know what to expect from Albie, after all. Whatever else had happened, he had been through hell the past seventy-two hours.

The thing that made Phantom such an incredible search dog was that I didn't actually have to tell her anything. She knew. She figured it out on her own every time, with a degree of empathy I had yet to see a human possess.

I looked at the GPS, my own heart hammering, and slowed when I realized that Phantom had done the same. Before long, she was in my sights once more. The mountainside had gone still, apart from a few lonely, isolated howls. I waited for Phantom to sound her alert—two sharp barks, and then she would lie down close to the subject of her search.

She just stood there, though.

I hesitated.

Something was wrong.

Phantom stopped, looked back at me, and whined anxiously.

"Easy, girl," I said quietly. "What have you got?"

I took another couple of steps. Phantom returned to my side, still whining. My body was rigid with tension. I felt another headache coming on, another psychic intervention from Brock, but this time I fought it. There was no time right now.

I focused on breathing, and took another couple of steps.

This time, Phantom got in front of me. She physically blocked the trail, and looked up at me with those soft, intelligent eyes.

No closer, she seemed to say.

"Okay, girl," I said. "I'm listening."

I cleared my throat, and called in as gentle a voice as I could manage. "Albie?"

There was no response.

I shone my flashlight around the area where Phantom had stopped. It was dense forest up this high, just off the trail but definitely not a place anyone frequented. I paused, swallowing hard. Someone was here. I could feel them.

"You're not in trouble, Albie," I said. "We just want you to be safe. Your brother's been out here looking, too. Everyone is just worried."

There was a rustling in the underbrush straight ahead, and I froze. Phantom returned to block my way again. I stayed rooted to the spot, her body warm against my legs. I pointed my flashlight beam again, just once more, and stopped when it was in mid-arc.

Something glinted off the light.

Everything inside my body went cold. I knew that glint—knew the shape, even in the darkness.

Light, bouncing off the barrel of a gun.

It was nested in the underbrush. When I looked closer, I saw the gleam of two eyes in the darkness.

"Hey, Phan," I said. My voice shook; I had to work to steady it. "Come on over here with me, girl."

I moved back, well away from the barrel of that gun; those two gleaming eyes. Phantom glanced back toward it, then trotted willingly to me.

"Sit," I said.

She sat. I took a moment and texted the IC my status and coordinates, but got no response. Then, I looked at Phantom steadily. "Now, stay."

She whined, but she remained where she was—safe, I hoped, from the range of gunfire should any break out. I walked back along the trail, talking all the while. I kept my voice light, friendly, and—ideally—reassuring. I didn't want to risk startling Albie, now that I knew he was armed. With everyone out searching for him in force for the past three days, it was a wonder nobody had gotten hurt.

I still hadn't gotten a reply from the incident commander. What if they came in with guns blazing, and startled Albie enough that he drew his weapon?

I closed my eyes, murmured a quick prayer, and kept on.

"I've never been up here before," I mused. "It's a good climb—the highest point on the whole mountain range. You have to be in pretty good shape to make it up this high. Strong."

I was babbling, I knew. I just hoped something I said got through to him. Or, at the very least, didn't set him off.

Back where she was seated, Phantom's whine got louder.

"I'm right here, girl. Just relax." Using the same tone, I

added, "Albie, I'm coming closer. Just so I know you're safe, I'd love it if you could say, 'I'm okay.' That's all I need from you."

I took another few steps. The bush with the gun was back in sight. I wet my lips, my mouth gone dry. "Albie?" I said. "Can you hear me? All you have to say is, 'I'm okay.'" I paused. "If you're not okay but you can talk, would you say 'I'm hurt'? That's all. I won't make you come out if you don't want to."

I risked another two steps. Ahead of me, the gun shifted. I heard Phantom get up, but I didn't dare to call her off, too afraid of spooking Albie.

"Albie, I'm just going to stop here, okay? I'm going to sit down and rest. It's hard work getting up this high. You must be tired by now."

I sat on the cold ground, paying no attention to whatever crawling things I might be parked on. I could hear Phantom creeping closer, the little rat. In ordinary circumstances, I would be one unhappy dog mama at her disobedience—and she would get the message, loud and clear. I didn't want to risk even the perception that I wasn't in control right now, though.

I looked back over my shoulder. Phantom slunk closer, her head and tail down. What was I supposed to do now? There still had been no response from command central. The protocol if you found a subject who was armed was clear: do not engage. Leave that to the police, and get out of there.

But Albie wasn't just a guy with a gun. He was a guy with the emotional maturity of a thirteen-year-old boy. He was terrified, he was armed, and he had either seen his mother murdered or he had done it himself.

"Come here, Phantom," I said to the dog. "How about if we just settle in, huh?"

She came over and lay down beside me without being prompted, though her attention was still on the gun pointed at us. I felt immediate peace when her body rested against me. I stroked her fur and looked at the stars above, and savored the quiet for a moment.

"We found Oswald in the equipment shed where you left him," I said conversationally, directing my words toward the bushes. "That was good thinking. Kind, too, you putting Oswald's safety above your own. He's okay. He's staying out on the island with us right now, but I bet he would like to see you. We gave him a bath yesterday."

I chuckled at the memory, honestly amused. "I'll tell you, he does not like baths. But you should have seen him, with all those bubbles. Afterward, he ran around like a crazy thing." I paused. "Actually, Sarah took some video of him after the bath and sent it to me. It's on my phone, if you want to see."

I glanced back toward the bushes when I heard a rustling again. The gun wavered—I saw the barrel move, and it nearly stopped my heart. A few endless seconds of silence followed. And then,

"I'm okay." The words came in a low, weary voice. My eyes welled. I smiled.

"I'm glad, Albie. Do you want to come out and see the video?"

There was a long pause. "Oswald is okay?"

"He is. I can show you."

"I didn't want to lock him in the shed. But he kept barking, and I didn't know if he'd be safe with me. I didn't want anything to happen to him."

"You did the right thing," I assured him. "I'm really proud of the kindness you showed him."

There was movement in the bushes, more pronounced this time.

"If you're coming out here, Albie, would you do me a big favor?"

There was no response for what seemed like hours.

"What?" he finally asked.

"Could you leave the gun there? I'm afraid of guns myself, and so is my dog. They make us really nervous."

"Guns keep you safe."

"They do sometimes," I conceded. "But they can also hurt someone very badly. I don't want anyone to get hurt tonight."

"You just want me to leave it here? That's not safe."

"No," I agreed. "But we'll have someone get it later. Just for now."

"I just put it on the ground?"

"Yes, Albie," I said quietly. "Just put it on the ground, and come out. I'll show you that video."

A full minute passed before I heard any movement. When it came, Phantom looked up anxiously. She whined in Albie's direction, then shifted focus back to me. I couldn't breathe let alone think a cogent thought, half convinced we were about to get our heads blown off.

"Easy, girl," I said again.

More rustling followed.

Finally, Albie appeared. He had his hands in his pockets, his body hunched.

"Thanks for coming out," I said.

He looked at me. In the moonlight, all I got were the

impressions: a pale, weary face; a man who could barely stand. No gun—or at least none that I could see.

"I left my rifle in there," he said. He indicated the underbrush.

"Thank you. I really appreciate that."

He looked warily at Phantom, who was still lying down beside me.

"I don't like German shepherds," he said. "They can be mean. One bit me, one time."

"Phantom doesn't bite," I assured him.

He nodded, then looked at me expectantly. "You said I could watch that video?"

"Yeah," I agreed. I pulled out my phone. "Come on over, Albie. Sit with me a while."

•

Twenty minutes later, Albie and I were bonding over post-dog-bath YouTube videos on my phone when Sheriff Finnegan arrived on the scene. I saw him pause at the head of the trail before he came to us, alerted when Phantom raised her head, her ears pricked forward.

"Someone's here to see us," I said to Albie, as quietly as I could.

He was on the verge of panicking again, until he spotted Finnegan.

"Hey, buddy," Finnegan said to him, in as gentle a voice as I'd ever heard from the man.

"Hey, Chris," Albie said. Any trace of the lightness we had just achieved was gone in an instant.

"I'm glad to see you," Finnegan continued. "We were really worried."

Albie nodded. He had his hands on Phantom, compulsively kneading the fur the more anxious he got. Phantom looked at him, and leaned up to lick his face. The man smiled, wiping the dog slobber away with the back of his hand.

And then, he began to weep.

17

ONCE ALBIE'S TEARS STARTED, there seemed to be no end to them. If anything, he got progressively more worked up as time went on. Phantom watched him worriedly as Sheriff Finnegan spoke to the man gently, reminding him of happier times—and assuring him with increasing desperation, that times would be happy again.

Finnegan didn't bother trying to question Albie at the time, and the bits Albie did reveal about the night were virtually incoherent. By the time a medic reached us, despite Finnegan and my best efforts, the poor man was on the verge of hyperventilating.

"I want you to take a breath for me, okay, Albie?" the paramedic asked, once she was on scene. She was in her early twenties, pretty and dark-haired and competent. It took a second or two for her to get through to him, but something about this woman seemed to reassure him in a way we had been unable.

"Now, I'm going to put this mask over your face," she continued. "Just like we usually do, right?"

"Like you're Nurse Hathaway," he said between gasps.

He took the mask from her willingly and placed it over his nose and mouth.

The paramedic smiled at my unspoken question, speaking to me in a soothing, conversational tone. "I've been over to Albie's house a few times over the past couple of years. Sometimes he has a hard time breathing, and I get a call. And what do we do then?" she asked him.

He removed the mask. "Just breathe," he said. "Like on ER. You give me the mask, and I know to breathe."

"That's right," she said. She helped him put the mask back on, and smoothed the hair back from his forehead. His eyes sank shut, utterly at peace.

It was eleven o'clock by this time. I could hear a few barks and the occasional residual shout from the search, but overall it seemed very still. Word must have spread that Albie had been found.

"Thanks, Keats," Finnegan said to the paramedic, as Albie continued to breathe. He was seated on a fallen tree, his face peaceful now. "I knew it was the right call bringing you in. Stacy Keats, Jamie Flint."

I nodded a greeting, my own focus still on Albie. I was happy that he was settling down, but one question continued to bother me:

How were we supposed to get him back down the mountain? He could barely stand, and while it was technically possible to carry him down, I wasn't in love with that idea.

Finnegan apparently had the same concerns. He got Keats' attention with a jerk of his head, indicating a spot just off to the side of our little clearing.

"Can I have a word with you two?" he said quietly.

Keats looked at Albie, who was still breathing into the

mask. She squeezed his shoulder. "Is it okay if I just go over there for a minute to talk to these guys?" He started to shake his head, but she smiled reassuringly. "Listen to me, okay? I'm going to be right there. I'm not leaving—I'm right here. Just give me two minutes."

She slipped a watch off her wrist, fiddled with a couple of buttons, and handed it to him. "Here—you can time me. Just raise your hand when there are only ten seconds left, and we'll wrap it up, okay?"

His focus shifted to the watch. He nodded, riveted to the numbers. Keats grabbed Finnegan and me, and we stepped just a few feet away and lowered our voices.

"How do you want to do this?" Keats asked. "He doesn't qualify for MedEvac—vitals are stable, and there's no immediate threat to his life. We can carry him down, but we'll need to put him out for that. Or at least heavily sedate him."

"I don't think sedation's such a bad idea, whatever we choose," Finnegan said. "He's a wreck."

"How would we do it if we just walked back down?" I asked. "We're not that far from the tower on Mt Battie, are we? From there, we can just get on the road and have the ambulance pick us up."

Keats frowned. "That's probably the least traumatic way to go. He stays upright... I can walk with him, keep him calm."

Albie's hand went up, a muffled sound coming from behind his oxygen mask. The three of us looked at one another, double checking.

"So, we walk out," Finnegan confirmed. We nodded in unison.

As soon as we set out, Phantom took a spot at Albie's left side, his arm hanging down with his hand on her sleek head. Keats walked at his right, Finnegan and I bringing up the rear. It was slow going, but eventually things opened up and I could see the old stone tower just up ahead. I smiled at the sight, erected in 1921 as a memorial to the soldiers from Camden and surrounding towns who served in World War I. This was one of the first places I took Bear, after Brock was dead and we were on our own. He had been broken then; this place had started the healing for him.

I hoped it might do the same for Albie.

An ambulance was already waiting for us—I could see the flashing lights through the trees. Albie caught sight as well, and stopped on the path as soon as they registered.

"What are they doing here?" he asked, voice tinged with panic once again.

"It's all right," Keats said. "They're here to help you."

"I'm not sick. I don't need that. I don't need them. They'll take me away—" His volume increased with his terror, and Phantom edged even closer to him. She whined softly, and the sound seemed to pull him back from the edge.

"Why's she crying?" he asked, turning to address the question to me.

"I think she's worried about you."

As if by magic, his fear was cast aside. He knelt beside the dog, brow furrowed. "You don't need to cry. I'm okay. Mom says, 'you be upset but do it quiet—don't upset all the other creatures who need you. You keep it together, for them.'"

He murmured this last as though talking himself down.

Phantom leaned the top of her head against his chest, and he sagged against her.

"You can be upset sometimes," I told Albie gently. "You can be afraid. Phantom can take it."

He pet her head, still kneeling on the path. Finnegan and I stood by, waiting, until he told us he was ready to go. Keats helped him up, and eventually we emerged from the trees to meet the emergency crew standing by.

As soon as we were visible, an ecstatic, high-pitched yapping cut through the tumult all around us. An instant later, I saw a bundle of fur dart toward us. Oswald leapt into Albie's arms, nearly knocking the man over.

Albie hugged the little dog tightly, sobs beginning anew. Bear stepped forward among the tide of paramedics, and nodded self-consciously when I smiled at him.

"Thank you," I said quietly.

He shrugged. "If it were me, I'd want Casper. More than just about anything." Casper's lean white body wriggled with his tail, and he grinned up at Bear upon hearing his name. Bear dropped his hand to Casper's head, and he smiled. I felt a weight lift from my shoulders at the sight.

Unfortunately, that weight wasn't gone for long.

Gradually, Albie came to himself once more, taking in his surroundings. He held Oswald tightly, and looked around. I saw his eyes when he registered Bear's presence. Watched the widening; saw him take a step back, nearly falling over in his desperation to get away.

"Albie?" Finnegan said, noting the reaction himself.

"Get him away," he demanded. "Take him away from me. I don't ever want to see him again. Never. Get him out." The words rose, ending on a scream. There were no tears now—only rage, and overt terror.

I looked at Bear, expecting confusion at Albie's reaction. Instead, what I saw stole something from me.

Understanding.

Resignation.

Guilt.

He stepped away, while Finnegan and the paramedic tried to calm Albie down. I followed Bear, but froze for an instant when Albie's words found me. They came with a howl of pain, the words more anguished than I had ever heard before.

"Take him away. I saw him. I saw him kill my mother."

18

IT WAS ELEVEN O'CLOCK when Jack returned to the Davis home that night. Though it was a Friday, he was surprised to see Barbara Monroe's silver Prius in her driveway, and all the lights in the house out. He wondered if Julie was home, or if she was out with friends—or possibly still helping with the search for Albie. He hadn't missed the way the girl looked at Bear, or Bear's own clear interest. Personally, Jack couldn't blame him. Regardless of how conflicted he might be, Julie was an attractive girl, and Bear was, after all, still eighteen.

On the other side of the Davis property, Nancy's neighbor Hank did not seem to be at home. Jack recalled hearing that the man was helping with the search. Hopefully, he would stay away long enough for Jack to finish what he was doing without being seen.

As he approached the house, he took a deep breath and instantly regretted it at the still-overpowering odor. He squared his shoulders, looked around surreptitiously one last time, and went to the front door. It was unlocked.

Jack could understand why—no one in their right mind would come in this place voluntarily. And yet, here he was.

He wasn't sure what that said about him.

It felt strange, surreal, to be inside under the cover of darkness. For one thing, the stench was no better now that the animals were gone. If anything, it seemed worse—stale, cloying. He should have a Hazmat suit, he realized, and could imagine what Sophie would say.

Have you developed a death wish, Agent Juarez?

He hadn't. Or he didn't think he had, anyway. He pulled on gloves and took a face mask from his pocket, placing it carefully over his nose and mouth and adjusting the elastic. Would a man with a death wish remember gloves and a face mask? Clearly not.

Once past the threshold, Jack moved forward carefully, his flashlight beam playing over ruined furniture and peeling wallpaper, chewed doorsills and windows patched with cardboard and plastic.

Nancy had died of blunt force trauma, or so it looked so far. Jack knew enough not to assume anything before the tox screen came back, but Dr. Fuller had seemed pretty sure of herself. And Nancy's skull didn't leave much doubt.

She had plenty of enemies. Albie could have done it. Talking to Mike and Mel over at the Loyal Biscuit, they'd come up with a list of names a page long without breaking a sweat. It was the other bodies in the house that were throwing him.

One female, two males. One identified as Fred's fiancé, the other an ex-con from Mississippi. The third still a mystery, but it wasn't Barbara Monroe's husband—whoever it was, he had been dead too long to be Tim Monroe. Were there other bodies buried in the basement? Or out in the field somewhere? Jack had an unpleasant thought about

Nancy feeding random passersby to the dogs, but dismissed it. The bodies in the basement had been relatively intact. Why leave them alone, and dispose of others some other way?

He was letting Barbara Monroe's imagination run away with him. There were no other bodies.

Probably.

He crept forward, tension climbing his spine.

The floorboards beneath his feet creaked as he moved deeper into the house. It had been beautiful once, no question. He doubted Fred wanted it now, though. He wasn't sure anyone would. Beyond the stench and the filth, there was something dark about the place. As though unspeakable things had happened here, over a long period of time. To his right was a staircase, the banister chewed through in places and two steps cracked through. He'd already seen the first floor when he came through with Sophie, but it had been a brief glimpse while he tried to keep pace with the woman.

Now, he took a moment to walk down the long entryway, through what must have once been a formal dining room and into the kitchen. Yellow police tape barred the entrance. Jack carefully untaped it and set it aside with a lack of guilt that surprised him.

A Formica-topped table laden with newspapers, dirty dishes, and a dog collar. A box of cereal—Froot Loops according to the box—had been ransacked by the animals, and now a few scant remnants were scattered across a grimy, curling linoleum floor.

His eyes were drawn to the stove. A small, cheap unit that fit about as well as anything else in this place. White tape had been used in place of chalk to show where Nancy's body had fallen.

Jack closed his eyes, trying to picture it. The woman he had seen on the exam table today, collapsed on the floor alongside twenty dogs.

Except the dogs weren't there—they had gotten out. Even Reaver, chained in the yard and unapproachable as far as Jack could see. Even he was gone.

Had Nancy done that?

Or Albie, maybe? Had he done something with the animals before he ran away? Had he found his mother on the floor—maybe even watched her die—and then, in a moment of panic, run out but forgotten to close the door or the front gate on his way out.

But that still didn't explain Reaver—a dog Albie was terrified of.

They were fighting at midnight, you could hear them all the way to my place, Barbara had said. *I saw Bear there. I wouldn't have wanted to get in his way, that's for sure.*

Bear could get close to Reaver.

Jack frowned. This wasn't good.

Before he could think any further on that, he heard something—a clatter and crash that sounded like it came from the basement. Where all the bodies were buried. Probably rats, he assumed. If possible, the idea made him even more uneasy than he'd been before.

He resumed his task, determined to find something that might prove helpful. His focus returned to the table. The newspapers were all *Courier Gazette* and *Downeast Daily Tribune*—the two local papers. Apart from what looked like rat droppings, they didn't appear to have been read. They were all recent.

The dog collar was the anomaly, he realized after a

minute. It looked brand new for one thing, and he recognized the red, white, and blue lobster pattern as belonging to a line of collars and leashes he'd seen at the Loyal Biscuit. Sure enough, a closer look showed a tag from the Rockland store. They weren't cheap, either. $14.99, according to the tag.

Nancy couldn't have spent that kind of money on a single dog, could she?

It was a large collar, too big to fit Oswald or any of the other ratty-looking dogs Jack had seen on that first day here. There weren't that many big dogs here, though. He recalled a giant drooling black thing; another dog he thought might have been a Doberman Pinscher. And Reaver.

Why did he keep coming back to that dog?

Another crash came from the basement, this one louder. Jack jumped at the racket, then tried to still his racing heart. Just rats. He went to the basement door and opened it despite the sound of his own heartbeat pounding in his ears.

"Hello?" he called down the stairs quietly.

There was no response, but he heard the scrambling of rodent feet when he shone his flashlight beam below.

He closed the door again, then shone his flashlight through the kitchen one more time but came up empty. No flashing red arrows pointed to clues he had missed, at least not here.

It would be too easy to leave now. Jack ignored his churning stomach and the knowledge that he could be in serious trouble for this if he was found out, and headed for the stairs.

It was more of the same, just multiplied by ten. Dog crap six inches deep, maggots crawling through. Jack kept his hands to himself despite his gloves, not for fear of leaving fingerprints but because he didn't want to risk catching God knew what if he touched anything here.

There were four bedrooms upstairs, three of them in total chaos. Albie's was the exception. Jack crossed the threshold, noting the splintered doorjamb and the door hanging off its hinges—it must have been locked, and the police apparently didn't have a lot of patience when it came to accessing the space. The room was easily identifiable as Albie's by the Georges Valley pennant flying on the wall, and the collage of photos that also appeared to be from high school. This was by far the cleanest room in the house, though it wouldn't win any prizes. A smell of human sweat and wet dog fur hung in the air, the bed clothes rumpled on an antique four-poster bed, all four posts chewed almost to the point of ruin. The only memento that was animal related was a photo of a scowling Albie—younger, but not by much, with a ratty little dog that Jack suspected must be Oswald.

Otherwise, it was painfully clear: for all intents and purposes, Albie's life stopped after high school. Yellowed articles about Buccaneer basketball, soccer, and baseball games covered the peeling wallpaper, all games dated 1987 – '90. The years Albie played. He'd apparently lost interest once his own career was over.

He left Albie's room and continued farther down the hall. The next door had been broken open in the same way that Albie's had, but that was where the similarities between the two rooms ended. The floor was caked in feces and what looked at first glance to be blood. Jack flinched, but kept going. A path had been cleared to a double bed with gnawed wooden posts and a filthy flowered bedspread. A lamp, a

Kindle, and several bottles of pills were on the bedside table.

Jack readjusted his face mask, grateful he'd had the foresight to bring it along this time. There wasn't much to see at first glance, or if there was he wasn't sure he had the heart to delve any deeper. Any investigators who had been here very likely felt the same. Regardless, he took another step into the room. Something squelched beneath his shoe. He winced. More animal feces he assumed, though he didn't have the stomach to check.

A large painting on the wall behind the bed held his attention. It made no sense in the room—in the house, for that matter. Any trace of interior decoration had long since been soiled or eaten or both, but somehow this had been spared.

Jack studied it from a distance. It showed someone he assumed was Nancy, as a much younger woman. Her hair was long, her build slender. She sat astride a roan-colored horse, her body draped over the neck and her head pressed to the horse's. It was an oil painting, and it had been well done. Someone must have paid good money for this. He tried to recall Nancy's background, but realized he hadn't even thought to ask. Had she come from a wealthy home?

Even in the portrait, something about Nancy's bearing chilled him. Her eyes were a little bit mad, her smile almost feral. The hold she had around the horse's neck didn't look gentle, either.

The only picture in the place, and it wasn't of Albie or Fred or their father—it was of Nancy and a horse. It wasn't surprising, but it did strike him as telling. She had clearly loved Albie, but it had been a selfish, debilitating love that may well have destroyed the man. Albie would have done anything for his mother; Jack had seen that when he'd held the gun to Bear on that first day here.

He thought of the bodies in the basement, and couldn't help but wonder. Had Albie killed for her?

Jack shone the light closer on the painting, studying it. There was definitely something odd. After a moment, it was clear.

The lack of dust or grime.

Brow furrowed, he took another step closer, until he was standing directly beside the bed. In the movie, this would be the part where a hand reached from below and grabbed his ankle or severed his Achilles. He grimaced. Jack hated those kinds of movies.

"What secrets were you hiding here, Nancy?" he mused aloud.

He knelt on the filthy bed for better access to the portrait. Another pair of jeans he would need to burn. At least he could expense this pair to Barbara.

With a gloved hand, he ran his finger along the edge of the painting. Then, he reached up and carefully removed it from the wall.

He set the painting on the bed—the cleanest surface in the room, though that wasn't saying much—and stared.

A recessed shelf had been built there, and effectively hidden from view by Nancy's portrait. The police hadn't found this, he had no doubt.

The first two shelves were a cluttered array of photos and macabre keepsakes from the animals Nancy had taken in: some photos framed, others faded and taped to the woodwork. Alongside were clumps of fur, three rabbit's feet, bleached bones and teeth… It was a grisly shadowbox, a tribute to the animals who had lived and died under her care.

It was the top shelf that held his attention, however.

There was a photo in a gilt frame, of Nancy in a wedding gown alongside a small, timid-looking man in suit and tie. He looked just like Fred. This, then, would have been her husband. And beside it... Jack looked away, stomach turning.

This most likely was also the husband. Sophie would be able to run dental records, but Jack had little doubt that the skull resting beside the framed photo belonged with the headless skeleton he'd found in the basement. Nancy's husband hadn't run away all those years ago at all, and Nancy had known it.

So, what had happened to him?

Jack was jolted from quiet contemplation by a crash downstairs, this one impossible to chalk up to a rogue rat or two. For the first time in months, he was grateful for the Glock holstered at his side.

He crept from Nancy's room, careful to replace the painting on the wall first. The house was still again when he reentered the hallway—eerily so, a silence that felt deeper than what he'd experienced when he first entered.

He started down the stairs, head up, eyes straining in the darkness. He was so intent on the world around that he forgot until the very last second about the broken stairs. His ankle twisted when he hit the broken board, but Jack recovered in time to keep himself from falling, a gloved hand grasping at the precarious banister. Once he'd found his feet again, he paused halfway to the first floor. His body tightened. This time, he actually reached for his gun. Drew.

Someone was moving downstairs. He heard a strange crackling. A distant murmur.

He considered calling out again, but if he wasn't supposed to be here, whoever was in the kitchen definitely wasn't.

Maybe Albie had returned.

Or Fred.

He continued moving quietly toward the sound, so focused on his destination that he paid little attention to his immediate surroundings.

That was his first mistake.

Because when the attacker hit, they came from behind. Someone moving fast, hurtling toward him, invisible to him in the darkness. He felt the impact of someone's hands on his chest. Smelled gasoline, even as his feet went out from under him. He realized then that what he'd heard downstairs wasn't a person at all—it was a thing.

A deadly, seething, violent thing.

Fire.

This time when he clutched at the railing, his weight was too much—he heard the splintering of wood, and crashed down half the flight of stairs before landing hard on the soiled floor below. He'd twisted his shoulder on the way down; hit his head hard on impact. He lay stunned for a moment too long—enough time for his assailant to follow him down the stairs. He was dimly aware of the rush of air as something darker than the black all around came toward him, and he felt the explosive pain when it crashed into his skull.

And then, he felt nothing.

19

I HURRIED AFTER BEAR as the ambulance left with Albie, and caught up to him and Casper just before he climbed into his truck. We were in the parking lot at the top of Mt Battie, a hoard of search teams all decompressing around us. I stepped in front of Bear's door before he could go anywhere.

"Why don't you ride with Monty and the others tonight? I'll take your truck back."

"That's all right—I'll just meet you later." He wouldn't look at me. Anger poured from him, so tangible that I could almost feel it. He looked like he would go mad, and I had no idea how to help him. When had he become so angry?

"It wasn't a suggestion," I said. I kept my voice even. In this state, there was no way I wanted him out alone on the roads.

"I'm eighteen—" His voice rose. I kept mine quiet, if only to provide some counterbalance.

"I know you are. So, I'm not ordering you—I couldn't if I wanted to. But I'm asking you: drive back to the wharf with Monty and the rest of the crew." I hesitated, grateful when he finally met my eye and I saw a glimpse of the boy I had raised. "Please, Bear."

Movement in my periphery pulled my focus for a moment, and I realized that Monty was standing by, Granger lying wearily at his feet. He made no move, though, letting Bear decide on his own.

Finally, Bear sighed. He looked exhausted, and as humorless as he'd been for the past month. "Fine," he grumbled. He pushed the keys at me. "Whatever. Don't wreck my truck, though."

"I'll do my best." On impulse, I pulled him to me in a crushing hug. "I love you, kiddo," I whispered in his ear. "We'll get through this."

He tensed, and pulled away with that damned mask still in place.

"Come on, sunshine," Monty said. He draped his arm around Bear's shoulders. "You're with me. Meet you back at the wharf?" he asked me.

"Meet you there," I agreed with a nod, then mouthed "Thank you" when Bear wasn't looking. Monty dismissed my gratitude with a wave of his hand.

"Nothing you wouldn't do for me," he said. I watched as he steered Bear away, the dogs at their heels.

I breathed a sigh of relief, and opened the passenger's side door of Bear's truck. Phantom leapt inside. I fastened her into Casper's harness safety belt, and took my own seat. My head was starting to pound again, but thankfully there were no voices. Before I turned on the truck, I remembered to turn the radio down—Bear tends to listen to music at three decibels above deafening.

This time, however, there was no music to burst my

eardrums. Instead, a woman's voice came on, so low I could barely hear. I turned up the volume.

"...I think you'd like it out here if you give it a chance," the woman's voice said. Not a woman, I realized immediately. Or, not just any woman. Ren. If I hadn't recognized the voice, I would certainly recognize the Nigerian accent. "I know we're young. I know everything I said before I left... It's still all true. We have to live our lives. Grow up. But..." She sniffed quietly. She was crying. "I just miss you, Bear. It's like I've lost a leg or something."

I turned the CD off quickly, ashamed to have listened even that much. I couldn't get the sound of Ren's voice out of my head. The tremor when she'd said those words. My own vision blurred as I blinked away tears.

No wonder Bear was having such a hard time. He was eighteen, high school behind him, with enough money to do whatever he wanted to. He put so many limits on himself, though. I knew he wouldn't use Brock's money, and academically he didn't have nearly the options that Ren had. She'd had colleges knocking down her door before she finally decided on the University of Southern California to be near her father. Bear had never done well with school. Dyslexia was just the first of many problems for him, and he seemed to view being in any classroom as some kind of punishment.

He had opted to stay on Windfall Island to pursue his own passion projects after finishing school, but I wondered now whether he was doing that because he truly wanted to, or because he didn't have the confidence to try something else.

I drove through the night with my thoughts whirling,

while Phantom slept soundly on the seat beside me. I kept one hand on her head, a grounding force as my thoughts shifted back to Albie. He'd seemed clear when he shouted the words.

I saw him kill my mother.

My stomach churned.

That was ridiculous, though. Sheriff Finnegan would have to see just how ridiculous—he had to know Bear wouldn't do this. He would never hurt someone.

You'll get this dog over my dead body, Nancy had said to Bear, on the night she died.

Fine with me.

Oh, God.

It looks like our son picked up your killing ways, Brock murmured in my ear. The usual accompanying headache rocked my skull. I kept my eyes on the road.

"Go away," I said aloud. Phantom woke and looked at me, head raised. If there were in fact some spirit here, she didn't sense it.

He's got that game down, James. Same as you, Brock said.

I didn't say anything, my head pounding now, but try as I might I couldn't just send him away.

"What game are you talking about, Brock?" I asked reluctantly.

I could feel his smile. He'd won. *The Redemption Game,* he explained. *You bust your ass, deny yourself all the pleasures you could have, in the hopes that maybe that will make you good enough. That will erase all those past sins.*

"We bust our asses because we believe in what we're doing," I said. Phantom lay her head back down with a sigh, now that she was clear I wasn't talking to her. "We have plenty of pleasure in our lives. Neither of us need all the crap you had when you were alive—the swimming pool and the helicopter and the tennis court. We both have what we need."

Liar, Brock said. *You're too afraid to take what you want. Every time you get close to it, you run like a beaten dog. You think if you keep working, keep doing all the good in the world, maybe someday you'll feel like you've earned something for yourself.*

"You don't know what you're talking about," I said, to the voice of a man I'd watched die nearly a decade ago. He laughed.

I ignored him, trying to push past the pain in my head and the ghost who wouldn't leave me be. Two minutes passed, maybe three, before the pain began to fade. Brock had gone back where he came from, at least for now.

I took a detour down the long lane to the Davis house, if only to pull myself together and buy myself a little more time before I had to face Bear at the wharf again. I still wasn't sure what I would say to him.

As I was driving in, I was nearly run off the road by a car driving like a bat out of hell, its high beams full on. I swerved off to the shoulder and into a ditch, cursing all the while. I turned to get a better look at the vehicle, but could make out nothing beyond a broken taillight on the driver's side. No idea of color, license plate, make or model. I couldn't even tell whether it was a car or a truck.

Grumbling, I got Bear's truck back on the road. If there was a scratch on the damn thing, Bear really would commit murder.

I was about to turn around and head back to the main road when an orange glow up ahead caught my attention.

Phantom was on her feet in the passenger seat now, straining against the harness.

"Easy, girl," I said. I put the truck in drive and continued on to the Davis house, my cell phone already in hand. I ordered the phone to call 911, and then slammed on the brakes at the overgrown drive leading up to the house. My stomach bottomed out.

I recognized Jack's car instantly, and was momentarily paralyzed by the sight of his Honda Civic against the growing flames inside Nancy Davis's house.

"I'm calling to report a fire," I shouted into the phone when the dispatcher answered. I made sure Phantom was secure inside the truck and safely away from the flames, ignoring her frenzied yelps when she realized what I was doing.

I gave the dispatcher the address. "Hurry," I said unnecessarily—like they would just sit on their hands without that added urgency. "I think someone might be inside."

I ended the call, stuffed the phone in my back pocket, and shouted Jack's name.

He didn't answer.

•

The whole front of Nancy's house was engulfed in flames by the time I got there. I ran around to the back, searching for any sign of Jack among the wreck and ruin that had been Nancy's home.

"Jack!" I called again.

I strained my ears, desperate for some sign that he was

all right; that he'd made it out of this hell.

There was no such sign.

I looked back over my shoulder, waiting for sirens and flashing lights. Nothing there, either.

He was inside.

I could feel it, could see him in there in a way that was so real, so tangible, that it was like I was watching the movie. I went closer, ignoring the heat and the smoke. The back door was already in ruin, half off its hinges and not yet touched by the flames.

I took a breath, whispered a prayer, and put my shirt over my face as I ran inside the burning building.

Once inside, it took a second to get oriented through the smoke. The house had already been in chaos, and it turns out that if there's anything worse than the smell of old dog crap and dead things, it's the smell of old dog crap and dead things on fire. I managed to keep down my dinner—just barely—and shouted through the fabric of my shirt, still using it as a mask over my nose and mouth.

"Jack! Are you in here? Please, answer me."

Still nothing.

I ventured farther in. The flames roared, the noise deafening. The heat was getting worse, the flames closer. I'd entered through a store room, and now made my way through to the hallway. Farther along, I saw a staircase already engulfed in flames. And at the bottom...

"Jack!" I screamed it this time, the word tearing at my smoke-filled throat.

He didn't move. I ran to him despite the flames, aware of nothing but him, bleeding and crumpled in a heap at the bottom step.

"Jack? Wake up. Please." I checked his pulse, and could have wept when I found it strong and steady. I shook him, hard. Nothing. Panic was definitely getting the best of me. Finally, I pulled my hand back and slapped his cheek, so hard that my palm stung. It may have seemed a little histrionic later, but it was the only thing I could think of at the time.

"Jamie? Ow. Damn it," he murmured, just barely out of his stupor.

"You have to get up. The house is on fire. Please."

I tugged at him, and an instant later he came to his senses. His eyes widened at the hellscape around us.

"What are you doing?" he demanded.

"I told you I'd save you someday," I said.

"You didn't tell me you'd get us both killed doing it," he said, coughing at the last bit. I pulled his shirt up over his nose and mouth the way I'd done with my own clothes, and tugged on him until he managed to get to his feet. He swayed there a moment, found his center, and surveyed our options.

I'd just started to panic when I saw a break in the flames, back the way I had come. I grabbed Jack's hand and held tight, pulling him along behind me.

It felt the like the devil was licking at my heels with every step. Beams crashed in our wake; sparks flew.

We kept running.

We didn't stop until we were back at Bear's truck, both of us gasping, and the fire trucks were just rolling up.

20

SHERIFF FINNEGAN AND A STATE DETECTIVE met Jack and me at the Penobscot Bay ER that night, and proceeded to grill me while doctors tended to Jack, then switched off to interview Jack as soon as they got the okay from the attending physician. I couldn't tell them much, beyond giving the description of the car with the missing taillight that had run me off the road as I was approaching Nancy's house.

Jack's interview took longer, and I could tell from the set of Sheriff Finnegan's jaw that he was none too pleased with the P.I.

"I should take you in just on principle," he told Jack as they were preparing to leave. The doctor had come to get me, and didn't look thrilled with the situation himself.

"I just wanted to get a look around," Jack said, somewhat painfully. He was bloodied and burned and bandaged, which probably went a long way toward convincing Finnegan to have some mercy. "I didn't disturb anything, took nothing from the scene."

"Yeah, well," the state detective said, "we'll never know that for sure, will we? The house is ashes now." He looked at Finnegan, his own mouth tensed to a thin line. "I still say we press charges."

"And I say it's my call," Finnegan said. "He didn't set the fire, and it sounds like he got some information your guys missed. He didn't have to tell us anything about that, but he did." I looked at Jack curiously, unclear on just what that information might be. Sheriff Finnegan continued, oblivious. "He shared the photos he took. My guess is, him going in there may end up being break for us. So, you can get in a pissing contest with me over this, or you can let it go and take what he brought us."

The detective contented himself with a few more stern words about Jack staying away from crime scenes, took down my number, and left us. Sheriff Finnegan remained just a few minutes more, but he looked dead on his feet.

"I wouldn't be feeling so charitable if Jamie hadn't helped bring Albie home tonight," he informed Jack wearily. "So, you can thank your girlfriend that I'm not dragging you to county lock-up or letting the Staties have their way with you tonight."

Jack nodded. "I appreciate that," he said. He didn't bother mentioning that we weren't together, which I could understand. This really didn't seem like the time to get into semantics.

Once the police were gone, the doctor returned his attention to Jack and me.

"You're lucky she came along when she did," he told Jack.

Dr. Phil Landry had been stitching up my crew and me since we'd moved to the area two years before. He was in his fifties, by far the oldest doctor in the emergency room, with an efficient air about him that had always endeared him to me.

"Your lungs might be a little raw for a couple of days," he continued. "And you'll have a headache for a while—the concussion is my major concern, though you'll likely experience some discomfort with the shoulder, as well."

"Sorry about that," I said to Jack. I hadn't realized until we were outside Nancy's house that I'd been dragging him by a dislocated shoulder.

He shrugged, then winced and rubbed his arm. "I'm alive. I can deal with a little shoulder pain."

"Take it easy tonight," Landry continued. He looked at me. "Are you staying with him?"

"I—uh—"

At the look on my face, Jack rushed in. "Don't worry about it. I'll be fine."

"You really shouldn't be alone," Landry insisted. "I could keep you here overnight, though I'm not sure how much your insurance will cover." He smiled suddenly. "I'm pretty sure I saw at least three nurses out there who would volunteer to keep you company—"

"That's fine," I interrupted, feeling a little dark myself by this time. "I'm staying. No need to recruit any nurses."

A grin flickered on Jack's lips, though he wisely squelched the expression. "Are you sure?"

"Positive. I just need to make a call."

"Good," Landry said. "Chances are you'll be fine, but I don't like to gamble where concussions are concerned."

"I appreciate that," Jack assured him. "Thank you."

•

Bear's truck had a crew cab, which was helpful in accommodating Jack, Phantom, and me. Jack got in and put on his seatbelt wordlessly; I was already in, the truck idling in the ER parking lot. Phantom had been asleep in the backseat, though she woke briefly to greet Jack before she settled back in. It had been a long day for all of us.

"You found Albie?" Jack said, once we were on the road.

"We did. He's okay—shaken up, but not hurt. He'll be all right. What was the sheriff talking about? He said you found something in the house...?"

He considered that for a few seconds before he said anything. "Yeah. I think I found Mr. Davis. Or...well. I think I found his head."

I glanced at him, just barely illuminated in the passenger's seat beside me. "Seriously?"

"Seriously."

I couldn't really think of a response to that, and we were silent for the remaining drive back to Jack's apartment. When we reached his building, he unbuckled his seatbelt and started to get out before I'd even come to a full stop.

"I'm fine," he assured me. "You don't need to stay—get back to things out on the island. I'll give you a call in the morning."

I turned off the truck. "You've got a concussion and smoke inhalation and a recently dislocated shoulder, Jack. Landry was pretty clear. I'm not leaving you alone for the night."

"You don't have to—"

"I know I don't have to," I said impatiently. "But I'm your friend. If it were me, would you just leave me in the parking lot and head off into the night right now?"

He didn't answer, but his silence was answer enough. Of course he wouldn't.

"I'll have to bring Phantom up," I told him. "If that's okay."

He didn't look sold on that. "The cats——"

"She'll be fine with them. She loves babies, doesn't matter if they're puppies or kittens or humans. And she knows enough to steer clear of Cash."

We made a sad-looking trio headed up the stairs, all three of us limping; Jack with bandaged head, the two of us smelling of smoke and whatever we'd waded through in Nancy's house. I waited by the door with Phantom as Jack unlocked the apartment and went in first. He checked to make sure the cats were secure, then stood aside as Phantom and I went in.

Cash went to Phantom immediately, hissing, his back up. The kittens had no such compunction, however. They took one look at the giant shepherd, and all five came racing over to greet her. Phantom looked overwhelmed for a moment, then lay down just inside the apartment and allowed the babies to explore. Cash looked on, his back still up, his tail puffed and his notched ear flat against his skull.

"He'll get over it," I reassured Jack. "They'll be fine."

I set aside all my own woes for a moment, and took stock of the man before me. His head was bandaged, his arm was in a sling, he smelled worse than the dead, and beyond that he looked plain beaten.

"Go get yourself cleaned up, all right?" I said, my voice

gentler now. "No shower since you can't get that bandage wet, but you can at least get washed up. I'll take care of these guys. Then we'll get you settled."

"There's tea in the cupboard, if you want." He started to go to the kitchen, but I headed him off.

"Jack. I'm a grown woman, I can make my own tea. Now, go on. I'll be here when you get out."

He nodded wearily, and shambled toward the bathroom.

I waited until I heard the water running before I dialed Monty. I'd let them all know what was happening as soon as we were out of Nancy's house, but hadn't checked in since. Monty answered on the first ring.

"The Davis house is flattened—did you hear?" he said.

"I was in it," I said. "I had a pretty good idea it wasn't going to end well. I'm at Jack's. The doctor said he needs someone to stay with him. How's Bear?"

"Surly and not a whole hell of a lot of fun. So, no change."

"If you need me to come back—"

"You've got a good-looking guy with a concussion who's crazy about you. Stay there and take care of him. I'll keep an eye on Bear."

"I'm not sure when I'll be back tomorrow, but I'll try to get there early."

"We'll be here, don't worry about us. We've got it under control."

"Any word on Grace and the hurricane?" I asked, before I hung up.

There was a long silence on the other end of the line, followed by a heavy sigh. "I haven't reached her yet. Her grandma's not answering her phone—it goes straight to voicemail now. I may need to head out sooner than I expected."

"I told you, family comes first," I said immediately. "Just let me know. Whatever you need, whenever you need to go... We've got you covered."

"I know it," Monty said. There was a smile in the words. "I appreciate that. Now, go on in and take care of the Fed, huh? I'm sure he could use a little TLC at this point. Maybe get some yourself, while you're at it."

"Goodnight, Monty."

"'Night, James. See you tomorrow."

I took a shower once Jack was done, and slipped into a T-shirt he'd gotten out for me, along with a pair of paisley boxer shorts that I cinched at the waist. I emerged refreshed to find Jack seated on the sofa with his eyes closed, Cash curled up beside him. The kittens were all settled around Phantom, who dozed contentedly on her side. If she minded five alien fuzzballs trying to nurse her, she didn't show it.

I went to Jack and stopped, hesitant—suddenly shy about the whole situation. He opened one eye, and smiled hazily at me.

"It's a good look for you."

"I don't know about that, but it sure is comfortable."

I reached for his hand—the one attached to the good shoulder this time—and squeezed his fingers. "Come on. You need rest."

"And you don't?"

"I'll sleep when you do."

He got to his feet and we stood there for a moment, our bodies close, gazes locked. "The couch isn't comfortable," he warned. "For sleeping, I mean."

"I can handle it."

"You don't have to," he said. His voice was dangerously low. "Come to bed with me. I'm concussed—I won't make a move."

"Jack—"

"It's not like we haven't shared a bed before."

That was true. In Bethel over the winter, we'd slept together in a little hunting cabin in the middle of the woods. At least, we had until I'd awakened from a dream so intense, so terrifying, that there was no way I could close my eyes again. Nothing had happened in that bed. At least, nothing physical.

"I'm not trying to pressure you. Or, I don't want you to feel pressured... You don't have to—"

"No," I said. "I know I don't." And I followed him down the hallway, my hand still in his.

Jack's bedroom was a soothing, masculine blue gray, the bed a massive thing that looked freshly made. Had he done that while I was in the shower, or did he always make his bed in the morning? The latter, I decided. Jack was former military; he was the kind of man who appreciated order.

He wore a T-shirt and cotton pajama pants. I watched, transfixed, when he took off the shirt.

"It gets warm in here at night," he explained, then looked uncertain. "If it makes you uncomfortable..."

I shook my head. I couldn't seem to look away from the smooth planes of his chest, the taut muscles in his stomach. "No," I said. My own voice was as low as his. "I'm not uncomfortable."

We got into bed. It was a king-sized—we could have

slept without touching easily enough. Hell, we could have slept three more people, Phantom, Cash, and all the kittens in here.

He rolled to face me. The bedroom door was open, a light still on in the hallway—for the cats, he explained. It meant that I could see him, which I suddenly appreciated very much. He was handsome in a way I hadn't even realized real men could be handsome, with the dark eyes and sculpted bones of a model. The bandage on his head, the scars and the self-consciousness and the lopsided smile, all made him slightly more accessible. Slightly.

It was two a.m. The night outside was quiet. It felt strange, without the sounds of dogs barking or donkeys braying. No birds, frogs, or crickets. Rockland was hardly a metropolis, but it still felt alien to what I was used to.

Jack reached out and touched my hair, brushing it back behind my ear. His eyes never left mine, a faint smile on his lips.

"How's your head?" I asked.

"It's fine. They gave me good drugs. I'm all right."

Of course, he hadn't taken the drugs they gave him. I didn't point that out. I thought suddenly of Albie's words, and the look on my son's face when he'd heard those words. I thought of the CD Ren had sent him.

I thought of Brock, and closed my eyes when I felt his voice edging into my mind.

How many reasons did I need to convince me this was a bad idea right now?

When I opened my eyes, Jack was closer. He ran the back of his hand along my cheek, his touch so gentle it was barely a touch at all.

We studied each other for a long moment, neither of us speaking. His thumb found my lips and brushed across the surface, still feather light. I don't know which of us moved next—it could have been me. Probably was. I wasn't breathing right. Every part of me ached, and it wasn't from the day I'd had.

Our lips touched. It was a gentle kiss at first—one I realized I had been waiting for from the moment we first met, up in Northern Maine while I helped him find the woman who would soon share his bed.

His hand slipped to the back of my head, fingers twined in my hair, and I moved against him.

It was another mutual thing when we parted, as though we'd both come to our senses at the same time.

"You have a concussion," I reminded him. My voice was husky. He smiled, I think at the sound.

"And you're exhausted." He sighed. "So, we sleep tonight."

"We sleep tonight," I confirmed, much as I hated to.

He pulled me into his arms, and I went easily. I lay with my head on his chest, his arms around me, and listened to his heart. Everything had changed—except that it hadn't, not really. Not yet. Everything was on the precipice, I realized as my eyes sank shut. It felt like the ground was shifting, like it could burst open, and I didn't know where to stand or how to prepare myself when it finally did.

I thought of Brock's words.

You're too afraid to take what you want. Every time you get close to it, you run like a beaten dog.

"Sleep, *corazón,*" Jack whispered to me. "Everything will be all right. We'll deal with tomorrow when it comes."

I closed my eyes, and I made a choice that my mind fought with everything it had.

I believed him.

21

AGAINST ALL ODDS, I did actually get some sleep that night. Of course, I had to get up every two hours to make sure Jack wasn't dead, but when he was right next to me in bed that proved to be pretty easy. My alarm would go off, I'd roll over and shake him awake, check his pupils and make sure he knew what year it was, and then we'd just go right back to sleep. At our seven o'clock check-in, he was the one to wake up first. I woke an instant later, and we just lay there for a minute, looking at each other across the pillow.

"I could get used to waking up next to you," he said. "It's kind of nice."

It was kind of nice, which frankly scared the bejeezus out of me. I spent the first fourteen years of my life sharing a bed with my sisters—I was the third to last of eight kids living in a two-bedroom shack in rural Georgia. Seven kids, after my little sister Clara went missing when I was seven and never returned. Later, I spent a few years co-sleeping with Bear before he decided he preferred the company of dogs to the company of his mama. Since then, I'd gotten very attached to sleeping on my own.

If I weren't so comfortable, I might have gotten up and

ended the conversation then and there. But Jack's bed really was remarkable.

Jack wasn't so bad himself.

"Do you know what year it is?" I asked.

He grinned at me, like he knew I was changing the subject. "I do. I know the president, the day of the week, and my social security number, as well. How are my pupils?"

I looked at them.

They looked good, and I told him so.

"I should get up," I said. "Phantom probably has to pee."

"We didn't get to bed until late," he argued. "Wouldn't she let you know if she needed to go out?"

"Not if she thought I was sleeping. I think she'd let her bladder bust before she bothered me—it's a matter of pride for her."

"Still… Get up if you need to, but she must be tired. We didn't get to bed until two."

He was right about that. Phantom had put in a lot of hours and a lot of miles last night, too—she deserved some peace.

"Fine," I agreed after a half-hearted debate in my head. "I'll give it a little while longer. Then I should definitely get up."

"Me, too," Jack agreed. His eyes drifted shut. "Wake me when you get up. There's something I'd like to talk to you about."

That piqued my curiosity, but not enough to push him on the subject. Instead, I re-set my alarm and closed my eyes again. There was no way I would sleep until nine, I was sure. Since Jack's bed did seem to have some kind of magical properties, however, I figured I should take precautions.

As it turned out, those precautions proved unnecessary. At shortly before nine o'clock, my cell phone rang. Jack was still out, snoring softly. Cash and three of the kittens had found their way to us, and I had to work to extricate myself. I grabbed my phone and reluctantly left the warm bed, checking the display as I slipped from the room.

"What's up?" I asked Monty as I answered. Phantom rose to greet me, tail wagging. The two kittens who had adopted her protested—loudly. I searched for my shoes, since Phantom definitely had to pee by now. So did I, but I usually took care of the dog first. Or else, just took care of it at the same time.

I probably shouldn't do that outside Jack's apartment building, though.

"I don't want you to panic," Monty began.

"That doesn't sound good." My shoes were by the sofa, but I saw no sign of my clothes. I didn't want to make Phantom wait, though. I checked the bathroom, and took advantage of the opportunity to use the toilet. Phantom and the kittens followed me in, lingering in the doorway so it was impossible to close the door. I crossed my fingers that Jack wouldn't come out, and scanned the room for any sign of my clothes.

"What the hell did he do with my pants?" I muttered.

"Well, that sounds promising," Monty said.

"Very funny." I wiped and flushed with one hand, pulled up my shorts, and left the room with Phantom and the kittens on my heels.

I managed to find Phantom's leash, though there still seemed to be no sign of my pants. I gave up, and snapped the leash onto Phantom's collar.

"What's going on, Monty?" I prompted. I had a brief flicker of concern, but there were a thousand reasons Monty could be calling me—many of them urgent, but few something to genuinely worry about. "Just spit it out."

"The police were just here," he said.

I was in the stairwell outside Jack's apartment with Phantom, still dressed in his T-shirt and boxer shorts. I paused. That flicker of concern intensified. "Why?"

He took a breath. Phantom whined, and I forced myself to keep moving. "They arrested Bear."

I froze. "They what?"

"They got a warrant last night—this is a stunt, Jamie. They waited till Saturday morning so there's no way to get him out until Monday. They want to scare him."

"What did they arrest him for?"

"They're saying he killed Nancy Davis."

I continued down the stairs and outside. Nine o'clock on a Saturday morning meant people in the parking lot, all of them wearing more than I was. I got some curious looks as I walked with Phantom over to a green space at the back of the lot. I couldn't think straight. This shouldn't be a surprise—I'd heard what Albie said the night before. I'd seen the look on Bear's face.

Why the hell hadn't I gone home last night? I should have been there.

"Before you start beating yourself up about not being here, stop," Monty said, reading my mind. "It wouldn't have made a difference. You should call a lawyer, though. They took him to the Knox County lock-up."

Phantom peed, then crouched and I realized I had no

bags on me for clean-up, and no keys to get into my truck for more. A couple of people were watching me, and I saw no sign of a doggie-bag dispenser anywhere.

"I don't..." I shook my head. "This is unbelievable. I should have come home. Do you know where the jail is?"

He gave me the address and directions, then added, "It's not a bad facility, James. They were good to him—polite. He's scared, but he's okay. Just get down there. He'll be okay."

My vision blurred. *I guess the apple didn't fall far from the tree after all,* Brock whispered in my ear. What felt like a knife point pierced my skull, nearly taking my knees out from under me.

"Are you going to clean that up?" an elderly woman asked, eyes narrowed as Phantom finished her business.

"I've got it," Jack said, appearing from nowhere with a plastic produce bag.

"We've got everything under control out here," Monty said, on the other end of the line. "Just go take care of the kid. Give me a call if there's anything I can do."

"Thank you," I said. "I'll call you when I know more."

I ended the call. Jack had bagged Phantom's poop, and was talking to the old woman. I watched him, detached. Brock wasn't talking anymore, but I could still feel him there. Waiting for me.

Bear was in jail.

I kept seeing that look on his face when Albie had said the words last night. *I saw him kill my mother.* There had been guilt there—no doubt.

You knew he had it in him, Brock said.

"Jamie?" Jack said.

I shook my head, trying to clear it. "It's Bear."

"I heard," he said. I looked around, but the old woman had gone and was nowhere in sight. When had she left? "Come on—come upstairs and get dressed. I'll go with you. We should talk."

•

"You had no right to take the case without calling me first," I said, barely ten minutes later. I was dangerously close to shouting. Dangerously close to violence, for that matter.

"He's eighteen, Jamie. It was his money. He came to me—you really would have had me turn him away?"

"No. That's not what I'm saying."

We were on Route 1 headed back to Nancy's house so Jack could get his car, with me behind the wheel. Saturday in July meant sixteen lawn sales on every side road all the way there, so the journey was painfully slow.

"What are you saying, then?" Jack asked. "I'm not clear on what you would have me do. I was bound by client privilege—I promised I wouldn't say anything."

"So why are you telling me now?" I bit out, still seething.

"Because I'm worried about him. He fired me—technically he's not my client anymore. He needs you to know what's going on."

"It would have been nice to know *before* he got arrested for murder."

He grimaced. "I know. I'm sorry, I didn't think the police would have a case pulled together so quickly."

"Well, apparently they do."

Silence fell between us. I finally made it to the

Thomaston bridge and headed across into Cushing, grateful when the road opened up and the lawn sales dwindled. It was a beautiful day outside, but I was having a hard time appreciating it at the moment.

"He'll be all right, Jamie," Jack finally said.

"You don't know that." When he offered no response, I dialed back my irritation and tried to get my head on straight again. I glanced at him. "Tell me more about the case. How do we figure out who the real killer is? I have a bad feeling that the police might have decided they've got their man."

"It's possible," Jack agreed reluctantly. "Does this mean I have a sleuthing partner now?"

"Just this once. I've got enough on my plate; I don't have any interest in starting a new career now."

"That's understandable."

He proceeded to run down the details of both cases he was working, so far as he understood them:

Three bodies, plus Nancy. Fred's ex-girlfriend, Nancy's husband, and a third victim killed within the past two months.

"And the most recent victim was an ex-con," I repeated, when he had finished.

"That's what Sophie said. No connection that we could find to Nancy or her kids."

"What about her animals?"

I felt his eyes on me again, before he returned his attention to the road. "What do you mean?"

"So far, pretty much everyone with a motive to kill Nancy ties back to her treatment of the animals. Barbara Monroe thinks Nancy killed her husband because of them, right? So... It makes sense that maybe the guy in the basement had something to do with them, too."

"He had a long rap sheet," Jack said. "Domestic violence, theft..." He hesitated. "Animal abuse."

My heart rate kicked up a notch. "Where was he from?"

"Down South. Mississippi."

I looked at him excitedly, thinking of the tattoo on Reaver's belly; my feeling that the dog had been trained for some kind of work. What had Albie said?

We saved him from down South. They would have killed him for sure.

That was possible. I'd heard stories about dog fighting rings looking for military dogs and police K-9s to train in the ring—there was a certain cachet to having a dog like that tear another dog to pieces, apparently. They'd steal the dog, then burn off any identifying marks and surgically remove any tracking device that might have been implanted.

I told Jack this, and he considered my theory for a full minute or more before I finally broke the silence.

"If Nancy killed all three people in her basement on her own, that doesn't do anything to clear Bear," I pointed out. "The police could just as well decide her death had nothing to do with the bodies in the basement."

"There's no way she could have taken out that ex-con on her own. And someone clearly wanted to wipe out some evidence that was in the house last night, and get rid of me in the bargain."

We reached Nancy's place, and I slowed to a stop beside Jack's car. The house really had been flattened in the blaze—it looked surreal, the once-beautiful Victorian home now nothing but a few charred boards and a gaping black hole in the ground. Jack and I both stared at it for a moment.

"You saved my life last night," he said quietly. "Thank you for that."

I looked at him. His eyes were dark and serious, but his lips were quirked up in an almost-hesitant smile. Despite everything else going on, I found myself returning the smile.

"You're welcome."

I thought of the dream or vision or whatever it was, that I'd had years ago of one day saving his life. Jack had once been obsessed with the idea, but he didn't even mention it today. Things got still between us, and I wondered for a moment if he was going to kiss me. In a normal relationship, that's what we would do. He would lean across the console, and kiss me. Tell me to have a good day; we'd talk later.

This wasn't a normal relationship, though. Hell, I wasn't sure it was a relationship at all.

"I'll go," he said, "and let you get over to Bear's. Give me a call if you need anything."

"I will. Thanks."

I looked straight ahead as he got out of the truck, and waited until he was safely in his car before I drove away. As I was leaving, I glanced in my rearview mirror and found that he was still in the parked car, staring out in the direction of the Davis house. I wondered what he was thinking, and I wished I had some idea how to ask.

And then, I drove away.

•

It was just past ten o'clock when I reached the Knox County Jail, where Bear was being held. I walked through the steel doors, claustrophobia setting in the second the door slammed closed behind me.

Bear stood on the other side of a long steel table, his

gaze fixed on the floor. He looked thin—had he lost weight recently? How had I not noticed that? Not only that, but he looked completely exhausted.

"Hi," I said. I wasn't clear on what else to say. Where do you even begin, when your only kid is behind bars on suspicion of murder?

"Hey," he said. "Is Casper okay? He was pretty shaken up when they took me away?"

My heart twisted. This was the boy I knew—the boy who would think of the dog first, forever and always. No matter what he might be going through himself.

"I haven't seen him," I confessed. "But I'm headed home after this. I'll give him some extra TLC."

"Good. Thanks."

He fell silent, his gaze shifting to the floor now that the most pressing business was taken care of.

"Do you want to sit?" I asked.

He shrugged, and sat in the plastic chair provided for him with a heavy sigh.

"Doug will be here soon," I said. Doug was our lawyer—the same lawyer I had used when police were investigating Brock's death. "We'll figure this out. This is all just plain nuts—the police will see that."

He grunted noncommittally, and anxiety ran through me in a wave.

"It is nuts, isn't it, Bear?" I asked. Another shrug. He had yet to look at me, his eyes now on his hands. I wanted to reach across the table and shake him. "What were you doing out that night?"

"I wasn't out." At least it was an answer, even if it was clearly a lie.

"Well, you weren't in your bed, either." I lowered my voice, glancing back toward the door. Could they monitor these conversations? I knew they couldn't if he was talking to a lawyer, but there was no such privilege when a boy was talking to his mother, was there?

"When Doug comes, I need you to tell him the truth," I said quietly. "I don't care what that truth is—we'll handle it. But no one can help you if you won't be straight with them."

"Yes, ma'am," he said numbly.

I hesitated. "There will be a hearing on Monday to set bail, but we can't get you out before then. You'll have to spend the weekend here."

"I know," he said. Did his voice break, or was I just imagining that? "Monty told me. I'll be okay."

"Just keep to yourself. If you don't mix with anyone else, they won't have a reason to bother you."

For the first time, he looked at me. He actually smiled. "I'm not in Alcatraz, Mom. All those prison movies don't apply here, okay? The guards have been nice to me, and there are only like five other guys in here. I can make it through the weekend. I'll be okay."

At his assurance, I felt that mask of reason I'd had in place since walking in here start to slip. My eyes welled, but I shut down the emotion fast.

"I love you, kiddo. We'll get through this. And if you need anything—anything at all—find a way to reach me and I'll be here just as fast as I can be. I promise."

"I know, Mom," he said. His voice was quieter now. For the first time, I saw genuine fear in his eyes. Pain. He looked away, pulling himself back together. "I'll talk to you again soon," he said, his voice low. "You better get going."

The guard came in, and I remained seated while the man escorted Bear away.

How was this happening?

How in hell was any of this happening?

22

FROM THE COUNTY JAIL, I returned to the Littlehope town wharf and headed back to Windfall Island. Which, it turned out, was a madhouse by the time I got home at noon that day. Casper was frantic at sight of me, and I spent ten precious minutes just comforting the poor pit bull when I first got through the doors of the galley, where I'd called an impromptu staff meeting. Therese, Monty, and Sarah were all there waiting for me, and I felt another wave of guilt at abandoning ship last night. Everyone looked exhausted.

"How's he doing?" Therese asked, before anyone else could get the same question out. There was no need to ask who she meant.

"He's freaked out," I said. "But he's okay. Jack's working on some leads, so we can get the real killer and get Bear out of there as soon as possible."

"It's crazy," Sarah said. "No way would Bear do this. He's the most peaceful guy I've ever met."

She wore cargo pants and a T-shirt with two kittens armed with machine guns, which I found disconcerting at best. She caught my look, and shrugged. "Sorry. It's laundry day."

"The press will be sniffing around today," I said. "I'm not sure 'arm the animals' is the message we want to put out there when one of our own is facing a murder charge because he threatened an animal hoarder."

"Something should be dry by now. I'll go change."

"I appreciate that," I assured her. "Any other day..."

She waved me off. "I know. Don't worry, I'm not feeling oppressed yet. Aside from a new uniform, what's the plan for today?"

"What's the status on the animals we've taken in?" I asked Therese, rather than answering the question.

The veterinarian consulted her notes. Her short gray hair stood straight up on end, and I caught a whiff of body odor that suggested she hadn't showered today. Or this week.

"Everybody's stable. We got the shearer out yesterday and he took care of Cornelius—"

I looked at her uncertainly. "Cornelius?"

"The big black and white sheep," she explained. "He was a mess under all that wool, but he's doing better. Farrier came out last night and took care of the goats and the donkey, and we've got somebody coming today to file down the llamas' teeth."

"And the dogs?"

"All good," she assured me, to my surprise. "We've got a slew with mange and parasites, but they've all been treated. The mange will take some time to clear up, but we're slowly starting them over to the Windfall diet. So far, they seem to be tolerating it well."

"Just be sure to go slow. And the worst cases of malnutrition shouldn't get it at all for now—just get them stable first."

The Windfall Diet consists of organic meat and a stew of vegetables and supplements, all of them mixed in our own kitchen. Depending on the dog's constitution, the meat is either raw or cooked. Either way, it works wonders for my K-9 team, and the diet shift is the first thing I do when newcomers came on board. However, any dog dealing with the kind of malnutrition Nancy's dogs were would have to build up to something like this over time. It definitely isn't a diet for sick dogs.

"What about Reaver?" I asked. The last I'd seen him, the pit bull had been on death's doorstep.

"Come see for yourself," Therese said. "I was worried, but Bear slept in the kennel with him last night."

It wasn't the first time Bear had done this, and I was sure it wouldn't be the last. I hedged, stomach turning. Unless, of course, he was convicted of murder and spent the next fifty years in prison. "This morning, he was up and eating. Bear even took him out for a run."

"How was he with the other animals?"

"Bear kept him on lead, but he seemed fine. He doesn't like loud noises, and he hates being chained up. But Bear had Casper with him at a safe distance, and Reaver barely seemed to notice."

"When you were writing up Reaver's report, did you do any research on that belly tattoo?" I asked.

"Whoever got to him did a good job burning it off," Therese said grimly. "I can't tell much of anything beyond a 3 that's on there, and even that isn't totally clear. Could be a partially burned 8. Maybe even just the letter 'b.'"

"Monty, when you were in the military did you ever work with K-9s?" I asked.

He looked up. "Sometimes. Why? You think Reaver could have been military?"

"I've got a hunch. Do you know anyone I could talk to to get that kind of information?"

"Let me make a couple of calls," he said. "There's a guy on the mainland who could probably help."

"That would be great." I paused. "What do you hear from Grace?"

"Nothing for twenty-four hours now. I haven't been able to reach Shonda's mother, either. They must have been evacuated."

"They should still have their phones, though," I argued. He frowned, eyes shadowed.

"Yeah, I know. The thought has occurred to me."

"Wrap up what you need to here. You should plan on going down there as soon as possible."

"Shonda made it clear. She doesn't want my help."

"Well, you can fight about that when you find her. This is your daughter we're talking about. The hurricane hasn't made landfall yet, but it will soon."

"Everything's gone to shit here—"

"Not your fault. Not your problem," I said firmly. I fixed him with a stern glare, unnerved at the depth of his uncertainty. Monty was my rock—he was never uncertain.

"I'm serious, Monty. Go. We'll deal without you."

He nodded resolutely, and didn't wait for me to resume my conversation with the others before he was on his way out the door.

When we were finished in the galley, I headed out to the kennels to check on the dogs. They started up with an ear-splitting greeting as I came through the door, and the headache I'd managed to shake returned with a vengeance.

"Easy, guys," I said, as soothingly as I could. "No reason to lose your minds. I'm just doing roll call."

Just as Therese had said, most everyone looked okay. Not great, but at least they were on the road to recovery. Some were better than others, and the fact that Nancy had worked primarily with smaller dogs worked in our favor. Even with behavioral issues or minor health problems, we would likely be able to find foster homes to ease their transition to a permanent placement.

I strolled past a kennel full of runny-eyed pugs, another with three yappy terriers—Oswald among them, and the next with the mangy Newfoundland, Cody. The massive dog had been shaved to treat the mange, and without the fur he was pitifully thin. He was lying down on the bed provided, and lifted his great black head to watch me as I walked by.

"Hey, Cody," I said calmly. "Don't worry, you've got a good home waiting for you. Life will get better, I promise."

He was likely two or three, possibly younger. Newfoundlands already live notoriously short lives, and the fact that his nutritional needs hadn't been met early on didn't work in his favor. Still, Hank seemed like a good man who was ready to put the time in. However many years Cody had left, they would certainly be better than the ones he'd spent with Nancy.

I continued on, speaking quiet words of encouragement to each of the dogs, evaluating as I went.

In the kennel at the end, I was surprised to note that the blanket between Reaver's kennel and the second to last had been removed. An odd-looking beagle/Dachshund kind of mix who was visibly pregnant watched me with wide, baleful eyes. Reaver sat at the door of the kennel, reminding me for all the world of a soldier at attention.

"Hey, sweet boy," I crooned through the gate. His tail waved, but he remained seated. "Mind if I come in for a second and check you out?"

I reached for the latch, careful to keep my movement slow and controlled. Reaver didn't seem concerned, though he stood and backed up to allow my entrance.

"How are you doing, Reav," I said conversationally. The kennel floor was clean, the door to the outside kennel open for him. I noted that the other area was likewise spotless. If he'd been housetrained early on, that training may be kicking back in now. For some dogs, a kennel situation can be incredibly stressful because the desire not to use the bathroom indoors is so ingrained that they actually make themselves sick trying to hold their urine.

"You want to take a walk, big guy?" I asked.

He stood eagerly, tail wagging harder now. I took the leash clipped to his kennel door, and called up the line to other workers in the area.

"I'm coming out with Reaver. Everybody else in?"

There was a pause before I got Sarah's response. "Everybody's in—go ahead."

There's a fine art to getting a dog-reactive or dog-aggressive dog past a line of occupied kennels. It's a dangerous business that can easily end in disaster if the handler doesn't know what she's doing. I was prepared for a fraught walk up the line. Instead, Reaver walked sedately beside me in a perfect heel, paying no attention whatsoever to the barking, occasionally lunging dogs on either side of him.

How could anyone have mistaken this dog for a killer? Had he truly given Nancy reason to, or was he just terrified, traumatized, and she reacted to that and his appearance in a way that just made his issues that much worse?

My hunch about the housetraining proved correct, because the moment he was outside Reaver lifted his leg and liberally christened the nearest pine tree. A few feet farther on, he crouched. His stool was still runny with a couple of flecks of blood, but it was worlds better than it had been just yesterday.

Phantom had spotted us when I first came out of the kennel. She minded my "stay back" command well, but still trailed after us with clear curiosity over the newcomer.

I was certain that Reaver was aware of her presence, but his posture remained relaxed. I hesitated. I wanted to know the extent of his aggression, but had to do so without risking Phantom's safety. Even on leash with Phantom free, an animal with real dog-aggression issues could do serious— even fatal—damage if she got close enough and he turned on her.

"Easy, Reav," I assured him in a soft voice. "I'm not bringing you back in yet. I just need to grab something."

I attached his leash to a line outside the building, checked to make sure no one was around, and darted into the kennel to grab a muzzle. Phantom watched me from a safe distance, her attention still split between me and Reaver.

"Hey," Sarah said when I stepped through the door. "I talked to Tracy, and she says she's got fosters for the pugs, the terriers, and a possible placement for that big lab-looking guy. Somebody else has volunteered to take Celia."

I shook my head, clueless. I'd been away for less than

twenty-four hours, and I felt like a stranger in a strange land. "Who's Celia?"

"Pregnant beagle-looking thing at the end of the line. They've fostered newborns before, are all up on early puppy care. Do you think Bear will mind?"

"No," I said, without hesitation. "He just wants what's best for everyone. He knows an actual home setting is the best way to train everybody, and get them acclimated to their future forever family."

"Yeah, that's what I figured," she agreed. "I'll let Tracy know."

"Perfect. Thanks—you're doing an incredible job with all this. I can't tell you how much I appreciate it."

She seized on that. "Do you appreciate it enough for a favor?"

"What kind of favor?" I asked. I was at the wall of leashes, Gentle Leaders, collars, and muzzles, but found the drawer that should contain muzzles for larger dogs frustratingly empty. "Do we have any more sixty-plus pound muzzles?"

"Check the next drawer. Things have been crazy, they may have gotten misplaced."

Sure enough, I found one crammed into the drawer for medium-sized muzzles. "Got it, thanks. Now, what can I do for you?" I shifted to take a quick look outside to make sure Reaver was still okay, and froze. "Sorry—it'll have to wait," I said hurriedly, and dashed out the door.

Too late, as it turned out.

Phantom had already decided she was ready for an introduction, and she wasn't waiting for me.

The shepherd lay down a couple of feet from Reaver—

close enough that the dog could easily reach her if he wanted. Reaver, however, was likewise lying down in the grass. Phantom crawled a little bit closer, belly never leaving the ground. My dog, the Ninja.

I watched Reaver's body language closely, poised to intervene if it became necessary. His tail waved, his body loose. He relaxed onto his side.

And then, he rolled onto his back, belly exposed. Phantom looked at me with a panting grin, and did the same.

I watched in awe as the two bicycled their hind legs in tandem, bodies wriggling in the warm grass. When they were done, they'd wriggled themselves close enough for a proper greeting. Reaver righted himself, and looked at me as though for permission.

"It's okay," I said. "You can say hello. Just don't eat her, please."

He did no such thing. Instead, he sniffed her backside briefly, bumped his body against hers, and lay back down. Phantom, well used to being taunted and tormented by Casper, looked utterly confounded.

She lay down beside the pit bull, closer this time, and relaxed with her head on her paws.

Huh.

I unclipped Reaver's leash from the line and set out again, this time with Phantom keeping pace beside the other dog. They walked easily together, bodies occasionally bumping together, tails at half staff and their mouths relaxed in open, welcoming grins.

My cell rang as we were approaching the galley. Reaver was still on leash, and I had no intention of letting him off until I had a clear idea of what I was dealing with, but we'd fenced a five-acre dog yard adjacent to the galley so staff and guests could let their dogs roam and play while they ate. That dog yard was currently unoccupied.

"Hello," I said into the receiver. I'd answered without checking the ID, too preoccupied to take the extra time. I let myself into the gated area with Reaver beside me. Phantom whined when I kept her on the other side of the fence. If something went sideways between the dogs, however, there would be no place for Phantom to escape to. For this meeting, I needed to be fully focused on the two dogs.

"Jamie?" a familiar voice said. I nearly wept upon hearing the Nigerian accent I'd come to love.

"Hey, sweetie," I said to Ren. I let Reaver off his leash. He stood still for a moment, as though confused. "It's so good to hear your voice."

"You too," she said. "I'm sorry I haven't kept in touch better. The time difference…"

"Don't worry about it, it's fine. It's just good to talk now." I hesitated. "What's up?"

There was a pause on the other end of the line, before she spoke again. When she did, her voice was hushed, as though she didn't want to be overheard. "I just wanted to check in. I…I was just wondering. Is Bear okay?"

"Why do you ask?" I said, rather than answering the question.

"I've tried to call him the last couple of days, and he's not answering. He's not answering his texts, either. That's not really like him."

"When was the last time you talked to him?" I asked. Reaver had ventured away from me, though he was moving very carefully, his attention riveted on the world around.

"Tuesday night," she said promptly. "It wasn't a good conversation."

Now why wasn't I surprised about that? "What time did you speak to him? Do you remember?"

"About eleven my time, so a lot later for him. Probably two a.m. He didn't sound good—he was very upset." She sniffled wetly, and I realized she was crying. "He wouldn't tell me what was wrong, just kept saying that we shouldn't talk anymore. He said it was messing with his head."

"He broke up with you," I said.

Another pause. When she spoke again, she sounded confused. "Well... No. We broke up before I left. He didn't tell you? I didn't want to," she added hastily. "But he kept talking about all these opportunities I would have here. These other guys I could date. I told him, I'm not interested in dating somebody else. But then I thought, perhaps he had girls he would like to see. I didn't want to tie him down."

"I understand, sweetie," I said. "It's not an easy situation for either of you. So, he didn't tell you anything about what had been going on that night? Where he'd been?"

"No, but I've never heard him more upset. It sounded like he might have been crying—and you know Bear just isn't that type of guy. He kept saying he'd messed up. That I shouldn't waste any more time on him."

It wasn't lost on me that none of this sounded good for Bear, and certainly didn't clear him of anything that had happened at Nancy's. An edge of my earlier headache returned.

"Ren, did he say anything about being at Nancy Davis's house that night?"

"No," she said. "But I saw everything that's been

happening, on news sites online. I can't believe it. Were you able to get any of the animals? There's a dog..."

"Reaver?" I asked.

She laughed, though it sounded a little bit sad. A little bit broken. "Yes. Reaver. Bear loves that dog—he's been furious with Nancy over him for months. I don't think I've ever seen him angrier."

Wonderful. I made a mental note to try and keep Ren from the witness stand, if it ever came to that.

"Well, we have him now. But there have been some developments that I wanted to talk to you about—I'm really glad you called, actually."

I went on to tell her about Bear's arrest, and my own suspicion that he might in fact have something to do with Nancy's death. Or, at the very least, be hiding something about that night. Ren was predictably horrified to hear that Bear had been arrested, but she couldn't give me much in the way of additional information that might shed light on what he'd been doing before he called her that night.

"I planned to stop calling," Ren said, when I was finished. "I really meant to, after our conversation that night. But I just had this feeling there was something he hadn't said, and I couldn't shake it. I know he wants me to leave him alone. I will after this, I promise. I don't want him to feel as though I'm some crazed stalker—"

"I promise you, sweetie. Bear doesn't think of you as a crazed stalker. I think he's trying to do what's best for you, but you should know that this is ripping him to pieces, too. You know how moody he can get, but he's taken it to a whole new level since you left. I agree with him—with both of you... You're young. The space to grow is important,

I think, even if it does hurt like hell. But don't think for a minute that he's not hurting too. That he doesn't miss you every day. I know he does."

She sniffled again, and took a deep, steadying breath. "Thank you. I've known on some level that he hasn't been coping well—I've been very worried about him, especially after our conversation the other night." She hesitated. "You said you were trying to figure out what he was doing that night, before he talked to me? The night that Nancy died?"

"That's right. Bear's treating it like it's some kind of state secret, but the police aren't going to take kindly to that much longer."

"You should talk to Julie Monroe," Ren said. There was no mistaking the disdain in her voice when she said the name. "If there's a chance that he was near Nancy's that night, my guess is that he was there to see Julie. She's been trying to get him alone from the day she first laid eyes on him. I know how happy she was to find out I'd left, and Bear has always been…" She paused again. "I think he might have had a crush, too. She's very pretty."

I fought the urge to say something about that—about how much prettier Ren was than her, and how if Bear really had any interest in a vapid little twit like Julie Monroe, he clearly had some growing up to do. But there were definitely some boundaries I should be maintaining in all this, and I had to keep reminding myself of just how young these two were. Bear was right: they needed time apart. They needed to grow up and see the world. The last thing either of them needed was me poking my nose in, trying to keep them together through all this.

"I'll look into it," I said instead. "Thank you."

We talked for a few minutes more, while I got updates on her father and Minion—her dog—and gave her all the latest news on Windfall Island. By the time I got off the phone, we'd been chatting for half an hour, and Reaver had found a spot in the sun and was resting peacefully on his side, his eyes closed. On the other side of the fence, Phantom had gotten as close as she could to the fencing and had likewise settled in. She didn't look nearly as peaceful, however. In fact, she looked more than a little bit peeved.

"If I didn't know any better, I'd say you've got a little bit of a crush, Phan," I said to the dog.

She didn't dignify that with any response, but she watched with interest as I approached Reaver with the muzzle in hand.

I definitely expected a fight this time around, but Reaver didn't even seem fazed at sight of the large plastic basket muzzle I was carrying. He sat obediently with his head up, and didn't so much as flinch as I strapped the bulky equipment over his face. It was an awkward fit because he had such a broad, short nose, but I managed to make it work.

With that added insurance, I went to the gate and let Phantom in. She went to Reaver without hesitation, and the two greeted one another with more polite sniffs. Then, Phantom blew my mind completely by lowering her aging bones into a play bow, her behind in the air and her tail wagging like she was a puppy.

Reaver took a short, quick step back, his own tail wagging. He pranced two steps forward. Lowered himself into a bow. The muzzle was clearly in the way, but I gave it another ten minutes of careful scrutiny before I went over and removed it from the pit bull.

Completely free now, he charged Phantom only to stop short with a quick, playful bark before he took off again. Phantom charged after him. He let her catch him, and the two collided. Growls erupted from both dogs, but it was clear that they were play vocalizations—there was no threat here. Quite the opposite. Phantom was four years old before I got her, so I never got a chance to see her playing as a puppy or adolescent dog, and she'd never been particularly interested in play with any other dogs. Apparently, she'd just been waiting for Reaver.

They played for only a few minutes more before Reaver was panting heavily, his thin sides heaving. Phantom settled herself back down without the need for any commands, and the two of them wandered the field together until they found a patch of sun big enough to share. Ignoring me completely, they lay down with bodies touching and closed their eyes.

I shook my head. How had Nancy gotten it so completely, devastatingly wrong about this dog?

23

WHILE JAMIE WAS BUSY doing whatever it was she needed to do to work through this whole nightmare, Jack returned to his apartment. He had a headache—a hell of a headache actually, but that was understandable given everything that had happened last night at Nancy's.

Thoughts of Nancy's inevitably led to thoughts of Jamie *after* Nancy's... Jamie, in his bed with him. Jamie, in his arms. They'd kissed. If he hadn't been concussed, he was willing to bet they would have done a lot more than that. Yet when he'd gotten up this morning, he was disappointed to find that the world hadn't had the decency to even pause to let them sleep in and revel in the moment. Instead, things had gotten exponentially worse while they were out. He knew from experience that life wasn't fair, but was it really necessary to hammer that lesson home with quite this much venom?

To distract himself—and because it was clearly necessary—he changed the cats' litter boxes, spent a few minutes playing with the kittens, and made his bed. His thoughts returned once more to Jamie and the time they had spent together, and he once more set that aside.

There were more important things to worry about right now. Chief among them, figuring out how to get Bear cleared of Nancy Davis's murder. Jack considered what had happened in her house. What he had found there. He'd taken photos of Nancy's bedroom—specifically, the skull in the secret hideaway behind her bed. Would they even be able to find it among the rubble now that the house had burned to the ground? It wasn't as though he could just hand Sophie the skull to test and see if it did indeed match the headless skeleton in the basement. It seemed like a safe bet, though.

Jamie's hunch that there could be a connection between Reaver and the Mississippi ex-con made sense. Now, Jack just needed to test that theory. Maybe taking out that single ex-con had been the thing that led to Nancy's death. If someone had found out…

He frowned, then thought the case through once more. Three bodies in the basement. There had to be more—he was almost positive of that. Were they buried in the basement? It seemed unlikely, considering the way the others had simply been left down there. No. Any other victims would have to be somewhere else on the property.

Was Barbara Monroe's husband truly among them?

Fred Davis was clearly still fond of Barbara. He may not have a relationship with the daughter, but Jack had seen firsthand how hard the man was trying to create one. Trying to insinuate himself into Barbara's life in whatever way he could. That hardly meant the man had killed Barbara's husband, though—if he knew about the deaths on the property, he would also know that evicting his mother meant any bodies would be discovered as soon as the place was vacated.

Unless he planned on going in before the house was sold, and cleaning up whatever messes had been left.

Jack frowned.

"But if he killed his mother, he had to know the police would come in and turn the place upside down," Jack said aloud.

"Prrrt," Cash replied, as he came into the office with the little black kitten close behind. The other four tended to do their own thing, but this little guy was never far from Cash. Always with tail puffed out and back up, a kitten with attitude from the get-go. Harvey Danger—that was the name Jack would call him, if he were to keep the kitten. Which he, of course, would not be doing.

"What do you think?" he asked Cash.

Cash wended his way over and hopped up on the desk. Harvey Danger couldn't make the leap, though, and instead sat at Jack's feet and mewed indignantly at being left behind.

Jack picked him up, smiling at the hissing little fuzzball.

"You need to chill out, Harvey," he informed the kitten. "You're cute, but you can't just trade on your looks. I don't know how many people will want to adopt a little black hellcat."

He stood, and went to the window with the kitten still in his arms. As though he'd understood Jack's warning, Harvey changed his tune and snuggled closer with a low, awkward purr.

"That's better," Jack said softly. He looked out the window at the street below. It was another gorgeous day, not a cloud in the sky. His thoughts shifted back to Bear, stuck in a jail cell right now.

They had to get him out. Some guys might be able to handle a place like that, but Bear wasn't one. He'd been ready to climb out of his skin just being stuck in Jack's office for those few minutes the other day.

In the street below, Jack watched idly as Mel emerged from the Loyal Biscuit and added water to a dog bowl on the sidewalk. There was a steady stream of customers going in and out—apparently, a sunny Saturday in July was prime shopping time for the local store. Suddenly, Jack remembered the collar he'd found in Nancy's kitchen.

He set Harvey Danger down, laced up his sneakers, and rushed out the door.

The Biscuit's Main Street entrance was open, but Jack had to wait for several people to come and go before he finally made it in. They were having a nail clipping clinic in addition to the usual Saturday foot traffic, which Jack supposed explained the rush. Regardless, he went inside gamely to see if he could find someone to help him out.

"Hey, handsome," Mel called from across the store, as soon as she caught sight of him. "How are the kittens doing?"

It took him a second to realize she was talking to him. "They're good," he said. A golden retriever puppy nearly bowled him over from behind, a little boy on the other end of the leash. Jack stepped aside. Several other kids were crowded around a large black cage, where two kittens slept snuggled together in a hammock while two others played with a plastic ball on the floor of the cage.

"Another couple of weeks, and you can bring your guys in here," Mel said. "I saw the pictures—between that and the press, I bet all five will be adopted out by the end of the day."

He frowned. A little girl stuck her finger through the cage, and Jack turned away. "Yeah. Maybe," he agreed reluctantly.

"Uh oh," Mel said with a sly grin.

"What?"

"You can't adopt all of them, you know. They have to go sometime. Trust me, I know—I've got a house full of fosters I couldn't stand to see leave."

"I know," he said. "I'm not adopting them all. I'm ready to give them up whenever Tracy says it's time."

"Mmhm," she said. Clearly, she didn't believe him. "How's the head? I heard about the fire last night. Nancy's got flattened, huh?"

"I guess so—I haven't seen it since Jamie pulled me out of there. How'd you know I was there?"

"Joel was at the station last night. He mentioned it."

"Oh." Jack had no idea who Joel was, but decided asking would mean getting more information than he really needed at this point. He was just about to change the subject by asking about the collar when several customers came up to the counter at once to check out. He stepped aside.

Across the store and up the stairs to the open second floor, he saw Heidi—the store owner—emerge from her office. Halfway down the stairs, she grinned at sight of him.

"Hey, Jack. How's the kitten business?"

Others in the store stopped to look at him, and he was suddenly very conscious of the bandage on his forehead and the sling on his right arm. He weaved his way through the crowd to the pretty blond woman, her eyes sharp when she took in his appearance.

"Joel mentioned you had a rough night. Everything okay?"

"It is," he agreed, then hesitated. "I'm sorry—Mel said the same thing. Who's Joel?"

Heidi laughed. "My husband. He's a cop—Rockland PD."

"Ah. That makes more sense."

Those keen eyes studied him a moment more, and her brow furrowed. "Is there something I can help you with?"

He hesitated, but only for a moment before he forged gamely on. "I hope so. If someone bought a collar from here, would you have a record of it? A way to trace who actually made the purchase?"

"Depends," she said. "If they're regular customers with an account here, we would. If they don't have an account, I might still be able to track it through a credit card."

"Would you do that for me? Find out who bought a certain collar, I mean?"

She hesitated. "That's all the information you're looking for? Just a name—no credit card info, no phone number, no address?"

"Just a name," he assured her.

She looked around the bustling store. "It's a little busy right now. Could I do it and get the list to you later?"

"Absolutely. That would be great."

"So... Which collar are we talking about?"

He went to the wall of collars and selected the red, white, and blue collar with lobsters that he'd seen on Nancy's table, making sure he'd gotten the correct size—large. Then, he returned to Heidi and placed it in her waiting hand.

"It's this one. That was the size, design, everything."

"It's a popular one," she said uncertainly. "Any idea how long ago this person got it?"

He considered. "Not more than three months, I think. Can you go back that far?"

She rolled her eyes, just a little. "Can I go back that far? Please." She grinned. "Yeah, I can go back that far. I'll give you a call once I get the list. If you don't hear back, check in before closing tonight. Sound good?"

"Sounds perfect. Thank you."

She waved off his thanks, and turned to answer an onslaught of questions from employees and customers alike. If this was what small-town sleuthing would be, Jack could definitely get used to it.

Jack was feeling far from at his best when he returned to his apartment. His headache was roaring, and he recalled the doctor's advice to stay quiet and resting for at least twenty-four hours with a grimace. Now hardly seemed like the time to take a break, but he did allow himself a few minutes on the sofa with tea, aspirin, and the kittens to take his mind off his troubles.

They seemed to be getting the hang of apartment living, and he was grateful that they likewise appeared to be shifting to a more people-friendly schedule. Phantom had been good at keeping the rowdy little fuzzballs quiet overnight; maybe it would be good to have her around on a regular basis. He considered that. Jamie had a lot going on out on the island—it wasn't as though she could just hop to the mainland whenever the kittens needed to be set straight again. Of course, he wouldn't actually have the kittens for that long...

The smallest of the five, a fuzzy orange female he'd taken to calling Jasper before Jamie gently explained that Jasper was a little girl, climbed up the leg of his jeans with pointy, newly discovered claws. She mewed the entire way, and then gazed at him triumphantly with deep blue eyes when she reached his knee.

"You're starting to get the hang of that," Jack congratulated her, and plucked her from his knee to rest on his chest. Two of the others—both tabbies, named

Marco and Polo—came barreling up his leg after her, and he winced when the sharp claws made it through the denim and into his skin.

"Ouch. See, this is why I got that climbing thing," he said. He stood, with Jasper in his arms and Marco and Polo clinging to his leg, while Cash and Harvey Danger watched him. The fifth kitten—a quiet, pudgy orange and white male Jack had taken to calling Zen—sat watching the action, apparently content to play spectator. Jack took the hangers-on to the cat tower he'd purchased from the Loyal Biscuit, and set each of them on a different limb.

While he watched them explore, his thoughts returned to Nancy Davis and the twin cases he was supposed to be solving. He still couldn't believe the police had already arrested Bear. Unless they had some ace up their sleeve they'd discovered at Nancy's, or else someone who had actually witnessed him killing the old woman, then they couldn't possibly expect to hold him. They were probably just trying to scare him, forcing him to spend the entire weekend behind bars to think about any lies he might be telling them. It was an old strategy, but not ineffective.

He sat around for a few minutes more before it became apparent that this wasn't a productive way to spend his time. At shortly past eleven o'clock, he locked up the apartment and headed out to meet with Barbara Monroe. The person he really wanted to talk to was Bear, but he decided to wait until he had an opportunity to talk to Jamie first. He resisted the urge to call her, knowing how much she had on her plate right now.

When Jack reached Barbara's house, her Prius was in the driveway. He parked next to it, then hesitated a moment before he got out. Julie was out back, tending a small garden patch in the sunshine. She wore short jean cutoffs and a sleeveless shirt that showed her belly, her hair pulled back in a ponytail. When she straightened, she stretched her body to reveal not just her flat stomach, but the lace-trimmed edge of her bra. There was no doubt in Jack's mind that she was well aware of his presence. She caught sight of Jack watching her, and smiled at him. Lifted a hand, and waved.

Jack looked away.

He waited a moment, hoping she would return to her gardening, but instead she started toward his car. He groaned inwardly, and got out.

"I heard what happened last night at Nancy's place," she began when she was a few feet away. "Are you okay?"

Had someone put out a press release without him knowing? "I'm fine."

She crowded closer, reaching up on tiptoes to touch his bandage. "Are you sure? This looks bad."

He stepped away, ducking his head to get away from her. "Positive—the doctor cleared me. No problem. Is your mother around? I was hoping to talk to her."

"She's inside." She jerked her head toward the house with a grimace. "Nursing a hangover. Don't tell her I said that, she'd kill me," she added, voice lowered conspiratorially.

"I won't," he said. She was waiting for him to ask questions about that revelation, but he remained silent. It wasn't his business if Barbara Monroe occasionally overindulged—hell, it wouldn't be his business if she got rip-roaring drunk and danced on tabletops every night.

Besides which, he wasn't sure how much of what Julie Monroe said he actually believed. She reminded him too much of the girls during the witch trials who sent innocent women to their deaths on a whim.

"I'll see you later," he said brusquely. "Enjoy the day—it's supposed to be beautiful again."

He turned from her and started toward the house. She called after him before he'd gone three steps.

"Mr. Juarez?"

He turned back around. "Yes?"

"Is it true that Bear got arrested this morning?" For the first time, he caught what appeared to be genuine emotion in her eyes.

"Where did you hear that?"

"Fred." She wrinkled her nose in distaste. "He was here this morning first thing, to let us know they found Albie. He said Albie told them that Bear did it—Bear murdered Nancy."

"Do you believe that's true?"

"I don't know." Her expression was guarded. "It's hard to believe, right? Bear's so gentle. I can't see him losing it so bad that he'd actually hurt somebody. Even Nancy. She was horrible, and I know Bear hated her. Still..." She trailed off, but something in her tone suggested she had more to say on the subject.

"Do you know anything more about what happened that night?" he asked.

"Me? No—I told the police, I was asleep with my headphones on. I didn't see anything. I didn't talk to anybody after it happened."

He registered the words, and kept his tone neutral when he followed up. "Did you talk to someone *before* it happened?"

The fear in her eyes was enough to tell him he was on the right track. "Did you talk to Bear that night, Julie? Did you see him?"

"Jack!" He heard a familiar voice call from behind him. The fear flashed deeper in Julie's face, and she shook her head.

"I have to go. I already told the police: I don't know anything." She hesitated. "If you talk to Bear, will you tell him I said hi? And...tell him I'm sorry, okay? I'm sorry about this whole mess."

And with that, she turned and fled, returning to her garden with a last backward glance. Jack suppressed the urge to go after her, since Barbara was already waving him inside from the front door.

Barbara wore snug-fitting jeans and a fitted T-shirt, her hair down around her shoulders. Her feet were bare, and—despite her daughter's words—her eyes were bright, and he saw no trace that she was suffering any ill effects.

"Can I get you some tea? The way Fred described what happened last night, I'm surprised to see you out and about. I would have thought you'd be in the hospital."

"No," he said, shaking his head. "I'm fine."

He followed her into the house. The date beside the door said 1790, and Jack shook his head as he passed the threshold and took in the details of the antique colonial.

"This is beautiful," Jack said honestly.

"Thanks," she said. She led him into a bright, spacious kitchen with checkerboard linoleum tiles and antiqued, custom cabinetry. An enamel Viking range stood at one wall, and Jack admired it from a distance.

"You should have seen this place when we first bought it. It was a disaster."

"You fixed it up yourselves?"

"Tim's a cabinet maker, and I always wanted to be an interior designer. It's been our pet project."

"I thought your husband was a salesman."

She shook her head with a sad smile. "That was what paid—he got a job with a company that makes these awful, cookie cutter kitchens... He's good looking, he knows what he's talking about. He does very well for them."

"He did the work in here?" Jack asked. He walked the length of the kitchen, running a finger along the cabinetry.

"All of it. We salvaged all the wood we could from an old three-story barn on the property, and used a lot of that. Tim didn't want to use anything new—he always says everything people make today is crap. He'd rather use boards fifty years old than something most lumber companies put out today. It's the way they harvest the trees or something." She shrugged, nostalgia in her eyes. "I don't know—he's given me the lecture a thousand times in the past twenty years."

Jack sat at a roughly hewn kitchen table, also homemade by the look of it, while Barbara put on tea water and set a mug and a selection of teas in front of him. He passed over the overwhelming array of herbal tea in favor of basic black, and waited for her to join him. When she finally sat down, after pouring hot water for him and then herself, she settled into her chair with the heavy sigh of a much older woman. She looked at Jack wearily.

"I saw you talking to Julie out there," she said. She looked away a moment, rolling her eyes. "I appreciate you not encouraging her. I don't know what's going on with her. She used to be this..." She shook her head, then looked at Jack full-on again. "All she ever used to do was read. All the time—we couldn't get that kid's nose out of a book. She started on Harry Potter when she was six or seven, and I don't think she stopped until she was fourteen or fifteen. She and Tim were inseparable. This job has been hard on her."

"So he hasn't worked for the kitchen company that long?"

"Three years in August. We were trying to build up our own business—we worked like dogs at that for fifteen years. When we first got together, we had all these ideas of what it would be like. We'd become rich and famous, have our own show on HGTV, our own line of books on colonial décor and renovation."

Jack flashed a sympathetic smile, thinking inexplicably of his own wife, Lucia. Of the daughter she was carrying when she was murdered; the dreams they'd whispered to one another across the pillow a thousand lifetimes ago. "Life doesn't always go the way you hope."

"No. No, it doesn't. Anyway, Julie started changing after he took the job. I don't know if it was because of that or just teenage hormones, or some combination of the two. It didn't help that all the ways she'd been awkward-looking and clumsy disappeared overnight, and suddenly the sweet little girl we had was…" She shook her head. "…gorgeous. We never really saw it coming—I wish I'd prepared her for the change better."

"You couldn't have known."

She laughed, fixing him with pretty green eyes rimmed with thick lashes. "Sure I could. I lived it. I know what boys turn into around that age, especially when they're around a beautiful girl; I know how crass and dehumanizing men can be to attractive teenage girls."

She sighed again, and took a sip of her tea before she set it down and looked at Jack again. "Anyway, that's not why you're here. Is there something I can tell you? I assume you would have stopped my babbling if you had news about Tim."

"Nothing yet," he said regretfully. "But I did have a couple of questions. Specifically, I wanted to talk to you about Fred Davis."

She looked surprised. "Fred? Sure. What can I tell you?"

"You dated when the two of you were in high school?"

She looked surprised at that, forehead furrowing. "No—we knew each other, but we didn't really move in the same circles. Later, we became friends. But we definitely never dated."

"Why would someone tell me that you had?"

"I don't know," she said. "Who did you hear it from?"

He traced the story back, considering. "I think someone said it over at the Loyal Biscuit. And Fred said something about your history, the other night."

"Our history? There's hardly enough between us to even use the word." She looked genuinely confused. "I'm sorry, but there's not a lot I can tell you about him. I know more about him from moving into this house than from any time we spent together in school."

"Such as?" Jack pressed.

"Nothing specific," she said. "I know he's always had a hard time holding down a job, at least until this latest thing. He's worked at the insurance place for a few years now. I'm happy for him—it seems like he's finally finding his way. I think he just needed to get some distance from Nancy."

"So, he's never asked you out on a date, anything like that?"

She hesitated. "When was the last time?" he pressed, reading her response.

"A couple of days ago," she admitted.

Jack stayed for another few minutes to ask more questions about Tim's co-workers and any contacts he might be able to reach to try and locate her missing husband, but he was going through the motions. There was no doubt about it: when it came to not only Nancy's death, but the other bodies in the basement, it seemed almost every road led back to Fred. The exception was the ex-con, but Jack hadn't investigated the man thoroughly enough to write that off completely. Finally, with more questions than answers, Jack finished off his tea and stood.

"You don't happen to know where Fred is staying right now, do you?" he asked at the door.

"He mentioned staying at a hotel in Rockland—Harborside. It's kind of a dive. I told him he could stay here, but he said he needed to deal with Albie first. Of course, as soon as Julie heard that, she threw such a fit that I'm hoping he doesn't decide to take me up on the offer."

"She doesn't like Fred, then," Jack said.

Barbara opened the door, and walked with him to his car. "She doesn't like a lot of people," Barbara said. "It doesn't necessarily mean anything. I think she's just afraid he's trying to take her father's place."

This made sense, Jack thought, considering that Fred clearly had designs on the woman.

A moment later they reached his car, and Jack noted that Julie was still in the garden, trying very hard not to look like she was watching him.

"I know I haven't given you much about your husband yet," Jack said, "but I promise, I am working on it. I have a couple of leads I'd like to follow over the next twenty-four hours. I should have a status report and some answers for you by Monday."

"Thank you," she said. She met his gaze, and for the first time he saw the weariness she hid so well. "At this point, I feel like I almost don't want to know. Like it would be better to just have the hope that one day he'll walk through the front door and we can be a family again. He'll tell us he was in a car wreck in the middle of nowhere and had amnesia, and then one day he woke up and it all came back to him."

Jack nodded soberly. "I understand. And that's your prerogative, if you'd prefer to have me stop looking."

"No." She shook her head, brushing at a stray tear. "We need to know. It's better for both Julie and me. It just doesn't feel like that sometimes."

"I'll be in touch soon," he promised.

He drove away with mother and daughter in the rearview mirror—Barbara watching from the driveway, Julie still covertly following his movement from the garden. He took a deep breath, trying to shake the look in both women's eyes. It would be wonderful to live in a world where husbands who went missing for months at a time simply returned one day, unscathed, to step back into their daily lives.

Jack had never lived in that world, though.

He turned on the radio, mouth set in a grim line, and set out to talk to Fred Davis.

24

HARBORSIDE WAS A HOTEL/MOTEL off the main strip in Rockland, with only a few cars in the parking lot despite the busy season. Once Jack stepped inside, he understood why. The lighting was dim, the carpeting was dingy, and it looked like the place hadn't had an update—or a thorough cleaning—since Nixon left office. According to the desk manager, Fred had checked out early that morning. He'd had his brother with him, and Albie was clearly agitated.

"I thought about calling the police," the man—Ralph—told Jack. Ralph barely topped five-foot-four, but easily weighed two hundred and fifty pounds, with sparse black hair and a thick mustache straight from 1970s-era porn.

"But you didn't call?" Jack asked.

Ralph shrugged. "Not my business."

"Was the brother here overnight, or did he just come in this morning?"

"This morning. He still had his hospital bracelet on. The way he was acting, I figured he just got out of the psych ward. And maybe they shouldn't have been so quick to let him go."

"Did either of them mention where they were going when they left?"

"Nope," the man said. "And they must've forgotten to leave a forwarding address. Imagine that."

Jack ignored his sarcasm. "Here's my card," he said, sliding it and a fifty-dollar bill across the counter. "Call me if you think of anything else, or you hear from either of them."

The manager took the money, flashing a smile that revealed yellowed false teeth and one glinting silver cap. "Sure thing."

Jack turned to go, then had a thought and turned back. "Has housekeeping been to the room yet?"

"Sylvia, you mean? She's my wife. She's not in yet."

"Any chance I could take a look?"

"Any chance you got another fifty in there?"

Jack took out a twenty. Ralph didn't bother negotiating, handing over the key without argument. "Where's the room?" Jack asked.

"Second floor, last door down. Elevator's broken, you'll have to take the stairs."

Jack was planning to.

Fred's bed was unmade, his sheets in a heap on the floor. Apart from that, though, there was nothing remarkable about the room. The bathroom was no dirtier than it had likely been when Fred checked in, and he found no notepad with an address conveniently left behind to indicate where the man might have gone next. Using a tissue, he picked through the trash bucket beside a well-worn desk in the corner. Three beer bottles—Budweiser—and a half-eaten bucket of KFC. He dropped it with distaste when he realized it was crawling with ants, and brushed himself off with a shiver. He'd survived all manner of horrors between the military and the FBI, but none of that had changed his distaste for bugs.

As he was stepping away, a blue slip of paper at the bottom of the trash basket caught his eye. Nose wrinkled, he pushed his way through until he reached it and pulled it out quickly, shaking the ants off before he looked more closely.

It was an envelope, issued by US Air. Two ticket stubs were inside, with today's date. Destination: Halifax, Nova Scotia.

Fred was leaving the country.

Jack took out his phone and scanned recent calls until he found what he was looking for, and pressed Send. It took three rings, but finally Sheriff Finnegan picked up.

"How's the concussion, Mr. Juarez?" Finnegan asked.

"It's fine," he said shortly. "Fred Davis is taking his brother and skipping town. Can you talk to someone about stopping him at the airport? He's got a flight booked for this afternoon."

There was a pause on the line. Finnegan said something to someone on the other end of the line, and he heard a door slam before the sheriff spoke again.

"You want to run that by me again?"

"Fred and Albie left—they're headed to Nova Scotia."

"And you know this how, exactly?"

Jack frowned. "I can't reveal my sources."

"Uh huh."

"It's already two o'clock—we don't have much time. They'll be checking in with security now, all it takes is a phone call. Unfortunately, it's not one I can make."

"I thought Albie was in the hospital."

"Fred must have checked him out this morning."

"I'll check into it," Finnegan said. He didn't sound happy. "But neither of these guys are under arrest. We asked them not to leave town, but it wasn't an order."

"They're not leaving town, they're leaving the country."

"Canada has extradition to the U.S. for criminals, it's not like they're off to Mexico or something."

"Maybe Fred doesn't know about the extradition laws. Either way, it's going to be a pain in the ass trying to get them back here, and in the meantime Bear Flint is stuck behind bars with a murder charge hanging over his head."

"That wasn't up to me," Finnegan said immediately. "That was the Staties."

"Well, they made the wrong call and you know it. As far as I'm concerned, Fred running now more than proves that."

Finnegan sighed over the line. "Let me make a couple of calls. I'll get in touch with you once I hear anything."

They hung up, and Jack took a photo of the tickets, returned them to the waste basket, and left the room. If the police ended up actually following up and coming here, he wanted to be sure they were able to find any evidence Fred had left behind.

He returned to his apartment at three-thirty to find Jamie's truck parked in front of his building and Jamie waiting for him at the street entrance, Phantom by her side. Phantom waved her tail at him and stood, which was about as much enthusiasm as he'd seen the dog greet anyone with. Jamie held out a coffee for him, and flashed a smile that made him pause. It was a good smile. Weighted, it was true, but definitely genuine.

"Thanks," he said, accepting the coffee. "I'm surprised to see you here—I thought you'd be back on the island. Is everything okay?"

At the look on her face, he amended the statement. "I mean, did anything else happen? I know everything isn't okay, obviously."

"No," she said. "I've been out there working since I left Bear this morning, but I feel like there are things I should be doing here. Something to get him out, instead of just trekking all over the island cleaning up dog crap and filing llama teeth."

"You file llama's teeth?" he asked. "I didn't even know that was a thing."

"I don't do it personally, I just helped out this morning. The point is…"

"You feel like you should be doing more."

"Or something else." She sighed. "I need to feel like I'm helping to get him out of there."

"How's he doing?" Jack asked.

She looked around, and hesitated. "Let's talk inside, okay? Small towns have big ears."

"True—and this town's ears are enormous," he agreed. He unlocked the door, and stepped aside as Jamie and the dog went up.

This time, Cash barely bothered getting his back up when Phantom came through the door. Now that was progress. The kittens rushed the dog immediately, but Phantom didn't seem particularly overwhelmed by them. Instead, she trotted into the next room with the lot of them in pursuit.

"You're sure she'll be okay?"

"She'll be fine," Jamie assured him.

They stood in the entryway to his apartment awkwardly for a moment before Jack ushered her in. "Can I get you anything? I was going to make a sandwich—I missed lunch. Have you eaten?"

"I have," she said. "But you can go ahead."

She followed him into the kitchen and sat down.

"So… Bear?" he prompted as he pulled out sandwich fixings. He got no response, and looked to find her seated at the table staring into space. "Jamie?"

"Sorry," she said, coming to. She shook her head, as though bringing herself back from somewhere very far away. She sighed. "I don't know. He's…different. Distant. He won't talk to me about anything anymore. It's not like he was ever a chatterbox when it came to his feelings, but when he was little he at least used to tell me some things. Now, everything's a secret with him."

"He didn't kill her, Jamie."

"I know that," she said impatiently. "I know he didn't. I just wish I knew what in hell he's thinking right now."

"I'm not sure *he* knows what he's thinking right now."

"Ren called me this morning," she said. He looked at her in surprise. "He was talking to her the night Nancy was killed—when I got the call from Tracy about everything, Bear was up. He said he'd been on the phone with Ren. She confirmed that, so at least I know he wasn't lying about that. It was good to talk to her. I'd been wanting to ask her some questions about him."

"And?"

She shrugged. "She misses him. He misses her. She thinks something happened that night, but she doesn't know what—when he called her, he was upset. But he didn't tell her why."

Jack nodded. He wasn't particularly hungry at this point, but he dutifully finished off his sandwich and put the mayo, mustard, bread, and cold cuts back in the refrigerator before he sat down beside Jamie. She looked at the sandwich, and smiled.

"What?"

"That's quite a sandwich," she noted.

"Gotta eat," he said with a shrug. "What did you have?"

"Clif Bar and some water." He frowned at that, cut his sandwich in half, and pushed one half toward her.

"Eat," he ordered.

"It's got meat in it."

He opened the sandwich up and took out the sliced turkey and ham, leaving the cheese and vegetables before he slapped the other piece of bread back on and pushed it back. "Okay?"

Her smile widened. "Thank you." She ate the half sandwich without complaint while Jack told her what he'd learned over the course of the afternoon. She was particularly interested in what he had to say about Julie, and he could tell from her reaction that she didn't trust the girl. What really made her sit up and take notice, however, was his news that Fred and Albie had apparently skipped town.

"I don't understand—the police told them not to leave, right? They must be suspects in at least one of these deaths."

"I don't know exactly what their thinking is, but they're not going to like the fact that Fred just took off like this." He hesitated, studying her a moment. "It could actually work in your favor, though. As far as I know, Albie is the chief witness placing Bear at the scene—Barbara Monroe said she heard fighting and saw Bear there, but Albie is the one who's tied him directly to the crime. If he's no longer in the picture, I don't think they'll be able to hold Bear any longer. I'm still not clear on how they were able to get a warrant in the first place, but no one in their right mind is going to actually move forward with charges on what little they have."

Her eyes widened, a flicker of hope there that brought a smile to his lips. "When can we get him out, then?"

"Not until Monday—he'll have to stay until then. I'm not positive," he added quickly. "They could have evidence I don't know about. But unless that's the case, I think you'll probably be able to get him out without the need to even post bond. He just has to get through the weekend."

"That's good." She let out a breath that he suspected she'd been holding for a very long time. "That's really good."

The front buzzer to his apartment sounded before he could reply. He went to the door and pressed the intercom button.

"Who is it?"

"I didn't know people had these anymore," a disembodied male voice said. "Only in Rockland. Heidi sent me over—I've got that list you asked for."

He glanced at the clock. It was quarter past five—he'd completely forgotten about his earlier visit to the Loyal Biscuit.

"Come on up," he said, buzzing the mystery man in.

"This is about the collar you found?" Jamie asked. She sat on the couch with Zen in her lap, while Marco, Polo, and Jasper chased Phantom's tail. Cash and Harvey Danger, meanwhile, continued to skulk around the perimeter of the room glowering at the dog.

"Yeah," he said. "I don't know if it will do any good, but I'm hoping it will give us some kind of information. I've got a call into a friend in the Army, too. He might be able to give us some information on Reaver."

"Without an ID number?" Jamie asked doubtfully.

He shrugged. "It's worth a shot."

A knock at the door interrupted the conversation, and

he opened up to find Mike waiting there with a manila envelope in hand.

"No tip necessary," he said when Jack opened the door, not bothering with a greeting, "if you'll tell me why you needed these names."

Jack looked at Jamie. Jamie looked at Mike. The kittens looked at the open door, and would have made a break for it if Phantom hadn't herded them out of the way. Jack quickly ushered Mike in and shut the door behind him.

"Heidi didn't say anything?" Jack asked.

"No," Mike said. "I had to give her five bucks to get her to let me bring these over. Hey, Jamie." He nodded toward the dog handler, who smiled at him.

"Hey, Mike. How are Tippy and Maggie?"

"Neurotic—no more than usual, though. Sounds like you guys are having quite a run over on the island. You coming to the fundraiser on Friday? Trackside's hosting, so there should be a good turnout."

"I'll be there," she promised. She stood and approached, eyeing the envelope he still held. "So, what have you got there?"

"It's a long list," Mike said.

"Why don't you come in," Jack said. "It's more comfortable in the kitchen. You want tea?"

"Do you have beer?"

"Sure." He squelched a smile. Anyone else and he felt sure Mike's shtick would get old, but he found himself inexplicably charmed. "Sam Adams okay?"

"Perfect."

The other man took in every detail of the apartment as Jack led him into the kitchen, where he and Jamie both sat while Jack served up a beer for each of them. He'd offered

Jamie more tea, and she had surprised him with a request for something a little stronger.

"Okay, so," Mike began, when they were all seated. "There's a whole page of names—that's for all the stores except Waterville. There's something going on with their system, so you'll have to wait a couple of days for that. But I'll follow up."

"And the time frame?" Jack asked.

"Past three months—that's what Heidi said you asked for."

"Can I ask," Jamie interrupted, looking at Mike, "why you're doing this? You don't even work at the store."

"I always thought I'd make a good detective," he said with a shrug. He looked slightly embarrassed. "This is a lot more interesting than the crap I do every day."

"Did any names jump out at you?" Jack asked.

"There are a few who had it in for Nancy," Mike said. "Not a surprise—she wasn't really topping anybody's Christmas list around here. But I took a few minutes and called most of the people who popped. Everybody could account for the collar they bought, so obviously they're not your guy."

Jack raised his eyebrows. Mike shrugged. "Sorry. Heidi told me what you told her; I figured out the rest."

"You said you called most of the people," Jamie said, steering the conversation back on track. "Who were the ones you didn't call?"

He frowned. "I'll let you take a look for yourself."

He took the list out, lay it on the table, and slid it toward her. Jack scooted closer and peered over her shoulder. About a dozen names were highlighted in yellow. Jack scanned them, aware that Mike had tensed perceptibly. At the last name, he understood why. Jamie looked away, and he knew she'd seen the same thing.

Bear Flint, right there in black and white.

"Bear bought one of these collars?" Jack asked Jamie.

"I don't know," she said. "He deals with a lot of dogs—it's not unusual for him to buy new collars or leashes from the store. This doesn't mean he was buying something for Reaver."

"Is there a way you can find out?" Jack pressed. "Would Monty know?"

"Monty's on his way down South to fish his daughter out of the belly of a hurricane. Therese or Sarah might know something, though." She looked at Mike. "Is there a way for you to tell what else he bought when he got this collar?"

"Sure," Mike said, with a nod. "I can look it up tonight if you want."

"This was two months ago," Jamie mused. "We had a shipment of dogs coming up from the South. A couple of them were pretty big. Bear might have gotten it for one of them."

"We'll check it out," Jack assured her.

"Any chance the police will be looking at this same list?" Mike asked.

Jack looked at him uneasily. "Not unless someone mentions it to them."

"Hey, I'm not going to say a thing. But... I mean, if someone asks me—"

"Tell them the truth," Jamie said quickly. "There's no reason to lie. Give them the same information you gave us."

"And if they ask why Jack Juarez was having the Biscuit look up this information?" he pressed, his sharp eyes scanning Jack's face.

"Whatever you need to tell them is fine," Jack said. He felt a momentary pang of unease, only slightly reassured when Mike shrugged.

"It's not like I know anything," he said. "Not really. I'll tell them you had us run the list—we didn't ask any questions beyond that. They're supposed to be the cops, right? If they want more answers than that, let 'em find them."

Mike's phone buzzed, and he checked his text messages with a sigh. "That's April. We're going out tonight—you two want to come? We could make a thing of it, I'll make some calls."

"We can't make it tonight," Jack said, with a shake of his head. "Another time, maybe?" He glanced at Jamie, encouraged when she nodded her agreement.

"Are you on stakeout tonight?" Mike asked. "Because I could tell April I've got something else to do."

"I'll let you know," Jack said.

"You've got my number."

After Mike had gone, Jack and Jamie dug into the list of Loyal Biscuit names.

"I didn't expect that," Jamie admitted. "It seems like you're making friends around here."

"It has gotten busy," Jack agreed. "I'm not sure what that's about, but I got very popular all of a sudden."

They were in the living room, surrounded by kittens and Cash and Phantom. Jamie sat on the floor with the lot of them, while Jack had taken the sofa. The evening air was just coming in through an open window, and it smelled like salt and summer. Jamie turned to look at him and tipped her head slightly, a little half smile on her lips. "I can't imagine why."

"No?" he asked. He slid to the floor beside her.

She studied him with a soft, frank gaze that seemed to miss nothing. "It could be the eyes."

He smiled. "Oh?"

She reached up and ran her hand along the side of his face. "Maybe the smile."

"I don't think Mike likes me for my eyes or my smile."

"Maybe not," she agreed, her voice quiet. She leaned in until their mouths brushed lightly, her hand still on his face.

And then, there was a knock at the door.

Jack groaned.

"Wow," Jamie said. She pulled away. "You really are popular. You think it's Mike again?"

"No," he said. "I'm actually expecting someone else."

She looked at him curiously, but he didn't reply to her unspoken question. Instead, he rose and answered the door. Jamie scrambled to her feet to follow alongside.

25

JACK ANSWERED THE DOOR a moment later to find a very uncomfortable-looking Julie Monroe standing on the doorstep. She'd changed out of her cutoff jeans and T-shirt, and now wore a pretty summer dress that he found considerably more acceptable than her earlier attire. He was struck again by just how much the girl looked like her mother, from her too-large doe eyes to her trim figure and casual grace.

"Thank you for coming," Jack said. "I really appreciate you taking the time to speak with me."

"Uh—yeah. Sure." She crossed her arms over her chest, easing herself forward enough to peer inside the apartment without actually stepping past the threshold. "I told my mom I had some stuff to do. She didn't actually care anyway. Did you, uh…want me to come in?"

"Of course," Jack said. He opened the door wider so the girl could see Jamie standing there. A mix of relief and perhaps a trace of disappointment crossed the teenager's face once she realized they weren't alone.

"Julie, you know Jamie Flint, I believe?"

"Sure," she said, with a friendly enough nod. "I didn't know you'd be here." A trace of guilt was next on her face.

Either Julie was a great actress, or she would never have much luck in Las Vegas; she was painfully easy to read. "How's Bear?"

"He's all right," Jamie said. Her smile seemed genuine, and served to set the teenager at ease. "He's pretty freaked out about everything, though."

"Sure," Julie agreed readily. "I mean, who wouldn't be? I'm really sorry if anything my mom said got him in trouble."

"She was only telling the truth as she knew it," Jack said. "We'd just like to get a better picture of what happened that night. Do you have a few minutes to sit?"

She looked around uncertainly. Jack half expected her to come up with an excuse and flee—she had yet to cross the threshold. "I didn't see that fight or whatever that my mom says happened," she said. "I already told you that. And the police."

If she folded her arms any more tightly around herself, Jack thought she might break something.

"So you've said," Jack said easily. "That's fine. I just had a couple of other questions I wanted to ask. I promise, it won't take long."

"Please," Jamie added, when Julie remained on the fence. After another moment of hesitation, the girl nodded.

"Yeah, okay. Sure. What can I tell you?"

Jack led her inside, and into his office. She looked around with a critical eye, but seemed to find nothing overtly offensive about the decor. Though Jack noticed that she didn't fall over herself to compliment him on the place, either.

He offered something to drink and was surprised when Julie asked what he had, then listened as though getting the drinks list at a fine restaurant before settling on lemonade.

Once they were seated, Jack with tea in front of him and Julie with the requested lemonade—Jamie had somewhat impatiently refused refreshments—Jack got started.

"Can you walk me through what happened for you the night Nancy Davis was killed," he asked. Julie eyed the tape recorder at the edge of his desk suspiciously.

"Why?" she asked, eyes narrowed. "I already told the police. I went home. Had dinner with my mother. Watched a little TV. Went to bed."

"What did you watch?" Jack asked. She looked confused. "Huh?"

"On TV. You said you watched something?"

"Oh—yeah, I don't know. YouTube stuff, whatever."

"With your mother?"

No, in my room. Mom was downstairs watching *Downton Abbey*—again. She loves that show." The way she said it, eyes rolled heavenward, Jack assumed Julie didn't share her mother's opinion.

"And what time did you go to bed?"

She shrugged, eyes darting away. "I don't know. Like eleven, maybe?"

"Was your mother still up at that point?"

"No. She was in bed by that time."

"Ah. Okay." Jack paused for a moment, studying the girl as she fidgeted under his gaze. "And you'd met Bear before?" he asked finally. "Before the day everything happened with the animals?"

"Sure," she said. She looked thrown by the question, which had of course been Jack's intention. "He came around to help Nancy sometimes, and I saw him then. He was always with that black girl, though—Robin, or whatever."

"Ren," Jamie said.

"Right," Julie said, waving the distinction off with a wave of her hand. "Whatever. But about a month ago he started coming around without her."

"And you talked to him then?" Jack asked.

Her cheeks colored. "I guess a couple of times, maybe. He seemed sort of...I don't know, lonely. I guess his girlfriend moved away or something?"

"He told you that?" Jack asked.

"Yeah. We got to talking one day, and I asked. Some girls can be so bitchy, they'll just steal a guy right out from under you. But I'm not that way—I just wanted to make sure he really was single, you know?"

Jack struggled to keep his face impassive, despite the revealing statement. He was pleased to note that Jamie had also managed to keep from reacting visibly to the girl's words.

"Did he ever ask you out?" Jack asked. "Once you had established that he was single, I mean?"

Her blush deepened, and she rolled her eyes. "What, you mean like on a 'date' or something?" Her fingers came up in air quotes around the word 'date.' "Kids don't really do that anymore."

The phrase "Netflix and chill" popped into Jack's head, though he said nothing. The world seemed like a foreign place to him sometimes these days.

"No, I suppose not," he agreed. He hesitated one more moment before he wet his lips and sat forward incrementally in his chair, fixing Julie with a pointed gaze.

"I've been trying to figure something out ever since this whole thing started," he said to her. "You know what that something is?"

"No?" she said—the word a question, her eyes locked

on his own, seemingly unable to look away. "What?"

"Why did Bear come back to the mainland that night? He'd had a long day with the animals, he must have been tired. Did he really just come out here to fight with Nancy again, when he knew they were coming back for the animals in the morning?"

Her eyes slid from his to the floor, hands knotted in her lap. "Oh. I—I don't know. I guess so."

Jack frowned. "Did you know Bear called his girlfriend when he got back to the island the second time, and told her he couldn't talk to her anymore?"

Julie's eyes shot to his, widening slightly. The first honest reaction he'd seen from her. "Really? He said that?"

"Do you know why he would have told her something like that?"

Mute, the girl shook her head. Jack's frown deepened. Time to bring it home.

"Can I tell you what I think happened that night?"

She nodded wordlessly, hands still gripped tight in her lap.

"I think earlier in the day, you and Bear talked. And he suggested, or maybe you suggested, that you meet up later that night. And that was why he came back to the mainland. That was why he was here and ended up fighting with Nancy."

Julie's voice was brittle, barely audible, when she spoke. "You're wrong."

He studied her quizzically. "Why won't you tell the truth about this? Because you're afraid your mother will find out you lied to her?"

Nothing.

She sat there, hunched and miserable, wrestling with herself.

"Don't you think your mother would want you to tell the truth about something like this? This could mean Bear's future..." he pressed. Jamie remained silent, intractable, in her seat, but Jack could feel her tension.

Finally, Julie broke.

Her eyes welled.

"I snuck out," she said miserably. "I talked to Bear earlier that day, and... I mean, I've kind of had a thing for him for so long. And we were talking that day, and I said maybe we could go for a walk or something."

"So he met you," Jack summarized.

"Yeah. We met out at the end of my driveway, and he took me to this place where you can see the stars—like, millions of them, up on Blueberry Ridge. He knows every single constellation. All the stories behind them and everything."

Jamie smiled sadly, but said nothing. Jack nodded.

"And then...?" he prompted.

Julie blushed. "I mean—well, you know. We kind of started...fooling around. Not sex or anything," she added hastily, looking at Jamie. "But—O.M.G. Maybe it's gross to say this to you, but your son is a really good kisser. Like... wow. Really good."

Jamie managed a somewhat sickly smile. "Great. I'm so proud."

"You should be," Julie said sincerely, totally missing the sarcasm. "I mean...wow. So, we're just up there in his truck making out and whatever, and it's getting kind of...um, you know. Hot, or whatever. And all of a sudden, he just stops. Gets out of the truck, kind of worked up, and walks away, says he's got to work something out and he can't do this and..." She frowned.

"Most guys, I would have been so pissed if they pulled something like that, you know? But I really felt bad for him."

Her frowned deepened, lips tightening.

"What happened after that?" Jack asked, careful to keep his voice neutral. "After he said he needed to stop."

She took a deep breath. "We decided it was late, so he drove me back to my house. And then we were just coming up over the hill to our property and he was like, 'Do you know where your dad is?'" She dabbed at her eyes, the motion reminding Jack of her mother once more.

"I mean—I know Bear isn't the best with social graces, but it was, like, completely out of the blue. And given the fact that my dad walked out on us just a few months ago, it was totally not a cool thing to ask."

"What did you say?" Jack asked.

"I said I didn't know and I couldn't care less, which is the truth. He can rot in hell for all I care."

"And what did he say to that?"

"He said I shouldn't talk like that—that my father probably loved me a lot, and I couldn't know what really happened. He was staring up at the top of the hill the whole time, and he was totally freaking me out. I don't know. It was creepy."

"So you said goodnight then," Jack guessed.

"Yeah. It was about midnight by that time. I told Bear he could call me if he wanted to go out again. I mean, he's tortured and kind of creepy, but..." She sighed. This time, the eye roll seemed to be directed at herself. "I can't help it. He's really hot."

"Plus a great kisser," Jamie said dryly.

"Right. Yeah, that too. And then I went inside."

"But Bear didn't drive away after that?" Jack asked.

"No. He parked at the end of my driveway, on the side of the road by Nancy's house, and then it got really weird."

"How so?"

"He got out of the truck, and it looked like maybe he was talking to somebody. The animals, maybe? He kept talking, the whole time while he walked up the hill to the spot he'd been staring at."

"And then…?"

"I went to bed," she said, with a shrug. "I put my headphones on because that's how I sleep best. So, whatever fight my mom saw with Nancy, I missed. That much at least was true."

Jack nodded. He paused a moment, waiting for her to volunteer anything further before he wrapped things up. "Is there anything else you'd like to say about this?"

"Not really," Julie said. She looked miserable, but a little bit lighter than she had when she'd first arrived. "Except, I'm sorry I didn't say anything sooner. I'm not sure how my story could have helped, but if you need me to testify or whatever… I mean, I'd definitely do that. Whatever you need. I'll deal with my mom, if I have to."

"I appreciate that," Jack assured her. "I'll let you know if I have any more questions." He handed her his business card. "Here's my phone number. Call if you think of anything else, all right?"

She nodded. "I will. Definitely."

26

WHEN JACK FINISHED HIS IMPROMPTU interview with Julie, he and I walked her to the door together. None of the information she'd given us was really all that mindblowing—apart from my newfound knowledge of my son's kissing prowess, which I could have done without. The rest, though, gave pause for thought but hardly busted the case wide open.

"I should get going, too," I told Jack at the door. "We have a million things to get done out on the island, and with Bear gone and Monty out..."

"If you ever need any help out there," Julie said, surprising me, "I'm good with animals. I mean, not as good as Bear, but they usually like me all right. And I'm a hard worker. I wouldn't mind mucking out stalls or whatever once Bear's out of jail. I'm sure he could use the help, now that his girlfriend's gone."

And there was the rub. She really didn't seem as bad as I'd thought at first—she was just seventeen, that agonizing in-between. Add to that the fact that her world had shifted completely off its axis when her father went missing, and it was no wonder she was a little bit horrible.

"I'm not sure how much Bear will be around," I said. "But it would be great to have someone cover for him while he's away."

Jack looked at me, surprised, but I knew Julie would turn me down. As expected, her face fell when she realized she would be stuck out on the island with a million animals and no Bear to keep her company. "Oh. Well… I should probably ask my mom first. Things might get kind of busy this summer."

"I understand," I said. And I did. I'd been seventeen once too, after all. Of course, I'd been seventeen living on my own with a toddler, but I got the gist. "Just call if you change your mind."

She left, and I went to retrieve my jacket only to have Jack beat me to it. He picked it up, but held onto it rather than handing it over.

"I really do need to get back," I said again. It's not like I was happy about it. I would have much preferred staying over with Jack Juarez to going back to the chaos on the island. He didn't relinquish the jacket, however.

"I was hoping you and Phantom could give me a hand with something."

"And what would that be?" I asked, immediately curious.

He hesitated. "Julie said she saw Bear out in the fields the other night talking to someone," he began.

"Someone who wasn't there—at least, not someone Julie could see."

"And he did ask some fairly pointed questions about her father…"

I'd had the same thought. In fact, it was one of the first things I intended to talk to Bear about just as soon as he was out of that damned cell.

"The police seem to believe they've found all the bodies they're going to over at the Davis place," Jack continued. "I think they're wrong. I'd like to go out to the property and search again."

"For bodies," I clarified. "After you were already bludgeoned and nearly burned alive over there, now you want to go back and take another look."

"I was hoping this time I wouldn't be alone." He paused. "Phantom is trained to find human remains, right?"

"She is, but we usually do so with the police and a search warrant and a whole team of law enforcement on board."

"Sure, I understand," he said, in a way that implied that was the end of the conversation. He wouldn't push any further, I knew. He handed over my jacket. "I'll walk you to your car."

I stared at him, unclear on what had just happened. "Wait—so that's it? What are you going to do?"

"Go by myself."

I frowned. "Jack—"

"It's all right," he assured me. "I'll be fine. Fred and Albie are gone—"

"You think. And you still don't know for sure that Fred was the one who attacked you the other night."

"I'll be careful."

Cash and the kittens had settled down, Cash and the little black kitten on the sofa together while the other four kittens were with Phantom. It was only five-thirty, the sun still bright outside Jack's window—it wouldn't go down for hours yet.

"I should go back to the island first. I'm assuming you don't want to do this in broad daylight."

I caught the flash of his smile, and just managed to suppress my eye roll. He'd known all along that I'd give in.

"I'll go with you," he said. I started to object, but he shook his head. "No arguments. I can help out there. And unlike Julie, spending time with your son is not a condition of my service."

As soon as we hit the island, we set to work feeding and exercising the animals and cleaning out the pens. Therese and Sarah and a few other volunteers had done an admirable job keeping up, but there was still no shortage of work to be done.

After the other dogs had been fed and were in their outside pens, I brought a bowl of food to Reaver. The kennel was eerily quiet now that the other twenty dogs were outside, and I reveled in the peace as I walked along the concrete walkway with Phantom by my side, Jack walking a couple of steps behind. As we approached the kennel, I could tell that the pit bull already looked a thousand times better than he had when he'd first come in. His head came up at my approach, though there was clearly tension in his frame.

"Maybe I should stay back," Jack said, remaining a couple of paces behind me.

"That would be good," I agreed. "Don't go far, though. I'd like to see how he is with men other than Bear. You mind just staying here?"

"Sounds good to me."

We continued on down the row of kennels. When we were two pens away, Reaver's ears pricked up when I spoke to him. Slowly, his tail began to wag.

His body changed completely the moment he saw Phantom, though. The slow tail wag became an all-out whipping, his entire body shimmying with it. He hopped forward with a few frantic, high-pitched woofs. Beside me, Phantom—usually completely intolerant of the multitude of dogs desperate to befriend her—was far from passive now that she'd caught his scent. She remained in the heel I'd ordered her into, but I could feel how desperate she was to break it. Tail waving, we approached the kennel.

Reaver greeted us with a play bow on the other side of the kennel door, then rolled over onto his back with his belly up, legs flailing.

"Wow," Jack said, still several paces back. "Have a little dignity, huh, guy?"

Reaver ignored him, which was good—it was what I'd been hoping. I was afraid the presence of a strange man would trigger the dog, but now that he'd been removed from Nancy's care and seemed to know he was safe, I'd yet to find anything that triggered this boy.

Each kennel had a small latched window that greatly simplified the process of feeding everyone, since it meant we didn't have to actually open up the kennel. I set the bowl of food inside Reaver's kennel, and he scrambled to his feet. I held onto the bowl for a moment longer than I needed to, again gauging the dog's reaction. He sat down politely, and waited.

No doubt about it, this dog had had some training.

"Good boy, Reav," I said. "Eat up."

I set the bowl down, but he still didn't move. I hesitated. "Go on, Reaver. It's okay."

At the word 'okay,' he sprang up. That must have been his release word, once upon a time—the command that signaled he could stop whatever command he'd been holding.

We stood by as he gobbled his food. His ribs were still visible and it would take time before he reached a healthy weight again, but he was well on his way. Once he was finished, I went into the kennel and snapped Reaver's leash onto his collar, and set out for a quick walk around the grounds. He and Phantom fell in together immediately, and he barely missed a step when Jack joined us.

"He's better," Jack noted.

"A lot better," I agreed. "I wish I knew what happened to him. I was hoping to talk to Albie, ask some questions now that I have a better sense of him. I'm almost positive that my theory is at least something along the lines of what happened: he was in the hands of a group that would have fought him, and Nancy got hold of him before they could actually do anything."

"That would explain Nancy feeling like she'd saved him."

"In a way, she did. I just wish he hadn't had to go through so much at her place before he finally found his way back where he belonged. He'll make someone a great dog."

Jack looked at me in surprise. "What do you mean? You're not keeping him?"

The pit bull bumped against Phantom like he was punch drunk, and that tail of his never stopped wagging. I shook my head, ignoring the pang in my heart.

"I can't keep every dog that comes along. That's how Nancy got started."

"This isn't every dog," Jack said. He nodded toward Phantom. "Look at her. I've never seen her react to another dog like this, have you? You really want to send him away? They look like they belong together."

I rolled my eyes, but I couldn't help but smile. "You're a romantic," I said, and felt silly for not realizing it before.

He shrugged. "Sometimes. Life is better that way."

"Yeah," I said, after a minute or two. I slipped my hand into his without looking at him, the heat rising to my cheeks when I felt his fingers grip mine. "I guess it is."

We continued on that way, the air taking on an evening chill, the sun sinking lower in the sky. The pit bull and my shepherd kept step ahead of us, oblivious to it all.

•

We returned to the mainland at just past ten that night, both Jack and me worn after putting in a full day's work. Phantom was restless, clearly eager to get moving once Reaver was returned to his pen. There was only one reason we'd set out this time of night, and she knew exactly what that reason was.

Jack drove his Honda Civic halfway down the lane to the Davis home, and pulled off to the side. It was the same place I'd found his car last night, and I shivered at the memory.

"Where do you want to start?" I asked.

"Near the barns," he said without hesitation. He'd clearly already been thinking about this. "Maybe they buried some of the remains around there."

I got out of the car, then released Phantom from her seatbelt in the back. Her ears were pricked forward, body already tensed. I might still be on the fence about this, but Phantom was more than ready to begin.

Dogs are trained differently to search for human remains, with unique commands used when they're looking for the dead versus a live find. They have to be, or else you'd have every K-9 going nuts every time a cemetery is nearby. Phantom had been trained on vomit and viscera, spare blood from the donor bank… Whatever we could come up with to make sure she knew all the scents she might come across when searching for a live find.

Training for the dead was a different process. We

used decaying bodies—or body parts—at all stages of decomposition. Bone fragments, adipocere, human teeth, death shrouds.... Whatever we could get. She got the same reward for remains that she did with a live find—an enthusiastic game of tug—but I far preferred looking for live people. Phantom seemed to sense that there was inevitably something sad, an ending she had brought home, when she alerted on remains. I didn't like to put her through that too often. Sometimes, however, it was necessary. Tonight seemed like one of those times.

The night was cool, a chilling sea breeze blowing off the water. Jack and I had both showered on the island, and he wore a spare Flint K-9 uniform—khakis and a black Flint K-9 T-shirt. I wore the same, though I had a jacket and Jack had left his in the car.

"We could go back and get it," I said, after we'd gone only a short distance.

"No need, I'm not cold."

"You're making me cold."

He laughed. "I can't help that. Do you want me to go get my coat so you can wear it?"

"No."

We walked on in a comfortable silence while I watched Phantom for any sign that she might be onto something. It was a warm night, which meant she would normally keep her nose up to catch any scent particles on the air. Since we were looking for a body, however, and most likely one buried below ground, her nose remained glued to the grassy floor.

"How's your head?" Jack asked, after half an hour of a whole lot of nothing.

"Fine. Yours?"

"Better. You know what I mean, though. That headache you keep getting."

"I don't have it right now," I said. "You're overreacting, you know. It's not like I have them all the time."

"When did you have the last one?"

I had to think about it. "During the search the other night."

"You were overtired then?"

"And now I'm rested."

"You don't think it might be a good idea to talk to a doctor about this?"

"It's a headache, Jack. I can handle it."

I couldn't actually see him in the dark, but I could sense his irritation. "It's not just a headache. What about the voices."

"Voice. Singular."

"Your abusive ex—"

"He's not my ex. It's not like Brock and I were high school sweethearts."

The tension went up a notch between us. "The abusive father of your child, then."

I stopped, the words and tone cutting deep. "I've barely heard him since this winter, when we were looking for a group of battered women. I'm no psychologist, but I think there may have been a link there."

Phantom was still doing her thing up ahead, though Jack and I stood facing off in the darkness. After a few seconds, he sighed.

"I just worry about you. You work too hard, have too much responsibility and nobody to help with any of it."

"I have people to help," I said. "Monty. Bear. Sarah. Therese. I have people, Jack. You're the lone wolf around here, not me. I've got my pack."

He didn't argue the point. To my relief, he resumed the trek behind Phantom. I kept step alongside him, willing the subject of chronic headaches and voices from beyond the grave to fade for at least the night.

Barely half an hour later, with Jack and me walking in companionable silence, I saw Phantom pause up ahead. Her head came up. Her body went still. Then, her tail lifted. She dropped her nose to the ground. And she was off, at a trot.

"She's got something," I said.

We followed the dog across the sodden pasture toward the tree line. Had Nancy and her accomplice—whoever that might have been—buried other victims out here? Jack seemed so certain, but I still wasn't sold. Her motives may not have been great, but there were definitely reasons for her to kill Nancy's husband and future daughter-in-law. And if the ex-con from down South had been abusing Reaver, that likely would have been more than enough to incite Nancy to violence.

But how many others could there possibly be, whose absence no one would have noticed? Locals couldn't just be killed and— literally—tossed out to pasture, could they? Not without someone asking questions.

We reached the tree line, and Phantom wavered. She retraced her steps, whining slightly. Something was confusing the scent. Understandable, since this entire property seemed soaked in every unpleasant odor known to man. Rather than going into the trees, Phantom loped back toward the pasture, then continued scenting along the fence line. At the far end of the fence, close to one of the ancient barns, I caught Phantom in the beam of my flashlight as she stopped. She barked twice, and lay down.

A very clear alert.

"She's got it," I said.

Jack and I ran to her, the smell of animals and decay getting stronger as we neared the barn.

"I thought they checked in there," Jack said. "Finnegan said they went through both barns."

"That's not where she's alerting," I said. "This is the spot, right here. If the scent were in the barn, that's where she would lead us."

He frowned. "So, you're saying someone's buried here."

"I have no idea, but that's a possibility." I looked at him when he didn't say anything, clearly unhappy. "What did you think, she was going to lead you to a cache of bodies like the one in the basement? Chances are, Nancy or whoever she was working with buried these guys a long time ago."

"Maybe," he said noncommittally, eying the barn. "With a smell like this, how thorough do you think the police were when they went in there, though?"

"Jack, I'm telling you. That's not where she's—"

"I know," he said, a bit impatiently. "But just because she smells something there doesn't mean there's not more to find inside here."

We walked past the dog and toward the lopsided barn entrance. I shone my flashlight through the doorway before Jack and I risked a step inside, to a dark cavern filled with cobwebs and filthy, abandoned dog crates, a pile of stinking blankets in another corner. Twenty-eight dogs had been pulled from here, six of them in such bad condition that they'd already been euthanized. The other twenty-two were malnourished and terrified, with sores all over their underfed bodies from lives spent in crates. Their muscles had atrophied; their bones were malformed.

My eyes filled at the reality of what these animals had lived through. Why hadn't I intervened sooner? Nancy might have saved lives in animal rescue once upon a time, but I should have seen how far from that she was now.

This shouldn't have happened.

"Jamie," Jack called, and I pried myself from my thoughts with effort. He was on the far side of the barn, looking at the crates. My stomach turned, as I tried to imagine what he might have found.

"What have you got?" I asked, shining my flashlight toward him. He shook his head.

"Nothing. Can we bring Phantom in, maybe have her check this out?"

I nodded, and went back to get the dog.

Suddenly, a man's voice cut through the night, echoing in the darkness. *You can't do this to living creatures. What in hell's wrong with you, Nancy?*

Not Brock. I didn't know this voice, but the anger and profound pity for the animals struck a chord with me.

Get off my property. Get out or you'll never go anywhere again.

That voice, I knew well. Nancy.

"Jamie?" Jack said.

"Just a second."

I stepped outside and gulped fresh air, grateful that this time the voices hadn't come with the feeling of a spear piercing my skull. Still shaken, I scanned the night for Phantom.

My shepherd was several yards away, still lying in the same spot. She looked at me.

"Here, Phan," I said.

She stood, but she didn't take a step toward me. Instead, she whined, circling twice with her nose to the ground, and pawed the earth. As if to say, *Come on, now—I did my job. Why are you over there? I already told you where to find them.*

"I know, girl. We'll get to it in a second. Come here first."

She didn't budge. I hesitated. I'd learned long ago to trust my dog—it's one of the most important lessons anyone working with K-9s has to learn. And she was clearly trying to tell me something here.

"Jack, can you come out?" I called. I went to the dog, whose tail whooshed excitedly when she realized I'd finally gotten the message.

I paced the ground, but it was hard to tell much, covered as it was in mud and feces.

I swept my flashlight beam across the area once. Then back again. I was just making my third pass when Jack came out, and my flashlight hit it:

A flash of metal, barely visible in the ground.

"There," I said. I hurried over, Jack close behind, and dropped to my knees to get a better look. It took some digging before we finally found it:

A door handle.

"What is it?" Jack asked.

"It must be an old root cellar," I said. "They're still popular around here. They're great for storing crops like potatoes and squash and other root vegetables, through the winter."

We worked together on hands and knees, our gloves and clothes soon filthy, until we'd cleared everything from an old wooden hatch built into the ground.

Jack's hand was on the handle, but he paused and looked at me. "What do you think?"

"I don't know. In another life, you would have said we needed to call someone right about now."

He nodded grimly, jaw set. "If I call someone, I'm out of the investigation. Who knows when I find out whether Tim Monroe is down there."

"You have your answer, then."

It still took him a few seconds before he worked up the wherewithal to pull up the door.

Or try.

It took several attempts, with both of us working together, before it even budged. On the second or third try, I heard another unfamiliar voice crying out in my head. And another. A third joined them, until it seemed there was a chorus of the damned locked inside my skull. Some were male, some female. Some seemed vaguely familiar, but Nancy's was the only one I recognized easily. She was there only occasionally, though. I heard Albie weeping. Begging to stop. Dogs barking in the distance.

Screams, echoing through the night as though they came from the very bowels of hell.

My stomach turned. That deadly, damnable arrow pierced my skull again.

Finally, we were able to haul the door open. Jack and I both backed off at the smell, so pungent that it felt like it was a living thing. I pointed my flashlight inside, illuminating a dark hole whose secrets seemed to rise up and surround us.

The voices got louder around me, but at this point the smell was the true enemy. I gagged, which is saying something considering where I come from and what I've seen over the years. Jack turned his head away, arm over his mouth and nose.

There was no question this time: we'd found Nancy's hidden cache.

"What do we do?" I asked.

He hesitated, clearly torn, but finally shook his head and stood up. He stepped away, pulling out his cell phone. "Let's get the police in here. There's nothing more we can do."

I fought to focus on him instead of the clamor inside my head, but suddenly they all went still.

Everything quieted.

He was already dialing when a single voice whispered in my ear.

Please. Don't leave me. I'm here.

It was so clear, I thought someone had actually spoken. "Did you hear that?" I asked Jack.

He looked at me, confused, and shook his head with the phone at his ear. "Hey, Sheriff," he began.

Don't leave me, the man said again.

A shiver ran up my spine. I shone my flashlight inside the hole again, until I found a ladder leading inside.

"I know," Jack was saying. "You said I should stay away from this place—but I didn't. I'm calling you now, though."

Trembling, head pounding, I put my flashlight in my mouth and swung my body down into the cellar.

"Jamie. What the hell are you doing?" Jack demanded. Above ground, Phantom whined.

I held onto the door for a second, until my feet found the rungs of the ladder. I hardly needed them—it was only a two- or three-foot drop down. I stepped in something slick and viscous, and my stomach lurched. I didn't even want to know what that was.

I'm here.

I trained my flashlight beam on the far wall, and ran it back and forth through the cramped space. One wall was lined with shelves, where canned goods and old glass jars had been opened and emptied. I put my arm over my mouth and nose, trying to block out the overwhelming stench of human waste. A couple of articulated human skeletons were seated together against another wall, as though the two had died together.

Here, the man insisted. *Don't leave me.*

I turned around, scanning the space.

At the far end of the cellar, there was a cavern—like someone had planned on adding another room, but gave up. My flashlight beam froze in place. My voice caught, before I could get the words out.

"Jack," I called. "He's here."

I went to him then. Tim Monroe. He didn't move, slumped over and inert. I put my ear to his chest, and then was on my feet again an instant later.

"He's alive, Jack! His breathing is shallow, but he's alive."

I heard Jack swear, and a moment later call for an ambulance. I remained where I was, my hand resting on the skeletal frame of Barbara Monroe's missing husband.

27

I WAS AT THE KNOX COUNTY JAIL Monday morning first thing, but barely had time to say hi to Bear before he had to go meet with counsel before his hearing at ten a.m. That gave me an hour to kill. I knew I could pay a quick visit to Jack and would likely be welcomed, but I wasn't really in the mood to be social. There were too many unanswered questions swirling in my head.

Tim Monroe still hadn't woken up, and was currently in Intensive Care at Pen Bay Medical Center. His prognosis was good, however—he had some superficial wounds, but overall he was in remarkably good health for a man who'd been kept underground for the past two months. The stored food had been his saving grace; living on canned beans and pickled beets may not be ideal, but it's sufficient to keep a body alive. The doctors suspected his body had shut down fairly recently, and with adequate nutrition, hydration, and rest, he would make a full recovery.

Barbara and Julie were beside themselves with relief.

Fred and Albie still hadn't been found, which meant without them and with Tim still unconscious, it was impossible to completely piece together everything that had happened. I still hadn't told Jack about the voices I'd heard that night in Nancy's yard. I'd replayed them in my mind, trying to identify players that as yet remained a mystery. I knew that I'd heard Albie's voice, and I was fairly certain Fred had been in there, as well. Had the three of them really been in this together all these years? At least according to the scenes that had echoed in my mind, Albie had been an unwilling participant. I couldn't get a handle on Fred, though. Had Nancy manipulated him the way she had Albie, or had he been the mastermind all this time?

At shortly before ten o'clock, I went into the courtroom and sat down. Court was already in session, with a surly-looking judge with thinning hair and glasses presiding. I waited for Bear to be led into the courtroom, but there was no sign of him. Ten o'clock came and went. I scanned the crowd in confusion. There was no mention of his case; no mention of him at all.

Finally, at quarter till eleven, my phone vibrated. I looked at it and caught my breath at sight of Bear's cell number. I answered as I was leaving the courtroom, but at least waited until the door was shut behind me before I spoke.

"What's going on?" I asked, already imagining the worst. He was sick; he'd been stabbed; they were foregoing the trial because they'd decided he was guilty and no one could change their minds.

"Can you pick me up?" he asked. "I don't have my truck."

"What do you mean, can I pick you up? I'm at the courthouse—I thought there was a hearing."

"Sorry I didn't call sooner. I thought there was, too; I've been freaking out, but I guess my lawyer convinced them that with Albie gone and only circumstantial evidence otherwise, there was no way the judge would even hear my case."

It took me a second to register that. "So, you're just... free?"

"I can't leave town," he said. "They're still investigating, and Doug says this doesn't mean I'm free and clear. I could still be charged."

"But you can come home now."

"Only if someone comes and gets me."

I smiled at that. Wonder of wonders, it actually sounded like there was some humor back in his voice. "I'll be right there. Don't go anywhere."

"Yeah, right." He hesitated. "And... uh, thanks, Mom."

My eyes welled, and I took a deep breath. "I'll be there in a few minutes."

Bear was sitting on a bench outside the jail when I arrived, wearing jeans and a Polo shirt I'd brought him for court. He had completely balked at the idea of wearing a suit to his hearing, and the lawyer had agreed that this would be acceptable. Personally, I wasn't sold on that—all the more reason to be grateful there would be no hearing. He was freshly shaven, and his hair neatly brushed. Maybe I was prejudiced, but I could understand why a girl like Julie Monroe might be taken with him.

"Need a lift?" I asked.

He smiled at me—the kind of smile I'd been missing in recent months.

"That would be good," he agreed.

He stood, and I pulled him into a bone-crushing hug. He tensed. Then, he didn't necessarily return the hug, but he didn't push me away, either. I counted that as a win.

"You ready to head back to the island?"

"Hell yeah."

We set out together, a thousand-pound weight lifted from my shoulders. He might not be fully cleared yet, but seeing Bear behind bars was something I would do just about anything to avoid repeating.

•

Three days passed before there was any word about Fred or Albie. Tim Monroe had woken by this time, and confirmed that Nancy had shoved him into the hole with Albie's help, though he believed he may have been drugged beforehand. He never saw Fred, but he couldn't say for certain that the man wasn't involved.

Jack went out to Philadelphia early in the week to dig deeper, and found that the insurance company Fred had listed as an employer had laid him off six months ago, and he'd left his apartment around the same time. He'd left no forwarding address, and when Jack spoke with the man's neighbors, he got a familiar line:

Fred was quiet, kept to himself. They supposed in hindsight that he could have been capable of something like this, but they'd never suspected anything at the time.

I learned all of this on Thursday, as Jack walked the island with me upon his return from Philly.

"So, what do you think happened?" I asked him, as we approached the kennels that afternoon. "Do you think Fred is the one who killed Nancy?"

"I do," he said, after a moment's hesitation. "I considered it when I first talked to him—his alibi was shaky, and he seemed more relieved than grief-stricken at his mother's death."

"That doesn't really mean anything," I pointed out.

"Families are complicated, especially one like that. He didn't necessarily have to kill her to feel some weight taken off when she was gone, considering all she put him through."

"So, you don't think he did it?" he asked, surprised.

"I'm not saying that. I just…" I shrugged. "Families are complicated," I repeated.

"I'm not sure that he was involved with the other murders, though," Jack conceded.

"He at least knew about them," I said, recalling the echo of his voice outside the old root cellar. "He may not have killed them, but he was aware of at least some of what was happening."

Jack didn't fight me on that, and he didn't question how I was so sure of it, for which I was grateful. I was still building up to telling him about the voices I'd heard that night, afraid he would insist I head to the nearest ER for every costly test on the menu. I would tell him eventually, no doubt.

Just not yet.

We stopped outside the kennel entrance, and Phantom immediately came to life. Her tail waved, ears pricked forward, as she waited impatiently for me to open the door.

"She's really got it bad," Jack noted.

"You have no idea. She whines when we leave Reaver in the evenings, and just about loses her mind when we get up to take him for a walk in the morning."

Sure enough, she pranced mindlessly beside me, then nearly bowled me over when I got the door open. Considering the fact that she'd been trained to wait beside me before going through an open door, I was not amused.

"Wow. What did you do with everyone?" Jack asked when he saw the empty kennels inside.

"Foster homes, mostly. The pugs and the Jack Russell went to breed-specific rescue, and Bear's dropping Cody—

that Newfie there—off with Hank tonight."

I nodded toward a kennel that seemed impossibly large for a dog that should have dominated the space. Cody had had a rough time of it since coming to us, though: he'd been shaved down to the skin to treat his mange and a series of lesions on his back and belly, and without all that fur it quickly became clear just how horribly underfed he actually was. Despite all that, the Newfie continued to maintain one of the best attitudes I'd ever seen in a dog, and I was grateful that a loving home was already waiting for him. Hank had been over to the island the day before to meet with Cody, and the dog's reaction was immediate and unequivocal: he knew Hank. What's more, he loved the guy.

"And Reaver?" Jack asked, as we made our way down the aisle of kennels.

"There's a guy Monty recommended from the Army. He's going to evaluate Reaver tonight, see if he can figure out what unit the dog came from and maybe help us find a placement from there. And there are people who foster or adopt retired military dogs, so I'm looking into that."

"So, you're really not keeping him," he said, clearly not believing me.

Phantom had reached the pit bull's kennel, and the two of them greeted each other with wagging tails and whines, both prancing impatiently as I opened the kennel door.

"I don't know that he'll be able to be a working dog again," I said. "I'm looking for a pup to take on and train so they can take over when Phantom retires. Reaver doesn't exactly fit the bill."

Unlike my dog, Reaver sat patiently inside his kennel until I released him. "Okay, Reaver."

He hopped up and rushed out the door to be with

Phantom. I didn't bother with a leash this time. I'd been working with him constantly over the last few days, and as far as I was concerned the dog was bulletproof, both on leash and off.

"So, maybe you don't adopt him for you," Jack suggested, eyeing the happy couple. Phantom play bowed like a puppy, tail whooshing, and then dashed away. Reaver loped after her, and I was awed at the progress he'd made in such a short time. His mange was clearing up, his body filling out, and he seemed to have a perpetual grin—as though he knew full well the second chance he'd been given.

"We'll see," was the only answer I would give Jack, though I think in retrospect my mind was already made.

It was six o'clock by now. My appointment with the Army officer was for seven-thirty, the earliest he could meet me. Bear had arranged to drop off Cody at the same time, so we wouldn't have to make more than one trip to the mainland. Overhead, the sky was dark, a balmy wind gusting in. The hurricane had finally hit the South on Wednesday, and we were seeing the residual effects now.

Monty had been gone for days now, and at last check-in had told me he was still searching for his daughter and the girl's mother. He had assured me then that he didn't need the team, but I didn't think that would last. Eventually, he would have to break and ask for help—it happened to the best of us.

Jack and I walked in silence behind the dogs, content to watch them play. When we were far enough away from prying eyes, alone on a wooded trail, Jack stopped walking and turned to look at me. He was smiling.

"You look happy," I noted.

"Do I?" He considered that. "Probably because I am.

I already have two new cases thanks to the publicity from finding Tim Monroe alive."

"That's not a surprise. Barbara sure talked you up, huh?"

"I'll take it if it helps me stay afloat," he said with a shrug. "It's summer, so I'm not freezing nearly as often as I am the rest of the year here. Cash and the kittens are settling in…" He trailed off. His eyes found mine, and I hurried to keep the conversation on safe ground.

"Have you decided who you'll keep and who you'll adopt out?"

"Cash and Harvey. They do well together—I think Cash would be depressed if I let the little guy go. The others deserve their own families. They'll do fine somewhere else."

"Cash and Harvey are lucky cats, then."

"You think?" he looked away self-consciously. "I actually… I was talking to my landlord. Have you ever heard of a catio? It's a patio, but for cats—an outdoor enclosure, so they get fresh air without the danger of being set loose outside."

I tried not to smile—I really did. I didn't succeed, though.

"And now you're laughing at me."

"No, I'm not." He gave me a look. "Okay, not that much," I conceded. "But I think it's nice. The cats would love that. I can give you a hand, if you want. I've built a few of them at different facilities over the last couple of years."

"That would be nice. Thanks."

Silence fell between us. Phantom and Reaver were still cavorting up ahead, crashing through the underbrush like pups. It really was incredible: seven years with Phantom, and I'd never once seen her behave like this.

"So…" Jack said after a moment, letting the word trail off. I shifted my attention from the dogs back to him.

"Yes?" I prompted, when he said nothing more.

He took a step closer. "I was wondering about... Well..."

Jack Juarez is, hands down, the most attractive man I've ever seen outside of Hollywood. He has the lean build of a serious athlete, with the dark eyes, sensual mouth, and strong features of a runway model. To see him fumbling for words, apparently for the likes of me, was a little mind boggling.

"Jack?"

He laughed, and rolled his eyes at himself. "Right. I was wondering if you're going to the fundraiser for Nancy's animals tomorrow night."

"I was planning on it."

"Do you have a date?"

Things got quieter between us suddenly, as though the world itself had paused to listen for my answer. I bit my lip. We'd been dancing around this for how long now? Something told me that my response to this question was important. Whatever I said, it would change things.

"Not yet," I said.

His eyes flashed to the ground a moment, then found me again. "Would you like one?"

"Jack—" I began.

He shook his head. "Don't. Just say yes—just this once. Don't overthink it. Don't panic. Just go out with me, one time."

I took a deep breath. I was thirty-four years old. I should be able to make a date without hyperventilating. He took a step closer, a half smile on his lips now.

"Be brave, Jamie."

That earned an eye roll from me. "So, by that logic, I'm a coward if I don't go out with you?"

He shrugged. "If the shoe fits."

Somewhere in the back of my mind, I heard Brock again. *You're too afraid to take what you want. Every time you get close to it, you run like a beaten dog.*

I pushed the voice away. Eventually, I would need to tell Jack the whole story—everything that had happened on the night Brock Campbell died. Everything I had done.

Not now, though. Not yet.

"Fine," I said. "I'll go out with you."

His half smile widened to a grin. "Good. I'll pick you up at the landing—say six o'clock? I thought we could go out to dinner first."

Dinner and a fundraiser—both of them very public. Right out there in the world. I pushed away any remaining misgivings, and nodded. "I can do that."

"Hey, are you ready to go?" Bear called, from just down the path. It wasn't like Jack and I had even been doing anything, but we still sprang apart like teens caught necking in the woodshed.

Phantom and Reaver came racing along to greet him, the two of them still grinning doggedly. Casper and Reaver hadn't hit it off so far, and I held my breath to see how they would do now. It wasn't like there had been an actual fight, but there had definitely been some posturing.

Reaver paid no attention to the younger pit bull now, though. Bear greeted the dogs with enthusiasm, pointedly ignoring whatever had or had not been going on between Jack and me.

"The boat's ready?" I asked.

"Boat's ready," he confirmed, squatting low while the three dogs circled around him.

"All right. Let's head out."

Bear strode on ahead with the dogs, while Jack and I lingered behind. No talking, no touching. Still, it felt more charged than it had before. I really wasn't sure I was ready for this, at all.

28

THE BOAT RIDE BACK WAS rockier than Jack liked, as the last of the hurricane that had done so much damage along the Eastern seaboard slowly wore itself to the ground. No one else seemed to notice the swells or the darkening sky; Jack could think of little else. Jamie piloted the boat, Reaver beside her while Bear remained with the Newfoundland destined for Hank's place. While Bear wasn't overtly hostile, he did seem to make extra effort to avoid actually interacting with Jack in any meaningful way now.

Once they reached the blessed mainland, they all would have gone their separate ways if Jack hadn't spoken up as Bear was unloading Cody.

"So, I guess I'll see you tomorrow," Jamie said at the dock, looking all too aware of her son's presence.

"Actually, I was hoping I could do a ride-along," Jack said.

Jamie's surprise was clear, as was her discomfort as she tried to find a tactful way to tell him he wasn't welcome.

"Not with you," he said, letting her off the hook. "I'd actually like to ride with Bear, if that's all right. I'd love to see what it looks like when one of the dogs finds their forever home."

Bear frowned. "You can see that kind of thing on YouTube whenever you want—there are a million videos of people adopting a dog."

"It's not the same as being there," Jack argued.

"I actually have some other errands to do," the boy said. Jamie stood to the side, watching wordlessly as the two negotiated.

"You can just drop me at the landing when we're done. Or I can come with you, give you a hand."

Bear looked pointedly at his mother, but she shook her head. "Oh no—leave me out of it. You're eighteen years old. If you don't want someone's company, tell them that."

"Fine. I don't want—" Bear began, but Jamie cut him off.

"However, I don't think it would be that horrible to just take him along, just this once. He's not that bad."

"And he's standing right here," Jack added.

Bear didn't acknowledge that, still glowering at his mother. "Fine. Whatever. Come on, then."

As soon as Bear was striding toward his truck, Jamie looked at Jack with a question in her eyes. "What are you doing?"

"Don't worry. I have a plan."

"Oh, good. That always ends well."

"Hey!" Bear shouted back at them. Cody was tugging at the leash, wriggling excitedly now that they were on solid ground again. "If you're coming, come on."

"We'll be fine," Jack assured her.

Famous last words.

●

"Listen," Jack said, as soon as he and Bear were on the road. It was a short ride to Hank's from the landing, and he wanted the chance to say his piece before it was too late.

"Is this the part where you tell me you plan to be part of my mother's life, and you hope I'm on board?"

"Uh—no. Why? Have you heard that speech before?"

Bear laughed shortly, his attention fixed on the road ahead. Rain had started, whipping at the windshield in bursts while the wind buffeted the truck enough for it to shimmy toward the center line. "I've gotten it more times than I can count. Of course, most of the time the guy got way, way ahead of himself, and my mom kicked him to the curb before he got through the front door."

Jack tucked this nugget of information away to consider later. "Oh. Well… I don't really know what the future holds for your mom and me, but that's not something you need me talking to you about. She's an amazing woman; I'm glad she hasn't kicked me to the curb yet." He paused. "And I would never hurt her—it's important that you know that."

"I do. You're not an idiot. You do anything to her, and you must know by now that Monty and I would kick your ass across the county."

"I figured."

They traveled for another few seconds of silence before Bear glanced at Jack curiously. "So?" he prompted. "If that wasn't what you wanted to talk about, what was it?"

"I wanted to apologize for breaking your trust. I never intended to tell your mother, but—"

Bear held up his hand, signaling Jack to stop. "Forget it," he said, a new tension settling in.

"I gave you my word—"

"And I said forget it," Bear said tightly.

"But—"

Bear slowed abruptly, and pulled onto the muddy shoulder of Route 97. A pickup roared past, blasting its horn. Bear raised his hand with middle finger extended as the truck rolled by, almost as a matter of course.

"Look," he said, when the truck was stopped. He turned to face Jack. Behind them in the crew cab, Cody whined. The wind rocked the truck back and forth, but Bear seemed oblivious. "I put my mom through hell with this whole thing, and it's not the first time—it's not like she ever had it easy with me. I hired you because I thought you could help, but it turns out I got myself in too deep for that. If you telling anything to my mom made her feel a little bit better while I was in jail, I'm fine with that. She needs to lean on somebody sometimes, and it seems like she's decided that's you." He hesitated. "Like I said, we'll break you if you hurt her. But right now, you talking to her about my lame-ass idea to hire you is the least of my worries."

"Okay," Jack said, honestly surprised. "It won't happen again, though. I mean, if you ever need to talk to someone about anything at all, I hope you know I'm around." He smiled, lightening slightly. "I won't work for you again, because I don't want to be in a position where I need to lie to your mother. But if you need something, I'm here."

Bear nodded briefly, and pulled the truck back onto the road. "Noted."

And that was that.

Five minutes later, they pulled up at Hank's place. The house was surprisingly neat, an old white colonial that was miniscule compared to the Davis and Monroe homes. The yard was freshly mowed, a flower garden in bloom out front and a vegetable garden at the side.

Hank met them out front. Cody was surprisingly wary when they got there, not nearly like the dogs in the YouTube videos Bear mentioned. The massive dog tugged backward on the leash when Bear tried to get him into the house, until Bear finally crouched down beside the animal and murmured something that Jack couldn't make out.

"Shouldn't he be more excited than this?" Jack asked.

"It happens this way sometimes," Bear said with a shrug. Cody leaned on him with a sigh, and the boy laughed. "Come on, big guy. You can do this."

"He's always been a little nervous," Hank said when they finally made it inside. He led them to a kitchen that was as neatly appointed as the yard. Jack surveyed the shelves, where spices and bulk goods were alphabetized and perfectly aligned.

"Were you military?" he asked.

Hank smiled affably. "Guilty as charged. Army, till some shrapnel in my hip took me out of commission in '73. I would've stayed longer if not for that."

"You've recovered well," Jack noted. "I barely see a limp."

"Push through, stop dwelling on it. That's all it is really."

Jack nodded, though he didn't have anything more to add. Bear was still working with Cody, who seemed just fine as long as the boy was with him. Who knew what would happen once they left.

"Why don't you sit," Hank said. "Have some coffee. Let Cody get comfortable before you take off."

"Sure," Bear said immediately. He straightened from where he'd been crouched next to the dog. "That will be good. He may have some trouble adjusting at first. I hope you weren't planning on getting a full night's sleep tonight."

"Nah," Hank said. "I don't sleep so well anyway. He'll be all right. Isn't that right, Cody?" he asked the dog.

Cody bumped up against him, his tail waving slowly as he mellowed again. Hank scratched the dog's ears, and it wasn't long before the Newfoundland abandoned Bear in favor of his new human. Jack remained standing while all of this took place, idly reviewing the shelves while Hank put on coffee.

"Nancy must have driven you crazy," he said, after a few seconds of silence.

Hank turned to look at him. "Why's that?"

Bear laughed. "You want a list?"

Hank joined in the laughter, though to Jack the man appeared distinctly uncomfortable at the subject change.

"I meant the way you're committed to order. It's pretty clear from the way you keep your home."

Hank shrugged, but something dark passed in his eyes. Jack felt a prick of uneasiness. "We had our moments. Everyone did, where Nancy was concerned."

"Sure," Jack agreed.

He took a chair next to Bear, and a moment later Hank set a steaming cup of coffee in front of each of them. For himself, however, he selected tea.

"You're not having any?" Jack asked.

"Can't handle the caffeine. Tea's good for me. I just keep the coffee around for guests."

"We could have had tea, as well," Jack said. "You didn't need to make a whole pot for just the two of us."

Hank waved off the protests. "That's all right. I like the smell. It's not a problem."

"Well, thank you," Jack said. He waited for Bear to acknowledge either of them, but the teenager was too preoccupied with the dog.

Jack started to raise his mug, but his cell phone rang before it got halfway to his mouth. He checked the display, and frowned.

"I'm sorry—I should take this."

Despite the drizzle and darkening skies, Jack chose to take the call outside, where he wouldn't be overheard. It was a warm night, humid enough that he could taste the ocean on the air. Illuminated by a motion-sensitive light that flooded the grounds, he followed a stone path to a series of raised-bed gardens, and pressed the button to accept the incoming call.

"What's up, Mike?"

"Hey. I wasn't sure I would get you. I was all set to leave a message."

"No need. I'm here—what's going on?"

"I was just looking at the list of people who bought those lobster collars, like the one you saw at Nancy's."

"What about it?" He looked around the gardens, marveling at the greenery. A coffee can of cigarette butts was the only hint that Hank Williams might be mortal. "I thought we already went through everything."

"Not for the Waterville store," Mike said.

Jack continued walking the grounds, then paused at a garage at the head of Hank's driveway. He peered through immaculate windows.

"Remember, there was a problem with the computer," Mike was saying. "I was bored, so I pushed Becky—she's the manager there—and she finally got it for me. One of the names that came up just struck me as a little off, so I talked to the girl who was working the day he bought the collar, and—"

"Who?" Jack interrupted again. Inside the garage were parked two vehicles: Hank's red pickup, and an ancient station wagon. From where he was standing, Jack could tell that the rear taillight was broken out. And he knew, before Mike had even gotten the name out, exactly who it was.

"Hank Williams. Not the—"

"I know who it is," Jack said. He lowered his voice. "I need you to call Sheriff Finnegan. You know him?"

"Sure."

"Great. Call him. Tell him to get a unit to Hank's house. Now."

He hung up before Mike could ask any further questions. Tensed, he remained where he was for a second, assessing his next step. Behind him, a branch snapped. He strained his ears for some sound from the kitchen, but he heard nothing beyond Cody's persistent barking.

He whirled, his body tensed, and raised his arm in time to block the blow that he was sure was about to land.

As predicted, Hank was there. He hardly looked ready to strike, however, his hands raised to show that he came in peace. "Sorry, I didn't mean to startle you. Bear's in getting Cody settled. I was just checking to make sure nothing was wrong."

"No," Jack said, his heart hammering. He slipped the phone into his back pocket. "Everything's fine. I just wanted some fresh air."

Hank glanced toward the garage. He was tensed, clearly aware that Jack knew something.

"The car in there," Jack began, nodding to the window. "The station wagon..."

"It's Nancy's," Hank confirmed. "I bought it off Fred, just before he and Albie left town."

"When was that?" Jack pressed.

Hank considered. "Uh... The morning after the fire, I think. Fred said he just wanted to get out of here."

"Not before the fire?" Jack said, recalling Jamie's story of the car with the broken taillight that had run her off the road that night.

"No," Hank said. He eyed Jack carefully. "Not before the fire. The next day."

Jack nodded. He tried to relax, thinking things through. "You and Nancy knew each other a long time," he finally said.

"A while," Hank confirmed. He studied Jack for a long moment before he sighed. He reached into his front pocket, holding up his other hand when Jack flinched. "Sorry, just getting a cigarette."

He retrieved the cigarette and offered one to Jack, who shook his head. The older man lit up, inhaled deeply, and looked at Jack with his head tilted, blue eyes keen.

"You figured it out, I guess. That's what that phone call was?" he asked, taking Jack completely by surprise.

"You killed Nancy," Jack said.

Pain registered in Hank's eyes at the words, but he didn't look away. "I did. Didn't mean to, but..."

"You bludgeoned her with a fireplace poker. How is that 'didn't mean to'?" Jack asked.

"Fair enough," Hank said, with an amiable nod. "I guess... I meant to. Didn't plan on it."

"You went over to get Cody that night," Jack guessed. "That's where the collar came from?"

"Yup. We'd been talking about me taking him forever— the damn fool was starving him. Slowly killing him, and here I was right next door ready to give him everything he needed. But since the cops were coming in the next day I figured, 'This is it. Now or never.' So, I go over there. She's all wound up because Jamie's kid had been there. And she's talking all over again, about how the place is hers. The animals are hers. Nobody has a right to them. Nobody will take care of them the way she will."

"And she refused to give you Cody. Again."

"Yeah. Again." He shook his head, and drew deeply on his cigarette once more. "I just... I don't know. I lost it. God only knew what she would have done that next day, but no way would she go down without a fight. The animals...the cops... She would have taken everybody out, I think."

"We'll never know that for sure," Jack said. "In all likelihood, she wouldn't have survived that night to begin with."

Hank looked at him with widened eyes. "Excuse me?"

"She was having a heart attack when you confronted her. The medical examiner thinks it probably would have killed her."

The older man's mouth twitched. His eyebrows went up. And then, catching Jack completely off guard, he began to laugh. "Are you kidding me? I'm going to prison for that old bitch...and she would have died anyway?" He laughed harder. "Oh, that's rich."

Jack was still trying to figure out how to broach the subject that he would actually need to call the police about all this when a sound like the clap of thunder echoed through the stillness. Jack hit the deck immediately, knowing the sound all too well. Hank, unfortunately, didn't fare as well.

When Jack looked up, the older man was on the ground.

"Get up," a familiar voice said behind him. "Slowly."

Jack twisted to look back over his shoulder. Fred stood with a gun trained on him, his eyes disturbingly calm. Hands raised, Jack got to his feet. He looked down at Hank. The man was still alive, a bloody hand clutched to his chest.

•

The next few minutes happened in a blur. Jack stood with the gun trained on him, Hank bleeding on the ground. Fred called for Albie, who appeared with a mad fire in his eyes.

"You got Bear in the truck?" Fred asked.

Albie remained focused on Hank. The man wasn't moving, but Jack could still see the pained rise and fall of his chest.

"Yeah. He didn't wake up," Albie said.

"Good," Fred said. "Get Hank in there too. I'll take Mr Juarez here. I want you to drive Bear's truck to the quarry."

Albie looked at him uncertainly. "But—"

"They hurt Mom," Fred said simply. "You know what she would say. She deserves justice, the same as all those animals she saved did. We're not killing them. If God wants to save them, he will. Same as with the others."

"Those others were bad people, though," Albie argued. "They hurt animals—"

"Hank killed our mother," Fred said. His voice rose to just south of a shout. "And then he laughed about it, I heard him. That's not bad?"

Albie nodded. "No. That is bad."

"So, it's the same game," Fred said. He was calm again—eerily so.

"The Redemption Game," Albie said softly. "God saves who's worthy. They just need to be sorry. They just need to mean it."

"Get him in the truck," Fred said. "I'll follow you out to the quarry."

Jack stood by, gun pressed to the back of his skull, and watched as Albie slowly, painfully, dragged Hank across the yard.

"I'm not going anywhere with—" Jack began. He fell silent at a crushing blow to the back of his skull. He went to his knees, the night swimming around him.

For the second time in a week, his world went black.

29

WHEN JACK AWOKE, he was behind the steering wheel of Bear's truck, his hands bound in front of him. His head throbbed, his mouth filled with foul-tasting cotton. Bile burned in his throat. When the world came back into focus, he looked to his right to find Bear slumped in the passenger's seat.

"You'll live if you're worthy," Fred said to him. He stood at the open driver's side door, watching Jack warily. "You made it through the fire... That may mean something."

"That was you, then?" Jack asked. "At your mother's house. You attacked me and set that fire?"

"No one was ever supposed to get in there. I was supposed to get my mother and Albie out, and then do what needed to be done to the house. But then Hank..." The man swallowed convulsively. "It's done, it doesn't matter. I don't think he stands much chance, but it's in God's hands now."

Jack twisted to look behind him. By the truck's interior light, he could just make out Hank's still form in the crew cab.

"What the hell are you doing?" Jack asked. The words

came out hard, and sounded like they'd been spoken by another man entirely.

"Just pray. We'll see how you fare," the man said. He slammed the door, and stepped away from the vehicle.

Awareness slowly crept in. They were in the woods, headlights illuminating a vast open space ahead. Rain spattered the windshield. Jack heard the roar of an engine behind them.

He looked back over his shoulder into the glare of high beams. His heart was pounding in time with his head now, panic pushing him to the brink. The car behind revved its engine. Jack looked to his left, but Fred was no longer standing there.

The car behind revved again, and the pieces clicked into place. *I'll follow you out to the quarry.*

Jack slammed his foot down on the brake.

Nothing happened.

Behind them, he heard Fred's car come to life. It sped toward them. He knew it was coming, but the impact still threw him into the steering wheel.

Bear's truck lurched toward the quarry's edge.

•

Jack braced himself for the fall that he knew was coming, but the force when they hit the water still rocked him so hard that he hit the windshield. Beside him, Bear hit the dash even harder, his skull cracking with a sound that made Jack's stomach roll.

He managed to get free of the ropes Fred had tied

around his wrists with a silent prayer of thanks, and turned immediately to Bear. If the boy had been close to regaining consciousness before, he was now once again fully out. Behind him in the crew cab, however, Hank groaned in pain.

He couldn't get all three of them out, Jack realized. There was no way. The cab was taking on water fast, already sinking below the surface. His head felt like it would explode, but it didn't matter.

He had to do this.

He pushed past the pain, and tried the truck door. With the weight of the water against it, it wouldn't budge. The power windows were useless, the engine quite literally flooded.

Jack maneuvered himself inside the limited space until his feet were jammed against the windshield, his back pressed to the seat for leverage.

He kicked out.

Kicked again.

And again.

Behind him in the crew cab, Hank's breath was an ominous rattle that Jack had heard before. The men who made that sound hadn't been long for this world.

He kicked again, fighting fatigue and a pain so great it seemed almost outside him now.

On the sixth kick, the windshield shattered. Water surged into the truck cab before Jack had a chance to prepare himself. He swallowed a lungful of water, but kept his head. He grabbed Bear around his middle, and tugged the boy free of the truck.

They weren't far from the surface. Jack took seconds to take in air before he oriented himself, scanning the night for some sign of shore line. He spotted dry land a hundred yards to his right, wrapped one arm around Bear's chest, and swam for shore.

Halfway there, Bear came to. He began to struggle, panic seizing him.

"Stop!" Jack ordered. "You're all right. We're almost to safety."

"What happened?" Bear demanded. "What's happening?"

Jack didn't answer, but he was relieved when Bear insisted he was all right, and swam the last few yards to shore on his own.

"We're at the quarry," the boy said. He dragged himself onto the granite rocks, his forehead leaking blood. "How did we get here?"

"I don't have time to explain. Just wait for me, okay? Hank is still in there."

Bear started to protest, but Jack ignored him. His body protested even more loudly. He ignored that as well, and waded back into the water.

Halfway back, he knew he was in trouble.

His body seized up with the truck just a few yards away, and his vision swam. Darkness crowded in.

"Just a few more yards," he whispered to himself. If he turned back, he might be able to save himself. He kept thinking of the gardens at Hank's house, though. Cody waiting.

"Keep going," he said aloud.

And he did.

30

I GOT BACK TO THE LANDING that night at eight-thirty, fully expecting to find Bear there waiting for me. Reaver sat in the crew cab of my truck, seatbelt buckled, dead to the world as I pulled in. Monty's friend had confirmed my suspicions, and I was still a little awed to know I had a genuine K-9 war hero by my side.

The moment I pulled into the town landing lot and found Bear not there, however, thoughts of my recent discovery faded.

Bear's truck wasn't here—and Jack's car still was.

It couldn't have taken that long to drop Cody off, even if Hank asked them to stay a while. I couldn't imagine the man would be all that talkative, and Bear wasn't exactly the social type.

I tried Bear's cell. It went straight to voicemail.

I got the same response when I tried Jack.

Get over there, Brock said to me, in a growl that nearly cracked my skull. Behind me, Reaver got to his feet.

"Get out of my head," I said aloud.

You know I don't give a rat's ass what happens to you, Brock said. *But you're supposed to take care of my son. Go do it.*

He was in trouble. I didn't need some voice from beyond the grave to tell me that—my racing heart should be proof enough. Since when had I needed Brock Campbell—or any man—to confirm the validity of my intuition?

Brock continued throwing out orders and dire predictions, but I ignored him. My palms were slick on the steering wheel, my head pounding. I pressed the pedal to the floor of the truck, fully aware of Reaver, still on his feet behind me.

When I pulled into Hank's driveway, there was no sign of Bear's truck. I grabbed my flashlight and told Reaver to stay put. Before I could close the door, however, the dog broke rank and bolted past me, headed straight for the woods dragging the seatbelt he'd gnawed through behind him.

I took off after him at a run, ignoring any trace of doubt that he didn't know what he was doing. Something was happening. I didn't know what in hell it might be, but I'd learned long ago to trust my dogs. With everything Reaver had been through, he deserved that much. I ran after him full tilt in the dark and the rain, and prayed that he wouldn't fail me.

No doubt Reaver could have covered ground a hell of a lot faster than I could, but he never got so far ahead that I lost him. Whenever I thought I had, I just had to call out and he would reply with a clipped, business-like bark while he kept moving.

He had something, I was sure of it.

Suddenly, after what could have been minutes or days of running blind, I caught sight of the dog stock still up ahead.

The woods had opened up to grass and rocky ground, and I stopped dead when I realized where we were. Reaver stood, body tensed, and barked ferociously at the abyss below.

The quarry.

I shone my Mag light down below, and fought a surge of terror so strong it nearly crippled me.

The rear end just breaking the surface of the water, was a pickup bed. I could read the license plate, but I already knew what it said.

FLINTK92

Bear's truck.

•

Jack reached the truck and had to hang on to the edge for a second, clinging to the steel body while he fought to remain conscious. Somewhere far, far away, he imagined that he heard Jamie's voice.

He had to do this.

He took a deep breath and dove under the surface of the water, managing to get back into the truck without incident. In the darkness, water closing in around him, he felt his way to the back of the cab. His hand closed around something fleshy. Human.

Hank.

With his lungs bursting, Jack wrapped his good arm around the dying man and pushed himself out with his legs.

Hank moved, but just barely. His body was lodged there.

Jack's vision blurred at the edges. He tugged again. The man was probably dead—he'd been shot in the chest.

But he had been alive when they went into the water.

Jack ground his teeth together, and with a fresh surge of energy hauled on the body one last time.

This time, Hank didn't move so much as an inch.

Before he could try one last time, he froze. From nowhere, a set of iron jaws clamped onto the back of his neck.

Jack had experienced terrifying things before. A lot of them, actually.

This was, without exception, the most terrifying.

The jaws shifted, until the beast found the back of his jacket. Jack fought as the animal tried to pull him up, until suddenly he felt a hand on his arm.

Jamie's face appeared before him, blond hair streaming around her in the water. She motioned to the surface. Jack's air had long since run out. With nothing more to do, he let go of Hank's body.

With no more resistance, the mysterious beast that had hold of him hauled him out of the truck and back to the surface. An instant later, Jamie popped up beside him.

"Go with Reaver," she said. He realized the dog was beside him, still holding to his jacket. Jack shook his head.

"Hank was shot. He's trapped in there."

"I'll get him."

"You can't do it alone—" Jack insisted.

"She doesn't have to," a voice said, just beyond them. Jack scanned the night, barely conscious of all that was happening around him. Above, he saw blue lights flashing. A diver appeared beside them. On shore, an ambulance crew and more police waited.

"Come on," Jamie said gently. "Take him in Reaver," she told the dog.

Jack sagged against the massive pit bull, unable to fight any longer. Eyes closed, heart still pounding, he and the dog made their slow way back to the rocks.

31

A WEEK LATER, Jack was waiting for me at the boat landing at six o'clock as promised. At news of all the drama that had taken place thanks to Nancy and her animals, the fundraiser on the animals' behalf had been postponed for a week. This was good, since neither Bear nor Jack were up for much in the way of moving after all Fred and Albie put them through.

You could hardly tell Jack had been through the ringer now, though. In fact, he looked almost unforgivably good. He wore jeans and a sports jacket over a black T-shirt, and I smiled at his idea of cocktail attire. Of course, it was probably dressier than anyone else would be tonight, so I didn't sweat it. Since it was Jack, it really wouldn't have mattered what he was wearing; I would still be with the best-looking man in the place, hands down.

He stopped at sight of me as I awkwardly got off the boat. Dresses aren't usually my thing, but at the look on Jack's face, I was willing to rethink that position. I wore a little black number with thin straps and a lower cut than I was used to. More shape-hugging, too. I resisted the urge to fiddle with the straps or pull it farther down my legs, and shoved my feet into black pumps once I was safely on the dock.

"You look good," he said.

"Thank you." I sounded more confident than I felt, which was good. 'Fake it till you make it' has been my motto for a very long time. "So do you."

He leaned down and kissed me lightly on the mouth, his hand resting on my bare arm. It felt natural and heated and…good, and I was smiling when he stepped back. Then, I studied his face with a critical eye, tipping his head with a hand to his jaw as I took in his remaining bruises from the night at the quarry. "You're healing nicely. Does it still hurt?"

"Only when people poke it." He gently pushed my hand away, but didn't relinquish it afterward, squeezing my fingers. "Are you ready? I made reservations."

I looked at him curiously. "Reservations? In Rockland?"

"At In Good Company—in Rockland. They've teamed up with the fundraiser. All proceeds tonight go to cover medical expenses for Nancy's animals. Mike said the food is good, though."

"It is," I agreed.

"You've been there."

"I've lived here a couple of years now," I reminded him. "I've been to a lot of places."

"I suppose so," he conceded. He took my arm when neither of us moved, and nodded toward his car. "Shall we?"

He opened the car door for me, then shut it when I was safely inside. I watched him walk around to the driver's side, waiting for some voice from beyond to shake my moorings loose. Nothing came, though. When he took his seat behind the wheel, it was just the two of us. It was refreshing, if not a little bit terrifying.

"How was your day?" he asked, once we were on the road. "Is Bear doing all right?"

"My day was good," I said. I couldn't hold back a smile when I said it. "Bear's…really good, actually."

Jack glanced at me, surprised. The weather had cleared since the hurricane swept through, the sun still bright despite the advancing hour. My smile widened at his look.

"Ren came home," I explained. "She was worried about him. I've been trying to get him to lighten up for months now, and all it takes is thirty seconds with her and he's a different kid."

"How long is she staying?"

"I'm not sure. I think we're all trying not to think about that." I hesitated, then opted for changing the subject rather than thinking about it any further. "Any word on Hank?"

"They're still not sure," he said with a frown. "He's awake, but he was without oxygen a long time. They're still trying to figure out what kind of mental deficits he might be facing."

"What do you think will happen to him?"

He shrugged. "He killed someone—they can't just let that go, even if there are extenuating circumstances. It's up to the judge, but I expect Cody will have to find a new home."

"I'm sure he won't have a problem," I assured him. "Everyone who meets him falls in love with that dog. My guess is that he'll have a home before the week's out."

"I got some other news today," Jack said. "I spoke with Sophie—Laurent, the forensic anthropologist." I nodded, but said nothing while I waited for him to continue. "She's identified three of the bodies in that root cellar. All of them had criminal records."

"Let me guess," I said, unsurprised. "Animal cruelty?"

"You guessed it." He shook his head. "They came

from all over the country. All those trips Nancy took over the years, all that good everyone thought she was doing... Apparently, she had some other business she was taking care of at the same time. Albie called it the Redemption Game."

I froze. Somewhere close, I heard Brock laughing. "What did you say?"

"The Redemption Game." He shook his head. "Apparently, they set things up to punish these guys, but they stopped short of actually killing them. The thought was that if they were sorry enough, if they were worthy of redemption, God would step in and save them."

Brock's words came back to me in a rush. *You bust your ass, deny yourself all the pleasures you could have, in the hopes that maybe that will make you good enough. That will erase all those past sins.*

"Are you okay?" Jack asked. He touched my hand, and I looked at him. "You look a little pale."

"Yeah," I said with a nod. I pushed the thought of Brock away yet again. This wasn't about him.

"Well, whatever they called it, there's no question that the two of them will be going to jail," I said. "Or Fred, at least. I heard they're trying to find a placement for Albie in Augusta."

"That's good," Jack said. "I feel bad for him in all this. Hell, I feel bad for everyone. It seems like Nancy did a number on everyone she touched."

"You can say that again," I agreed.

I was pleased when the conversation turned from Nancy to happier topics. While we drove, I gave Jack the short version of my meeting with Sergeant Roy Redaker, the military man Monty had recommended I reach out to. As we'd suspected, Reaver had been a military dog, and Roy had been able to tie him to an Army K-9 unit that had been stationed in Afghanistan.

"He was retired a year ago when his handler was killed in the line of duty," I told him. "He was starting to show signs of PTSD after that, so he was supposed to come home and live out the rest of his life in peace. Somehow in transit, Reaver got rerouted during that hurricane last summer. They lost track of him in Atlanta."

"Well, I for one am grateful he ended up with you. You two saved my ass the other night. Did you find out his real name?"

"Archie," I said. "I tried it out on him, and he was definitely enthusiastic. So, Archie it is now."

"Does that mean you've finally given up the pretense that he's not staying with you."

I laughed. "I guess I have. I don't think Phantom would forgive me if I sent him away now."

"Neither would I," Jack said.

I considered that. "That other name: Reaver. It's from a TV show called *Firefly.*"

"Reavers are some kind of cannibalistic pirate," Jack said. "Nancy certainly got it wrong with that name. They're beyond animals—kind of the worst of the worst."

I looked at him in surprise.

"Erin was a fan," he explained, referring to Erin Solomon. "That and *Buffy the Vampire Slayer.* Whenever there was a marathon on, we'd watch."

"Ah," I said. "I've never seen them. I'm kind of behind on pop culture, I guess."

"That's all right," Jack said. "TV's overrated. It's nice curling up sometimes on a rainy day, though."

I considered that, and tried to push aside an unexpected

twinge of uneasiness. Jack glanced at me when I didn't say anything, one eyebrow quirked.

"What just happened?" he asked.

"Nothing."

"Something just happened. Is it because I mentioned Erin? Because things are way, way over with her. They barely even got started—I'm very happy for her and Diggs."

"That's not it," I said. We were getting into Rockland now, traffic picking up now that it was both summer and a Friday night.

"Then what?"

I hesitated. Jack took a left onto Main Street and turned into his parking lot, since In Good Company was just a couple of doors down from his apartment. He stopped the car, and turned to look at me expectantly. Clearly, we weren't getting out of the car until I explained.

"I don't know if I've ever curled up on a rainy day before," I confessed. "There's always work to do. I'm not good at just…relaxing, and being with someone. If that's what you're looking for—"

He actually smiled at that, which wasn't the response I'd been looking for.

"How is that funny?"

"Do you really think I want to date you because you're so laid back?" he asked. "Because I'm imagining all those hours we're going to spend vegging out in front of the TV?"

"Well… No," I said. Defensiveness crept into my tone. I glanced away from him, hating the heat I felt rising to my cheeks. "I guess I just…" I bit my lip. "I'm not totally sure why you want to date me. It's not like I don't have any baggage."

"I have baggage, too," he reminded me. "Lots of it."

"I think you carry it better than I do."

"I think you're wrong."

We remained that way for a moment, at an impasse, before Jack sighed. He got out of the car without another word, and came around to the passenger's side. Opened the door for me. Stood aside, waiting for me to get out. When I had, he closed the door behind me and then remained there, his body close to mine. He caged me there with his arms outstretched, hands resting on the car on either side of me.

"You're thinking again," he said quietly. "Just for tonight… Let it go. Trust me."

I took a long, deep breath, and nodded. "Okay. I can do that."

•

In Good Company was busy when we got there, and only got busier as our meal progressed. The food was incredible, the company even better, and the wine went straight to my head. Afterward, Jack and I walked the scant half mile from the restaurant to the bar where the fundraiser was taking place. Conversation flowed easily, and the night was perfect: warm and breezy, with a backdrop of sailboats and summer traffic and tourists wending their way through town.

Trackside was packed when we arrived. Somewhere in the background I could hear live music playing courtesy of a local folksinger by the name of Paddy Mills, but it was drowned out by the sound of laughter and conversation. Jack got us both a beer and I found a much-prized table toward the back. I sat down, and watched with a combination of amusement and awe as the locals gathered around my date. April, Heidi, and Mel were working the event, but they all managed to take a minute to say hello. Mike cornered him, and Jack laughed at something the man said. It struck me that none of this was forced for him—he wasn't dutifully enduring the locals, for my sake or anyone else's.

He actually liked it here.

He might even stay.

"Hey," a familiar voice said, just behind me. I turned to find Bear standing there. His eyes were bright, his jeans were clean, and the grin he gave me didn't even seem forced.

"Hey," I said in surprise.

"Mind if I...?" he said, gesturing to the seat next to me.

"Yeah. Of course. What's up? Where's Ren?"

"Over there," he said, nodding vaguely toward another table. I looked, and saw Ren seated at a table with Sarah and Therese and a few others I didn't recognize. She wore a red summer dress that went beautifully with her skin, her hair up and just the right amount of makeup tastefully applied.

"Listen, I was hoping I could talk to you for a second," Bear said. I shifted my focus back to him.

"Isn't that what you're doing?"

He rolled his eyes. "Right. Yeah. Well... Um. I just... Ren and I were thinking, and I guess we're just going to stay over here for the night. On the mainland, I mean."

All my goodwill vanished into the night at once. "Oh? Where were you planning on doing that, exactly?"

He wet his lips. Cleared his throat. "We're eighteen, so... It's not like I'm asking. I just wanted to make sure you could cover me if I wasn't there tonight. I already talked to Sarah and Therese, and they said they could handle it."

"Well, then, there you go. I guess you're good."

He bit his lip. "And you're cool with it?"

I laughed at that. I couldn't help it, thinking of the eighteen years we'd spent growing up together. All the agony he'd put me through. All the agony I'd put him through, for that matter.

"I'm cool with it, Bear. You're going to a hotel?" I guessed.

"Yeah. I got reservations."

"And you have protection?"

The eye roll this time wasn't nearly as dramatic as I'd expected. "Of course."

"And you remember our talk about consent?"

He sighed, but his eyes remained serious when he replied. "She can say no anytime. Doesn't matter where we are or how far we've gotten. The choice is always hers." He frowned briefly. "I wouldn't hurt her, Mom. Not for anything."

"I know that." I reached across the table and squeezed his hand. Jack was still talking to the others, so I took advantage of the extra minute or two. "Have you thought about what happens next? When she goes back to California?"

He hesitated, but I could tell that this wasn't a new question for him. "We actually wanted to talk to you about that."

"We?"

"Ren and me. She... Well, she was going to tell you herself. But she's decided to take a gap year. You know—not go to school for a year?"

"I know what a gap year is, thank you. What does her father say about this?"

"She hasn't told him yet," Bear admitted. "But... I kind of was thinking maybe I could do the same thing. I know I've started all this stuff out on the island, but ever since Ren left it's been..." He stopped, searching for words.

"Awful?" I supplied.

He laughed. "Yeah. Kind of. I just... There's all this stuff I want to see, and I want to do, and she's been talking a lot about the, uh... You know, the powers or whatever? The things I can see. And you and I never really talk about that, but...I kind of want to know more. Like... I saw Mr. Monroe that night, at Julie's place? And I freaked out... I thought he was dead. But if I'd understood what was going on, if I had actually talked to him, maybe we could have gotten to him sooner."

"He's all right," I reminded Bear. "He's going to be fine."

"That's thanks to you and Phantom, not me. I just need to figure out what it's all about. What I can do. And if I can help people, somehow."

"And you're going to do that with Ren? Where?"

He shrugged. "I'm not sure yet. She's got a couple of places she wants us to visit. Some guy she wants me to talk to. I guess mostly it's just...us, figuring out what we want and who we are."

I nodded, fighting an unexpected surge of emotion. I stuffed it back down, and kept my voice even when I looked at him. "When would you go?"

"We were thinking we'd work here together through the summer, and that way I can make sure everything's set and the animals are taken care of. We can help train anybody new you want to bring on board." He looked at me seriously, his brow furrowed and his dark eyes that much darker. "If you don't want me to go... I mean, if you need me—"

I squeezed his hand and shook my head. "No. It's good that you're doing this—this is what you should be doing. I mean, I don't know if talking to a shaman and traveling the globe with your girlfriend is exactly what you should be doing... But you should be exploring. You shouldn't be worrying about me. I'm okay."

Jack had finally extracted himself from the others, and was headed our way. Bear caught sight of him, and gave me a look.

"I told him if he hurts you, Monty and I will beat the snot out of him," my son said.

I laughed, taken aback at that. "I don't think you need to worry about that."

"No," he said. He eyed Jack speculatively as he stood, surrendering his seat to the older man. "I don't think so, either. Ren and I are gonna get going. See you out on the island tomorrow?"

"You will," I confirmed.

"How's it going, Bear?" Jack asked.

"Can't complain. Don't keep her out too late, okay?" he said. I watched him walk away, and I barely recognized him as the awkward, shaggy-haired little boy I had raised.

Jack looked at me. "What was that about?"

I took my beer from him, and took a long, long pull before I set it back down again. "It seems like we're both growing up," I said.

"Oh?" He sat opposite me, in the stool Bear had vacated. "Is that a bad thing?"

I studied him a moment. A lock of dark hair had fallen over his forehead, almost in his eyes. I resisted the urge to brush it away, and contented myself with settling my hand in his on the table top. "It has its good points." I hesitated. The tables had been cleared away on one side of the bar, and a growing knot of people had gotten up to dance. I watched Bear and Ren leave the building, hand in hand. I took another pull from my beer, and a long, steadying breath.

"Do you know how to dance?" I asked.

He smiled. "I do. Did you want to...?" He nodded

toward the dance floor, and I hesitated. He caught on after a second and tightened his hold on my hand, studying me all the while. "You don't dance?"

"I grew up in a house where dancing was off-limits, because of Jesus." He raised his eyebrows at that, and I waved him off. "A story for another time. But then I had a baby when I was fifteen. And then I raised that baby, and started a business... There hasn't been much time for dancing, so far."

"I can see how that might happen."

I bit my lip. There was a spark in his eye, a hint of danger there that was more intoxicating than the beer. "But you know how to dance."

"I know how to dance, *corazón*," he said softly.

"Good." I stood, allowing myself one more steadying breath, and pulled him to his feet. "Then you can teach me."

More Mysteries from Jen Blood

In Between Days
Diggs & Solomon Shorts
1990 - 2000

Midnight Lullaby
Prequel to
The Erin Solomon Mysteries

The
Payson Pentalogy

Book I: All the Blue-Eyed Angels
Book II: Sins of the Father
Book III: Southern Cross
Book IV: Before the After
Book V: The Book of J

Flint K-9 Search and Rescue

The Darkest Thread
Inside the Echo
The Redemption Game

ACKNOWLEDGMENTS

Thanks go to my family, always, for the love, support, and kind words when it seemed this book would never be done. To Heidi, Mike, Mel, April, and the rest of the gang at the Loyal Biscuit for helping me with the intricacies of solving this case and for being the very coolest of friends, and to my readers for their patience in waiting for the story to come together, I offer my heartfelt gratitude, always.

I always love to hear from readers! Email me at jen@jenblood.com or follow me on Facebook at www.facebook.com/jenbloodauthor or Twitter @jenblood, and don't forget to join the mailing list for all the latest news on projects and upcoming releases.

ABOUT THE AUTHOR

Jen Blood is a freelance journalist, certified dog trainer, and author of the bestselling Erin Solomon Mysteries and the Flint K-9 Search and Rescue Mysteries. She holds an MFA in Creative Writing/Popular Fiction, with influences ranging from Emily Bronte to Joss Whedon and the whole spectrum in between, and teaches workshops on writing, editing, and marketing for authors. Today, Jen lives in a big old farmhouse on the coast of Maine with a puppy named Marji, a Maine coon cat named Magnus, and a lovely bearded man called Ben.

Made in the USA
San Bernardino, CA
16 December 2019

61623947R00219